Adrian Boult

ADRIAN BOULT

by

MICHAEL KENNEDY

HAMISH HAMILTON · LONDON

HAMISH HAMILTON LTD

Published by the Penguin Group
27 Wrights Lane, London W8 5TZ, England
Viking Penguin Inc, 40 West 23rd Street, New York, New York 10010, U.S.A.
Penguin Books Australia Ltd, Ringwood, Victoria, Australia
Penguin Books Canada Ltd, 2801 John Street, Markham, Ontario, Canada L3R 1B4
Penguin Books (N.Z.) Ltd, 182–190 Wairau Road, Auckland 10, New Zealand

Penguin Books Ltd, Registered Offices: Harmondsworth, Middlesex, England

First published in Great Britain 1987 by
Hamish Hamilton Ltd

British Library Cataloguing in Publication Data

Kennedy, Michael, 1926–
Adrian Boult.
1. Boult, *Sir* Adrian 2. Conductors (Music)—Biography
I. Title
785'.092'4   ML422.B79

ISBN 0–241–12071–3

Typeset and Printed in Great Britain
by Butler &·Tanner Ltd, Frome, Somerset

For
GWEN BECKETT

List of Illustrations

Table of Contents

Preface   ix

CONTENTS

PART III
AT THE BBC, 1929–1950

PART IV
FREELANCE, 1950–1983

Preface

Writing to me in 1976 after an article I had written about him had been published, Sir Adrian Boult said he had sent copies of it to some of his young relatives: 'It will be their version (if they want) of my contribution to things and quite *enough* (J.B. with a whole book was an exception in many ways – I'm much too boring!).' As usual, Sir Adrian was too modest. His career, though so different from Sir John Barbirolli's, is no less interesting and deserves to be recorded in a biography, since so much of what he did is not known to the younger generation. Also, the public image of him as a reserved English gentleman, the antithesis of the stereotyped view of a conductor, while not a distortion is only half the picture. He was as complex, sensitive and, at times, insecure as many of his colleagues. The difference is that he never wore his heart on his sleeve.

A biographer's principal acknowledgment must go to Sir Adrian himself. He was a meticulous keeper of diaries and maker of lists. It is no exaggeration to say that one can discover from his papers what he did, where he had lunch, tea and dinner and with whom he had meetings on almost every day of his adult life. He was also a splendid and prolific letter writer and wrote many broadcast talks and articles for periodicals, all of which are characteristic of him and usually contain some precious nugget of information or comment.

I am profoundly grateful to Lady Boult for handing over to me the whole of her husband's documentary archive, for putting no restrictions on its use and for helping me by her patient answering of innumerable questions. Similarly, Mrs Gwendolen Beckett, Sir Adrian's loyal secretary for over 50 years, has been kindness itself in digging into her memory and her own archive to help me in every possible way. She better than anyone knew Sir Adrian's passion for accuracy and if I have slipped from grace in this respect it is emphatically not her fault.

My thanks go also to Mr Christopher Bishop for much help and advice and for so generously making his correspondence with Sir Adrian available to me. For similar help I am grateful to Mr John Warrack, Mr Trevor Harvey, Mr Raymond Monk, and the late Mr Bernard Shore. Invaluable information came from Mr Adolph Borsdorf and from Mr Beresford King-Smith of the City of Birmingham Symphony Orchestra. I express my gratitude to Mr Donald Mitchell for much kindness and to the Trustees and Executors of the Britten Estate for their permission to quote from the diaries kept by the late Lord Britten of Aldeburgh. Others who have been helpful to me are Mrs Ursula Vaughan Williams, Miss Audrey Napier-Smith, Sir Keith Falkner, Sir Colin Davis, Sir Michael Tippett, Sir William Haley, Sir Yehudi Menuhin, Mr Vernon Handley, Mr Robert Ponsonby, Mr Felix Aprahamian, Dr Alan Bush, Professor Ian Parrott, Miss Ashley Ringshaw of the Royal Opera House archive office, Miss Frances Cook, publications officer of the London Philharmonic Orchestra, Miss Annette M. Kennett, Chester City Archivist, Miss Eileen Simpson, Mr Timothy Day, curator of Western Art Music, The British Library (National Sound Archive), Mr Meirion Bowen, Mr D. A. Dunckley, deputy editor, *The Birmingham Post*, Mr and Mrs Jeremy Boult, the Library and Department of Portraits, Royal College of Music, and Mr Hugh Graham of EMI (UK) Ltd. Mrs Jacqueline Kavanagh and her staff, particularly Mrs Clare Brown, at the BBC Written Archives Centre, Caversham Park, extended me exceptional help and courtesy. Dr Joyce Bourne has typed my manuscript and given invaluable help and encouragement.

Michael Kennedy
Manchester, 1987

PART I

The Making of a Musician
1889–1919

CHAPTER 1

Blundellsands

ADRIAN Cedric Boult was born at 1.55 am on 8 April 1889. He weighed 9 lbs. These precise details are recorded in a diary kept by his mother. In 1926 she wrote an account of her son's childhood from which he quoted extensively in his autobiography *My Own Trumpet*,[1] but the immediacy of the diary presents a more vivid picture of the development of a child who was cherished but by no means pampered by his parents. The birth took place in 4, Abbots Hayes, Liverpool Road, Chester. This was a small terrace of houses, now demolished. The child's father was Cedric Randal Boult, an oil merchant, who was born on 10 September 1853 and died on 2 March 1950. On 17 May 1881 Cedric married Katherine Florence Barman and their first child, a daughter, Olive Isabel Eileen, was born in May a year later. The Boults were comfortably placed financially and the children were brought up in the English upper-middle-class style. In religion they were strict Unitarians and Adrian remained one all his life, being very generous to various Unitarian appeals. There had been Boults in Chester for at least a century. William Boult, who died in 1811 aged 77, his wife Hannah, who died in 1814, and their son William, who died in 1822, were all buried in the Unitarian 'Matthew Henry' Chapel, Trinity Street. (The burial ground was cleared for a ring road in 1964.)

When Adrian was about nine weeks old he developed whooping-cough but by 8 September he weighed 19 lbs and on 26 December he 'got three teeth at once and developed a temper. Could crawl.' In March 1890 he would call 'Woggie' and could walk seven steps alone. On his first birthday his height was 2 ft $7\frac{1}{4}$ in, he had found out how to open drawers and he 'loved looking at himself in the glass.' A month later he could crawl upstairs. From the age of eight months he reacted to music and would stop whatever he was doing to listen. An entry for January 1891 says: 'Showed great love for music, always played piano with one finger at a time and could imitate fairly tunes sung to him. If he

3

had poetry said to him, he would repeat the sounds with the exact metre.'

By the time Adrian was two, the Boults had moved to Lancashire, to Brooke House in Blundellsands. Now in the county of Merseyside, Blundellsands is on the Irish Sea coast, eight miles north of Liverpool. Like Southport, 13 miles further north, its seafront is a maze of sandhills. In the 1890s, an era of prosperity for some Lancashire industries, it was a favourite residential suburb of Liverpool's successful businessmen who, like Cedric Boult, travelled by train to and from their offices. Brooke House was plain and unostentatious, adjectives which could equally describe the life style of the Boults. It had a billiards room and quarters for the maidservants and the German nurse. (Most of Adrian's first utterances, noted down by his mother, were in German.) Once a week Cedric's business took him to Manchester. Adrian, asked when he was seven and had missed the school fireworks on 5 November because of a cold if he would like a bonfire at home on the following Tuesday, replied with the consideration for others that was to be a lifelong trait: 'No, because Papa is tired on Tuesday with Manchester.'

At two the boy could sing what he heard 'fairly well.' He would 'sit for an hour at a time playing quietly or watching me play. He would say "C D E F" and play them like five-finger exercises.' In January 1893 he could play the whole of Edward German's *Shepherd's Dance* with one hand. 'He picked it out quite alone. I only told him once that the note he was hunting for was a black one but did not go near the piano to show it to him.' On 17 November 1893 Katherine Boult recorded: 'He knew five duets and parts of two Reinecke duets with me. On this day he was cross and would not let me come and play Olive's accompaniment, so I sat on the edge of the chair and played on both sides of him. Of course it was difficult to play arpeggios so I missed a C sharp near the end. When I had finished he said: "Mammie, you played a white note instead of a black one, you should have played that (touching the sharp) and you did play that."' A few days later when he was playing some of his pieces he said, 'Now I will play them minor,' which he did correctly.

Some entries in the diary were made by Adrian's father and disclose the child's nascent sense of fun, something that he never lost. For example, on 25 November 1893:

He took an 'animal' biscuit out of a box, held it up and said 'Sis, what's this?' 'A parrot,' was the reply, 'and you see it is on its wooden stand ...' He chewed violently and made such faces that all present exclaimed 'What's

4

the matter?' 'It's this wooden stand. It is *very* hard.' The first sentence was spoken without moving a muscle, but he then burst out laughing.

20 December. At breakfast he began 'playing the piano' on the table and singing as loud as he could. I said 'Oh, Baby, don't make such a noise.' He covered his face with both hands and bursting into tears said: 'Music is *not* a noise, Papa.'

10 April. He came flying out to me in the garden, flushed and eyes sparkling. 'Papa, Papa. I have played an octave!'

Though musically precocious, he was in other respects a normal if highly strung little boy. When he was five he broke a little terra-cotta pot his mother had liked very much. When she remonstrated with him, he replied defiantly: 'Well, you should have put it on a high shelf so that I couldn't reach it.' 'But, Baby, you might say sorry for breaking it.' 'Well-l-l-l!!! (most indignantly) you should have known I was sorry because I – cried.' All of this was shouted except the last word, which was whispered. When Adrian's parents wanted to talk about him when he was present, they would refer to him as 'Brooks of Sheffield.' Once, when he asked them who Brooks of Sheffield was, they replied, 'Oh, just a friend of ours.'

On 27 October 1894 he was taken to his first concert, a recital in Liverpool given by the baritone Harry Plunket Greene accompanied by H. S. Welsing, a Viennese émigré who was Adrian's godfather. He 'clapped enthusiastically and when Mr Greene sang a song about a crocodile he went into fits of laughter much to the amusement of people in the next box.' In January 1895, the month in which he first attended a day kindergarten, his mother noted that 'he composed quires of music, but Mr Welsing says there is no coherence in it although it is quite correct. It is simply his repetition from memory of what he has seen or heard. He usually composes up in the play-room – *never* at the piano – and then brings the things to me to play. Very often I can't, they are so difficult.'

An entry in the diary for 17 February 1895 is amusing in view of the famous moustache which was a Boult trademark in later life: 'He came up to me with a solemn face and puckered forehead. "Mammie, I can't think what to do when I grow up about shaving." "About shaving? Oh you need not trouble. I never bother myself about shaving." "You stupid," (great indignation) "of course you don't 'cos you're a girl." So I assumed an air of becoming concern and asked what he meant. "Well, you see, Papa has a moustache and I can't think whether to have one too or not." We referred the momentous question to Papa when he came home and he decided that under *no* circumstances was the moustache to be cut or shaved.'

> *21 February 1895*. He looked at the beginning of *Tannhäuser* ... and said sighing: 'Oh, I wish I could play that!' I said 'Well here it is, play it.' 'But I want to play it on the orchestra.' I explained that only the conductor played on the orchestra, all the players only did each a little bit. So he took *Tannhäuser* and muddled away at the overture. I said 'Shall I play it? ...' Then I played the beautiful piece in the second act where the singers' names are drawn and asked: 'Wouldn't you like to be able to compose lovely music like that when you grow up?' 'Didn't I tell you' – savagely – 'that I am going to be a musician and play the piano like Mr Welsing when I grow up? Then I shall play at the [Liverpool] Philharmonic and' – relapsing into mildness and looking up in the little shy way he does sometimes – 'I shall say to the people, please will you let my Mammie come and sit beside me while I play.'

On Adrian's sixth birthday his father was awakened at 6 am by two warm arms round his neck and a sleepy voice saying: 'I have wakened up a little six-year-old boy.' By now he could skate and he was given a telescope so that he could look out at the sea. He could sing a high E clearly and his lowest note was the G of a violin string, a compass of three octaves all but two notes. Like most Liverpool and Manchester families in those years, the Boults spent their summer holidays in Wales. There was no piano at their holiday home, but the minute they returned home Adrian went straight to the piano. He had now taken to calling his mother 'Mummie.' 'Our fights over scales still continue,' she wrote, 'however, we have plodded on to five flats. He can do them charmingly when he chooses!'

On Saturday 26 October 1895 he was taken to his first orchestral concert, at the Philharmonic Hall, Liverpool. This, as it happened, was an historic occasion, for Sir Charles Hallé had died in Manchester the previous day. By strange chance Dr Hans Richter was touring the provinces with his 'London Orchestra of 90 performers' and was opening each concert with the fortuitously appropriate Symphony No. 6 in B minor (*Pathétique*) by Tchaikovsky. This was performed in Manchester on the night of Hallé's death. Next afternoon the programme was repeated in Liverpool. Mrs Boult's diary recorded that her six-year-old son 'was most excited – not fidgety nor noisy but his eyes sparkled and his cheeks got so red. The first piece was the Siegfried *Trauermarsch* for Hallé's death. After it he turned round to me and said, "Oh I *do* like it, Mummie." He was very bothered by the 5 time of one movement of Tchaikovsky's symphony. [The second movement of the *Pathétique* is in 5/4.] He had tried to beat time with Richter and was evidently puzzled (for over ordinary tempi he never has the slightest difficulty) but he got it right soon. At the *Tannhäuser* overture he gradually rose from his seat as it worked up until, when the clash came, he sat down *hard*. Needless to say, his clapping was vigorous in the extreme.'

At Christmas 1895 he went to several parties and, his mother noted, 'got dreadfully grown up and all the baby has gone. Mr Welsing ... very kindly gave him some lessons and started him in the right way and he is coming occasionally to see what I am doing with A. and to put us both straight.' Then follows a remarkable entry:

> I brought home the 1st Suite from *Peer Gynt* [Grieg] for violin and piano for Olive. Adrian seized on it and wanted to play the violin part on the 2nd piano. All went well until he came to *Ases Tod* which – being easy – he wanted to stump and bang through. I said: 'Oh, don't. Remember she is a poor old woman dying and her nasty wicked son has made her a lot of trouble and has run away from her.' He played it very quietly and then jumped down and ran out of the room, banging into Olive at the door. Although it was quite accidental he flew in a rage and stumped off, refusing to be comforted. After some time we looked for him and found him in the bathroom nursing a finger, which he said Sis had broken, the tears pouring down his cheeks. Of course he was duly consoled with an arnica-dolly, but he was very mournful and finally went to bed. This was very unlike him for he rarely makes a fuss when he is hurt. However when I went to kiss him and tuck him up, just as I was going away he called me and, putting his arms round my neck and pouring floods of tears over me, he whispered: 'Mummie, it isn't my finger that makes me cry, it's the poor dying woman who sighs so.' Of course I told him it was only a story and not true and that when he grew up he would read it and understand that it was only meant for a picture of something else, but I shall have to be very careful what I say if he is going to be so sensitive.

His next musical treat was his first visit to the opera on 29 February 1896. He heard the Carl Rosa Opera perform *Tannhäuser*, with E. C. Hedmondt[2] in the title-rôle. 'He was rather overcome and had his eyes full of tears several times, but he enjoyed it immensely and was most intelligent over the story.' A week later he was taken to *The Flying Dutchman* with Ella Russell as Senta. At this time he was composing his own piano sonata in C major – 'he was very much exercised over what keys he should put the different movements in – he wants relative keys.' In April, for a birthday treat, he went to London for the first time, visiting the Tower and the zoo and, that summer, while his parents went to New York, he developed a passion for golf. On returning, his mother observed that he was going through a curious phase. 'He practises and composes but does not seem to have the passion for music that he had, and certainly does not play as well as he did a year ago. I think all his other studies, arithmetic, geography and particularly Latin, take up his thoughts and crowd out the music. I am curious to see whether it will come back again or whether his early promise was only a fizzle.'

Music is mentioned less frequently in the diary for the next year or so, although he went to dancing classes. In April 1897 he and his sister put on a musical entertainment for their parents at which Adrian's setting of Edward Lear's 'Mr and Mrs Discobbolos' and his *Dance of the Fairies* for violin and piano were performed. The programme for this still survives, printed by Adrian on his toy printing press, which also survives. A few days later, the children were taken by Mrs Boult for a short holiday in Boulogne. Asked at bedtime during the week if he had had a happy day, Adrian replied: 'I feel like Charles the First felt to Buckingham.' 'How is that?' his mother asked. 'When Buckingham brought Henrietta Maria to be Charles's wife, he felt he couldn't thank Buckingham enough and that's how I feel to you for giving us this treat.'

If his compositions contained mistakes, he would not revise or alter them. He insisted on destroying them and starting again. This happened to a string quartet. On another occasion a musician friend 'whose breadth was nearly as great as his length'[3] went through one of Adrian's compositions, correcting mistakes and pencilling in a few notes. The boy thanked him and went to dress to go for a walk with his tutor. He was found in a towering rage exclaiming, 'To think I have to go for a walk with a sausagey dumpling! A sausagey dumpling that alters one's things.' The composition was burnt. Another side of the child's character emerges from an incident on 16 June 1897, arising from his afternoon walks with boys who boarded at his school. He went to his mother and shamefacedly asked her for money to buy a Jubilee medal, explaining that the other boys always bought something and he wanted to be like them. 'I said, "Well, darling, you know it's rather weak to want to do just what other people do." "Yes, I know, but then, you see, I'm not very big yet." "No, and that is why you certainly shall buy your medal if you want it. Some day you'll be stronger and won't care what other people do. Will you have the money now and go and buy it?" "Mummie," in calm desperation, "you don't understand one little bit. I don't want the jubilee medal, I want the excitement of buying it with all the other boys. *Don't you see??*" I *did* see and gave him the money ready for next time.'

On 1 January 1898 Katherine Boult wrote:

I had better tell a little of how his music stands at present. His compositions are wonderful for his age, the *Merman's Song* composed last Sept. and the *Air with Variations* given me for Xmas particularly. He wrote *big* orchestral things with all the instruments in their right compass too. His reading is very good also, but he is just as slow at learning a piece as any ordinary child. He gets to a certain point and then sticks. The last week or two he has begun to grasp the idea of *practising* and goes over and over a little difficult piece, so that I have hopes of him. He knows the thing by heart quite as soon as with the music. His poor little fingers are stiff and unwieldy and he gets impatient that they will not go as fast as his brain wishes. In health he is much better and not quite so thin. He has also quite conquered his temper. Of course his teeming brain is always inventing something new and marvellous.

He had gone to her one morning the previous summer and announced that he was 'just crammed full of bad temper.' She advised him to leave it on the sandhills on his way to school. This, he afterwards told her, he did. Some orchestral musicians in later years might not have been convinced by this!

On his ninth birthday, in 1898, his height was 4 ft 8 in. With his sister and parents he went to Bonn, where he was taken to the Beethoven house. At the end of this visit a dance was given for Olive, who was approaching 16. As Adrian was put to bed, his mother asked if he had enjoyed himself. 'Oh yes, *very* much, it only wanted one thing to be perfect – a little girl for me to dance with.' And an anecdote from his Blundellsands school suggests that teachers' political prejudices entered the classroom even then. He asked his mother if Gladstone had been a bad Chancellor of the Exchequer. No, she replied. 'Oh, Mrs Lovegrove [his teacher] said he was. That's because he was a Liberal. I believe Mrs Lovegrove hates teaching us Anne and George I, because Whigs began in those reigns and Whigs make her perfectly sick.'

Katherine Boult's diary of her son's progress ends there. But in her later account of his life she tells how the Viennese Mr Welsing had wanted to turn Adrian into a *Wunderkind* performer. 'It could have been so easy,' she wrote, 'but we knew he was far too nervous; it would have meant an unbalanced sort of genius, a misery to himself and a worry to everyone else. We preferred a normal, sane boy.' Adrian Boult could count himself lucky in his parents, in the good and kind father whose business was in shipping and Valvoline Oil and who returned from Liverpool each evening and played billiards, and in the mother who was as handsome as she was understanding. She collected stamps and antiquarian books and wrote a novel, under the pseudonym Newton

Stewart, about Frederick II of Prussia. Both she and her son were martyrs to Cedric Boult's mania for punctuality. His life was lived to an ordered pattern and woe betide anyone who upset it. Adrian would tell in later life how he and his mother were playing a piano duet when the gong for lunch was struck. They were on the penultimate chord, but Katherine stopped abruptly, leaving her son raging at the abuse to the music.

Adrian's sister Olive spent a year in Brussels working with a pupil of the violinist Ysaÿe, a fortunate event for a biographer for it means that Adrian's regular letters to her convey his impressions at 11 years old of musical matters. For example, in a letter from Brooke House dated 16 February 1900 he tells 'dear Sis' that a relative of theirs who was at Antibes had written to say 'they have Massanez [sic], the French composer, there. He has a bad cough and goes down to dinner in a shawl.' Other entertaining extracts from this correspondence follow:

> *February 1900.* I have Bach's Preludes and Fugues, Mummy bought them for me. It is such a nice edition, all German. We are having lovely high tides now and that big pile of sand – at the bottom of Brooke Road – where you used to jump Kate [her horse] makes a splendid island.

> *November 1900.* I went to a Philharmonic concert. We had Van Rooy[4] (singing) and Rosenthal,[5] he had an encore. There was a piano concerto of Schumann's which he played beautifully ... They played the Polish Symphony of Tchaikovsky which began this way [and he then wrote out the opening theme in notation].

> *24 February 1901.* The concert yesterday was lovely ... First they played *Leonore No. 3.* Then Dr Richter said something which no one could understand. Anyhow they played the *Pathetic* then[6] and after the interval *Don Juan* (Strauss) then Charfreitagszauber from *Parsifal* and then *Rienzi* ... I followed 3 of them and only got lost once and then found the place very soon ...

CHAPTER 2

London

ADRIAN left his dame school at Easter 1901 and was sent to London to
Westminster School. His parents regarded him as a delicate child for
whom the rigours of a boarding school might prove harmful, so he was
enrolled as a day boy in Grant's House, said to be the oldest school
boarding house in Britain, and his mother rented a small flat, 13, St
Thomas's Mansions, near the hospital. At the flat he was looked after
by Mabel Green, a cousin of one of Katherine Boult's oldest friends. He
described himself in his autobiography[1] as 'badly overgrown' – he was
six foot at the age of 15 – 'a pretty weedy sort of individual in spite of
careful feeding and the most strict discipline over things like bedtime.'
He knew a London that has changed much since the year Elgar's
Cockaigne (In London Town) was composed. He remembered how The
Mall was then 'an apology for a processional road with the processions
slinking along on either side of the trees, and at night it was a dark,
unsavoury and sometimes unsafe haunt.' A farmyard stood where
Admiralty Arch stands now: pedestrians on the way to Trafalgar Square
walked through the mud and manure and could buy milk 'warm from
the cow' for a halfpenny. The Westminster schoolboys went daily to
Vincent Square to play football or cricket and were not allowed to go
directly through 'what was then a very slummy part of London.'

The first boy to whom Adrian spoke at Westminster was Lawrence
Tanner, son of the housemaster, Ralph Tanner. Lawrence was to become
an historian and Keeper of the Muniments of Westminster Abbey. Their
friendship was to last 78 years until Tanner's death. Other school friends
were J. Spedan Lewis, later to inherit John Lewis's of Oxford Street,
and Douglas Dickson, who played the violin and might have become,
Boult thought, a Kreisler instead of head of a firm which managed many
of the great Scottish estates. Of Dickson's four children, Joan became
a leading cellist and prominent teacher and Hester (Boult's goddaughter)
an excellent pianist. Later, a younger boy, Robin Barrington-Ward, who

was to become editor of *The Times* in 1941, was a close companion. At school Adrian acquired two nicknames, one of which – 'Daddy' – stuck to him most of his school life though he did not remember how it came about. The other, 'Boosey', was the consequence of two operations for adenoids, the first of which had been crudely done and had left his nose 'a colour that is usually associated with the bottle.' One day when he was being ribbed about his musical activities someone mentioned the publisher Boosey – and the name stuck.

Music did not loom large in the curriculum. The music master was J. G. Ranalow, father of the baritone Frederick Ranalow. Each evening the boys sang a Latin psalm to his accompaniment on an ancient harmonium. His 'lessons' were a quaint combination of piano and singing. When Katherine Boult discovered that Adrian had been given Chopin's A major *Polonaise* as his 'first piece,' she intervened to stop it, regarding it as the least suitable work for a boy whose natural inclination was 'to hammer away with a stiff wrist.' Once a year the school concert included extracts from Gilbert and Sullivan or, as Boult remembered, 'a ghastly cantata by Cowen called *The Rose Maiden*.' There were no voice tests and 'everybody sang the top chorus line at any octave that suited him, and this was conducted by Ranalow with an enormous silver-mounted ebony club.'

However, a young physics master, H. E. (David) Piggott, was intensely musical and, in the time he was at Westminster before becoming second master at Dartmouth naval college, gave Adrian weekly guidance in harmony and counterpoint. They went to concerts and Piggott showed his pupil how to analyse the scores of what they were about to hear. 'He made me write a violin sonata following, bar for bar, Beethoven's F major, and introduced me to Tovey's Meiningen programmes, the first annotations, I believe, that he ever wrote.'[2] Adrian spent his pocket money on miniature scores – Beethoven symphonies could be had for three shillings each (15p) but with student's discount this was reduced to 2s 3d (just over 11p). Despite this preoccupation with music, he still managed to win a prize for French, though his housemaster told his mother in 1903 that 'he is apt to be a bit dreamy in form and comes back with a start to everyday life and the relentless questions forced on his unwilling brain.'

The musical scene in Britain during Adrian Boult's childhood and adolescence differed greatly from today's, quite apart from the non-existence of radio, television and state and municipal subsidies. London had only one orchestra in which the personnel had some consistency, Henry Wood's Queen's Hall Orchestra. The orchestra at Philharmonic concerts was an ad hoc affair, as was that at Covent Garden. Apart from Wood and the occasional composer–conductor such as Parry, Stanford or Elgar, British names were rarely encountered on the rostrum. Weingartner, Richter, Nikisch, Steinbach – these were the conductors who drew the crowds. Thomas Beecham did not come on the scene until 1905. Bournemouth's small municipal orchestra had been founded by Dan Godfrey in 1893. The Scottish Orchestra, founded in 1891, was conducted by a foreigner. Like the Liverpool Philharmonic, the Scottish shared several players with the Hallé. When Hallé died in 1895, Manchester invited Hans Richter to succeed him. The negotiations to capture the erstwhile director of the Vienna Opera and conductor of the Vienna Philharmonic dragged on until 1899: Liverpool grew impatient and gave its rostrum to Frederic Cowen, keeping faith with him even when Richter arrived. The Hallé was perhaps the best-rehearsed orchestra in the country, but it existed only from October to March, as did Liverpool and the Scottish. In the summer its players scattered to the seaside pier orchestras of Scarborough, Blackpool and Llandudno. Even when Richter retired in 1911, the Hallé did not even consider engaging a British successor. As for Covent Garden, the Edwardian years were a 'golden age' for singers – Caruso, Melba, Destinn among them – but the conductors, apart from Percy Pitt, were also the bearers of foreign names. Only in organ-lofts and academies did native musicians hold sway.

The education which was to stand Adrian in the best stead was obtained at the weekends. He had a season ticket for Henry Wood's Saturday and Sunday concerts and rarely missed one. While most schoolboys hero-worshipped Ranjitsinhji, Fry and MacLaren, he hero-worshipped Steinbach, Nikisch and Strauss. In various of his notebooks, in diary form, are his comments on most of the concerts. Olive in Brussels received weekly reports during 1902. Thus:

9 *March*. Yesterday's prog. was Choral Symphony ... Beethoven, Piano Concerto ... Saint-Saëns, Symphonic poem *Don Juan* ... Strauss, Quartet *Rigoletto* ... Verdi, Overture, *William Tell* ... Rossini. Mr Mark Hambourg, Mesdames Ella Russell, Kirkby Lunn, Messrs. Lloyd Chandos, Ffrangçon-Davies. The Choral is *very* heavy and lasted 1 hr 20 mins! E. Russell and K. Lunn had one a light blue and the other a light purple dress on. They clashed. E. Russell sang out of tune. We went to the pantomime at Drury Lane on Wednesday week. Dan Leno and Herbert Campbell acted ...

23 *March*. Have you seen Ysaÿe yet? Or rather has Ysaÿe seen you yet? He

is going to play and conduct at the festival at the end of April and beginning of May ... Have you heard of Herr Nikisch? He is going to conduct at the festival...

During the Easter holidays at Blundellsands he had measles, convalescing by helping his mother with her stamp collection and by riding his horse. He told Olive: 'I have given Dorothy Couper measles and she has most probably given them to Marjorie. I have not given it to Leslie Vey although he has got it and it amuses Mrs Vey to think that I gave it to him, but if I gave it to him when I saw him at Marina the day after I came home surely someone else must have got it and he developed it too soon after I went there to tea.'

The holidays ended with his attendance at what 65 years later he still described as 'the most important concert I have attended from my own point of view.' This was Arthur Nikisch's appearance at the London Musical Festival on 30 April. The programme included extracts from Wagner's *Tristan und Isolde* and *Die Meistersinger* and two Tchaikovsky works, the B flat minor Piano Concerto, with Mark Hambourg as soloist, and the Fifth Symphony. Adrian had never heard such playing and he noticed how Nikisch drew a totally different sound from the orchestra and threw a totally different light on the music. That day, at the age of 12, he knew that the only thing he wanted to do in his life was to be a conductor.

He was still composing. His first entry in his diary for 1903 is 'Have composed an *Impromptu* of 40 bars, Op. 4, today. I think it's for Mummy's birthday on the 20th. Went to badminton in the afternoon.' 2 January: 'Am copying my *Impromptu* out, and am not quite sure it is music.' Back at Westminster, on 17 January he heard Wood conduct Schumann's Fourth Symphony which was 'magnificent, magnificently played.' Kreisler in Beethoven's Concerto was also 'magnificent – he is the best violinist after Ysaÿe ... *Tod und Verklärung* is very clever indeed, it is nicer though not so involved as *Ein Heldenleben* but is not as good as *Don Juan* or the love scene from *Feuersnot*.' Hearing Brahms's Second Symphony for the first time on 31 January he deferred judgment until a repeat performance on 8 February when he rated it 'splendid. I enjoyed it ever so much more than on Saturday week. They played it better too.' 14 February: 'When I hear *Hebrides* [Mendelssohn] it always strikes me how unequal an orchestra is – somehow the woodwind always seems so weak.' 16 February: 'I was not very well so got leave from football. I wandered in the Abbey and began copying "A Canon in four parts in one, by Dr John Blow" on his tomb, but I had done 2 bars when I gave it up.' On 16 March Richter took the Hallé[3] to Queen's Hall: 'Richter's *Meistersinger* [overture] was magnificent – brought out points which Wood does not ... *Francesca* [Tchaikovsky's *Francesca da Rimini*] magnificent, nearly equals No. 5 in E minor ...' On 22 March, it was back to Wood and to his first hearing of Beethoven's *Eroica* Symphony. He liked the *scherzo* best.

As an early birthday present on 27 March he was given a miniature score of *Ein Heldenleben* which he heard under Wood the next day: '*Heldenleben*! Oh! I should like to hear it every day for a week and then I should begin to know something about it. I have never seen such terrific polyphony ... Mr Piggott thinks that it is a mystery how a man could write such a horrid noise. Dickson thinks it a mystery how a man could write such a huge score and know what it sounds like ... I think it a mystery how a man could write such terrific discords without them sounding wrong ... I heard Strauss do it at the 1st performance in England on December 8th but I hadn't the score then.' Evidently this inspired him, for on 30 March he composed two pages of a symphonic poem. 'It is getting on fine.' But by 3 April he was stuck at the 94th bar for want of a new melody. Two days later he had got a melody but was 'not quite satisfied with it.' His 14th birthday present from his parents was *Grove's Dictionary of Music and Musicians*. On 5 May he went to the start of a Covent Garden *Ring* cycle conducted by Richter, with Ernest van Dyck as Loge and Olive Fremstad as Fricka in *Das Rheingold*. 'Awfully pretty' was the incongruous verdict, with the rider, 'How anyone can put a cut into that lovely thing is a mystery (I should have said "make a cut out"). Richter managed his *98* orchestra admirably ... We have a box on the 2nd tier ... The King, Queen, Henry J. Wood and A. E. Rodewald[4] were there.' *Die Walküre*, with Van Rooy as Wotan, van Dyck as Siegmund and Milka Ternina as Brünnhilde followed two days later – 'splendid, although not as good as *Rheingold*. Could not go to *Siegfried*.' But after *Götterdämmerung* on 9 May: 'Ternina and Ernst Kraus [Siegfried] simply magnificent and so was Richter. We are all quite willing to go to the 3rd cycle next week!?' After this, Felix Weingartner conducting Beethoven's Triple Concerto ('rather long') was tame.

Boult completed his symphonic poem on 13 July. A few days later he was on a field day in Epping Forest. He had been surprised that his parents, 'stern radical anti-conscriptionists,' had welcomed the formation of a cadet corps at Westminster. He joined it, becoming a lance-sergeant in October 1906. He was a good shot. His other school activity was carpentry, which he found 'great fun.' But success in making toolboxes rated only one line in his diary, whereas hearing Liszt's *Les Préludes* on 11 October led to this: 'It is the first time I heard it and I think it very fine indeed. It is – barring rhapsodies – the first Liszt I have heard and if I had not known what it was should have declared it the work of a Russian or Pole. You can trace his influence over the later Wagner, Grieg and Richard Strauss, as much as Berlioz, although he and Berlioz I think have little in common. His influence over Richard Strauss is not so marked as I had expected, although you can certainly trace it. I am dying to hear it again as, as it was at the end of the concert, I couldn't study it as much as I wished, although the concert lasted only $1\frac{1}{2}$ hrs – what a mistake $2\frac{1}{2}$ hr concerts are!'

On 17 November, with his parents and Edward J. Dent,[5] a new friend, present, Adrian sang in Westminster Abbey in a Gregorian service. 'I was in the choir next to Mr Piggott ... We did not have the Abbey choir this time and managed very well ... After the service Mr Ranalow (conductor and music-master) went up to the Dean (Armitage Robinson). "Well, Mr Dean, what did you think of our humble attempt?" The Dean: "Very humble" and proceeded to blow him up – why didn't he make the boys sing up etc. etc. (all because his wretched choirboys were not there).' On 28 November he heard Muriel Foster sing Strauss's *Hymnus* (op. 33, No. 3): 'I don't like the *Hymnus* as much as the *Apollopriesterin* [op. 33, No. 2]. It goes on about nothing. She sang it beautifully. Wood made the fiddles stand up to play the Bach [Brandenburg Concerto No. 3] ... what a wonderful thing it is!' The future champion of English music was a harsh critic on 29 November when Rutland Boughton's *Songs of the English* and Sullivan's *Overture di Ballo* were in Wood's programme: 'The Sullivan is very pretty (that is all that can be said). The Boughtons were too feeble for anything.' Better fare, though, on 6 December: '*Till Eulenspiegel* I place before *Ein Heldenleben* and second only to *Don Juan* of Strauss's works. It is magnificent. At the beginning I roared with laughter. I have never heard anything like the way he treats the woodwind. He seems to have created them again.' Five days later he heard Strauss himself conduct the Queen's Hall Orchestra in a Berlioz centenary concert: 'A lovely concert. Half the stalls were full, 1/3 grand circle, 1 row of the balcony!! Wood sat behind us with Percy Pitt. Berlioz is marvellous. If I ever become a conductor (!!) I must revive some of his works – oh, if only I could!!! I like "Carnaval" [*Carnaval Romain*] very much, also the three movements from *Romeo* – they are exquisite, but *Francs juges* I must hear again. It is magnificent but I don't yet understand it.' At the penultimate concert he attended in London on 12 December before going home he heard Ernestine Schumann-Heink sing *Non più di fiori* from Mozart's *La Clemenza di Tito* – 'wonderful, $2\frac{1}{4}$ octaves and a marvellous trill' – but he found the basset-horn obbligato 'curious, I don't like its tone as much as the clarinet.' And there was Teresa Carreño, 'very fine' in Grieg's Piano Concerto.

In 1904 Boult began to analyse 'in depth' and in formidable technical detail works by J. S. Bach, Mozart (Symphony No. 40 in G minor) and Beethoven (First and Second Symphonies). By now his handwriting was taking on the shape familiar to the many correspondents of his maturity, a bold, individual hand, unmistakable for anyone else's and on the whole easily legible. From now on, his comments become sharper and more perceptive. Fewer works are merely 'magnificent,' but the enthusiasm of this remarkable 15-year-old persists. His biographer needs no excuse to quote liberally from these vivid, amusing and informative diaries. One is glad to note, too, that sometimes there were cakes and ale, as at home for Christmas in 1903:

> *21 December.* Sis and I were taken by Mr and Mrs Nicholl to the Ball at St George's Hall given by the Liverpool Scottish. First they had speeches by Col. Macfie and received their prizes. Then they all came in in couples and had a terrific march round – and then the Lancers began. Sis taught me how to waltz.

The next day, after hearing *Elijah*, he wrote that he was 'studying the arrangement of orchestras.' There follow plans of Wood's at Queen's Hall, Cowen's at the Liverpool Philharmonic, and Richter's at Covent Garden for *The Ring* the previous May and with the Hallé in Manchester. Wood was alone in having first and second violins grouped on his left, with violas on his right and cellos and basses behind the violas. Cowen and Richter had first violins on the left and seconds on the right, but whereas Cowen had violas and cellos in front of him with basses divided left and right alongside cellos, Richter at the Hallé had two rows of basses on his left behind first violins and alongside woodwind and another row on his right behind the bassoons. At Covent Garden Richter had violins, cellos and basses all on his left, violas ahead of him and woodwind and brass on his right. Boult's interest in and experimentation with the positioning of the orchestra remained for the rest of his life, and he felt strongly that for certain works – Elgar's Second Symphony, for example – the score demanded that first and second violins should be to left and right of the conductor and had been conceived with that seating in the composer's mind.

On Christmas Eve he had evidently read a report of the 'illegal' performance of *Parsifal* in New York when Heinrich Conried, director of the Metropolitan Opera House, defied Wagner's ban on performances of the opera outside Bayreuth, for the diary comments: 'I think Conried got hold of the full score and smuggled it into America, where it is not copyright. Of course Frau Wagner is an old idiot not to want it taken out of Bayreuth.' On 6 January 1904 he heard Richter conduct the Hallé in his favourite *Don Juan* and Beethoven's Fifth Symphony. 'In *Juan* I had never noticed two commas which are put over two bar lines. In the symphony he gave me a new idea of Beethoven especially of the slow movement. Wood is not good for Beethoven.' Back in London Emil Paur conducted the Queen's Hall Orchestra while Wood was in the United States; 'undoubtedly a great conductor,' Adrian thought, 'he is able – like Weingartner – to get much finer crashes than Wood does. I should like to have heard him in Beethoven ... Those idiots Chappell's, who lease the hall now, won't let you hang your coat over the front of the balcony.' He developed what the doctor called congestion of the lungs a few days later and was sent home. His diary comment was a rueful, 'Oh, the concerts!' But at Blundellsands he was told 'a lovely story about Richter. He had just tried the first Brahms Symphony on the Liverpudlians and they clapped furiously. So in the interval Mr Welsing went to congratulate Richter, and the first thing he heard when he got into the Green Room – "Ha, Welsing! Look at me, what you think of me and my new vite vaistcoat!" So Mr Welsing had to finish his congratulations on the waistcoat before he could begin about the Brahms.'

Before returning to Westminster he heard Frederic Cowen conduct the Liverpool Philharmonic in Beethoven's Seventh Symphony, the Grail Scene from *Parsifal* and some Strauss. 'Cowen is offensive! His Wagner is awful. Richter keeps strict time without making Wagner sound like a sort of dance, and Cowen accents the first beat so that it is awful. The chorus are excellent ... The Beethoven was disgraceful – I wonder Cowen dare do anything after the way he does some things (that sounds very funny, but I think the grammar is all right) ... *Tod und Verklärung* gave me one of the greatest surprises I've ever had. Cowen and the orchestra did it magnificently. It is (so far) the only thing I've heard him do worthy of praise (I think somebody else must have given them a secret rehearsal on the sly!!).' Back at the Queen's Hall he found Brahms's *Variations on a Theme by Haydn* 'lovely but I don't understand them yet – I think I was listening too much for the double counterpoint. *Don Juan* was still more lovely. The performance of it bears out what I say about the restlessness and unceasing energy of Strauss's music being caused chiefly by the way he rushes through his harmonies. Beethoven has (generally) one harmony a bar. Strauss has at least four. The reason it struck me specially yesterday was because I heard it last done by Richter, who takes it at a slower tempo than Wood and it does not sound nearly so restless as Wood's does.'

This concert he later discussed with the teacher H. E. Piggott, who had thought it 'abominably played' and that this was because 'there is a terrible fight going on at Queen's Hall – Wood has dismissed half the orchestra.' This was when new contracts for the orchestral players stipulated that Wood would not allow them to send deputies to rehearsals or concerts. He thereby signalled his intention to end the pernicious system whereby an orchestral player could send some, possibly inferior, player to take his place while he took a more lucrative engagement elsewhere. The ill effects of this practice on the standard of performance can easily be imagined; economically, of course, the players regarded it as something to preserve. On the other hand, many of the players had become bored with Wood and wanted the chance to play under other conductors. The result of the 'terrible fight' was that the players who broke away from Wood formed the London Symphony Orchestra as a self-governing body and gave its first concert on 9 June 1904 with Richter as conductor.

Hearing a performance of Saint-Saëns's Fourth Piano Concerto at a Wood concert on 23 March 1904, Adrian judged it as 'glorious – the changing of the hymn tune of the first andante to the splendid theme of the finale is marvellous.' But he was disappointed in the last two items of the concert; 'I suppose I was looking forward to them.' One of the items was Elgar's *Enigma Variations*. The diary contains few references to Elgar performances and it is clear that Boult was much more impressed by Strauss, Liszt, Wagner and Tchaikovsky than he was by Elgar. He had heard the two part-songs of op. 26, *Fly, Singing Bird* and *The Snow*, on 12 March and had found them 'delightful, a little commonplace perhaps, but they were so truly Elgarish.' Some weeks later the *Three Bavarian Dances* were 'pretty, but not up to much.' A second hearing of the Brahms *Haydn Variations* on 13 March, however, 'sent thrills through me. I like the horn one best ... I like *Heldenleben* more and more – it is glorious! I don't understand it all yet, but I am getting nearer.'

Westminster boys inevitably became involved in state occasions. Thus on 17 March from 12 to 1 pm Adrian's form were having Greek conditional sentences – 'very dull except when Fox gets angry. Well, they were *very* dull, so I was three parts asleep (letting my mind run

19

on – or rather off – the lesson) and suddenly I jumped up, wide awake, for I had heard that *dreadful* Abbey bell that tolls for royalty and deans and archbishops. The Duke of Cambridge, the King's uncle, was dead. His funeral is to be in Abbey on Tuesday, we are to be there.' At the funeral Adrian first heard Purcell's *Funeral Music for Queen Mary* ('splendid') but *Onward, Christian Soldiers* with trumpets and drums was 'magnificent and sent cold shivers down my back.'

Another memorable occasion was at St James's Hall on 30 April when the Joachim Quartet marked the diamond jubilee of its leader's first appearance in London (when he had played the Beethoven Concerto with Mendelssohn conducting). The quartet played three Beethoven string quartets, op. 18, No. 3, op. 135 and op. 59, No. 2. 'Oh what a heavenly quartet,' Adrian wrote, 'they all play different tempo rubato (moderate) and they are always together. It's marvellous. Joachim ought to change places with Haliř, he is getting very old and shaky, 73 years old! ... The quartets were glorious but I cannot and never will like chamber music as much as orchestral.' In *My Own Trumpet* Boult recalls that 'it was an example of perfect loyalty to hear how the whole Quartet brought their tone down to balance that of their leader. I still remember the slow movement in Beethoven's op. 18, No. 3 when Haliř's second violin rose to the surface above the first violin for four bars and let us hear a beautiful cantabile which came from him at no other time.'[6]

During 1904 he was still composing – a Minuet in C minor, 'the best thing I have ever done,' a setting of Herrick's *Daffodils* for Piggott 'will be very good with little alteration,' and 'a prelude for Mr Piggott after J. S. Bach is in binary form and completely founded on 3 figures which appear in double counterpoint inverted, written backwards, etc. etc. I think it very good.' He went to listen to debates in the House of Commons, and on 18 May scored for his form's cricket match after which he felt 'influenzaish.' A temperature of 105°F next day was the start of pneumonia and pleurisy and he went home for the rest of the summer term. On recovery he was taken to Liverpool on 11 July to see Sarah Bernhardt in Sardou's *La Sorcière*: 'her voice has gone and she rants, but in certain places one can tell what the real Sarah Bernhardt must have been.' On 19 July Edward VII was in Liverpool to lay the foundation stone of the new Anglican cathedral, a huge building which was not to be completed until 1980. A week's stay at Swettenham in the last week of July included watching the local rifle corps competition and his 'first invitation' to play a piano recital at someone's home – some Liszt and Grieg and his own Minuet in C minor. Helping at a school treat at Swettenham Hall he was 'struck in their garden and house how every flower or piece of furniture was put all alone, separate by itself, giving its full effect – whereas in the Tippings' [where he had given his recital] everything, old oak and lovely china amongst others, was piled together.' On 28 July he returned not to Brooke House, but to a new home, The Abbey Manor, at West Kirby.

CHAPTER 3

Schuster

FROM his new home, Adrian went to New Brighton on 7 August to hear Adolph Brodsky[1] conduct an orchestra (presumably drawn from the Hallé) in a Tchaikovsky programme. The soloist in the Violin Concerto had been one of Brodsky's pupils at the Royal Manchester College of Music, Arthur Catterall. He was now 21 and a quarter of a century later he was to be Boult's first leader of the BBC Symphony Orchestra. 'Very laudable and praiseworthy' was his 15-year-old future chief's verdict on this occasion.

Back at Westminster School in September he recorded an amusing incident when he was asked at the last moment by a monitor to play the harmonium for prayers.

> He told me to pull out all the stops but the 16 foot ones and it would be all right. So I went and pulled out all the stops as he said and consequently couldn't hear a word they were singing. I was much too flurried to try and think of remembering the words, and so I went on, and they went on; we were together sometimes! ... Afterwards Dr Gow said 'Why ever don't you sing? I never heard such a disgraceful exhibition in my life. Let your voices out. I shall keep you all in if I don't hear any improvement.' I felt awful. If I had played properly I am sure they would have sung up more. However better luck next time!

On 2 October he heard the New Queen's Hall Orchestra for the first time – 'trumpets are disgraceful, nothing but bubblings and cracklings. Horns little better.' An improvement was reported week by week.

The concert in Queen's Hall on 24 October was of more significance for Boult's future – his first encounter with Elgar's *The Dream of Gerontius*, with the London Choral Society conducted by Arthur Fagge, and Marie Brema, Gervase Elwes and David Ffrangçon-Davies as the solo singers. This was only its second London performance.

> I was very disappointed. It is a very aimless wandering. The closing scene is

22

exquisite, and the demon chorus is good, but Gerontius takes much too long dying, although phrases (e.g. *Sanctus fortis ... Domine*) are lovely. Elwes has too small a voice for Queen's Hall, Ffrangçon-Davies was magnificent, Marie Brema, though getting old, was good. Rehearsals were too few with orchestra, there was a lot of raggedness. Will Elgar live? His *Variations* (op. 36) will, I am certain. Will *Gerontius*? I am *not* certain by any means. I fully believe that if I knew the poem better I should understand the music more: I should like to hear it again. Parts of it are wildly exciting, but a lot is deadly dull. I believe the performance had a lot to do with that, though. Fagge doesn't understand an orchestra ...

He returned to West Kirby in mid-term to attend the wedding of 'Clara (our dear parlourmaid for 15 years)' on 1 November, a date deserving its place in Adrian's biography because he notes in his diary entry for that day: 'Alas, shaved for first time. Absurd at $15\frac{1}{2}$! but necessary.' In London he was now attending meetings of the Concert Goers' Club, where discussions followed a lecture. In this way he met Rosa Newmarch and Edgar Jacques, both active as writers of programme notes for London concerts. But a more important meeting awaited him. Living near the Boults when they were at Blundellsands was a widow, Mrs Wood, 'a wonderful example of the type which modelled itself on Queen Victoria,' Boult described her in *My Own Trumpet*.[2] Adrian paid her regular visits and on one of these she told him that her nephew Frank Schuster lived near Westminster Abbey and knew a great many actors and musicians including Elgar. 'I will write and tell Frank he must ask you to some of his parties.'

Leo Francis Schuster lived at 22, Old Queen Street and also had a riverside house called The Hut on the Thames at Bray. He was a tireless and generous host and he enjoyed being 'in the swim' and patronising new artists. He was a close friend of Gabriel Fauré, who always stayed with him. He was homosexual and was described by the poet Siegfried Sassoon, whom he befriended, as 'a social impresario of "artistic events" ... He was something more than a *patron* of music, because he loved music as much as it is humanly possible to do. In the presence of great musicians he was humble, bowing before them in his semitic way and flattering them over-effusively because he knew no other way of demonstrating his admiration. With first-rate people he became, in his way, first-rate ...'[3] In 1967 Boult wrote:[4] 'I remember a chap saying that there was nothing like Frank's *welcoming mouth* except his sister's! They were *both* amazing hostesses.' Schuster had worked for a short time in his father's bank in the City of London but decided that all he needed was his portion of the family inheritance. With this he entertained hundreds of friends and helped as many.

Boult first met Frankie Schuster[5] on 12 November 1904 when they went to the Queen's Hall to hear Beethoven's Fifth Symphony, Brahms's Violin Concerto (soloist Maurice Sons), Wolf's symphonic poem *Penthesilea* and Max von Schillings's melodrama of Wildenbruch's *Hexenlied* recited by Tita Brand. Schuster had written to him the previous day from the Midland Hotel, Manchester, enclosing a ticket for the concert, 'a very interesting programme.' Boult's diary says:

> I sat with Mr Leo Schuster ... who financed Elgar and without whom the Elgar Festival [at Covent Garden in March 1904] would never have taken place. He is extremely interesting and knows everybody worth knowing in musical London. He was most amusing about the Elgar Festival. Elgar was staying with him and though he stayed in bed most of the time to get rid of the reporters etc., Mr Schuster says that one day he was shut up in a little room – a photographer on the stairs, an interviewer in the dining-room, a man who wanted to make his bust in the drawing-room and they would not go away – so poor E.E. to get rid of them retired out of the window! He is going to ask me to tea next time Elgar stays with him.

That meeting was soon to follow, but in the meantime, on 26 November, he heard Debussy's *L'Après-midi d'un faune* ('very difficult, though not much in it') and Busoni ('clean-shaven, by the way') play Beethoven's *Emperor* Concerto 'beautifully.' Also, at the same concert, *Ulalume*, a 'poem' after E.A.Poe by Joseph Holbrooke. 'By a long way the vilest piece of music I have ever heard. Every instrument possible (from fiddle to tuba, muted throughout with horrid effect). Not a tune in it. Clever orchestration, but not used to any effect. Two men near me hissed and I joined them lustily.' Adrian's invitation to an evening dinner party at Schuster's came on 11 December. There he found Elgar, Theo Lierhammer, the Austrian baritone, Fritz Volbach, *Generalmusikdirektor* at Mainz where he had recently conducted Elgar's *The Apostles*, Claude Phillips, Keeper of the Wallace Collection and art critic of the *Daily Telegraph*, and Edith Clegg, a young contralto.

'Introduced to all but Volbach,' Adrian wrote that night. 'Had a long talk with Lierhammer about translations of songs, operas etc., audiences, lozenges. He said if he were born again he would never be a singer ... With Elgar and Miss Clegg I had a little talk too. Lierhammer sang Handel's *Largo*, Grieg's *Im kehn* and two songs by Hugo Wolf *divinely* and Miss Clegg sang well. Volbach accompanied perfectly.' One of the Wolf songs was *Anakreons Grab* and Edith Clegg sang Elgar's *After*. It was on this occasion that Boult was shocked by a characteristic outburst of Elgar's petulance. He and the composer were looking at the recently published score of *The Apostles* when Schuster asked Elgar to meet Miss Clegg, who was about to sing *After*. Elgar strode towards her and shook her hand with the remark, 'Well, you have spoiled my evening for me.' When the song was over Elgar said to Boult: 'Aren't the *words* beautiful?' – 'How to answer that remark was a bit of a conversational problem for a lad of 15,' Boult wrote years later.[6]

Four days later Boult wrote: 'Oh what an orchestral performance! Finest I think I have ever heard.' He had heard Fritz Steinbach conduct the London Symphony Orchestra in Bach, Beethoven and Brahms. 'The performance of the Brahms [Symphony No. 4] was magnificent. One always heard the woodwind. His arrangement of the Brandenburg [No. 3] has his own phrasing and expression marks, leaving out the two middle chords between the movements.' And he sketched Steinbach's arrangement of the orchestra. What a contrast three evenings later when he was scandalized by Wood's savage cuts in Tchaikovsky's *Francesca da Rimini*. That was to be the last London concert he would attend for some months. Doctors had advised that, after his pleurisy earlier in the year, he should spend the winter abroad. His father needed to go to South Africa on business, so on 7 January 1905 the family, excluding Olive, sailed from Southampton in the *Durham Castle*, landing in Cape Town on 31 January. On the voyage Adrian twice played piano solos at ship's concerts and took part in shipboard activities. At first, his mother wrote, 'he was inclined to go off alone to write, but we told him it would be wiser to mix with people and learn their ways, since he had to live in the world.' Touchingly, there still exists the writing he did – on ship's notepaper: a list of the variations of dynamics in Brahms's Fourth Symphony. The echoes of Steinbach's performance would not be stilled.

CHAPTER 4

Opera Nights

In South Africa the Boults visited Johannesburg, Durban and Ladysmith. The names in the church of the 3,030 men who fell at Ladysmith moved Adrian to anger and to blame of 'pigheaded Downing Street and drunken generals (Buller chief among them) and most of all Chamberlain and Kruger.' He managed to hear some recitals while in South Africa. On 5 March they sailed in the *Galeka* with 300 troops of the Royal Irish aboard. A week later he went ashore at St Helena. On 21 March it was 'too rough for fancy dress dance – what a relief!' After calling at Tenerife they returned to Southampton on 30 March 1905.

His concert-going was resumed in London on 2 May. 'Second impressions of *Gerontius*. After studying vocal score I am convinced that a good deal I thought at first must be modified. The whole idea and carrying out of the words is magnificent, and to me the "deadly dull" parts are much fewer and further between. His treatment of orchestra and chorus is excellent all through, except at the first appearance of the "grand mysterious harmony" which, though the chords are lovely, seems to me not *grand* enough, ie. full enough scored; it may be done to give additional weight to its subsequent appearances, but I don't quite like it. But yet, there is still something just missing to me – I don't know what, unless perhaps coherency and definite ideas but then that is exactly what should be lacking in a correct setting of the poem. I give up ... The performance, with the same artists, was better. Elwes, though his voice is too small for Queen's Hall, is a fine singer ... Marie Brema was awful. She has no idea of the work, the hot potatoes in her mouth are much worse, and she wow wows worse than ever.'

A week in camp at Aldershot in August with the Public Schools Brigade was followed by a holiday in Scotland, with grouse-shooting. He was back in London for the end of Wood's Promenade Concerts and a performance of Elgar's *Introduction and Allegro for Strings* which had had its first performance while he was in South Africa. He noted and disapproved of Wood's new arrangement of the orchestra with all the violins on his left. The diary entries at this time are highly critical of Wood, who 'would take a prize for making nonsense of Brahms.' Adrian was in the Abbey on 20 October for Sir Henry Irving's funeral service – 'all well-known England was there.' Hearing Elgar's *The Apostles* on 30 October he declared it 'a wonderful work – the proportions are very fine and the last scene is magnificent ... The Mary Magdalene scene is dreadfully slow. Alice Lakin sang it very poorly ...' At the first concert of the Queen's Hall Orchestra's season on 4 November, 'the Elgar Variations were well played (Mr Schuster was quite pleased)' but 'last but not least my first hearing of Strauss's *Symphonia Domestica*. Under his direction, 2nd performance in England, altogether 7th perf. The harmonies are disgusting but there is something in it which excites you extraordinarily, it makes the work sound 5 minutes long instead of $\frac{3}{4}$ hour. But still it is not worthwhile spending all the time and trouble over it.'

These judgments are those of a 16-year-old schoolboy, but a very exceptional schoolboy, whose natural enthusiasm was tempered by discrimination and whose animadversions did not preclude fairness and generosity. He was also, of course, privileged, not least in his introduction to Schuster's social world. But he was not spoiled nor did he abuse the privilege of his position. And he was a Liberal. He was overjoyed on 4 December when Balfour's Conservative Government resigned and the Liberal leader, Henry Campbell-Bannerman, formed a government. 'Perhaps we shall have a little less muddling now. Chamberlain is still dangerous because he intends to fight the next (not this one just coming) General Elec. for Tariff Reform.' A week later: 'The Cabinet is settled. It ought to be very powerful – H. Gladstone as Home Secretary seems rather a mistake but Asquith should be good with the Exchequer and most of the others are good. Winston Churchill is not in the Cabinet – I'm so glad.' When the election came in January 1906, Adrian was at West Kirby. On the 9th he went to the Sun Hall in Kensington, a Liverpool suburb, to hear Campbell-Bannerman speak – 'no orator' – and several women suffragists 'made nuisances of themselves.' On 15 January: 'Balfour defeated at Manchester. All 9 seats swept by Liberals and Labour men. If only they keep on like this! Later: They *have* kept on and we've got a large majority over Labour, Irish and Conservatives put together.'[1]

The year 1905 had ended with some fine musical experiences for him. In November and December he heard Richter conduct Strauss's *Also sprach Zarathustra*, Kreisler play Viotti and Mozart concertos, Wood conduct Schubert's Great C major Symphony (16 December, 'I have not heard it before, it is very fine') and, on 19 December, a Chopin recital by Busoni: 'I had no idea a piano recital was like that, or that Chopin was like that. It was a revelation.' At Schuster's home on 26 November his fellow guests were the critic and translator Alfred Kalisch, the composer–conductor André Messager, the composer Baron d'Erlanger and the French baritone Victor Maurel, creator of Verdi's Iago and Falstaff. Maurel sang and Adrian noted that Schuster had described him as 'a wonderful wreck.' Then he went home for Christmas and at a dance in the dining room of The Abbey Manor 'had a list of ladies on the back of my card and danced with every one.'

Mozart's 150th anniversary was marked on 27 January 1906 by concerts and talks which Adrian attended. On 3 February he heard Strauss's *Don Quixote* for the first time: 'very mad but exceedingly clever. The solo part well played by Hugo Becker.' When he heard Strauss conduct the piece a few weeks later he found it 'magnificent. He reduced the sheep etc. to reasonable and harmless proportions.' In the summer he took to watching billiards matches and often went rifle-shooting. Nikisch conducting Brahms one evening and accompanying Elena Gerhardt at the piano the next, and Caruso and Scotti in *Pagliacci* were all eclipsed, in spite of their celebrity, by the experience on 26 June in Queen's Hall: 'Had an extraordinary revelation in orchestral playing by the Vienna Philharmonic. They sounded quite different from our London orchestras and play magnificently. The tone of the brass is beautiful, and timpani are also very fine – the note being very easy to distinguish even when *ff*, when most timp. degenerate into a row no more musical than Gran Cassa. Wagner's *Meistersinger* overture, Mozart's G minor and Beethoven's C minor symphonies, the *Oberon* overture and Elgar's *Variations* were all played equally well in the several styles. Schalk[2] is a great conductor and they understand him perfectly.'

In the second half of the year theatre-going predominated in his activities. He went to his first ballet on 21 July, *Coppélia*, at the Empire Theatre with Adeline Genée ('I enjoyed it awfully, Genée is fascinating and acts marvellously'). On the 24th at Covent Garden he heard Gluck's *Armide* conducted by Messager. He thought the music 'wonderful – it expressed the words so admirably. That last scene with Armide alone is magnificent. The tunes are all so graceful without being commonplace.'

On 6 October at Covent Garden he saw *Madama Butterfly* with 'Giachetti and Sammarco fine and Zenatello good but rather excitable Yank naval officer. Mugnone fine conductor, works up splendid climaxes without ever drowning singers. Scene at end of 2nd act impressed

me exceedingly.' A week later the same cast in *Tosca* were 'all magnificent,' but *Rigoletto* on the 20th was 'so funny and silly, but I am
glad to have seen it.' (Between *Tosca* and *Rigoletto* he had seen Ellen
Terry in *The Winter's Tale*!). On the 27th he heard Melba and Zenatello
in Gounod's *Faust*: 'Once is enough, thank you! Though I am glad to
have heard it. Melba can't act a bit but has a lovely voice.' Adrian heard
Elgar's *The Kingdom* for the first time at 'rather a poor performance'
in London on 10 December. 'It is very finely balanced and doesn't drag
like *Apostles* – altogether an improvement.' He had been alerted to the
beauties of *The Kingdom* the previous August by Schuster, who wrote
to him on the 29th: 'I received yesterday another precious instalment
from Ed Elgar of first proofs of his *Kingdom*. This is a work of
extraordinary subtlety and delicacy and of more than usual "intimacy"
of atmosphere. Heaven help it when produced in the respectable *stodgy*
manner of a Birmingham Festival – but of course I can't resist going for
all that ...' Schuster mentioned *The Kingdom* again in a letter a year
later (19 September 1907) when he described the Hereford performance
as 'really perfect ... It is assuredly a work destined to a glorious
immortality. I don't believe that people so close to its inception can
properly appreciate its rare beauty.' Boult remembered all his life how
Schuster said that 'compared with *The Kingdom*, *Gerontius* is the work
of a raw amateur!'

New Year's Day 1907 saw the arrival of Boult's driving-licence 'and
I had my first lesson ... Went nearly to Heswall.' His comment on a
New Year dance at Oxton is a reminder of how social mores have
changed. He sat out three dances and noted that 'all the ones I sat out
there were lots of ladies also sitting out, but nobody introduced us!' It
just was not done to approach a girl direct and ask her to dance. On 14
January he waited three hours for a ticket for his first *Meistersinger*.
'All sold out so gallery my only chance. Got there at 4. On the stairs
5.15. Seats 6.15. Performance 6.45 ... What a splendid thing it is. I had
no idea there would be anything so farcical as Beckmesser's serenade.'
The next evening he was at *Tristan* conducted by Nikisch: 'he's wonderful at concerts but in opera he's perfectly extraordinary.'

On 19 January he heard his first *Jupiter* Symphony of Mozart and
Sibelius's 'very interesting' *Finlandia*. He heard *Tristan* again, as well
as *Der Freischütz* and *The Flying Dutchman*, and on the 26th attended
his first ballad concert with Kreisler playing and the veteran Ben Davies
singing. *Die Walküre* and another *Meistersinger* followed, then Ysaÿe
conducting *Fidelio* on 31 January and 2 February ('the whole thing
wonderfully dramatic considering the relapses into trios and quartets').

And so it continued, night after night. On 9 February he was overjoyed to learn that Theo Lierhammer would give him singing lessons and on the 27th, the day of the first lesson, he learned he had been promoted to full sergeant in the cadet corps and appointed quartermaster – 'entire charge of armoury and stores at camp.' Recitals by Godowsky and Pachmann, winning the inter-house drill competition, Richter conducting *The Ring* and *Die Meistersinger*, Safonoff conducting Tchaikovsky's Fourth Symphony ('he makes you so wildly excited without making half the noise H.J.W. does') and on 5 May at the Albert Hall 'a good tenor named McCormack' – life's richness must have seemed inexhaustible. On 17 May he heard Destinn as Butterfly, with Caruso and Scotti and conducted by Campanini: 'It is delightful while it's going on, but how worthless and feeble after 10 hours! They all acted wonderfully well, especially Destinn in spite of her hopping between here and Paris, where she is doing *Salome* at its initial performances there with Strauss.' On 4 June he shot at Bisley for the first time and for the next few weeks shooting matches and the camp at Aldershot took priority over music. Boult's memories of Safonoff[3] were still fresh 67 years later. Writing in January 1974 to John Warrack he said:

> He was among the greatest of my experience and I have splendid memories of things like Beethoven symphonies as nobly done as by anyone at that time, BUT – a very comic thing: he latterly only used his hand – no stick – I maintain this *can* be effective on up to 20 people but no more. It *won't* work at a distance (*pace* Boulez, but he rehearses about three times as much as most people, I believe!). Well, Safonoff gave an electric performance with the LSO of the MND [*Midsummer Night's Dream*] overture (*on* the string – very fast – no spiccato) but before he got there he rehearsed the opening chords for 12 minutes, and they weren't together at the concert! I was about 18 at the time and it impressed me terrifically from a man who was a real top-notcher but couldn't see that simple limitation. He was, by the way, the very greatest Tchaikovsky conductor of my experience: the emotions of the *Pathetic* were those of a great nation, whereas Nikisch's Tch. was neurotic, and 'feminine' weakness seemed often there too ... I once met him in Liverpool – he often came there during the '14 war and I had a very exciting evening with him at the home where he always stayed. He also was a lovely pianist – the same pearly touch as Previn when he plays Mozart. I don't think he ever played in public in England. I heard him at that house.

Early in his London years Boult was apprenticed to the Worshipful Company of Musicians, specifically to its Junior Warden, the Rev.

Robert Hadden. When Hadden died in 1910 (Elgar's *Elegy* for strings is dedicated to his memory), Boult was 'adopted' by John Clementi Collard of the piano firm.

CHAPTER 5

The Year 1908

IN addition to having lessons from Lierhammer, Boult occasionally accompanied him. This led to the occasion on 7 December 1907 when they were summoned to Lymington to the house of Colonel and Mrs Cornwallis-West to perform for Kaiser Wilhelm II who had been convalescing at Bournemouth. 'We got to Newlands Manor about 2. They came out of lunch at 2.30 and we began with Handel's *Largo* and a song by Henschel ... Then the Kaiser planted a tree and went off ... They say that [Dan] Godfrey sent up to know whether the Kaiser would conduct the Bournemouth orchestra, if only for five minutes. Stuart-Wortley wouldn't let him. I expect if they'd told him he'd have gone like a shot.'

The musical experiences of these next few months and Boult's comments on them are of such interest that some of them should be listed:

23 *November*. Tetrazzini in *Rigoletto*. She is far finer than Melba, but still I think rather overrated. Her voice is worn, but her runs are beautifully clear still and she acts well. John McCormack and Sammarco both splendid.

14 *December*. Pugno in the D minor Mozart; 5th Brandenburg; Franck's *Variations* ... His reading of the Bach was an artistic triumph. The figured bass parts were played so softly that one never noticed anything but a support to the solos, and his *cadenza* was a perfect marvel, he worked it up with such power and yet at the end was not playing above a good *f*. Elgar's baby suite [*The Wand of Youth*, op. 1A] was produced. It is quite uninteresting, I think ... it got a bad place in the programme and Wood is always rather tinkly with baby things.

16 *December*. Gorgeous performance under Richter of the B minor Mass by the Huddersfield choir trained by Coward.[1] Their *pp* was superb and their fortes never oppressive.

1 *February 1908*. Debussy's first appearance in London. He conducted an

exquisite performance of *L'Après-midi* and a new thing *La Mer* which seemed too long.

3 February. Rheingold: second cycle of the first complete *Ring* in English. It might as well have been in Choctaw. No one – except Mr Hedmondt (Loge) – sang a word audibly or rather intelligibly ... Orchestra fine but not quite so gorgeous as in the summer. Richter very energetic, even going so far as to wave Alberich across the stage in the middle of the curse!

4 February. Walküre: Borghild Bryhn a very nice Brünnhilde ... Walter Hyde [Siegmund] and Agnes Nicholls [Sieglinde] very nice voices in first act, but A.N. is *so* fat!

8 February. Götterdämmerung: P.[erceval] Allen very Melbaish and horrid. Frederic Austin as Gunther acted and sang very well indeed. The whole thing was very *creditable* and spoke very well of Richter, Pitt and Mr Hedmondt.[2] Mr. H. had a new dragon in *Rheingold* which was not pulled across the stage with a string but came out of a rock and waved about beautifully. Then the Closing Scene was very clever. The house collapsed without dropping anything – the walls fell outwards, and the roof was pulled up and left jagged ends of rafters. Then at the end of *Siegfried,* when he broke the spear, the way he ran up right into steam and red fire was very clever. The place was packed and the audience enthusiastic, though the papers were ridiculous. The general average of singers was far lower than that in the summer, and again the orchestra was not so big and not so fine.

15 March ... In the evening at Mr Schuster's. Gabriel Fauré accompanied Mrs Swinton and Mme [Jeanne] Rauney in several charming songs ... Grainger played the first nocturne charmingly ...

26 March. Landon Ronald's[3] début at the Philharmonic. *Oberon* overture, *Tristan* Vorspiel and Liebestod, and Tchaikovsky F minor which the Berlin critics cracked up so ... *Tristan* much too matter-of-fact – especially after Nikisch last Sunday – the symphony in a way better than Wood, in a way worse – of course nowhere near Safonoff is or (I should imagine) Nikisch would be. An interesting but long viola concerto by York Bowen well played by Lionel Tertis ...

1 April. Le Société de Concerts d'Instruments Anciens gave a concert at Bechstein Hall. They are four violas – Quinte, d'amour, de gambe and basse with clavecin ... Hasse, de Montclair, Rameau were all beautifully done ...

8 April. In afternoon went to Palace to see Maud Allan. She doesn't dance a bit, but her arm work is rather good.

11 April. Rather disappointing concert. Sheffield choir sang splendidly in *Gerontius* but – (except certain scenes) the better done I hear Elgar the worse I like him ...

9 May. Nikisch in an irresistible reading of *Carnaval Romain* – he is supreme
at working up a thing like that, and the Brahms C minor, which I disliked
before when he did it. Is it that he has changed or that I am becoming too
much of a Nikischite? I want a dose of Steinbach to make me see straight!

16 May. Richter's *Tristan* for the first time. Not all one would expect
particularly after Nikisch in Jan. 07. HR is too steady and smooth, and
he makes his singers obey him while half Nikisch's excitement and tension
is produced by the orchestra's never knowing when they won't be hung
up waiting for, or rushed in after, the singers. The soloists: [Edyth] Walker
as Isolde, although the papers raved about her, was not good. She sang
well in the low notes and is a better actress than Litvinne or Gulhausen.
But she was a contralto 6 years ago, and is still, though she pretends to
be a dramatic soprano and consequently her high notes are appalling. Her
Cs may be B flats or Ds but they were never nearer than a semitone ...

17 May. May Harrison dabbled in the Beethoven concerto today with
cadenzas written by herself this morning and consequently thoroughly
well practised! The result was too awful for words.

23 May ... Aida. Very fine performance gorgeously mounted. Destinn,
Kirkby Lunn, Zenatello and Scotti, all in splendid form. After *Tristan* I
was particularly struck by the difference in the general idea of opera. In
Aida the whole is vocal and yet finely dramatic; the orchestra is far above
mere accompaniment though it doesn't speak like Wagner's. But the drama
seems to move so much better than *Tristan*, hardly perhaps *Meistersinger* –
in spite of less orchestra. Of course Richter's *Tristan is* dull, there is no
doubt; it wants a man like Nikisch to make it live whereas Richter's
Meistersinger (the only one I've heard) is supreme and will never be beaten.
Perhaps this is heresy, but somehow *Aida*, as seen at C.G., seems to me a
better combination of drama, music and spectacular art, ie. colour and
grouping and scenery, than Wagner at C.G. Possibly it will not compare
with Wagner at Bayreuth but there the singers are bad.

29 May. Great event. School concert. *Merrie England* (German) rather good
on the whole – at any rate *not many* of the basses sang the thing an octave
lower. I had drummed their own part thoroughly into them.

6 June. Armide in German at C.G. After the charming performance with
Bréval in French under Messager two years ago, it was decidedly unsuc-
cessful. Richter was quite bad; he has not the sympathy for accompanying
his singers – he always wants to rule, and the Gluck conductor should not
rule. Then again there was a sort of heaviness in the orch. which made
the whole thing drag badly. Of the singers Destinn was magnificent, but
French is the language not German ...

18 June. To the Palace ... Yvette Guilbert is charming. We were all so glad to have heard her before she retires. She sang 'La fille de Partheaz', 'Les cloches de Nantes' and 'The Keys of Heaven' . . .

23 June. A wonderful example of the powers of personality. In the afternoon, Paderewski's recital. His playing is fine, but there are several fine players – if playing were all – but his magnetism is so wonderful that he holds one spellbound and one is conscious of no effort whatever in following the course of the movements. The Beethoven Sonata E flat op. 27 impressed me wonderfully, and it was the Beethoven – never the Paderewski – that attracted me, so great is his power . . . His Chopin was not so great.

11 July . . . Barrington-Ward and I went home to early dinner and *The Huguenots* – a performance I shall never forget. The old and – in places – cheap music seemed to live again and glow with a force far greater than anything Puccini can do. A fine orchestra with Campanini but, above all, cast which won't often be collected again. Tetrazzini (Margarita), Destinn (Valentina), Fely Dereyne (Urbano), Zenatello (Raoul), Scotti (de Nevers), Nivette (St Bris) and Marcoux (Marcello). Tetrazzini was superb . . . She only had one act to do and so she seemed to work all the harder. Then, too, there was competition with Destinn. The curious irregularity of her voice I never once noticed – it was as even and clear as a girl of 20's is (is if properly trained!). Dereyne sang the song in the first act admirably and will soon be in the front rank of florid sopranos. Then Destinn – I think it would be impossible to have that last act more wonderfully done. During the plotting she slid up and down the left wall with always a new gesture and always intensely dramatic and expressive . . . the old recitatives she made as forcible as the Wagner declamation . . . After the performance B.W. and I were so wide awake that we walked right along past the H. of C. and over Lambeth Bridge and back down the Albert Embankment. Then we discussed things artistic until nearly 2.

Two days later Boult went to Bisley as one of the school eight. They did badly; on the third day rain and wind 'put us all off.' Although he himself shot well, they finished 40th out of 57. Even there he got up early to work and composed a setting of a poem by Barrington-Ward 'with the poet asleep on the ground beside me in the tent.' The evening they returned from Bisley, he and the captain of the eight 'went and drowned our sorrows at C.G. *Otello* was done, a fine performance under Campanini. Zenatello a splendid Otello and Scotti (his voice weak again – I wonder what's happened) an excellent Iago. The sticky nondescript part of Desdemona, who stands in the middle of the stage and sings lovely music, suited Melba absolutely and she did far better than anyone could have expected, particularly in the last act where the "Salce" song was a triumph of pure – but expressionless – beauty of tone ... I believe the opera is really as fine as *Aida* ... Boito certainly is a very clever librettist.'

Some idea of Edwardian social life can be gained from the entry for 21 July: 'After school, to tea with Mrs Whitelegge; Hubert Bath was there and played a good many of his things ... Then to Mrs Benvenisti's to dinner, and afterwards to Mrs Du Cros in Addison Road. They have a charming music room and there were only about a dozen other people there. Miss Hincks – Mrs Du Cros's daughter (she was a great society woman in New York) sang with Gordon Cleather the great scene between Salome and Jochanaan [from Strauss's opera]. I had never heard any *Salome* before. It is wonderful but with a piano a lot of it sounds so complicated that it is impossible to get a real idea of it ... We adjourned to supper and found the room darkened, the only light was from two candles on the table, one on each side of a huge dish on which was – John the Baptist's head, a trifle, which we ate and found very nice. When we got back to the music room we found the carpet rolled back and proceeded on one long hilarious waltz which lasted at least half an hour ... Of course I took a turn at the piano.' And next evening he was at the Duke of York's to see Isadora Duncan. 'She is a *wonderful* dancer, far finer than Maud Allan, because she is more classical. She continually reminds me of a piece of classical sculpture – she has copied a lot from vases, I have since heard. She was doing a lot of the ballets from Gluck ... It was so restful to have no talking and no scenery (all dark green curtains). Just a good orchestra and something nice to watch all the time.'

His last day at Westminster was 28 July – 'not nearly as upset as I thought I should be – the service was bad and the anthem atrocious.' He went to OTC camp on Farnborough Common until 5 August. 'All the horrible goodbyes. It was like a sea-voyage – you know so many people so well and like them so well for the week and then you say goodbye and never see them again probably. I felt it a lot more than leaving school ...'

He had been to Oxford in March of 1908 to sit his entrance examinations. In October he went up to Christ Church ('the House'), where the Dean was the music-loving Dr Thomas B. Strong (who four years later was to notice and nurture the talent of one of the cathedral choristers from Lancashire, William Walton). When Adrian, like all freshmen, called at the Deanery for his entrance interview, Strong asked him 'What career do you mean to follow?' 'I am going to be a conductor.' 'Conductor!' the Dean said, 'what do you mean?' 'I mean,' Adrian said, 'a conductor of orchestras.'[4] It was the first time the Dean had

encountered such an ambition and he was much concerned. But he lived
to see Adrian's hopes fulfilled. Not many schoolboys in England in
1908 can have had the wide experience of music in performance that
Adrian Boult had gained while in London. His diary entries suggest that
if he had not had other talents he could have become a critic. It is
significant that, relatively rarely among conductors, he formed genuine
friendships with several critics. He understood the nature of their work
and he would often help them in their researches. He wrote in 1962:[5] 'It
is my firm rule never to quarrel with press criticisms: after all, they are
opinions to which people have a perfect right!' (As will be seen, this
was not a view he held during his unhappy experiences when he was at
Birmingham.) What emerges from his adolescent diary is that opera was
the subject that lit him up most brightly. He responded enthusiastically
to Strauss, Tchaikovsky, Wagner and Brahms. With the exception of
works by Parry, notably the *Symphonic Variations*, his encounters
with English music usually elicited a derogatory comment. Stanford,
Mackenzie and Cowen were all dismissed as 'dreary' or 'awful.' Most
surprising of all, especially since Frank Schuster must have tried to
influence him, is his relative coolness to the music of Elgar.

CHAPTER 6

Oxford

As early as August 1905, Boult's mother had written to Ralph Tanner, his housemaster at Westminster: 'It is quite evident that Adrian will never do anything that makes money and as Mr Piggott thinks that he really will be a musician the only thing is to prepare him for that thoroughly. It is slow work and meantime we think that he had better go to Oxford – for he can work at music in conjunction with – oh, – ordinary work. What is your idea of a college? We should like Christ Church or Balliol, the first preferably if it has really (and I am told it has) outlived its evil reputation.'

Boult wrote in his diary that his first term, 'as usual at Oxford, I believe,' was almost wasted. He planned to do Pass Moderations and 'got on with Logic ... but did practically no work besides.' One reason for this, he told Lawrence Tanner in a letter dated 29 October 1908, was 'the awful sociableness of the place' which 'nearly kills me although I love it. I think I have had two or three breakfasts alone in my rooms this term and not a single tea! My rooms (which are quite respectable, by the way – although the furniture is of the rather ancient and shabby splendour order, and consequently rather rickety) are in the most access-ible place in College – consequently they are always full of people. This of course I enjoy hugely, but work is *rather* difficult, as you may imagine. Then the iniquitous system of freshers having to call and call again until they find people in is rather a trial. I'm sure I've paid about thirty calls in consequence!' He had been pleased to find that 'quite a lot of people neither drink nor smoke here.' His abstemious habits were often the butt of humour among colleagues more addicted to the fleshpots, but he was in no way priggish about it. He had been encouraged to look after his health and he genuinely disliked the taste of most drinks – in July 1905, at a London wedding, he tasted champagne for the first time and declared it '*BEASTLY!*' His first action was to join the Oxford Bach Choir which was conducted by Hugh Allen, who had also been

conductor of the Bach Choir in London since 1907. The choir was due
to sing Bach's Mass in B minor in Reading on 21 October and would
accept no new members until after that concert. 'I was determined to
sing at Reading. So I bearded the lion in his den and, without a test or
question, he booked me in, out of pure kindness of heart, I suppose, as
he *can't* have known anything about me ... Words cannot describe the
first experience of singing in a big choir in a great Bach work: it is
overwhelming.'[1] The soloists that evening were Ruth Freeman, Edith
Clegg, Gervase Elwes and Campbell McInnes. Adrian told Lawrence
Tanner: 'I was singing lustily near two of Blackwell's (booksellers)
assistants who have voices like bulls of Basan so I had only a *partial*
idea of what was going on at the front of the platform!'

Hugh Percy Allen (1869–1946) was a major figure in English music in
the first half of the 20th century. Born in Reading, he was a church
organist there at the age of 11. At Cambridge he soon showed that he was
more concerned with practical music-making than with the academic,
making an early reputation as a conductor by his performances of Bach
church cantatas. After holding cathedral-organist appointments at St
Asaph in North Wales and Ely, he was appointed organist of New
College, Oxford, in 1901. With the chapel choir he performed a wide
range of music from Palestrina and Schütz to contemporary composers,
with Bach as the staple fare. In 1909 he was appointed Choragus of the
university and he made radical changes in the music examinations,
particularly where the practical side was involved. He conducted the
London Bach Choir from 1907 to 1920, the year in which he was
knighted. In 1918 he became Director of the Royal College of Music
and also Professor of Music at Oxford. To both these posts he brought
immense energy and organizing skill, always with the emphasis on the
practical. He was a bluff, breezy man, very keen (like Parry) on sailing.
He has been blamed for encouraging a parochial, blinkered view of the
European musical scene while he was director of the RCM, fostering
the English school represented by Vaughan Williams and shielding
students from the 'pernicious' influences of Stravinsky, Schoenberg and
Bartók. Yet his musical tastes were wide and catholic and it is fatally
easy to simplify and overgeneralize in this controversial matter. Boult,
however, was later to encounter Allen's chauvinistic side at the BBC.

Boult also joined the Musical Club, which organized excellent recitals
where celebrated recitalists and singers were usually partnered at the
piano by one of the university musicians such as Ernest Walker, organist
of Balliol, and Henry G. Ley, organist at Christ Church. He attended

Union debates, was a founder-member of a debate-cum-lecture society called the Martians, and joined the OTC Cavalry because his doctor had forbidden him to row because of his heart. (His father had suggested that for exercise he should take up hunting or rowing.) A major musical experience awaited him on 2 December when Allen put on an Oxford Bach Choir concert in honour of Parry, who had just retired as Professor of Music at the university (he was succeeded by Sir Walter Parratt). The composer conducted his 'English' Symphony, *The Glories of our Blood and State* and the oratorio *Job*, but Allen had rehearsed them. Boult recalled:[2] 'This too was a revelation. I had been brought up to think of English music as rather small beer, and as the magnificent choruses of *Job* and the beautiful little *Glories of our Blood and State* were rehearsed again and again, getting finer and finer with repetition, I rubbed my eyes, for I could hardly believe that it really was great music, and wondered somehow whether Allen's dynamic rehearsing was filling the music with a power it didn't really possess. Allen's rehearsing was certainly terrific, but 20 years later when the Oxford Bach Choir came to the Maida Vale Studio to sing *Job* with the BBC Orchestra, their equally convincing performance put *Job* for me, once again, on the map as a work of the future.'

He still went up to London to attend recitals and concerts, and was at Schuster's on the evening of 6 December to hear Elwes and others sing Fauré songs and the *Pavane*, accompanied by the composer, and some of Roger Quilter's *Elizabethan Lyrics*. This was on the eve of the first London performance of Elgar's A flat Symphony at an LSO concert conducted by Richter. Boult attended the rehearsal and could remember Richter making his famous comment to the orchestra ('Now let us rehearse the greatest symphony of modern times and not only in this country'), but curiously he makes no reference to the occasion nor the work in his diary.

In his second term he was elected a member of Oxford University Dramatic Society and invited to sing in the chorus of the Greek play (*The Frogs*, with music by Parry). The stage chorus was led by F.H. (Freddie) Grisewood, later to be a BBC colleague. Boult also conducted the first (frogs') chorus off-stage, peering through a hole in the scenery. 'I found that unless I was beating a quaver ahead of the conductor of the music I could hear, I could see dirty looks coming up in my direction, and I realized that in the theatre it is essential that distant sounds should "anticipate" to an extent which is really uncomfortable for the people concerned.'[3] Allen conducted most of the performances and Parry a few. 'I shall never forget Parry's happy smile when I got my frogs to sing well ahead of the accompaniment they could dimly hear.' Boult's rooms were now in Tom Quad, with space for two pianos, and he had a 'thirder,' a rare third room which looked across to the cathedral and Staircase Tower.

At Easter 1909 Boult passed Mods and began to read History. But extra-curricular activities claimed most of his attention. In the last term of his first year he was elected president of the Martians, secretary of the Musical Club and treasurer of the Oriana Society of about 25 members which read papers out and then discussed 'really deep and interesting musical subjects.' His mother and sister with friends took a house in Iffley Road for Eights Week, in which he took no part (Christ Church stayed Head of the River). He missed the last day (26 May) because Allen asked him to assist at a concert at Newbury. Allen was one of the pianists in Bach's Concerto in C (BWV 1064) for three pianos and Mozart's in E flat for two pianos (K.365) and Boult conducted both works. He was soon in demand as pianist and singer at the many 'open houses' in Oxford where musical undergraduates were welcome. Most of his Sundays were spent in this way and he watched wistfully as friends departed on early trains for a day in the Cotswolds. But music came first. One house to which he was invited many times (after a first meeting in November 1910) was that of the poet Robert Bridges at Chilswell. One of Bridges's daughters, Margaret, was a good pianist and introduced Boult to many Mozart concertos he had never heard. These were rarities in the concert-hall in those days. He had heard Raoul Pugno play the A major (K.488) and the D minor (K.466) in Queen's Hall in 1905 as great novelties.

Boult's notebooks enable us to appreciate the high standard and variety of Oxford music-making at this time. The baritone Campbell McInnes sang Brahms's *Four Serious Songs*, for example, in an Oxford University Music Club recital, and Frederic Austin sang Schumann's *Dichterliebe* at Balliol. The cellist Robert Hausmann played Beethoven cello sonatas with Donald Tovey for OUMC, so did Pablo Casals, and a string quartet whose members were Maurice Sons, Tom Morris, Frank Bridge and Ivor James frequently gave concerts, on one occasion performing the Debussy quartet. The pianist Fanny Davies played Beethoven concertos with Allen's amateur orchestra; Godowsky, Paderewski and Carreño gave solo recitals; Allen conducted Vaughan Williams's *Toward the Unknown Region*; and Stanford conducted his own works.

In the summer vacation he went as usual to the OTC camp at Farnborough and then on to Scotland, sharing the driving with a new chauffeur aged 18 who 'had the knowledge of a man of 30 and far more commonsense and is more of a gentleman than 2/3 of the people I meet in Oxford.' In retrospect Boult wished he had made better use of the long vacations and gone abroad like many of his friends. But he liked to be with his family. His mother would have preferred a holiday abroad but 'hated leaving my father, who tied himself perhaps over-conscientiously to his business.' The six weeks in Scotland were enjoyed by all but Mrs Boult who 'as mothers do, entered into everything with us and never let us see how much she was hankering after Spain or Italy.'⁴

During this first Oxford year, Boult renewed acquaintance with Marie Hedmondt, wife of the tenor E. C. Hedmondt. She was teaching singing at Leipzig Conservatory, where Gerhardt had been one of her first pupils. After a Gerhardt–Nikisch recital in London on 20 March 1909, she invited Boult to lunch with her, Gerhardt and Nikisch at the Savoy. Also present was Robin Legge, music critic of the *Daily Telegraph*, who invited Boult to send him news about Oxford music for his Saturday column which covered events generally. When his second year began in October 1909, Boult wrote: 'Getting more to work on History this term. But it's awfully hard to find time for it with so many other things.' One of the other things was a resumption of rowing, now permitted by his doctor.

Just how much he crammed into his time is evident from a letter he wrote to Lawrence Tanner from Oxford on 14 November 1909: 'I'm just off (did you ever hear of such a thing on Sunday?) to town for a Covent Garden Sunday evening concert. I meet the Infant [their nick-name for Guy Chapman, a school friend] – who is dinner-eating – at 9.50 and we journey home the worse for wear, getting here 11.33. Tomorrow I row in freshers' fours!! I am truly foolish but then with Richter and *such* a programme what could I do?'⁵ He had hoped to go over to Cambridge for its Greek Play performance (26 November) of *The Wasps* by Aristophanes with Vaughan Williams's music. 'It was piggy not being able to see *The Wasps*,' he wrote to Tanner on 3 December. 'I *do* know a little of the music. Vaughan Williams brought it in to Allen's one Sunday morning last term when I was there and he played, Allen sang tenor and I bass. We had great fun and Allen and I sang *far* better than V. W. *played*, although it was his stuff. Allen told him to go and learn the piano! I trust my inability to attend *The Wasps* will not prevent you taking the intention for the deed (this is getting involved) and paying us a return visit for *The Tempest* [OUDS pro-duction for which Boult was arranging the incidental music], but do not save your "talk loud and continuous" till the orchestral breathing-spaces. *During* the overture is the time – it will be ghastly! I believe

Olive is coming to play Ceres. She ought to look rather well as a Greek goddess (in spite of being *ex machina*) (that sounds grand) and has a jolly duet to sing with Juno.'

Boult did not mention to Tanner that in November he had also read a paper on 'Some Notes on Performance' to the Oriana Society. This is a remarkable document, which may be read in full in *Music and Friends*,[6] but some extracts from it have their place here. It was written, it is hard to remember, by a 20-year-old undergraduate:

... The name of the performer does not live long, his work is ephemeral ... Everything changes – the quality and often the whole system of the instrument, the surroundings and acoustic properties of the music-room, and above all the intelligence and point of view of the performer himself, until the performance of music much more than one hundred years after its inception under so-called 'original conditions' seldom has an interest more than historical, and even then the interpretation is controlled by modern and not contemporary brains. An invention which will actually show our great-grandchildren exactly how we perform our things today has recently been brought to a very fair state of perfection. It is a pity that this – the gramophone – is being confined almost entirely to extracts from operas or drivelling ballads, sung by so-called star singers at a time when the art of singing is perhaps in a worse condition than it has been since the science of voice-production was first considered. [That in 1909, the era of Caruso!]

He then set out his idea of the principles of a good new interpretation of modern works:

1. They must give the impression that they are being played exactly as the composer wished ... It is my firm belief from experience – though of course this extends a very short way – that composers are the best performers of their own work. That generally-accepted theory that composers never can play or conduct their own things is, in my opinion, entirely due to the fact that a great many of them do not take the trouble to make themselves technically efficient ...

2. The reading must be clear ... Clearness is an essential of modern quite as much as of classical polyphony ...

3. Another principle is that the work must *sound easy* ... However much a man may know or think about the music he is playing, he cannot make it sound easy unless his fingers will do exactly what his brain requires ...

Boult then touches on songs and music for two pianos before coming to the orchestra, which he saw was 'entering upon a fresh stage of development' through the advent of the virtuoso conductor. He contrasts the London Symphony Orchestra, 'a musical republic' which chose its conductors, with the Queen's Hall Orchestra, 'a permanency [which] will always remain firmly fixed in the readings of Mr Wood ... The greatest provincial orchestra – Dr Richter's – is also the same. But surely this is wrong – it cannot be good for the orchestra, for where is the conductor who can ever do justice to all the different schools of orchestral music? – and it certainly is not good for the conductor to have no change of interest and environment.' He proceeds to divide the conductors of the day into three schools:

> ... there are the men who beat time, like Dr Richter; who guide the orchestra, like Mr Safonoff; and who hypnotize the orchestra, like Mr Nikisch. It seems treason to say anything against Dr Richter, but I must confess that I cannot help feeling that he is the last of his line. No one who has ever heard him can forget the magnificent breadth, dignity and power of his performances of the classics, and his steady beat which produces an absolutely even tempo, unbroken sometimes from beginning to end of the longest symphonic movement ...
>
> [In the second school] the impression is that the conductor is leaving the orchestra to supply their own force and interpretation, himself only giving occasional suggestions for them to follow, and it is just in these suggestions that he brings the orchestra to his own way of thinking and his personality and impression of the work is stamped on the players, and thence on the audience ...
>
> The third school is exceptional, and I only know one man who can be said to belong entirely to it. But hypnotism or personal magnetism plays such an important part in conducting that anyone who makes use of it to such an enormous extent as Mr Nikisch does must be studied very carefully. It is, of course, incompatible with the performance of anything but music of the most nervous and intensely emotional character ... but in things of this kind his grip of the orchestra is so complete that he is able to alter the tempo several times in one bar without the slightest loss of ensemble ... The virtuoso conductor ... is developing into the man who will guide the orchestra. He must be endowed with a large measure of magnetism, and if he feels that by this he can lead the orchestra to emotional crises in the style of Nikisch where such are suitable, by all means let him do it, provided he does not have to exaggerate his gestures.

We must regret that Boult had not seen Mahler conduct. But the 25 members of the Oriana Society on that Edwardian November evening had heard an exposition of the principles on which the BBC Symphony Orchestra of 20 years hence was to be founded.

His sister Olive had spent two months in Leipzig having singing lessons from Mrs Hedmondt and in December 1909 Adrian went there to escort her home for Christmas. On arrival on the 8th she waltzed him straight off to Dresden for a *Fidelio* because she had heard he was to sing in it at Oxford shortly. The cast was headed by Marie Wittich (the first Salome) as Leonore, with Karl Perron as Pizarro, but the performance was memorable 'for the marvellous atmosphere of the whole thing and particularly the gorgeous orchestra – the horns are absolute perfection.'

At the Gewandhaus next day he heard Nikisch conduct the First Symphony of Robert Volkmann (1815–83) and Berlioz's *Carnaval Romain* overture 'which I have heard Nikisch do in London with *better* results. Wonderful though he is, it seems to me that he is too exciting to be a good permanent conductor of an orchestra. The LSO have to mind their technical Ps and Qs when playing under Richter and people and the result is brilliant when Nikisch gets hold of them ...' Motets in the Thomaskirche were 'in a way quite a revelation in choral singing' and on the 14th he attended 'a lovely recital [Schubert, Brahms, Wolf, Strauss] by Julia Culp and Erich Wolff at the end of which the audience rushed to the platform and shouted out the names of songs for her to sing which she and Wolff, being blessed with memories, sang on and on, about six or seven!' On returning home he noted: 'Olive quite above her boots, I longing for the time, if it ever comes, when I can go permanently to Leipzig for a bit.'

In the term which began on 14 January 1910, Boult concentrated on the incidental music for the OUDS production of *The Tempest* – 'a grossly inefficient orchestra of 18, eight strings passable, and a vile lot of wind, saved from utter perdition by the horns ... Everyone talked loud, so it was all right ...' Prospero was played by W. Bridges-Adams, later to be a pioneering Shakespeare producer and director of the Memorial Theatre at Stratford-upon-Avon.

Allen encouraged Boult to train a ladies' choir to compete in the Berkshire, Buckinghamshire and Oxfordshire festival in May, when they beat the holders from Windsor and the shield was presented by Gervase Elwes. (The test pieces were Vaughan Williams's *Sound Sleep* and Parry's *Pied Piper*.) He made his first public appearance as a solo singer at Reading on 1 March in the bass solo in Bach's *Magnificat*, conducted by Allen. 'It was a jolly concert and I made quite a fair amount of noise.' Part of the jolliness was his first meeting with the composer George Butterworth, who played the two-piano accompaniment with Henry Ley of Stanford's *Ave atque Vale*. A few days later he himself was playing with Ley in Schubert and Brahms, and then singing Handel's *O ruddier than the cherry* and settings of Beddoes poems by Richard T. Woodman, whose rooms were back to back with Boult's. ('He is very quiet but knows a lot about things and has written some beautiful songs.') In this spring, too, he first took part in the Petersfield Festival with which he was to be associated for many years and where he enjoyed the 'free and easy' mood.

But the most important event of the spring of 1910 was his talk with Hugh Allen in which he decided that an Honours school was a hopeless proposition for him at Oxford and he should go for a pass degree. Allen sent him to see the Dean, Thomas Strong, who said he could not see that Boult's music could benefit from a longer study of history. The point was whether the time saved could be usefully employed. Boult contended that anything he did with and for Allen was the finest preparation he could have, and he won his case. His study for that summer was Political Economy.

The winter term ended on 12 March, allowing Adrian and his sister to be at Covent Garden that evening for the first performance in England of Strauss's *Elektra*, conducted by the composer. He had already been alerted by Robin Legge who, in a letter on 17 February, said he had spent all day at rehearsal:

> Wonderful, but not at all new – that I can see! By that crass something that buzzes in all our bonnets, I am prevented from being in the least alarmed by it. It is not as new in the 20th century as Berlioz was in the 19th. It is not inventively, creatively great at all that I can see *so far*. But it is MAR-VELLOUSLY effective and it's a Meisterstück of competence – it all comes off.

On 8 April Boult was 21 but makes no mention of it. Birthdays meant little to him. When he became eminent he asked *The Times* and *Daily Telegraph* to exclude him from their 'Birthdays' entry.

CHAPTER 7

Singing Days

BOULT sang in Brahms's *Requiem* under Allen in Oxford on 20 May, the day of Edward VII's funeral. There was further gloom some days later when Christ Church came third in Eights Week, but brightness returned on 1 June at Newbury when he again conducted the Bach three-piano concerto and Mozart's in F (K. 242) for three pianos ('probably first time in England,' he believed),[1] and with the three performances of *Fidelio* at the Oxford Theatre on 9, 10 and 11 June, conducted by Allen, with Campbell McInnes as Pizarro and Boult singing Don Fernando in the final scene. 'Went off well . . . it paid, too – Grand Opera!!!' He got through his Political Economy group and rowed for the Old Westminster eight at Molesey, 'getting used to a slide and doing a lot of work,' and winning the Juniors. On 20 June he had heard Debussy's *Pelléas et Mélisande* at Covent Garden: 'too lovely to discuss. There is not a flaw anywhere and the performance – Edvina [Mélisande], Symiane [Yniold], Devriès [Pelléas], Marcoux [Arkel] and Bourbon [Golaud], cond. Campanini, as perfect as could be.' Two days later he saw Pavlova dance at a matinée and in the evening was at His Majesty's for 'a really good and bright performance of *Figaro* under Beecham in English. Agnes Nicholls [Countess], Beatrice La Rahne [Susanna], Maggie Teyte [Cherubino] were all excellent.' He noted that as an entr'acte between scenes 1 and 2 of Act III, Beecham conducted the *Adagio* and *Minuet* for four horns from the *Divertimento* No. 2 in D (K. 131). In July he attended three more of the Beecham season operas, including *Die Fledermaus* conducted by Hamish MacCunn, with Carrie Tubb as Rosalinde.

October found him at the Leeds Festival.

We heard a rehearsal of the second part of *Matthew Passion*, also of Rachmaninov's symphony [No. 2 in E minor] . . . Mr [Robin] Legge danced about the Midland Hotel raving at Stanford [conductor of the festival], in which all Leeds agreed. His behaviour was absolutely disgusting. Not only did he show himself incompetent every minute, he seemed to revel in it, and added bad manners to people like Rachmaninov and never looked at the chorus. Rachmaninov was a great success and both his works [the Symphony and the Second Piano Concerto] were very good indeed; also he was by far the best conductor who appeared at Leeds. But *the* new work of the festival was Vaughan Williams's *Sea Symphony* which we are to do in Oxford next March. He conducted it badly and resulted in muddling it a good deal and there was far too much noise.

Boult got through his History group in the Michaelmas term and stroked a college four in the races known as Toggers. On 3 November, at the Musical Club, Casals and Leonard Borwick played Beethoven and Brahms cello sonatas and Casals's 'playing of an unaccompanied Bach suite [C major] was – like *Pelléas*, only of course totally different – absolutely perfect. One can never want to hear anything better.' A week later he went to Queen's Hall 'to hear Kreisler play the Elgar concerto for the first time and to sup with them at Mr Schuster's afterwards ... The Concerto is better and more mature than the symphony, but ...' The symphony occupied the second half of the concert. At Schuster's party the guests sat at three separate tables, the menu at each being headed by a theme from each of the concerto's three movements. Boult heard Elgar ask the art critic Claude Phillips, 'Well, Claude, did you think that was a work of art?'

During the Christmas holidays, Boult went from West Kirby to Manchester to attend a Hallé concert conducted by Richter, who had announced his retirement at the end of the season in March. The programme was mainly of extracts from *Die Meistersinger*, 'very fine indeed. It was R. at his very best and one almost wishes not to hear him again after so splendid an impression.' Boult was now president of the OUMC, which entailed his engaging the artists and making arrangements for them to be entertained. He had arranged for his first concert on 24 January for George Butterworth to be pianist in Beethoven's 'Archduke' Trio and Brahms's op. 8 but Butterworth 'cried off' two days beforehand and Ernest Walker stepped it. A young pianist, later to be a conductor, Lawrance Collingwood, played pieces by Scriabin and Medtner, unusual fare for 1911.

On 31 January a young tenor, Steuart Wilson, sang only the fourth performance of Vaughan Williams's Housman song-cycle *On Wenlock Edge*. 'V.W. was there. Highly delighted,' Boult recorded. He never forgot from these Oxford days 'the impact of Vaughan Williams, this magnificent-looking young man, and his fresh and vital music.'[2] At one of Allen's concerts at which Bantock conducted his *Pierrot of the Minute* overture and Parry his *Symphonic Variations* on 8 February, Boult played the triangle (in the Bantock). He brought off quite a coup for the OUMC on 28 February by persuading George Henschel, the great baritone and conductor who was then 61, to sing Schubert, Schumann, Loewe and one of his own songs to the club, after which they made him an honorary member. Boult kept his letters from Henschel fixing the visit. 'I do not think I will trouble your treasurer at all,' must have been a welcome sentence, but there was a sharp lesson in the letter from St John's Wood on 17 February: 'I do sincerely hope enclosed is the *proof* I asked for and not the printed thing. It is always a great nuisance to have the audience turn the pages in the middle of a song and I took it for granted your printer would know that.'

The diary continues:

> *1 March 1911.* Sousa came to Oxford. When one gets used to the noise it is marvellous. The players are such virtuosi technically and the rhythmic feeling is extraordinary.

> *6 March.* Richter once more – this I expect really the last time (although he is going to Bayreuth in August). It was the last LSO concert but one that he conducted and he got an ovation. Berlioz *Faust* with ... the Hanley choir, a most wonderful performance, chorally, although H. J. W. feels the sense of a thing like that better than the Old Man.

> *8 March.* Second performance of V. Williams's *Sea Symphony* (in Oxford). We have rehearsed it for months and it certainly seemed much better balanced than at Leeds. V.W. was delighted and came and sang in the Choral Symphony afterwards.

On 25 March Boult sailed from Harwich to stay in Schwerin for lessons in German 'from a nice old lady.' Needless to say he found some concert or recital to attend almost every evening; on 7 April, an opera gala in honour of the Grand Duke's birthday, which included the first performance there of 'a rather witty operetta *Susannens Geheimnis* [*The Secret of Susanna*] by Wolf-Ferrari'; on the 9th, with his mother in Hamburg, Wagner's *Rienzi* conducted by Gustav Brecher, 'a very fair performance spoilt by the tenor.' The next evening they planned to hear Strauss's *Der Rosenkavalier* (which had had its first performance in Dresden the previous January) but found all seats sold so went and saw *Torquato Tasso* (Schiller) – 'My first German play, and an eyeopener. It was *perfect* from beginning to end.' He attended a performance of J. S. Bach's *St John Passion* at Schwerin. 'I am not at all sure that in many ways it is not greater than the *Matthäus*.' On the 18th they went to Copenhagen, saw *Pagliacci* and *Fra Diavolo* ('delightful ... one can see what rot it is if not done very well') and returned to West Kirby on the 24th. Two days later he was in Oxford for Eights ('... I am stroking the Second ... a crew who ... were all jolly keen') and to get down to some work. On 2 May, he noted, 'first Mus.Bac. Got through by a fluke.'

At the OUMC on 16 May, in a recital by Campbell McInnes, nine settings by George Butterworth of Housman's *A Shropshire Lad* poems received their first performance, with the composer at the piano. A letter to Boult from Butterworth at 19, Cheyne Gardens, Chelsea, the previous week, interestingly sets out the songs in the order they were sung: 1. O fair enough are sky and plain. 2. Look not in my eyes. 3. When I was one-and-twenty. 4. When the lad for longing sighs. 5. Think no more, lad. 6. Loveliest of trees. 7. Is my team ploughing? 8. With rue my heart is laden. 9. In summertime on Bredon. Only six of these were later published as the song-cycle *A Shropshire Lad* (1911); the remaining three (Nos. 1, 4 and 8) were included in the cycle *Bredon Hill* (1912). Adrian himself sang four of the songs (1, 4, 6 and 7), with Allen accompanying, at Allen's house ten days later. During Eights Week his 'baby eight' did well, ending in the first division and winning a cup for being head of the Second Eights. During the week he performed in three musical events, including playing the bass drum in Elgar's *Cockaigne* for Allen's orchestra. His Oxford activities this May were so strenuous that not even he managed to be in London on the 24th for the first performance of Elgar's Second Symphony. On 15, 16 and 17 June he sang Zamiel in Weber's *Der Freischütz* in English at the Oxford Theatre. Allen conducted. 'I got to the theatre at 9.30 am,' Boult wrote on the first night, 'dressed and stayed so – painting or moving scenery or doing something until the show was over at 11.'

Part of his summer holiday was spent in Truro. One of his Oxford friends was Robert Trefusis, who invited him to stay with his brother, Lieutenant-Colonel the Hon. Henry Walter Trefusis, and sister-in-law Lady Mary, formerly Lady Mary Lygon of Madresfield Court, near Malvern. She was, at any rate partially, the subject of the asterisked *Romanza* variation in Elgar's *Enigma*. 'It is a most lovely place, sub-tropical, the garden running down to the Fal near its mouth. They have a motorboat moored at the bottom of the garden and we went to Falmouth and Truro in it. Had a jolly time, very lazy ... We played a lot. Lady M. plays very well indeed.' In the vacations from Oxford he also had lessons from Gordon Stuteley, conductor of Liverpool city police band and a violinist in the Philharmonic Orchestra. Stuteley was an expert on each instrument in the band and instructed Boult on *embouchure* and fingering of them all.

The year 1912 began with Boult attending Max Reinhardt's production of *Oedipus Rex* at Covent Garden, 'full of wonderful lighting and effects of different kinds which the classicists hate.' He also saw Reinhardt's famous production of *The Miracle* at Olympia ('the most heavenly music by Humperdinck, and it is equally fine'). That term at Oxford he played the Soothsayer in the OUDS *Julius Caesar* and arranged the music for it. 'We had Monteverdi, Schütz etc., played by 3 trumpets, 3 trombones, a tuba and drums. They make a jolly noise.' There was rowing and, at the OUMC, the first performance of the *Two Idylls on English Folk-Tunes* by Butterworth. This was conducted by Allen and the second Idyll was encored. A few days later Boult went to Queen's Hall to hear Willem Mengelberg rehearse the LSO in Strauss's *Ein Heldenleben*. 'It took him nearly 3 hrs ... It was great fun, and the changes he made in them were splendid. Drilling like that does them a world of good.' In the summer term he again stroked the second boat, ending in the first division, and passed the second part of his B.Mus. After term there was Henley: 'Christ Church i raced Christ Church ii before the King in the final (I stroked ii as usual!). They gave me 1st Eight colours after the race.'

An evening at the Russian Ballet at Covent Garden, with Nijinsky and Karsavina dancing and Beecham one of the conductors, preceded 'a jaunt' to Germany with his mother. Heidelberg castle lit up at night was 'one of the most gorgeous sights I have ever seen.' In Munich they saw Reinhardt's production of Offenbach's *La Belle Hélène* and 'the most perfect Mozart possible under Bruno Walter. I expected performance, but not singing as well, and we heard no less than 5 absolutely first-rate soprano Mozart-singers *and* actors ... in the course of the 3 3-prima-donna operas, *Figaro*, *Così fan tutte*, *Don Giovanni*. And *all* Müncheners.' These performances, 'given in the exquisite little Residenztheater, unaltered since Mozart conducted *Idomeneo* in it in 1788,' were the first of Walter's directorship of the Munich Opera. Boult was captivated by Munich, 'that lovely city with its great broad avenues always culminating in some handsome building, and its magnificent River Isar.'[3] On to Nuremberg ('vastly overrated; the old is jolly, but is always cheek by jowl with the filthiest decayed tawdry new') and then to Bayreuth on 8 August for *Parsifal* conducted by Richter's successor in Manchester, Michael Balling, with Richard Mayr as Gurnemanz and Heinrich Hessel as Parsifal. Boult described it as 'the most colossal artistic crime ever perpetrated. It is certainly the real apex of the absolute

51

barbarity of a monopoly. The pretentiousness of the whole affair, the blatant carelessness of *Regierung* [production] coupled with one of the worst opera choruses I have *ever* heard and a good deal more than respectable soloists and a magnificent orchestra. One thinks all the time: "what it *could* be" and let's hope what it *will* be when they attack it at the Prinzregenten next year, which let's hope they'll be allowed to.'

CHAPTER 8

Leipzig and Nikisch

HENLEY, Boult wrote in his diary, was 'a very jolly end to Oxford, if the end of Oxford can ever be jolly.' He then went to Scotland for the grouse-shooting and in September to Leipzig 'to start the next stage – the next act. What will happen, no one knows.' He had realized that he could not study the art of conducting in England and that Germany offered an altogether wider chance of further musical education. In February 1912 he had written to Edward Speyer, the German financier who lived at Shenley, Herts., and was a friend and adviser of Schuster, Strauss and Elgar, to inquire about Cologne and Leipzig Conservatories. Speyer had recommended Frankfurt, where Iwan Knorr was teaching, but Boult preferred Leipzig, where there was the supreme bait of being able to study Nikisch at work with the Gewandhaus Orchestra. At their meeting at the Savoy, Nikisch had told Boult that he would help him to obtain passes for admission to rehearsals.

Boult entered the Conservatory on 25 September. The previous evening he went to see Jakob Feldhammer's *Hamlet*, which he persisted in regarding as the finest he ever saw. 'O if only the English would learn to act!' was his diary comment. At that time the Leipzig theatre 'was enjoying one of its greatest periods and the performances of Shakespeare, Schiller, Goethe and Hebbel were unequalled in Germany.'[1]

If the strict rules had been followed, two years would have had to pass before Boult was admitted to the weekly conducting class. This comprised about a dozen students, all of whom were given a chance with the baton during the two hours. No discussion of mistakes or difficulties followed. Somehow Boult managed to persuade Hans Sitt, who had recently succeeded Nikisch in charge of the class, to let him join after six weeks. As soon as he had the baton in his hand, he corrected three false entries without stopping the orchestra, consisting of students. 'I learned a lot,' he wrote in his diary, 'not so much from Sitt as from the orchestra, which was bad enough to make one thoroughly foolproof – they couldn't half grasp what the Oxford amateurs would tumble to at once.'

Within three days of arrival he had attended a choral concert and opera performances of *Les Huguenots* and Lortzing's *Undine*. And on 2 October he was at his first Nikisch rehearsal in the Gewandhaus. As far as it lay within his nature, Boult hero-worshipped Nikisch, but it was not blind worship nor did he overlook his hero's failings. The magnetic power whereby the man could put his stamp on an orchestra within a few seconds transfixed Boult the first time he experienced it in 1902 and it continued to do so. At Leipzig Nikisch would rehearse the choir on Monday evening and the orchestra on Tuesday morning with a few students present; on Wednesday morning there was a public rehearsal, and the concert was on Thursday evening. Boult went to the Wednesday rehearsal and thought Nikisch got better results in London. A week later, the untidiness of the playing of Mozart's *Jupiter* Symphony at the rehearsal was such that Boult left the hall in angry disgust. However, Marie Hedmondt gave him her ticket for the evening concert. At the first note he was entranced by the beauty of the performance.

Boult's pass for Nikisch's private rehearsals

Soon after that he obtained his pass for the private rehearsals and was able to study Nikisch's methods. (During his year in Leipzig he attended 16 of these rehearsals.) He also sang in the Gewandhaus Choir in Beethoven's *Choral Symphony*, extracts from *Parsifal*, Reger's *Die Nonnen* and Brahms's *Requiem* in which the organist was Karl Straube from the Thomaskirche. Nikisch, Boult wrote later,[2]

> made his stick say more than any other conductor that I have ever seen. Its power of expression was so intense that one felt it would be quite impossible, for instance, to play staccato when Nikisch was showing a legato. There was no need for him to stop and ask for a sostenuto – his stick had already pulled it from the players ... When verbal explanation was necessary, Nikisch would rarely pull the orchestra up, then and there. He would play on probably to the end of a movement, by which time there might be several passages to be discussed ... He would often trust his players to remember a point once he had spoken of it, and saw no need to insist on hearing it again ... It was said that the first bar of *Tristan* was enough to enable anyone to recognize blindfold the warmth and beauty of the tone which unmistakably showed that Nikisch was conducting ... Once he knew an orchestra he would rarely demand any special tension at rehearsals ... Nikisch's rehearsals were always peaceful, almost uneventful; only once did I see him lose his temper.

For all his admiration, Boult came to the conclusion in Leipzig that if he were to make a list of the music he would prefer to hear Nikisch conduct, it would be short. It was as a magician working his spell on the players rather than as an interpreter that Boult admired him. Among the symphonies he heard rehearsed in 1912–13 were Schumann's First and Second, Mahler's Fourth, Brahms's First, Tchaikovsky's Fourth, Berlioz's *Fantastique*, Schubert's Great C major, Bruckner's Sixth and all Beethoven's.

But it was not only Nikisch who could be heard in Leipzig. In his time there Boult heard Karg-Elert play the organ; Gerhardt sing; piano recitals by Schnabel and Carreño; the Bohemian and St Petersburg String Quartets; Huberman in Beethoven's Violin Concerto; Georg Göhler conducting Berlioz's *Requiem*; Cortot in Saint-Saëns and Chopin; Fritz Busch (then at Aachen) conducting Brahms's Fourth Symphony; an Yvette Guilbert recital; and one by Ludwig Wüllner accompanied by Edwin Fischer. He heard Göhler conduct Mahler's *Das Lied von der Erde* and Ninth Symphony in one concert, and went to *Tristan* and *Fidelio* conducted by Otto Lohse. On 7 December 1912 he went to Dresden when Strauss conducted the first version of *Ariadne auf Naxos* (its first performance, in Stuttgart, had been six weeks earlier) and next day to Prague for *The Bartered Bride*, with Emil Burian in the cast and Marie Hedmondt's daughter Ilva as Mařenka. In January 1913 in Leipzig he heard Anna Bahr-Mildenburg as Amneris in *Aida* and as Isolde (in

March he heard Wittich as Isolde) and he went to Prague again in March for Dvořák's *Rusalka*. An orgy of opera-going in Leipzig in the spring holiday in 1913 included Berlioz's *Beatrice and Benedict*. And Nijinsky and the Russian Ballet, with Pierre Monteux conducting, were in Leipzig in January 1913 with *Cleopatra*, *The Spectre of the Rose*, the *Polovtsian Dances* and *Carnaval*. He went to Meiningen for a festival conducted by Reger and to Cologne in June 1913 for the South Rhine Festival, where he heard Mahler's Eighth Symphony and Steinbach conducting Beethoven's Ninth ('the adagio as played by that orchestra of 200 players was a revelation'). Six days later he was in Berlin for Mengelberg's interpretation of the Ninth.

On 13 February 1913, after singing in the choir in *Parsifal* extracts conducted by Nikisch on the 30th anniversary of the composer's death, Boult was taken ill with what was diagnosed as a strained heart. He woke in the night, he said, 'with thumps of irritating irregularity.' He ascribed it to 'going out of training' when he embarked on a 'life of sightseeing and stodgy food' two days after the Henley races. However that may be, his energy seemed undiminished and when his mother and sister arrived in Germany before Easter he took them sightseeing and to operas. During his days at the Meiningen festival he met the director of Göttingen Conservatory who, he discovered, had played the cello in the first performance of Wagner's *Siegfried Idyll* on the staircase at Tribschen in 1870. He returned to England at Whitsuntide for two days' Eights and his Bachelor of Music degree. His last week in Leipzig in July he spent on a walking tour. 'I got a great deal of good from Leipzig,' he noted in his diary. 'Of course I had the great advantage of being put with the best people to start with.'

He had seen the Germany of Goethe and Schiller, 'peaceful, easy-going Saxony,' where life was incredibly cheap and you could buy ten good meals for 50p. 'Passportless, happy Europe,' he called it, and was anxious to remain there, contemplating a career in the German opera houses. But because of his heart ailment his parents wanted him to return home. One of his first journeys was to Leeds in late September for festival rehearsals where Hugh Allen was joint conductor with Nikisch. 'In later life,' Boult wrote,[3] 'Nikisch had a curious aversion from studying scores. He was always ready to do new works, but said that he could not think out his interpretation from the cold print, but must have the living sound under his hand. I sat next to George Butterworth when Nikisch took a second rehearsal of the *Shropshire Lad* at Leeds. At the first rehearsal he had gone through it and afterwards Butterworth had asked for several slight modifications. Nikisch agreed, but did not re-rehearse then; however ten days later he had remembered them all and George could truthfully say that he had nothing further to suggest: the performance was exactly as he wished it.'

'Taking it easy' for Boult involved attendance at orchestral rehearsals in London and Liverpool – Safonoff and Mengelberg – and becoming an extra member of the Covent Garden musical staff during the 1913–14 season. There the principal occupation was preparation for the first London performance of *Parsifal*, conducted by Arthur Bodanzky on 2 February 1914 – 'a remarkable example of incompetent management,' Boult described it.[4] At the rehearsal the chorus, who had been kept hanging about all day, could not keep pitch and it was found necessary to station several viola players behind the pillars. The instruments made a bigger contribution to the ensemble than the chorus of knights. Boult played some of the bells in the performance itself.

Later in the year he was again an assistant ('doing odd jobs with lighting cues') at the Garden when Nikisch conducted *The Ring* and Albert Coates *Tristan*. On 17 January he went to Queen's Hall when Schoenberg conducted Wood's orchestra in the *Five Orchestral Pieces*. As soon as it was over he was thumped on the shoulder and looked up to find Parry there. 'Bless my soul that's funny stuff,' he said. 'I must say I rather like it when they do it loud like Strauss, but when it's quiet all the time like this, it seems a bit obscene, doesn't it?' From 18 to 24 February he was at Oxford for the Greek play, *The Acharnians* of Aristophanes, with Parry's incidental music. Parry and Allen conducted eight of the nine performances. Boult conducted on 23 February. 'I'm comfortably confident that you will put lots of go into the Music, & am much obliged to you!' Parry wrote to him.

More significant, however, for Boult's future was his decision to conduct a professional orchestra in public for the first time. He gathered together 40 members of the Hallé and Liverpool Philharmonic Orchestras, led by Arthur Catterall, with Agnes Nicholls (a friend of his mother) as the solo soprano, in the Public Hall, West Kirby, on Friday, 27 February 1914. The programme was:

Brandenburg Concerto No. 2......Bach (in Steinbach edition)

Aria, 'Marten aller Arten'
(*Die Entführung aus dem Serail*)......Mozart
Soloist......Agnes Nicholls

Idyll, The Banks of Green Willow......Butterworth
(first performance)

Piano Concerto in A minor (2nd and 3rd movements)......Schumann
Soloist......Dr. W.B. Brierley

Siegfried Idyll......Wagner

Aria, 'Ah! fors è lui' (*La Traviata*)......Verdi
Soloist......Agnes Nicholls

Italian Serenade......Wolf

Overture, *Don Giovanni*......Mozart

The arias were substituted for compositions by Hamilton Harty, Agnes Nicholls's husband, who was to have accompanied her at the piano but was ill. The *Liverpool Daily Post* noted the occasion. Its critic found the programme 'so very, very proper and safe' but thought that the conductor was 'well-read in his scores ... appears at all times to have control over the instrumental forces under him and the ability to impart here and there a delicate touch or to proceed to a bold, effective climax. Amidst all this – perhaps it is the most thankful point of all – his manner is devoid of all ostentation.' While Boult was rehearsing the *Italian Serenade* the first oboe, Charles Reynolds of the Hallé, came in a bar late. Boult admonished him, to be told by Reynolds that he knew the piece well and was right. 'I am afraid I knew very well that the piece had hardly ever been played in England before so I thought the appropriate answer was "I am sorry, Mr Reynolds, we must all of us have been a bar early then." This intrigued the orchestra and I suppose it got round to the Liverpool Philharmonic management.'

Towards the end of March Boult went to Paris, where he heard Debussy play some of his own preludes and accompany the first performance of his *Trois poèmes de Mallarmé*. The Petersfield Festival followed in April; the Oxford Bach Festival in May, with Elwes among the singers in the Mass in B minor, Sir Walter Parratt and Henry Ley the organists, W. H. Reed solo violinist and Boult playing the continuo. In June Nikisch was in London conducting the LSO in Wagner and on 26 June Boult went to the Queen's Hall when Strauss conducted. Of this he wrote sixty years later,[5] 'He did *Don Juan*, *Till Eulenspiegel*, *Tod und Verklärung* and the Mozart G minor. I was told that [at rehearsal] he polished off his three in an hour and spent the remaining five hours on the Mozart. It sounded like it – the end movements were amazing: for 10 bars you thought it was slow; it was, but you forgot it after 10 bars because the rhythm and accentuation were so astonishingly light and lively ...'

On 25 and 26 July Boult conducted two concerts in the Judge's Lodgings, Oxford. This beautiful building in St Giles was occupied by two sisters, Mabel and Alice Price, the former a fine contralto, the latter a violinist. At the beginning of each vacation they invited a group of friends, headed by Hugh Allen and Ernest Walker as the two pianists, to perform a wide selection of music with Bach cantatas as the backbone of the programmes. Thus on the 26th Boult conducted what must have been the first performance in England – albeit without an orchestra – of Mahler's cantata *Das klagende Lied*.

CHAPTER 9

Boots and Ballet

NINE days after that Mahler performance a real 'song of sorrow' began when Britain declared war on Germany. Boult wanted to join the Liverpool Scottish but his father persuaded him to wait until his heart was better. In any case, despite the embarrassment of looking healthy and strong, his medical category was C3. So in October he returned to Oxford to work with Ernest Walker and Donald Tovey for his first Doctor of Music examination, which he sat and passed in November. Returning to West Kirby he heard of the plight of some of the players in the Hallé and Liverpool Philharmonic whose income had been diminished by a reduction in the number of concerts and of private pupils. So, with financial support from his father, he formed an orchestra of 30 players, who included Archie Camden as bassoonist, and organized a series of four concerts in the large Sun Hall (capacity 4,000) in the poor Liverpool suburb of Kensington. Admission was from twopence to 2s 6d (12½p) and smoking was allowed. The concerts were given on Fridays from 13 November to 4 December. The highest audience figure was 399 (at the third concert) and a full call was made on the guarantors. The programmes were popular, from 'Your King and Country Want You' and 'Tipperary' to Tchaikovsky's *Rococo Variations*, Beethoven's First Symphony, Vaughan Williams's *Wasps* overture and the first performance of *New Forest Rhapsody* by Boult's Oxford friend Richard T. Woodman.

'Undeterred by local apathy and imbued with a high ideal,' as the correspondent of the New York *Musical Courier* put it, Boult conducted a further six concerts between 20 January and 24 February 1915. Out went the patriotic ballads. The Woodman and Vaughan Williams (twice) were repeated, Mozart's G minor Symphony, some Wagner and Beethoven's G major Piano Concerto were played. Audiences steadily increased to the thousand mark and the press comment, lavishly generous in space by today's standards, was favourable, especially towards the conductor. The *Courier*'s correspondent went so far as to suggest municipal subsidy, but added: 'No! Such a thing as official recognition of music as a civilizing agency does not come within the purview of our municipal satraps ... Liverpool is probably the most unmusical place in the British Isles. This, of course, is due to the people themselves, who elect men to represent them who have no artistic perception ...'

While rehearsing and organizing these concerts, Boult was also spending five hours a day drilling recruits belonging to the 16th Service Battalion of the King's (Liverpool) Regiment at West Kirby. These were mainly Lancashire miners billeted in the Public Hall near to The Abbey Manor. In May 1915 they were moved to St Asaph, Denbighshire (now Clwyd), and Boult was asked to go with them to act as an orderly officer in the headquarters of the Rhyl Reserve Centre. His office was just opposite St Asaph Cathedral, but the camp was a few miles away in Kinmel Park. This continued until the summer of 1916 when the centre was dispersed.

In the autumn of 1915 Boult resumed his Liverpool concerts, this time in a more central venue, the theatre of the David Lewis Club in Great George Place. The young warden, Frederick Marquis, was a friend of Cedric Boult and had been impressed by the Sun Hall concerts. The club was part of the philanthropic enterprise of David Lewis; Marquis was in due course to become managing director of Lewis's and eventually Lord Woolton, Churchill's Minister of Food in the 1939–45 war and later a highly successful chairman of the Conservative party. Among the works performed during the six concerts between 6 October and 15 December were Brahms's Second Symphony, Mozart's *Prague* and G minor Symphonies, Haydn's 102nd Symphony, Beethoven's C minor Piano Concerto and short pieces by Grainger, Glazunov, Holbrooke, Fauré, Bantock, Arensky, Holst, Ravel and Scriabin. Again, the enterprise and execution were alike welcomed. Incidentally, Boult by now looked like the conductor audiences came to know so well: before leaving Oxford he had grown a moustache and had begun to lose the hair on his head. A few days after launching this new series he asked Landon Ronald to give him some advice on conducting. Ronald agreed to go through scores with him, 'making things clear' about technical points. For this he charged six guineas (a guinea was 21 shillings, or 105p) an hour. One six-guinea hour, Boult drily remarked, produced a good hint: to stop the orchestra, strike the baton on the flat of the desk and not the edge. The stick will not then break.

These successes led to his first appearance as a guest conductor of the Liverpool Philharmonic Orchestra on 25 January 1916. He opened the programme with the Belgian national anthem and included a suite by Arthur de Greef based on Flemish folk tunes. Bach's Third Brandenburg Concerto, Haydn's 99th Symphony and Parry's *Symphonic Variations* were the principal works, with the 14-year-old pianist Solomon as soloist in Liszt's *Hungarian Fantasia*. The critic of the *Musical Standard* (5 February 1916) was present:

> ... The programme revealed the catholicity of his musical tastes and his ability to interpret widely differing schools. His lead is clear and convincing if somewhat lacking in that magnetism which holds in a relentless grip both orchestra and audience. There is no doubt but that this musician is destined to do much in the cause of native orchestral composition.

When Boult was at home he attended the Liverpool orchestra's rehearsals under such conductors as Mlynarski, Safonoff, Wood, and Gabriel Pierné. For Pierné, who did not speak English, he acted as translator – Boult spoke fluent German, French and Italian.

In the summer of 1916 he was asked to take a job in the War Office, translating the German Press and writing a weekly account of how the Germans, for propaganda, were presenting reports in English newspapers. In a London street he encountered Fred Marquis, who was also working for the War Office in control of the country's leather resources. 'I'm overworking and you must come and join me.' The transfer was arranged inside a week and Boult joined the contracts department as Marquis's personal assistant. He was able to fit in concerts and rehearsals, and perhaps the most far-reaching rehearsal he attended was in London on 27 November 1916 when he heard Landon Ronald rehearse the orchestra of the Royal Philharmonic Society in Elgar's Second Symphony. This was the first time Boult heard a work with which he was to become so closely associated, and it was a performance that evidently did no more justice to it than its first performance, for a member of the audience, Frank Bridge, wrote to Edward Speyer: 'Poor Elgar – the orchestra positively scrambled through the Symphony as they had never before seen it ... As I had never heard the work before I felt quite sick about it. Performances of this kind do far more harm than good.'

In 1916, too, his friendship with Gustav Holst began. They had corresponded the previous year when Boult asked him which of his works might be suitable for his Liverpool concerts and Holst told him of the *Somerset Rhapsody* and the *Country* and *Marching Songs*. In London Holst took Boult on what he called his 'London country walk', a clever amalgam of Kew Gardens, Sheen Common, Richmond Park and other beauty spots, linked by the Thames towpath. He also went to Holst's soundproof room at St Paul's Girls' School (where Holst was director of music) and heard on two pianos the big orchestral suite that he had just completed, *The Planets*.

Marquis devised a scheme for a 'standard wartime boot' to suit all pockets. He dispatched Boult in January 1918 with 18 samples to tour the West Country and to 'discuss any difficulties' with local retailers. He had also given him permission to organize four Queen's Hall concerts with the London Symphony Orchestra for February and March in each of which contemporary English works would be included. While Boult was fortunate enough to have the private means to undertake the venture, he was unknown to the London public and to make one's début in the capital as a conductor with such programmes was either 'a splendidly plucky enterprise,' as Holst[1] described it, or foolhardy. Before it would agree to the concerts, the board of the orchestra required a reference for Boult from the Liverpool Philharmonic Society. The biggest work he was to do was Vaughan Williams's *A London Symphony*, which had had only two performances (in Bournemouth and Harrogate) since its first in London on 27 March 1914. He had neither heard nor seen it, but felt it was due for its second London performance. Having obtained the score, he studied it on his train journeys to his boots sessions.

Slowly, in the years leading up to 1914, and accelerating during the war itself, the cause of English music was gaining adherents, though the public was slow to join the bandwagon. Wood had now been joined by Landon Ronald, Beecham, Geoffrey Toye and Harty as native conductors. Beecham's principal championship was reserved for Delius, who lived in France. A venture to establish a kind of English Bayreuth at Glastonbury centred on the Arthurian operas of Rutland Boughton attracted support and interest, ludicrous though it may seem today. The cause of folk music and folk dancing was espoused not merely by Cecil Sharp, but by Vaughan Williams, Holst and Butterworth. The name of Edward J. Dent cropped up in association with several ventures to promote English music and music-making. Perhaps most significant was the establishment in 1914 of the Carnegie United Kingdom Trust, which awarded grants to organizations and competitive festivals and in 1917 began to publish works by composers who were little known to the public or which were unlikely to be taken up by commercial publishers (the first score to be published by the Trust being the Piano Quartet of Herbert Howells).

Dent wrote the programme notes for Boult's four LSO concerts which were given on Mondays 4 and 18 February and 4 and 18 March. The orchestra was led by W.H. Reed, a close friend of Elgar and thenceforward a close friend of Boult. The first programme[2] opened with the Third Brandenburg Concerto and included Beethoven's Fifth Symphony. The soloist was the viola player Lionel Tertis, who played the Bach *Chaconne* and Benjamin Dale's *Romance*. The other English works were the *Country Song* by Holst (still von Holst at this date) and the *Rhapsody* by Richard Woodman. The critics gave Boult full marks for enterprise but were less impressed by his conducting. The *Daily Telegraph*'s man mentioned 'unusually slow tempi' in the Beethoven which robbed it of 'much of its vitality.' A long report in the *Christian Science Monitor* complained of a lack of 'nuance, detail and polish' but decided that Boult, if not remarkable, was at least capable. The audience was small, and even smaller for the second concert. There had been Zeppelin raids on London on the two previous evenings and there was a third during the concert. 'At the end,' Boult recalled,[3] 'orchestra and audience (about equal numbers) collected in the basement bar at Queen's Hall until the "All clear" had sounded.' The programme began with Elgar's *In the South* and on 17 February Boult went to tea with him at Severn House, Hampstead. 'Quite a nice man,' Lady Elgar confided to her diary. 'E. went through *In the South* with him – he seemed to understand ...' Also in the programme was the first performance in England of *Asie*, from Ravel's *Shéhérazade* song-cycle, sung by a tenor, Yves Tinayre. But it was the Vaughan Williams symphony that took most space in the notices and was generally acclaimed. The composer, who was still in the army, wrote to Boult from the Royal Artillery mess at Bordon, Hampshire: 'It really was splendid; you had got the score right into you & through you into your orch. May I say how much I admired your conducting – it is real *conducting* – you get just what you want & *know* what you want & your players trust you because they know it also ...'[4]

At the third concert Boult had three soloists: Louis Fleury and Gwendolen Mason were flautist and harpist in Mozart's Concerto (K.299), and Beatrice Harrison played Lalo's Cello Concerto. He conducted Butterworth's *A Shropshire Lad* rhapsody (which had now acquired the additional poignancy of its composer's gallant death in action in 1916), his old master H.E. Piggott's *In Shakespeare's Days*, and the Prelude and Dances from Bax's ballet *Between Dusk and Dawn*. (Bax complained that the side-drum 'was apparently seized with a maenad fury.') Boult's heart, one suspects, was most fully committed in Parry's *Symphonic Variations*. The composer went to the rehearsal because he had

had 'such sad experiences with those variations ... I hope you spotted that the tune is very slow.' At rehearsal he asked for it to be 'still slower.' Next day he congratulated Boult 'on the good hold you have on the performers.'

At the last concert Boult elected to repeat the Vaughan Williams symphony. In the intervening month, the composer 'came to my room in a distant outcrop of the War Office and sat among the samples of boots ... and made some cuts in the score ...'[5] He deleted a 'hymnlike third subject' in the finale and made some cuts in the second movement.

The programme also included Harty's *With the Wild Geese* and Ireland's *The Forgotten Rite*. For this last concert Boult had 48 string players compared with 28 at the preceding concerts and it was agreed that the symphony gained immeasurably. 'We look to Mr Boult to reveal to the nation its own music,' was the verdict of the *Musical Standard*. As a *succès d'estime*, the venture was a feather in Boult's cap. But Francis Toye in the *Nation* of 3 May 1918 summed it up: ' "Surely," we say to ourselves, "the day of English music has dawned at last! What could be more representative? What more hopeful?" And then we look round the empty seats and recognize with a sigh that if this be truly the day of English music, it sadly needs a little sun ... The fact of the matter is that these several isolated experiments, wholly admirable and stimulating as they individually are, scarcely count from the public point of view.' Boult himself was pleased by the way the concerts had been welcomed by the musicians. He had 'the curious feeling, after all these years of work and preparation, that at any rate I was now good enough, or thought to be, to be at any rate a useful musician. This and the satisfaction of CIR [*Commission Internationale de Ravitaillement*] work – where one was at last a responsible officer [June 1918] – almost dwarfed the longing for peace, for there was the feeling that the moment it came one *could* make good; and before it had been that when it came one might be found useless.' His next act as a 'useful' musician was to step in at short notice on 6 September to conduct the first performance in London for four years of Diaghilev's Russian Ballet at the Coliseum, when Lydia Lopokova made her début in the city in *Cleopatra*. Henri Defosse, the regular conductor, had been delayed on his journey to England and Boult rehearsed the company.

CHAPTER 10

The Planets

HOWEVER little English music counted with the public, its adherents were undeterred. In July 1918 the British Music Society was founded, with Lord Howard de Walden as president and a committee which included Dent, Boult, Bernard Shaw, Walford Davies, W.W. Cobbett and Geoffrey Toye. Boult tried in vain to persuade Elgar to let the Society have the first performance of his Violin Sonata. But an historic and unusual first performance was about to come his way. In mid-September his War Office sanctum was invaded by an excited Holst. 'I've been ordered to Salonika in a fortnight, and Balfour Gardiner has given me a wonderful parting present. It consists of Queen's Hall, full of the Queen's Hall Orchestra, for the whole morning on Sunday week. We're going to do *The Planets* and you're going to conduct.'

The Planets, for a huge orchestra, had been started in 1914 and completed in 1916. The parts were now copied by Holst's pupils at St Paul's Girls' School where Boult was again played the two-piano arrangement. Dining with Holst the night before the performance, Boult remembered:[1] 'Geoffrey Toye pointed to the combination in *Neptune* of the E minor chord with G sharp and D sharp in the bass and said to him "I'm sorry, Gustav, I think that is going to sound frightful." Gustav's answer might well have come from Ralph [Vaughan Williams] ... "Yes, I know it will, but what are you to do when they come like that?"' The performance was on 29 September (among the most interested listeners was Henry Wood) and when it was over Norman O'Neill, honorary treasurer of the Royal Philharmonic Society, invited Boult to conduct two concerts in the forthcoming season. Holst wrote:[2] 'I have discovered that there is no need for me to thank you or to congratulate you. It would be as ridiculous as for you to tell the Queen's Hall Orchestra that you didn't know the scores! You covered yourself with glory ...' When the score of *The Planets* was published, Holst wrote in Boult's copy: 'This score is the property of Adrian Boult who first caused *The Planets* to shine in public and so earned the gratitude of Gustav Holst.'

But before the Philharmonic concerts there was the sadness of Hubert Parry's death on 7 October. Boult was at the Royal College of Music memorial concert on 8 November, which opened with the first performance of the *Elegy for Brahms* Parry had written in 1897, destined to be one of the last works Boult was to record over 60 years later. Then came the Armistice. Boult had escaped the horrors of the trenches, but he had lost Butterworth and the Australian pianist and composer F. S. Kelly among his friends. 'What a joy it was a few days ago,' he wrote a few months after the end of the war, 'to walk past the CIR and realize I had forgotten their telephone number! All the same, I've had a very much better time than most of my friends, and the war has only really thrown me back 2 years as a conductor. It may have stopped me composing, but perhaps that is a blessing to the world! The indoor life and companionship only with indoor friends are really what I have felt most, after the musiclessness.' He divided his friends into indoor and outdoor, the latter being those with whom he rowed or shot or walked, 'ordinary people in brain, but Robin [Barrington-Ward] is the summit of both – brains and splendid health and spirit.'

'The two Philharmonics (Jan and Feb) with that marvellous orchestra ... seemed to put the lid on to the way people spoke,' Boult wrote in his diary, 'for in both there was heaps of immaturity and heaps that another rehearsal might have done; and everything was found perfect (when the conducting wasn't taken as a matter of course).' In October 1918 he had approached Henry Wood for conducting lessons. 'How can you teach Conducting except with an Orchestra in front of you, to play on?' came the reply. 'No! No! No! certainly not – ridiculous.'[3]

Boult's début at the Royal Philharmonic was on 30 January 1919. Although he conducted Schumann's First Symphony and Mozart's *Serenade* in B flat, the significant event was the first performance of Delius's Violin Concerto ('one long gorgeous melody from beginning to end,' *The Times* critic wrote) which was received with tumultuous applause for the composer. The performance was nearly jeopardized by the reluctance of a music-hating colonel to release Albert Sammons, who was still in the army, to play the solo part. Holst wrote[4] from Salonika with some hints about *The Planets*: 'Mars. You made it wonderfully clear ... Now could you make more *row*? And work up more sense of climax? Perhaps hurry certain bits? Anyhow it must sound more unpleasant and far more terrifying ... *Saturn*. Make the climax as big and overwhelming as possible. Then the soft ending will play itself as

long as there is no suggestion of crescendo. *The organ must be softer
... Jupiter.* As long as he gets the wonderful joyousness you gave him,
he'll do ...' Boult decided to include only five of the seven movements
at the concert on 27 February (he excluded *Venus* and *Neptune*), explaining to Holst's friend Vally Lasker that he felt that when the public were
being given 'a totally new language like that,' half an hour of it was as
much as they could take in. 'I am quite sure that 90 per cent if not 95
per cent of people only listen to one *moment* after another and never
think of music as a whole at all.' It was for this reason, he explained,
that he had asked Vaughan Williams to cut his *London Symphony*.
Boult evidently took Holst's words on *Mars* to heart for *The Times*
called it 'as bad an exhibition of frightfulness as the modern orchestra
can produce.'

Inside a year, as one newspaper remarked, Boult had risen from
obscurity to a leading place among British conductors. More was to
follow. A consequence of Parry's death was the appointment of Hugh
Allen as his successor as Director of the Royal College of Music. Allen
at once invited Boult to join the staff to start a class for conductors. He
began work in February 1919. Among the first students were Leslie
Heward, whose early death in 1942 prematurely ended a brilliant career;
Boris Ord, later organist of King's College, Cambridge; Armstrong
Gibbs, the composer; Constant Lambert; Richard Austin; Herbert
Sumsion, later organist of Gloucester Cathedral; and Patrick Hadley,
composer and professor of music at Cambridge University. When Boult
was away, the class was taken by Arthur Bliss. Allen also revivified the
college's Patron's Fund, founded in 1903 through the generosity of Sir
Ernest (later Lord) Palmer. Instead of two annual concerts, there were
10 public rehearsals with a professional orchestra (LSO) at which British
compositions were performed. The composers could conduct if they
wished, or Boult did so.

Boult's reaction to his academic rôle was quizzical.

The first few lunches at the RCM were a succession of people whose names
were well known (but their faces not to this benighted provincial) introducing
themselves ... It is touching the kindness of Stanford to me (*cf.* his reputation) – even writing a note after I had helped (at a rehearsal) with the part
corrections of his *Agincourt.*[5] And at the Savile 2 days later he said so much
to Sir William McConnell (of Carnegie fame) and McC. talked so openly
about Carnegie and Government plans for music that I feel as if I were 50
and an old friend of them all.

Boult still went to as many concerts as he could, and now he took students to rehearsals. He gave Albert Coates credit for restoring London orchestral standards after the war and remembered his taking 50 minutes to rehearse the *Meistersinger* overture with the LSO (29 April 1919), 'every moment badly needed.' Others were less enthusiastic about Coates's zeal in this respect – Elgar, for example, whose Cello Concerto received a disastrous first performance on 27 October 1919 because Coates used most of Elgar's rehearsal-time on other works.

In October 1919 Boult took over the conducting of the Russian Ballet at the Empire Theatre from Ernest Ansermet, who was contracted to open the Suisse Romande season in Geneva. Ansermet 'was kindness itself and took endless trouble to enable me to get the hang of things and learn the tempi,' but there were 14 ballets in the repertoire none of which Boult knew more than casually. They included *Petrushka*, *La boutique fantasque*, *Thamar*, *Scheherazade*, *The Three-Cornered Hat*, *Les Sylphides*, *Parade* (world première), *The Good-Humoured Ladies*, and *Firebird*. Boult found he had to have a good row with Diaghilev every three weeks 'to get any peace.' He also found after the first four weeks that there was no sign of any salary (20 guineas a week), so after the second ballet of a triple bill he sent a message to the impresario saying he was going home there and then if no money was forthcoming. 'Round he came instantly, his pockets bulging with £20 notes, and asked me what I wanted.'

Ernest Newman, in the *Manchester Guardian* of 17 December 1919, described the *Firebird* revival as 'a triumph' for Boult 'who is the most gifted of our younger conductors. He has both temperament and technique, and above all an aplomb that is invaluable in those moments of stress and strain that are all too common under our English system of running risks with new and difficult works.' Leigh Henry, however, ballet critic of the *Musical Standard*, thought Boult's engagement 'a blunder' on Diaghilev's part. 'Not that Mr Boult does not beat very correctly – he is too emphatically English, even to the extent of being one of the staff of the Royal College of Music, not to do everything he undertakes with the acme of correctness.' Henry believed that the English could only bring 'earnest solemnity' to their music-making and 'to the infusion of these necessary qualities in the shamelessly unbridled music of the uncultured Russians Mr Boult has applied himself with commendable zeal – ardour being too reckless a word to apply in such a well-bred instance.' This critic much preferred those performances conducted by Edward Clark. He pointed out that Clark had conducted most of the *Firebird* rehearsals.

The benefit of this young conductor's preparation, informed by his thorough conversance with modern orchestral technique in general, and that of Stravinsky in particular, was so great that the most unsympathetic or unintelligent after-treatment could not reduce the orchestral rendering to the banality which has marked the musical side of many of the present ballet season's productions. Nevertheless, Mr Boult did his best to secure the average result.

Another writer referred in the *Sketch* to Boult's 'genial back (Christ Church Cathedral in every curve of it, except those severer parts that are more reminiscent of Westminster Abbey) ...'

Boult admitted that he was slow to grasp the art of ballet conducting:

Dancers cannot initiate a tempo as a singer or concerto soloist can; they can only take the tempo a conductor gives them ... Only one dancer in my experience had the initiative power to show me if I had taken a wrong tempo, by stepping ahead of my beat or behind it, and that was Massine ... It was madness to expect a newcomer to gauge all the tempi correctly when they change every few minutes in 14 ballets, some of them 40 minutes long!

For one ballet, 'thrown on with a minimum of rehearsal,' Boult asked Diaghilev to send someone to sit at his feet and tap his leg at the right tempo whenever there was a change. Diaghilev himself performed this strange function. Boult was now able to take the Doctor of Music degree for which he had passed the examination in 1914. In congratulating him on his work with the ballet, Henry Wood joked: 'This settles it, you can never be a Doctor of Music after this, can you?'

At 30 years of age, Boult had now 'arrived.' Yet what had happened to his ambition to conduct opera? As he became more enmeshed in the work of the College and of promoting the cause of English music the real purpose of his Leipzig year was disappearing over the horizon.

PART II

RCM and Birmingham, 1920–1929

CHAPTER 11

British Symphony Orchestra

THE year 1920 began for Boult with a repetition of Delius's Violin Concerto at a Royal Philharmonic concert on 29 January in a programme that included Holst's *Beni Mora*, Bantock's *Hymn to Aphrodite* and Brahms's Fourth Symphony. In February he went to Amsterdam to hear Mengelberg conduct Mahler's *Das klagende Lied*, remembering his own Oxford performance with two pianos nearly six years earlier. His main energies, however, were concentrated on Elgar's Second Symphony, neglected since its early performances in 1911 and 1912, which he was to include in an LSO concert at Queen's Hall on 16 March to mark the reappearance in London of the Polish violinist Samuel Dushkin. He went through the score with Elgar in the previous month, and the composer went to the rehearsal on the 15th. The performance was a triumph and the critics were almost unanimous in wondering why so great a work had been allowed to fall out of the repertory and in acclaiming Boult's 'revelation' of it. But for one listener in particular, Lady Elgar, with less than a month to live, it was a fulfilment. 'It seemed absolutely to penetrate the audience's mind & heart,' she wrote in her diary that evening. '... Adrian was wonderful ... E. was so happy & pleased.' She wrote to 'Dear Mr Adrian Boult' on the 17th to thank him 'from my heart ... I cannot describe the delight to me of hearing that great work so splendidly rendered ... I rejoiced in your triumph ...' From Elgar himself there came a laying-on of hands: 'I feel that my reputation in the future is safe in your hands. It was a wonderful series of sounds. Bless you!'

In the spring of 1920 Boult was in Holland from 26 March to 4 April with Bliss and some of his RCM students, – Armstrong Gibbs, Scott Goddard, Boris Ord, and Leslie Heward. They heard Mengelberg conduct Bach's *St Matthew Passion* twice, on successive evenings at the Concertgebouw, Amsterdam. 'The perfection of ensemble simply bowled one over after our scratch English performances, and it was a

73

very beautifully thought out interpretation. The recitatives were frightfully slow and seemed endless.'

Boult returned to Amsterdam on 13 May when he went to the famous Mahler Festival which Mengelberg mounted there to mark his 25th anniversary as conductor of the Concertgebouw Orchestra. He reported the occasion for the *Daily Telegraph* (22 May) and wrote that the festival committee had 'expressed to me their grief that so few visitors from England had been able to accept their invitation. I saw, indeed, only two that I knew.' He heard the Sixth, Seventh and Ninth Symphonies, *Das Lied von der Erde* and the *Kindertotenlieder*.

> The wonderful finish and uniform bowing of the strings, the perfection of ensemble, and balance of woodwind and the fine chording of the brass can only be achieved when orchestras are able to rehearse works until they know almost by heart not only their own parts but everyone else's as well ... The splendid power and strength of the performance of the Seventh Symphony last Saturday was probably accounted for by the fact that the Amsterdam orchestra had given it no less than fifteen times in the last ten years, under the direction either of Mengelberg or Mahler.

He diagnosed the reason for English neglect of Mahler as the length of the works.

> One feels that Mahler is master of his structure, whether he uses the traditional forms or not, and it is impossible to question the orchestration of a man who was one of the greatest conductors of his age, although one must confess to an impression of over-scoring in much of the purely orchestral work.

Not many other Englishmen at that date would have recognized Mahler as a master of structure. Talking to Christopher Bishop about Mahler towards the end of his life, Boult remarked that it was 'odd music, but great fun to conduct.'

During the summer Boult typically found time to conduct the music Armstrong Gibbs had composed for a play by Walter De La Mare, *Crossings*, which Dent produced at a Brighton preparatory school in June. He was also involved in the reorganization of the British Symphony Orchestra. This had been founded in 1919 by Raymond Roze, son of Marie Roze, a famous Carmen, from professional musicians who had served abroad in the Services during the war. It had given a few concerts under Roze, including two in Liverpool. The honorary secretary of the orchestra was Eugene Cruft, the double-bass player, who was to become a principal in the BBC Symphony Orchestra and one of Boult's dearest friends. Roze died suddenly and the orchestra was taken over by Thomas

Quinlan who invited Boult to be its conductor. He met them first on 3 July 1919. The orchestra made its début under him at the Kingsway Hall on 16 October, Tchaikovsky's Fifth Symphony being the principal work, but the programme opened with a Boult favourite, the Third Brandenburg Concerto. Among the cellists was ex-Lance Corporal John Barbirolli. Boult had high ambitions for the British Symphony Orchestra. In its second concert he included Debussy's *La Mer* and in the third Elgar's Second Symphony. But even these programmes, as the critic of the *Saturday Review* noted, were 'too dependent as yet upon the adventitious aid of "stars."'

Boult was now seeing more of Elgar, lonely after his wife's death. They met frequently at The Hut, Schuster's Thamesside house at Bray. Looking afresh at the symphony led Boult to the conclusion that 'I knew precious little about it when I did it last March, although it was such a success.' His diary continues with this frank self-assessment:

At the time I realized I was really far too busy to get a real grip of so big a work quickly, and so concentrated on the architecture of the whole thing, and rise & fall to and from climaxes, and so on. The result quite justified this, but it is a rotten and unprincipled way of going about, and if it hadn't been a first-rate orchestra, things might have been very different. Elgar's scoring (and how often it is more registration than scoring!) is so telling, and comes off with so little trouble that it (the detail) spoke for itself. Passages like cue No. 17, and the centre of the last movement (145) meant nothing at all to me and I just drove through them like a snowplough. It will have to go a bit different next time, when I do it with the BSO. I really must keep things clear in order to have plenty of time in hand to work quietly – even in London. The Patron's Fund is of course very insidious, because in the time at one's disposal one *can* only skim over the stuff, but perhaps it is as well there because, as Rimsky [Korsakov] says, the test of good orchestration is a scratch performance, not a fully-rehearsed one (in the continental sense of the term); and we mustn't pamper the Patron's Fund composers!

During this year he had been writing 'A Handbook on the Technique of Conducting' and finished it on 6 August, sending it to a printer in Oxford. 'It will be useful for RCM of course,' he wrote in his diary, 'but I wonder what certain conductors will say. I mean to send it round for comments. Coates told me not to write it as "everyone must go his own way," but I think it is time to lay down certain things. Whether I've done it right or not is another matter.' The text was divided into 11 sections and gave hints on how a conductor should stand, hold and handle the baton, and how to produce maximum effect with minimum effort. Something of the atmosphere of Boult's conducting classes was vividly captured by Katherine Eggar in an article published in January 1921:[1]

> Mr Boult moved about the hall smiling, helpful, observant, unfussy, now and then jotting down the notes which in the afternoon would reveal the shortcomings of the novices ... The chief feature is a sort of gay earnestness. There is no relentless pounding through in spite of bewilderment. When it is better to stop and start again, this is done ... At three o'clock came the Day of Judgment ... 'Brown, your *rehearsing* was really excellent. You show them how. But you had no control at change of time. Now why was that? ... You stopped the stick between the beats. You see, your too definite beat stopped the swing. You had got to arm's length and had left yourself nowhere to go ... You've got to contend with the player who looks up *between* the beats. Remember page 17, last paragraph, in our famous book. Green, you and the band couldn't agree; you remember the place? You must count out loud if you can't get them with you.' 'But I did.' 'Yes, but they couldn't hear you. You must bellow if necessary. Black, you were put out because the desk was too high. If you find yourself in that difficulty it does not solve the problem to conduct from the trouser pocket as you were doing ... Miss Grey, where do you beat the "and" in six time? ... and those grace notes ... And White, you got into difficulties in the last movement and looked very fierce – not that that mattered, but why didn't you *do* something? ... You must practise everything, bullying included, you know! ...' 'What happens, sir, when you're conducting a professional orchestra and you miss a beat? ...' 'O, the professional orchestra will carry their conductor over a misbeat; they'll save you from a catastrophe, unless it happens that you've ruffled them beforehand ... But talking of misbeats, did you notice what happened at the concert on Saturday?'

About this time, too, Boult was asked to help a Christ Church under-graduate, William Walton. In 1912 Walton, aged ten, had won a choral scholarship to Christ Church Cathedral choir school and, like Boult, had been befriended by Dr Strong. Walton was sent down from Christ Church for two terms in 1920 after failing the first part of the Responsions examination and it was at this point that Boult, as he wrote later,[2] 'got a passionate letter from Henry Ley about this wonderful Lancashire boy who had been kept at Ch.Ch. by the Dean and was now to come to London and MUST find a job – could I do anything? ... Anyhow I fixed up an interview (with Goodwin and Tabb, the publishers) and I thought W.W. nicely started proof-reading for a go-ahead publisher etc etc. A few days later a letter arrived: "Thank you for the introduction but I'm afraid I have decided to starve in a garret and compose all day rather than enjoy a nice job." Three weeks later he took up residence with the three Sitwells!! Some starving! And the "garret" was a jolly little house just off Chelsea Embankment.'

Another landmark in Boult's progress during 1920 was his first contract to make gramophone records for His Master's Voice. This was announced during the summer and the first results of it were issued in the spring of 1921. The records, with the British Symphony Orchestra, were of Butterworth's *A Shropshire Lad* rhapsody and two ballet suites, the Scarlatti-Tomasini *The Good-Humoured Ladies* and the Rossini-Respighi *La boutique fantasque*. Thus began a career in the recording studio which was to continue for 59 years. Like so many other great recording artists, Boult was 'signed up' by Fred Gaisberg, the American who was manager of HMV. Gaisberg had heard Boult at the Russian Ballet and asked him to record some of the music. Boult recalled:

> We trekked down to Hayes one morning, and found ourselves in a studio so small that it would hardly have held a full-size billiard table besides the essential chairs and music stands and an enormous gramophone horn ... Immediately in front of this sat the leader of the orchestra with his fiddle as nearly inside the mouth of the horn as he could hold it. He was surrounded by a few strings, but in those days, apparently, the low tones of the double bass were an impossible proposition and the double bass part was in the hands of a gentleman with a tuba who puffed away in the furthest corner of the studio with remarkable results. I always longed to hear him operating on the arpeggios in the last movement of Beethoven No. 5 ...

One of his early recordings was of Bliss's *Rout*:

> The moment the final chord had been sounded our gallant composer shouted at the top of his voice 'By Jove, you fellows, that was grand.' This was, of course, immortalized on the hot wax and had to be scrapped, to our great grief. I tried to persuade Mr Gaisberg that to have the voice of the composer would surely stimulate the sales of the record, but it was decided that this would not do.

His holiday in September was a journey with Robin Barrington-Ward to Holland, Germany, Czechoslovakia, Austria and France. Barrington-Ward, on demobilization, had joined *The Observer* as second-in-command to the editor J.L. Garvin and was visiting the paper's pre-war foreign correspondents to re-establish contacts. Among Oxford friends they met was Kurt Hahn, at Salem, home of Prince Max of Baden, who was beginning the educational experiments he later transferred to Gordonstoun. In Prague Boult went to four concerts, hearing Bruckner's First and Second Symphonies and two works by Förster, and a recital by Destinn (who now called herself by her real name, Destinnová). On returning to London he resumed his round of RCM, British Symphony Orchestra and LSO. A Patron's Fund concert in November at which Albert Coates conducted the orchestral epilogue to his proposed opera *The Myth Beautiful* prompted some tart comments in Boult's diary:

> It is a melancholy fact that *really* the executive artist lives for applause. The four big shows I can remember are the *4 Planets* at the Philharmonic, the Elgar 2nd Symphony, my return after the first *Firebird* and now on 9th November the reception given me by the LSO when I went back to do the second half of the Patron's Fund concert after Coates's performances with (not 'of') his work. No need to put down details, but it was very grateful [*sic*] and comforting to get that from the LSO of all people. It would be a difficult choice, if I ever have to make it, between them and the BSO. Let's hope I shan't. Of course it was largely their annoyance with Coates – they'd have welcomed the most incapable creature at that moment – what a pity A. C. can't carry corn.

Boult was severe on himself, too. Two days after the Coates episode he went to conduct the Portsmouth Philharmonic, of which Bliss had recently been appointed conductor:

> A very successful British programme given by Arthur Bliss on 11th Nov. I conducted the Stanford first Rhapsody disgracefully; had no idea where I was a lot of the time (high pitch may have helped this, and a very short rehearsal) and never helped anyone to do anything. It is becoming a very serious problem how to find time to get up my scores, for I have done some very bad things at the Palladium, and it is even worse to come down to a country town and do things badly. My rule about knowing the melodic line by heart is a dead letter, and unless I can make time to revive it, I must start refusing work, which seems silly to put it mildly.

He obtained advice and help wherever he could find it, such as from one of his staff colleagues at the College, the pianist Fanny Davies. This celebrated pupil of Clara Schumann was now 59. During 'a delightful evening' at her Kensington home she

> shed me a lot of light on Schumann symphonies – we played I and II as duets and then she played the concerto. She can't explain a thing but, in hand words, the way she played things like the very difficult (bumpy) start to the last movement of II, brought one always back to the broad view. She made the greatest possible difference in each bar of the ♪| ♩ ♩. ♪| : made it seem like one line and made it sing as a tune in minims (or anything else) first, and then superimposed the rhythm. It was wonderful, and I left at 12.50, after a struggle to prevent her tackling a symphony by Suk!

Boult's special concern was to discover from her how far she felt orchestral performance of romantic music might go in the direction of the freedom to which the piano recitalist inclined. Some other female member of the college staff, who was notorious for importuning her colleagues for concert engagements, led Boult to seek advice from H.C. Colles, chief music critic of *The Times* and also on the RCM staff. Colles wrote to him:

> I have had it all in even greater doses. She has plenty of means of intelligence about new works if she really wants them. The point is, are you to be an amateur concert agent or a musician? It is the latter we want of you. When I go to a concert and see your name on the programme as a musician I know I'm in for a good thing; when I go to one and see your name as a member of a committee it tells me nothing, except what I knew before, that you are kindhearted and a little pliable. Forgive my brutality. This has nothing to do with one show as against another; it is a question of doing your own work or buttressing up other people's.

At home in West Kirby for Christmas, Boult looked back on 1920, the year in which, incidentally, he had conducted for the first time Elgar's Violin Concerto (RCM 5 June, soloist Manus O'Donnell):

> I hope to be able to order my time better next term ... it is the strain of doing these unrehearsed Palladium things for the first time in my life that is so telling. The Quinlan concerts have gone well, artistically, for me and for the BSO. But the admixture of the ballad concert element has been ghastly. It has been interesting this term to compare the standards one aims for with the RCM orchestra, with the BSO, and again with the LSO. It is curious how they vary ... The only time I have felt a bit helpless was with the LSO – ie. the problem of how to find a way of improving things (particularly with Patron's Fund music, which may not be of the highest value) from the remarkable condition they are already in as read at sight by the LSO. I do not think it is my fault: the LSO know they read marvellously and therefore think that a thing as sight-read by them is ready for performance, and even Coates has trouble when he wants some hard work out of them. It is a certainty that the Mengelberg standard of ensemble, for instance, is unknown to them: they don't believe they've anything to learn in that or any other way, but worse than this, when they hear it (as when the New York Symphony-Damrosch-people came[3]) they talked about the mechanical precision in a superior way and didn't realize that precision could be learnt from them and need not be mechanical ... Thank goodness the BSO are free from this and (like College) are delightful to rehearse with ...

It was probably about this time that Boult's mother gave him a little orchestra of silver figures dressed in 18th-century clothes, with knee breeches, long coats, waistcoats and tricorn hats. The figures were studded with coloured stones and were on a wooden two-tier base with a glass cover – 'an orchestra always ready to rehearse and who will never send deputies,' Mrs Boult told her son. (After Boult's death, the 'silver orchestra' was accepted as a gift by Charles, Prince of Wales.)

At the British Symphony Orchestra's December concert, Boult conducted the first British performance of Bax's *The Garden of Fand*. In January 1921 Boult conducted this orchestra in Vaughan Williams's *London Symphony*, prompting the *Observer* critic to write that 'one could hardly have imagined that a brief three months' work' would have brought the BSO to the standard of this concert. A few days later Boult repeated the symphony in Oxford (with Debussy's *La Mer*). On 9 February he appeared as guest conductor of the City of Birmingham Orchestra in its first season (Elgar had conducted its first concert on 20 November 1920). The main works were Hamilton Harty's Violin Concerto, played by Murray Lambert, and Brahms's Second Symphony. A.J. Sheldon of *The Birmingham Post* thought Boult's handling of the Brahms was 'a triumph of flexibility, suggestion and control.' A few days later Boult went to Kingsway Hall to hear Coates conduct the Beecham Orchestra in Brahms's Fourth Symphony. The orchestra had just been on a provincial tour and the symphony, he thought, 'glowed with life' and was 'played with amazing (for England) ensemble, due to their having done it on tour many times, the only way things can get really rehearsed in this country of ours.'

March saw the abandonment of the BSO concerts when Quinlan went bankrupt. The critics blamed the unsuitability and poor acoustics of Kingsway Hall, the extravagant publicity (what today would be called 'hype') and the attempt to appeal to two audiences, the 'stargazing' public and the serious-minded. Boult pledged himself to preserve the BSO and meanwhile, on 18 March, conducted at the opening of the RCM's opera theatre. 'I did *Figaro* [Act II] and never felt so incompetent in my life ... I had thought beforehand of all the essential differences except one: the stupidity of singers which is so curiously uncertain. I suppose I shall get used to it in time.' He went to Amsterdam in April, hearing three performances of Mahler's *Das Lied von der Erde* conducted by Mengelberg ('I must say its beauty was striking, though it has its bare patches'). With Arthur Bliss he also went to Cologne where they spent a week listening to Otto Klemperer rehearsing. They were astonished to hear him admit that he could not beat the irregular metres in Stravinsky's *The Rite of Spring*. These visits were followed by the annual Petersfield Festival, an event Boult loved.

Boult and his friend Steuart Wilson, the tenor, were the linchpins of the festival. Since Wilson had sung Vaughan Williams's *On Wenlock*

Edge at Oxford in Boult's undergraduate days the two men had kept in touch. Only three months separated them in age. Wilson and his wife Ann Bowles, daughter of a naval officer (they were married in 1917), had lived at Steep, on the outskirts of Petersfield, since 1918. Ann Wilson sang in the Steep choir (a majority of its members was staff and families from Bedales School, a 'progressive' establishment where Steuart was music director from September 1921 until January 1923). Boult and Wilson made the Petersfield Festival more ambitious and they were able to persuade artists of the quality of Plunket Greene, John Coates, Myra Hess and Dorothy Silk to take part. Malcolm Sargent, who burst on to the London musical scene in 1921, was often enrolled as conductor, judge or pianist. In 1921 the festival, Boult wrote, was 'simply wonderful. I have rarely enjoyed anything like the village day with 2 rehearsals (the second public) of the *Songs of the Fleet*. The town choirs were a bit sticky in comparison but with gorgeous weather (we bathed after the rehearsals!) it was a delightful time.' At Petersfield, as at Dorking's Leith Hill Festival, the village choirs spent the winter rehearsing the selected work with the object of joining together on the festival day and, after a morning of friendly competition, becoming one large chorus. Boult much preferred the atmosphere there to that at Morecambe which he visited next as an adjudicator and regarded as 'a gladiatorial show ... It really doesn't seem to matter whether it is music, boxing or spillikins. I offered once (after judging mixed choirs) to take a little combined rehearsal. The only people who stayed were – the winning choir!'

Boult's views on adjudicating were amusingly expressed in a letter to Bernard Shore on 24 April 1963. Shore hated it and Boult said:

> I do so agree with you, but I did learn a very great deal about it from Sidney Nicholson a great many years ago. He treated it as a glorious game – a sort of jigsaw puzzle – and got enormous fun out of it. I think the only thing to do is to keep it very lighthearted and to remember this, that if the competition were repeated two or three days running with a different judge, or even with the same judge, the results would almost certainly be very different. We know how music critics contradict each other, and this is the same sort of thing. So the great thing, which I know is just as hard for you as it is for me, is still to keep in mind the Irish saying: 'If you can't be aisy, be as aisy as you can.'

During the first half of 1922 Boult's parents left West Kirby and moved to 'Northlands' at Landford at the edge of the New Forest near Salisbury. His father had retired early through ill health and was thereafter on a diet suggested by Dr (later Sir) John Weir, who was physician to both father and son. (People who knew Cedric in these years cannot remember his ever having a day's illness!). Adrian arranged for two friends to propose Cedric for membership of the Savile Club, with himself as 'supporter'. He received a circular asking what he knew of the candidate and replied: 'I have known him for thirty-one years during which he has performed the duties of a father to my complete satisfaction.' Cedric became the country squire at Landford, taking a keen interest in the smallholdings and cottages on the estate. In September and October each year he invited friends to shoot pheasants and partridges, occasions which his son risked displeasure by doing his best to avoid, though not always successfully.

Boult found work for the British Symphony Orchestra in a concert during the second congress of the British Music Society at which he conducted (14 June) *The Planets* and the first London performance of Vaughan Williams's *The Lark Ascending*. Thirteen of the players, reinforced by piano and organ, were engaged for a curious experiment in *opéra intime* at the Aeolian Hall. This was the brainchild of the tenor Vladimir Rosing, with Komisarjevsky as producer and Boult as conductor. Four operas were produced at three performances, Tchaikovsky's *Queen of Spades* (score reduced by Leslie Heward), Rossini's *The Barber of Seville*, Leoncavallo's *Pagliacci* and Mozart's *Bastien und Bastienne*, all in 'potted' versions. Not surprisingly, only the Mozart trifle was regarded as artistically successful. The waits between scenes were very long, the *Daily News* reported, but because of the heat they were not unwelcome and 'the very fashionable audience paraded Bond Street.' Boult conducted his second Liverpool Philharmonic concert on 15 November 1921, when Pablo Casals was soloist in Schumann's Cello Concerto. Casals began their long friendship by asking 'Have we time to work, or must we go straight through it?' 'His knowledge of the thing is complete,' Boult wrote, 'and he ran the rehearsal for $1\frac{1}{2}$ hours.' (This led a member of the committee who was present to remark that Boult seemed 'out of his depth' in the concerto since the soloist did most of the talking.) 'I tried to collect the result of the long rehearsal and found that it had consisted entirely in playing (1) the notes (2) the expression marks as Schumann had written them.' At this concert Boult conducted the first Liverpool performance of Vaughan Williams's *A London Symphony*. Casals invited him to go to Barcelona, where he conducted orchestral concerts. 'It will be a great experience watching him work out his things: he has twelve rehearsals for each concert.' Another helpful musician was Albert Coates. When Boult in June 1921 heard him conduct Scriabin's *Prometheus*, Coates invited him to stay with him in Italy 'as he had a great deal to talk about.' Boult's diary continues:

He was so nice that at any rate I decided to see him off on the 8.20 [from Victoria] next day. He then said that I had been on his mind a great deal, and said that I was stagnating in London instead of going ahead (?abroad) and suggested that I should let him find me a berth in a first-class opera house in Germany as first conductor and Operndirektor. Of course I should hate leaving London, but it is true that everything I'm doing is second-rate and that the whole rehearsal-time is devoted to getting the notes right: interpretation has to look after itself, and a break of this kind would let me take a very different position when I came back. Allen is against it, as he says it would make me feel so helpless when I came back to the old scratch conditions which nothing will ever change in London.

Hugh Allen's counsel of despair, one feels, was perhaps not unmotivated by a vested interest in having Boult at the College. But as 1922 dawned, Boult knew in his head and heart that a crisis in his career had arrived: he must break away or conform. But this had not prevented him launching a new philanthropic venture involving the British Symphony Orchestra – a series of Sunday afternoon concerts in the East End of London at the People's Palace in the Mile End Road. He promised a symphony and a British composition at each concert. In addition to writing the programme notes, he gave an introductory talk on each item, sometimes with brief orchestral illustrations. Seats were as cheap as they could possibly be made. Smoking was allowed. The programme of the first concert on 16 October opened with Bach's Third Brandenburg Concerto and continued with Butterworth's *A Shropshire Lad*, Brahms's Second Symphony and Tchaikovsky's *Francesca da Rimini*. Nearly every seat in the large hall was filled. At later concerts, Beethoven's Fifth and Elgar's Second Symphonies and Strauss's *Don Quixote* were performed. Boult abandoned his introductory talks when he discovered that most of the audience had come from the West End and knew the music anyway. 'One other pleasant thing about the place,' he noted, 'was the swimming pool next door.'

The Elgar performance was on 1 December 1921 and afterwards the composer, who had attended with his daughter Carice, wrote:

It was wonderfully good yesterday and you did the thing splendidly and I thank you for your interest in and loving care of the work. Will you thank the orchestra for the thrilling (no less) playing: unfortunately we had to get back here [37 St James's Place] but I took an ungloved part in the ovation you received. I wish I cd. have seen you to speak to.

Elgar's words were support for the judgment on Boult (after an earlier performance of the symphony) expressed in *The Times* by H.C. Colles: 'When you listen you find yourself listening to Elgar or Wagner and not to Boult ... It is a great thing to have begun with the fixed belief that the conductor does not know better than the composer; it may lead to the composer's firm belief in the conductor.'[4]

CHAPTER 12

Restless

ALTHOUGH his engagements reduced his free time, Boult remained an assiduous attender of concerts. Thus in 1921 he heard Coates conduct several times at the Queen's Hall; he attended the concerts of contemporary works conducted by Edward Clark; he heard the Sevčik and Flonzaley String Quartets and piano recitals by Harold Samuel and Myra Hess; he heard the first London performance of Stravinsky's *The Rite of Spring* conducted by Eugene Goossens; and he attended song recitals by the tenor Steuart Wilson at which new Vaughan Williams works were performed. Wilson's vocal sextet, the English Singers (three men, three women), who performed madrigals and folk songs with a popularity of the kind enjoyed half a century later by their all-male successors the King's Singers, had given their first concert in February 1920 and were already very much part of the post-war renaissance of English music. They went with Boult and Bliss to Prague in January 1922, where on the 5th, in the Smetana Hall, Boult conducted the Czech Philharmonic in Butterworth's *2 Idylls*, Bliss's *Mêlée fantasque* and Elgar's Second Symphony, with the English Singers following after the interval. Undoubtedly the singers had the biggest success. There was unanimous praise for Boult's conducting and a rather cool critical response to the music (one writer finding excessive Brucknerian influences on Elgar).

Boult had ten hours' rehearsal for the 80 minutes of music. He wrote in his notebook:

> The orchestra put their backs into things in a remarkable way. In particular Hoffmann and Suk (of the Bohemian Quartet) were enthusiastic and it was a great pleasure to get to know Václav Talich, a conductor of the first rank. I went to Pilsen next day to hear *Ma Vlást* complete and it was a marvellous performance. Talich said he had not rehearsed it for two years, but the ensemble was marvellous (quite different from our English idea of ensemble) although they had often rehearsed and played it under other conductors in

between: a real case of what the Germans mean when they say a thing 'sitzt'. When can this be done in England?

He was back in London for two important events. On 17 January Strauss returned to London for the first time since 1914 to conduct the London Symphony Orchestra in the Royal Albert Hall in three of his tone poems (*Don Juan, Tod und Verklärung* and *Till Eulenspiegel*) and some songs. Boult always liked to recount how Willie Reed said to him after the first rehearsal: 'I have been playing the passages for the first time for years.' Strauss, Boult pointed out to me on one occasion, had 'a wonderful knack of *just* giving people time to play things, while during the war we had all been rushing them.' Five days later, at a Royal Philharmonic Society concert, Boult conducted the first performance of Vaughan Williams's *A Pastoral Symphony*. 'I think he was pleased. I certainly never expected such a reception for it.' He conducted the second performance at the RCM on 17 February.

In the spring Boult, Bliss and the English Singers went abroad again as musical ambassadors, this time to Vienna where Boult conducted the Symphony Orchestra on 6 and 10 April in four English works, the Prelude to Act II of Ethel Smyth's *The Wreckers*, Bax's *November Woods*, four of *The Planets* and Elgar's Second Symphony.

> The orchestra was not like Prague, they are tired out; but they did their best … I made a stupid mistake in technique through not being used to so many rehearsals (I had 4×2 hours to which 2 more hours were added owing to late starts). We ran through everything to get a general view, and then we messed about with Mercury, for instance, playing it through and through instead of dissecting it properly: wind and strings separately etc. I feel that once one has covered the whole ground, one can best dissect the most difficult things, and leave (as Coates often does) the easier things to look after themselves, for the last rehearsal is always a run through everything again. I'm sure my method of playing a large slice and then talking about it in detail worries them far less than keeping on stopping.

Boult enjoyed meeting colleagues on these visits. On 31 March he heard Wilhelm Furtwängler, three years his junior, conduct Beethoven's Ninth Symphony. Furtwängler had just been appointed conductor of the Leipzig Gewandhaus Orchestra. He got 'the last ounce of meaning out of every bar,' Boult noted, 'making it warm and vital to an amazing extent. Sometimes one felt it was in danger of falling to pieces, but one must not compare it with the monumental performances of Richter and Steinbach. The art of performance of classics, as of other things, must go forward like the art of composition, and perhaps architecture will go further into the background. I am inclined to think that Furtwängler is leading the way.' When Furtwängler made his London début in 1924 few of the critics shared Boult's admiring view of him. Boult and Bliss also went to the Opera to hear Strauss conduct *Der Rosenkavalier* and heard Weingartner conduct the Philharmonic in a Brahms programme.

> He took the C minor [symphony] fast, but the playing of the orchestra, who obviously knew it by heart, never let clearness be sacrificed, as was the case when he did the D major in Prague – they hadn't time to straighten out anything. He is very much liked by the orchestra, people say, and they always give him their best, and it was perhaps the tradition in them rather than the mind of Weingartner that made such pure Brahms playing of it.

In the following month he took up Casals's invitation to go to Barcelona. He went there for a month and attended rehearsals twice a day. 'I diligently learnt Spanish,' he wrote,[1] 'in order to study his rehearsal methods, but found he always spoke Catalan, a very different proposition ... In Barcelona I had to be very quick off the mark ... my musical ear had to do it all.' He made

> a lot of notes on technical things in case a full edition of the conducting book is needed. It was interesting that his power was more felt in rehearsal than in performance: he taught the orchestra to play as he plays himself, but especially in the modern things he failed to draw the last ounce out of things for want of stick technique. But the rehearsals were always amazing, and the performance of the Schubert C major quite the finest performance (of anything) that I have ever heard. It thrilled me so I quite forgot I had to come on next ...

Although he was admitted to a Fellowship at the RCM on 7 July 1922, Boult's discontent with his lot in England was fuelled by experiences such as Barcelona. Only this can explain how that summer he involved himself in the affairs of the Hastings municipal orchestra after the death of its conductor, Julian Clifford. There was a plan that it should give concerts in the winter (previously having existed only for summer visitors) and that he should be 'musical adviser' with Dan Godfrey Jnr. (son of Bournemouth's Sir Dan) as deputy conductor. Boult offered to conduct at least 10 concerts, to open rehearsals to the public and to give introductory talks. The scheme was rejected by the council. The debate at which the vote was taken makes depressing reading today, not because of what was said but because much the same thing is still being said by councillors over 60 years later.

With Frank Schuster, Boult went to Munich for the opera festival in August 1922. He was reporting it for the *Daily Telegraph* and Robin

Legge gave him a letter of introduction to the *Generalmusikdirektor*, Bruno Walter. He wrote in his notebook: 'Wonderful performances of things as different as *Meistersinger, Tristan* (where the white heat in the 2nd Act – 2nd scene – made me glad for the first time that the big cut was not being made), *Seraglio, Figaro*. Got to know Walter better: he is a delightful creature and what an artist!' As he told *Telegraph* readers, he also heard Karl Muck conduct *Parsifal* and *The Ring*. But it was Walter's *Meistersinger* that was 'the crowning point of the festival,' its 'glorious humanity' standing out more than ever before.

In England that autumn the British Symphony Orchestra was disbanded after the failure of the People's Palace series – 'I wish I could have given more time to running round on the management side,' Boult wrote. 'I think we could have filled the house if the advertising had been better.' There was compensation of a sort in conducting the first London performance of Bliss's *Colour Symphony* at the RCM on 5 December. The work is dedicated to Boult, who commented afterwards: 'What I understand I like – he has written since to say he is altering the scoring in certain places to make it sound less strident. I think it will be a fine work.'

Boult's next major hurdle was his first *Dream of Gerontius* with the Royal Choral Society and Sir Landon Ronald's Royal Albert Hall Orchestra on 3 February 1923. He wrote to Elgar about his concern over the higher pitch to which the hall organ was tuned. 'I detest the high pitch,' was the reply. 'Why could not the *organ* play $\frac{1}{2}$ tone lower? You cannot do *Gerontius* (in that hall especially) without the O. I suppose the O. is tuned to equal temp. – but the whole thing is so disastrous that it is quite easy enough to believe it is not tuned at all.' With which helpful encouragement, Boult launched himself on *Gerontius* and Holst's *The Hymn of Jesus* with three choral rehearsals of 90 minutes each and one orchestral rehearsal of three hours – and no time when choir and orchestra rehearsed together. 'It is an appalling affair,' he wrote.

I felt very ineffective somehow. Many tiny points of detail were missed – perhaps I hadn't looked at the score enough through a magnifying lens – and in the Holst (which came second) we were all dead tired and pitch came sadly to grief, as well as a bad mistake of mine at 'Holy Spirit' on the last page. The orchestra played well at the concert but were very sticky at rehearsal. Ronald never stretches them ... The choir were keen but unwieldy – there are so many places where one must give in to a choir that size: nothing will move them and if they get a beat behind they do it together and are unperturbed because they do not understand conducting.

As 1923 progressed, Boult became increasingly restless. He was always busy. With Stanford growing older, more of the RCM conducting came his way. He was in demand as an adjudicator at competitive festivals and he enjoyed making music with amateurs at such summer festivals as Petersfield. But it must sometimes have seemed a long way from Nikisch's Leipzig of 1913. Boult's diary at this time grew increasingly analytical. Sir Hugh Allen had bemoaned the post-war students' attitude in a talk he had with Boult, who wrote afterwards:

It is a difficult problem ... if the discipline of College is relaxed in any way for anybody, this is expected in every way by everybody. Make the thing a hard and fast mould and in the long run it is good for them – with certain (grave) exceptions. It all applies to me very much and particularly with odd-and-end people who come and play concertos. If I treat them like Stanford: never budge an inch and at the end tell them they've got no rhythm, they go away feeling perfectly miserable *but* are thoroughly well equipped for concerto-playing next time – all except the very thick-skinned, who probably never play again with orchestra in their lives. I give them heaps of consideration and at the end they say 'they had no idea it was so easy' and – come to grief next time ... Ever since Allen has let me devote the whole of the Friday rehearsals at RCM to concert music, and the work has therefore been much more rehearsed, I have had trouble with myself, that is, most classical things I have been still rehearsing at the concert. There is a little more in it than just the 'engine-driver and guard' contrast, it is that the mind is trying to pilot them through details which ought to be left to themselves. The 4th Beethoven on 8th June 1923 seemed (to myself too) so long and dull for this reason and the Brahms D major last autumn the same ... At a show one must *supply* the motive power, even if the mind is on detail most of the time.

For three weeks from 22 September Boult travelled in Canada and the United States. He sailed with Robin Barrington-Ward and while the journalist visited politicians, Boult inspected musical life in the New World. His long letters home to his parents – 'dear people,' he addressed them – survive and give a detailed account of where he went and whom he met. Toronto he found the most interesting town and there he formed a lasting friendship with Vincent Massey, Dean of Victoria College of the University of Toronto and later Canadian High Commissioner in London, and his wife Alice. Barrington-Ward and Massey had been at Balliol together. 'We are touring in very grand company,' Boult wrote home, 'Melba sings here tonight, Clara Butt next week, Lloyd George comes next week and Birkenhead [F. E. Smith, 1st Earl of Birkenhead] has just left. They say he (B'head) is usually drunk and spoke very

poorly here though he had a terrific success in British Columbia ...'
While in Toronto, Boult met Ernest McMillan, who had taken his
Oxford doctorate while interned at Ruhleben during the war. Within
three years, McMillan was to be principal of Toronto Conservatory of
Music and later conductor of its symphony orchestra. He was the first
Canadian to be knighted for services to music.

Boult left Toronto on 9 October by train for Rochester, NY, travelling
'with a car load of the most *awful* businessmen: their voices here are so
much worse than the Canadians, they seem to go through one like a
knife.' His hosts there, the Warners, were musically influential and he
found Eugene Goossens and his wife as fellow guests at dinner that
evening. The Warners wanted Boult to become conductor of the Rochester Philharmonic Orchestra and his eventual refusal led to Goossens
holding the post from 1923 to 1931. 'It is a marvellous place,' he told
his parents. 'Everything money can buy.' While there he was shown
round the new Eastman School of Music, endowed by George Eastman,
who owned the Eastman Kodak Company. Arriving in Chicago on 12
October he went straight to the public rehearsal of the first-concert of
the season by the Chicago Symphony Orchestra under Frederick Stock.
'It is the same orchestra Gustav [Holst] had at Ann Arbor.[2] A solid
classical programme *very* finely played – such string work and ensemble
though I don't agree with G.H. that the wind soloists are as good as
ours.' After visiting Charlottesville and Washington, he went to New
York and then on to Philadelphia to hear the orchestra under Leopold
Stokowski. After a Haydn symphony he heard an 'amazing' performance
of Stravinsky's *Song of the Nightingale* and Tchaikovsky's *Casse-
Noisette* 'done with the loveliest light touch and freedom. We went to
see Stokowski afterwards (he was once at the RCM, you know) ...'
Boult liked to say in later years that what he heard in Philadelphia that
day knocked the conceit out of him for years.

Back in London, Boult pondered the Rochester offer. It is probable
that he would have accepted it – he later told Gwen Beckett he had his
bags packed – had not Sir Henry Wood resigned in November as
conductor of the Birmingham Festival Choral Society and nominated
Boult as his successor. The prospect was not all that enticing: Wood
resigned because the orchestral conditions prevailing were so bad and,
like Boult with *Gerontius* in London, he had attempted to rehearse
Beethoven's *Missa Solemnis* when orchestra and chorus did not perform
together until the concert. In his autobiography Boult says: 'I was in no
mood to pick or choose and cheerfully accepted the difficulties.' But
reject an American orchestra in a rich town in favour of prehistoric

English provincial music-making? Two other factors were exerting pressure on this decision. One was that Boult had learned that the orchestral scene in Birmingham might soon alter dramatically; the second was that, even at the age of 34, Boult was still very much under the sway of his parents and could not bring himself to snap the thread.

Possibly, too, Boult realized that he needed a challenge of a kind that wealthy Rochester would not have provided. He was well aware that life had been easy for him. In a loving home, he had been rushed to the doctor for every minor ailment and this habit persisted when he was adult. He had not been sent to a preparatory school but went direct from a dame school to Westminster as a day boy. No roughing it as a boarder; instead, he had lived in a flat with a housekeeper. Christ Church, Oxford, at the height of the Edwardian era was a privileged world and the authorities there had connived at his pursuit of a musical career rather than insist on his studying hard for a degree. As aide-de-camp to Hugh Allen he gained an entrée into the English academic musical establishment. An attempt to break away in Germany had been thwarted by the war, which otherwise affected him only to a minor degree. After the war, Allen's appointment to the RCM ensured Boult a base from which to operate in any direction he chose. Luckily he had real talent, which was recognized. He chose to take risks by promoting the unpopular cause of English contemporary music, but knew that if he came to utter grief, his father's money was behind him. Yet he was also unspoiled by success or privilege; when abroad, he could always expect hospitality from the upper echelons of society, while back home his musical activities often showed him to be socially conscientious. His first Liverpool concerts in 1915 were given in a poor district, his People's Palace venture was guided by the same desire to take good music to the less fortunate among his fellow-countrymen and in the summer of 1923 he eagerly took on the conducting of the first series of Robert Mayer children's concerts.[3] As his diary indicates, he was both self-critical and aware of his shortcomings. The chance to struggle and to build something from very little in Birmingham was just what he needed at this stage in his career.

CHAPTER 13

Leaving London

BIRMINGHAM'S musical history[1] is like that of several other British provincial cities: a few enlightened men struggling to keep a flame alight, with varying degrees of success. In Birmingham's case, its musical fame began in 1768 with the foundation of the triennial festivals, inaugurated to finance the general hospital. During the 19th century this became England's leading choral festival (rivalled by Leeds) at which major works by Mendelssohn (*Elijah*), Sullivan (*The Light of the World*), Dvořák (*The Spectre's Bride* and *Requiem*), Gounod (*Rédemption*) and Elgar (*The Dream of Gerontius*) had their first performances. Sir Michael Costa and Hans Richter were among its principal conductors. The orchestra on these occasions was an ad hoc body, with players drawn from London and Manchester. The Festival Choral Society gave concerts annually, its conductor from 1855 being William Stockley. These were with organ accompaniment; Stockley founded an orchestra from local freelances and in 1878 he began a series of purely orchestral concerts. It was 'Stockley's Band' in 1882 that Edward Elgar joined as a violinist; some of his early works were given first performances under Stockley. The Stockley concerts foundered in 1899. George Halford then gave a series of orchestral concerts but soon gave up, 'crushed between the upper millstone of expert criticism and the nether millstone of choral society prejudice,' as it was delightfully described.[2]

With first Elgar then Granville Bantock occupying the chair of music at the university and Bantock principal of the School of Music (incorporated 1886) from 1900, pressure for an orchestra and a hall more suitable than the Town Hall increased, aided by Neville Chamberlain, a leading figure in municipal politics. During the war, Bantock and Chamberlain persuaded Sir Thomas Beecham in 1916 to finance and direct a New Birmingham Orchestra for a three-year trial period. This collapsed in 1918, but Beecham had already caught a financial cold and never forgave Birmingham for its failure to support his venture. He was at this time offering to build Manchester an opera house and conducting the bulk of concerts by the Hallé, London Symphony, Liverpool Philharmonic and Royal Philharmonic Society Orchestras, sometimes for no remuneration. Obviously box-office receipts alone could not sustain an orchestra in Birmingham. Undaunted therefore, Chamberlain and Alderman Sir David Brooks, spurred by Bantock, persuaded the city council in 1920 to make an annual grant of £1,250 for an experimental five years to a new orchestra to be called the City of Birmingham Orchestra (the word 'Symphony' was not added to the name until February 1948). Thus Birmingham became the first British city to subsidize orchestral music from the rates. It was made plain that the CBO was not to be a municipal orchestra such as existed in seaside resorts but an independent body. Two active proponents of the scheme were Birmingham's chief constable, Charles Rafter, a very keen flautist, and the conductor of the City Police Band, Appleby Matthews, a violist and pianist who also had his own choir and since 1918 had run a series of Sunday orchestral concerts in the Futurist Cinema, John Bright Street. Rafter re-equipped the police band with low-pitch instruments so that it could supply the wind section of the new orchestra, but this led to protests from the Musicians' Union and a compromise whereby the police band would be called in only when triple wind was needed.

Matthews was appointed first principal conductor of the CBO and 45 players were engaged on contracts lasting from September to March. In the summer, like the Hallé and Queen's Hall players, they migrated to the summer-resort orchestras. Matthews 'ran in' the orchestra with two months of weekend concerts in the city's old Theatre Royal, beginning on 5 September 1920. Holst came twice, conducting five of *The Planets* on his second visit, Bantock conducted his *Hebridean Symphony* and Sibelius conducted his Third Symphony. The orchestra's first Town Hall Wednesday concert on 20 November was conducted by Elgar (*Falstaff*, the Cello Concerto, only 13 months after its first performance, and the Second Symphony). The hall was by no means full.

Matthews's programmes were remarkably ambitious and enterprising, and the guest conductors from 1920 to 1924 included Albert Coates, Harty, Vaughan Williams, Ronald, Eugene Goossens and Boult who, in the 1923–4 season, conducted Parry's *Symphonic Variations* and Stanford's Seventh Symphony. Not surprisingly a financial crisis occurred and the Sunday concerts became increasingly 'popular.' There was trouble, too, between the committee and Matthews, which ended in the courts with Matthews being awarded damages and costs. It was against this background and in this context that the negotiations with Boult were conducted.

One of Boult's first concerts as conductor of the Festival Choral Society was the revival on 7 February 1924 of Ethel Smyth's Mass in D. As this was the occasion of one of the most celebrated Boult anecdotes, it is worth looking at it in some detail. (Boult himself, incidentally, vouched for the accuracy of the anecdote.) Dame Ethel was relentless in her pursuit of conductors who might conduct her works. Bruno Walter was an early victim. In 1922 she latched on to Boult when he became a governor of Lilian Baylis's Old Vic, trying to push him into involvement with her opera *The Boatswain's Mate*. Later in the 1920s, John Barbirolli was her quarry. Boult's secretary, Gwen Beckett, remembers her as a 'perfect pest' at the BBC at Savoy Hill, pestering all and sundry to include her works in programmes and waiting for hours to waylay likely victims. Describing the Mass performance at Birmingham in his diary Boult wrote:

> She came to 4 or 5 rehearsals – I did everything I could to give *her* performance, out of which two things arose. 1. She was very keen about 'iron rhythm,' no *rubato* (although her mind changed several times over what the pace should actually be in places). This is *most* inadvisable because it makes it impossible to underline certain things which a first-performance audience should have underlined; it is also extremely difficult to *do* in English rehearsal conditions. 2. There is a point beyond which it is impossible to go on following composers' wishes, particularly when they change their minds – the *Et vitam venturi* I wanted slower than she does. She begged me to race it, but about a week before the show she said she wanted it much slower. Having with great difficulty got it *fast* into my mind, I found it almost impossible to get it slow again, although it was what I had originally wanted and still felt to be right; the moment I took my mind off to attend to detail, the pace quickened, and I had to pull it back again.

On the morning of the final rehearsal Boult walked into Birmingham Town Hall to find the composer already in her seat in the stalls, score at the ready. 'Good morning, Dame Ethel,' he remarked. 'And what are your tempi for today?'

When next he saw her, after the performance, she told him she had decided that, as he noted, 'all the fast movements were too fast and would stand being taken a lot slower!!! How is one ever to arrive at a fixed impression? If all composers were like this, one might make a rule to pay no attention to them . . .' The Mass was repeated in London with different soloists later in the month. To study the score again with her, Boult met her at the home of her sister Mrs Charles Hunter, a widow who lived at Hill Hall, Theydon Mount, near Epping. Mrs Hunter was a friend of Schuster and is described by the poet Siegfried Sassoon in his diaries[3] as 'a jolly old Jingo ... elderly and gold-haired, in gardening gauntlets.' He also described Hill Hall as 'a delightful house to stay in. Leaning out of my window this morning I watched two peacocks trailing their plumage on the upper branches of an immense cedar, while a swan ferried its reflection across an Elizabethan fish-pond unruffled by wind and guarded by stone statues stained green with damp.' Boult wrote to his family:

> On Sunday we had our 4 hours on the Mass (the others played golf) and I caught a 5 train back. She has given way over a good deal and I have made it plain I can guarantee none of these changes at such short notice. She is frightfully apologetic about it all, and has insisted on my borrowing her metronome in order to make it easier for me! She implored me to try and do it her way this time and I think it is really wiser, as I haven't time to think out my own way.

This same letter of Boult's sets out his schedule for this last week or so of February 1924. It is worth quoting (he was, by the way, learning the viola at the time):

Monday, 25 February. 2¼-hour soloists rehearsal with Dame E.

Tuesday. 6 conductors at RCM concert at 4.45 ... Then to the wilds of Old Kent Road to take a S.E. London Festival rehearsal.

Wednesday. Angus [Morrison] at 10 to go through his Brahms. Then choral class as Allen had an awful cold. Then B'ham. Night train back to London.

Thursday. Patron's Fund rehearsal in the morning and a run-through the *Sea Symphony* with RVW in the afternoon. Dinner at St Gabriel's, Camberwell, an *enormous* girls' school, with the head mistress in state at high table. Then rehearsal.

Friday. RCM as usual, with viola lesson to top up with. Dinner with Dyneley Hussey, the critic, who lives in Lincoln's Inn. Then walked with him to Wigmore Hall to a recital but left him there to walk home ...

Saturday. BMS annual meeting in the morning ... Lunch at Savile and Q.H. concert in the afternoon. Rather dull; tea with the Colles at the Langham and then to Liverpool Street to meet Dame E. at 6.3. Hill Hall is 3 miles from Epping, a wonderful house, Elizabethan and William and M.

Monday. The Taylors to dinner and then to Mrs Morley's. She had a very small party to hear the Hungarian Quartet.

Tuesday. Soloists at RCM this morning ... then home to lunch. RCM show.

Wednesday. RCM (Malcolm [Sargent] away). 5 pm Sir George Henschel wants to see me. 6.30 RCM Board of Professors (Mackenzie coming as guest).

Thursday. 12. Verdi Requiem soloists. 1.30 lunch with Pedro Morales.

Friday. RCM.

Saturday. 4.30 I have to talk (10 minutes) at an Anglo-Czech Society tea-fight on the Smetana Centenary. Then to Cambridge for Greek Play.

Monday. First rehearsal with Royal Choral Society ...

Ethel Smyth bore no grudge over these tense rehearsals. Something of her leathery, breezy character emerges from a letter she wrote to Boult from her home, Coign, Woking, on 14 November 1924 – and she rather neatly scores a point over another of his criticisms of her work:

Reflection: ... born of programme of Norwich Fest. and hearing the B minor [Bach Mass] in its gorgeous *profane hilarity* (woven in with the deepest religious sense art has registered) last night. Why do you all fight shy of *cheerful* joie de vivre, strong, jolly, vitally *gay* music? Why do budding composers write shimmering harmonic chords for strings – wrigglings about in the ether? Why is everything full of bass clarinet wailings? Why do people who, bless them, are not too proud – or something – to play a woman's music always play the *Cliffs*[4] and not the *Wreckers* overture – which personally I *prefer* at this moment, because it has *not* got 'atmosphere' of a certain kind ... and *has* got blood and bones and thumps and fun in it *without labelling itself as a chartered expression of lightheartedness*, as of course an overture to a comic opera does (in which case the highbrow condescends for 5 minutes to tolerate what he considers frivolity??) Why! even our choruses who can and do sing things like the Crucifixus in the B minor as if they were singing about a talk they had had with a very dull neighbour, even they wake up and *sing finely* and *feel* go and hilarity! But no! mirkiness, they are taught, is the higher expression of music – and tragedy, which doesn't come natural to them to express, the Real Thing. Look at the soldiers in the trenches, their jokes, their brave hilarity. That's English! 'Heynonnyno! Men are fools that wish to die.' I found an old letter of mine, 1889, in which I describe the state of unutterable excitement the (then) new-to-Europe Roumanian band put us into at the Paris Exhibition: 'One of the most exciting things is the way that, before the leader has decided (one dance being finished) what shall come next, the little orchestra just plays rhythmic chords – any of their dance rhythms will do – your heart beats with expectation! *What tune now*?? You know one is coming, and wild invisible dancers are keeping the thing going till it starts! I can't tell you how exciting this is ... I suppose because so frightfully true to nature' – There now!! I had forgotten all about this experience – as much so as if I had never had it. And lo! it was there in my veins all the time and ... *that's what made the 8 bars you say you don't like in the Wreckers Overture*!! Now mark this – the PUBLIC rises to that

Overture! and I believe that makes people think it must be of the 'Land of Hope and Glory' brand. But it also rises to gorgeous things like the finale of the 1st act of *Ruddigore* and to all Sullivan Tunes. O! ghost of modest Arthur S.! Do you know how immortal your *gay* music is? Dear Mr Boult – forgive Ethel Smyth for such an outburst.

*   *   *

Boult's appointment as Matthews's successor as conductor of the City of Birmingham Orchestra was not clear-cut. He was not first choice. There was a move to appoint Eugene Goossens who, because of his recent Rochester appointment, would necessarily be away a lot and it was mooted that Boult might be joint conductor. Writing to his family after a Smyth rehearsal in Birmingham before catching a 2.35 am sleeper to London, he confided:

> ... I saw Gustav [Holst] at lunch and he told me he'd had a long talk with Gerald Forty[5] about me and the orchestra. And that F. was very keen about me. Now Professor [Ernest] de Selincourt [of Birmingham University] said that F. was rather the pivotal person as he believed he was a great friend of Eugene G.'s So I instantly wired and asked him to dine tonight. He couldn't, but left a masonic show for $\frac{1}{2}$ an hour in order to see me. He is absolutely as convinced as de S. that the joint scheme would be hopeless and that they all got rather thrilled that night, so I feel very much easier in my mind and think I can go to G. knowing that the committee are behind me, although I can't of course say so. Forty was *very* nice and said that he had been wishing someone would be very indiscreet to me and was glad the opportunity had come to him!

By 12 March matters had improved:

> I saw Forty and de Selincourt this evening, dear people. Forty did write yesterday, but I haven't got it yet. The committee passed everything and probably would agree to my wind scheme. A technical mistake in the delivery of the notice to M. [Appleby Matthews] makes it *technically* invalid, but if he takes it into court they don't think he can get more than $\frac{1}{4}$d damages. [They were wrong!] The professor rather dwelt on this as another example of the orchestra's bad luck ...

A few days later Boult's appointment was announced in the Press. Among the first to congratulate him was Granville Bantock. 'It has long been my dream to make this city our English Weimar,' he wrote, 'and the prospects for the realization of this idea were never brighter than they are today. Your advent will bring new life and culture into the place ... Would you have any time or inclination to help us in any way at the School of Music?' Boult taught a chamber music class for a while but, as he told his parents, Hugh Allen's reaction to his new post was to say: 'What about your work here though? I'm not going to let you go without a struggle.' In April he conducted the music at Stanford's funeral and said au revoir in May to his pupil Leslie Heward, who had been appointed musical director of the Cape Town Orchestra. 'How funny we should have thought it when we were there,' he wrote home, 'that in 20 years a pupil of mine should be there as musical director!' The Masseys were his guests on a visit from Canada in June. Meanwhile he was attending meetings at Birmingham, planning the programmes for his first season and engaging soloists.

In 1920 Boult had begun a long association with music in Wales when he conducted at the first Aberystwyth Festival organized by Sir Walford Davies, Professor of Music at the University of Wales at this date. Boult, Elgar and Holst were among the visiting conductors at these festivals, at which Boult first came into contact with the two remarkable sisters, Gwendoline and Margaret Davies, the owners of the beautiful Gregynog Hall five miles north of Newtown in Montgomeryshire, and generous patrons of the arts. Boult succeeded Davies as conductor of the festival in 1925, remaining in the post until 1937. The programme usually contained a major choral work, such as Haydn's *The Creation* or Brahms's *Requiem*, and visiting soloists included Jelly d'Arányi, Isobel Baillie, Elsie Suddaby, Dora Labbette, Steuart Wilson, Parry Jones, Keith Falkner and many others. Boult enjoyed both the music-making and the countryside. In 1924 he wrote to his parents on 22 June: 'Went a real good walk after breakfast yesterday – piping hot: they dropped me at the Devil's Bridge about 10.30 which is a wonderful place you must see someday and I climbed two hills and walked back getting in at 6, almost 18 miles I think. Then after bath and change the rehearsal of Verdi *Requiem*, in which I sang in the chorus. Today I leave at 10, getting to Birmingham in time for committee.' He ended the week in Arundel where 'they have arranged for a run-through of Holst's new choral symphony and want me to conduct' (the first performance was at the Leeds Festival the following year, when Albert Coates was the conductor). During this summer, too, he attended the Three Choirs Festival at Hereford. It was on this occasion that he heard the performance of *The Kingdom* in which Elgar, who was conducting, gradually lost interest (because the choir were singing badly) until Agnes Nicholls sang the soprano aria 'The sun goeth down' so beautifully that he and the performance sprang back to life and intensity. Boult recounted the story in several articles and broadcasts but never as fully as in a letter he wrote in 1976:[6]

It was a rather terrible festival. Hull [Percy Hull, organist of Hereford Cathedral] wanted a change of personnel (not himself of course) and imported a lot of Covent Garden people who one by one threw their hands in. I believe it was [Florence] Austral who was to sing *The Kingdom*!!! Of course she defaulted (it may have been someone else equally impossible) and A.N. was pressed into service, *I think*, well after she had retired because she began singing a bit out of tune. Afterwards she said, 'The Pentecost choir were badly out of tune and I saw that E.E. had lost his temper & it got worse & worse & faster & faster and when "The sun goeth down" came I wondered if I could do anything, but I shut my book and I shut my eyes and prayed – and it happened.' It was extraordinary how vividly I remember Willie's [Reed's] instant response to her dedication. Almost at once the orchestra followed with a sort of change of colour and finally E.E. decided to join in and the performance flowed from then to the finish ... The Elgar performances at the Three Choirs were nearly always very good, in contrast to the way Atkins or Hull would CHARGE through the B minor Mass with H. P. Allen blaspheming in the cloisters refusing to go in!!

It is curious that after his early successes with the Royal Philharmonic Society Boult did not conduct one of their concerts between January 1922 and March 1934. He had attended the RPS concert on 24 January 1924 when Furtwängler conducted Strauss's *Don Juan* and Brahms's First Symphony, his first London engagement. Afterwards at a reception given by the soprano Dorothy Moulton, who married Robert Mayer, Boult 'asked him about the Beethoven 7th which we are doing at RCM: how the rhythm becomes ♪♪♩ instead of ♪♪♩ and whether it was the Breitkopf and Härtel bowing ♪♪ that was responsible. He thought not and said that thorough rehearsing was the only cure together with an upward jerk of the stick at each beat – this I should have thought to have the opposite effect (of inducing the quaver to come early). But I have Ivor James and Eugene Cruft's opinion that ♪♪ ♪♪ is workable, and am finding it so.'

CHAPTER 14

With the CBO

BOULT's first Birmingham season began on 7 October 1924. It comprised eight Tuesday[1] and six Saturday concerts in the Town Hall, five Sunday concerts (more popular design) in the Futurist Cinema, and six Saturday-afternoon children's concerts. The Sunday concerts were played by an orchestra of 33. Boult recalled later[2] that he had 'a great affection' for the Futurist.

> There was no artists' room at all and I used to walk in through the ordinary door, walk down the hall, take off my coat in the front row and climb on to the platform, all in full view of the audience. I remember one day I had just finished conducting the overture when Paul Beard leaned over and said 'Do you know you've got your rubber Wellingtons on?' I was a great walker in those days and used to walk the two miles to the concerts and on wet nights wore the Wellingtons to preserve my dress trousers. There was nothing I could do but get down and take them off. My dress shoes were there so I put them on. Those were the sort of things that happened at the Futurist and no one minded.

Boult said that his six Birmingham seasons were the only time in his life when he planned his own programmes (though presumably he had planned his early Liverpool concerts in 1915). His first CBO concert (which was broadcast) comprised *The Flying Dutchman* overture, Strauss's *Don Juan*, a work by Armstrong Gibbs (*A Vision of Night*), and Brahms's First Symphony. There were many empty seats. The *Dutchman* overture was one of the works which he maintained Nikisch could do better than anyone else, so there was perhaps a sentimental element in its choice.

Boult invited Sir Landon Ronald to conduct Elgar's Second Symphony at the second concert. He assigned a revised version of Bliss's *Colour Symphony*, another of his own specialities, to Eugene Goossens and, to the same conductor, Bantock's *Hebridean Symphony*, which Boult and the orchestra recorded the following day for Columbia (an acoustic recording which was never issued). Bruno Walter was guest conductor on 9 December, a generous gesture from this eminent colleague. Another colleague to support Boult was Fanny Davies, who played a Mozart Piano Concerto. Among the works Boult conducted were *The Planets*, Schumann's First and Fourth Symphonies, Bax's *Symphonic Variations*, Debussy's *Nocturnes*, Ireland's *Mai-Dun*, Dohnányi's Violin Concerto and Beethoven's Seventh Symphony. But he risked too much by having no soloist in five of the eight Tuesday concerts. In the Saturday and Sunday programmes he included Wagner extracts, Beethoven's Violin Concerto and, of course, Butterworth's *A Shropshire Lad*. Not surprisingly, perhaps, Boult was able to persuade the RCM to give a Patron's Fund rehearsal at the Midland Institute, the first to be held outside London. This was on 3 March 1925 and among the students involved was a conductor, Guy Warrack, and a violinist, Marie Wilson, later to be a stalwart of the BBC Symphony Orchestra under Boult. Sir Hugh Allen and other VIPs travelled to Birmingham in Sir Ernest Palmer's personal railway carriage!

Ensconced as music critic of *The Birmingham Post* since 1919, when he succeeded Ernest Newman, was the 50-year-old A. J. Sheldon.[3] Although its stablemate *The Birmingham Mail* printed long concert notices, Sheldon's were the Midlands equivalent of those by Samuel Langford in the *Manchester Guardian* and Herbert Thompson in the *Yorkshire Post*. They all wrote as if they had a direct line from Mount Olympus. Sheldon kept his powder dry on this first encounter. His impression of the playing was that Boult's aim was 'precision and the development of sonority to the limit possible with the forces under his command.' He shared the then prevalent view of Brahms as drab in texture. 'High as was the standard of proficiency in the playing, there was little sense of music quickened to vitality by the pulsing of a soul within it ... On the whole, though in the technique of conducting he is a master, Mr Boult's Don Juan was too sober a rake to be a likeable fellow.'

Before the orchestral season had opened, Boult had conducted the first performance of Bantock's opera *The Seal Woman*, produced by Barry Jackson at Birmingham Repertory Theatre. 'There were some awful moments for all of us,' said Boult, describing the first night to his family, 'but after the first act people seemed so gripped that there was dead silence – it is a custom of the theatre that the house lights only go up after the applause begins, and so nothing happened – it seemed like $\frac{1}{2}$ an hour. There was great enthusiasm after the show and Jackson had to make a speech ...'[4] The theatre felt awfully cold one night, Monday

I think, and we had a 4-hour rehearsal beginning 6.30. So I drank hot milk when I got in and ate Gels, and though I still felt rather tame next day I was all right the day after . . .' Well enough, indeed, to bicycle for 30 miles through the Warwickshire countryside, one of his favourite relaxations wherever he was. His first concert of the season with the Festival Choral Society was to lead to a direr consequence for him than any Bantock opera. This was Elgar's *The Dream of Gerontius* on 16 October. Sheldon was not impressed.

> If a devotional rendering of a religious work is merely a matter of being very solemn and very slow, then Mr Boult, his singers and his players were masters . . . But of the nervous energy which lives in the music and the composer draws from it when he is himself directing its rendering . . . there was hardly a trace.

However, it was not Sheldon's disapproval that hurt Boult but Elgar's. Meeting Elgar at the Hereford Festival five weeks earlier, Boult had told him that because of the high cost he was having to conduct *Gerontius* with reduced woodwind. Far from showing sympathy, Elgar was hurt and angry. The memory of the near-disastrous first performance in Birmingham in 1900 still rankled after 25 years and here was a young conductor whom he admired conniving at another affront to the work. Earlier in the year Elgar had written warmly to Boult congratulating him on his election to the Athenaeum. Elgar had proposed him for membership in August 1920, asking Hugh Allen to second it. The nomination was under Rule II which provides for the annual admission of 'a certain number of persons of distinguished eminence in science, literature, or the arts . . .' Elgar himself had been elected under this rule. For the next seven years his relationship with Boult was frosty and distant. The thaw came in April 1931 when Elgar explained to Boult:

> My feelings were acute: I have never had a real success in life – commercially never; so all I had (& have now) was the feeling that I had written *one* score which satisfied R. Strauss, Richter and many others; it was the discovery that no one in that very wealthy city – which always pretended to be proud of the production of *Gerontius* – cared a straw whether the work was presented as I wrote it or not: *there* at least I hoped to be recognized. Now let us forget it.

Ironically, Boult had in any case engaged the extra wind players and paid them out of his own pocket.

His first purely orchestral Elgar in Birmingham was the *Enigma Variations* on 21 December in a concert which included the orchestrated version of Vaughan Williams's song-cycle *On Wenlock Edge*, performed in London for the first time the previous January. Boult opened 1925 with the second English performance of Delius's Cello Concerto (soloist Beatrice Harrison) – 'the loveliest work of its kind in existence,' Sheldon declared. Later in the season came Vaughan Williams's *A Sea Symphony* and *A London Symphony* and Delius's Double Concerto. He also – rarity indeed in 1925 – conducted a symphony of C. P. E. Bach. These works were played at the Sunday concerts, which were the success of the season. Also popular was Boult's institution of lunchtime orchestral concerts. He, Neville Chamberlain and Professor de Selincourt all urged the need for a new concert hall to replace the Town Hall.[5] Although no move was made in that direction, the season ended encouragingly with the doubling of the city's grant to the orchestra to £2,500 for a further five years. It was a vote of confidence in Boult which meant all the more if he looked back to London. The music critic of *The Times*, writing in praise of Birmingham on 28 February 1925, quoted a musician's forecast that

> there will be no orchestral concerts in London in a few years, only an ever-increasing supply of performances by 'international celebrities' ... In London, the success of every performance has to be measured by box-office returns ... We have seen the oldest of our concert-giving institutions, the Royal Philharmonic Society, forced to restrict its activities to a wretched minimum of half a dozen concerts ... in the hope that by a rigid economy of means it might be able to produce a respectable balance-sheet ... No one knows precisely by what shifts the London Symphony Orchestra ... has managed to keep its head above water, but it is an open secret that its crises have been warded off from time to time by the personal sacrifice of its members ... It moreover has the advantage of being the chosen vehicle for those 'international celebrities' who wield the baton. Now apparently the same pressure affects the New Queen's Hall Orchestra ...

Not such a bright scene; only in Manchester, where Harty was on top of the world with the Hallé, were prospects brighter than in Birmingham, but Manchester still gave no municipal aid nor, apart from some schools concerts, was it to do so until after Barbirolli's advent in 1943.

Sheldon summed up the first season in two long articles in the *Post*. Birmingham, he said, had not yet seen the best of Boult but 'if at 35 you arrive at your best, there is not much use in living until you are 50.' He then gave what still reads like a very fair assessment of Boult's qualities.

> It is a rare event in our concert life to find one of our local conductors attending a concert run by anybody else. Mr Boult, on the other hand, is to be found supporting by his presence concerts of all kinds to an extent equalled by only one other conductor within the writer's experience – Mr Michael

Balling during his direction of the Hallé Concerts [1912–14] ... Though it is by no means for a critic to plead for the appearance of hackneyed music in concert programmes, there is room for speculation as to how many more people might have been attracted to the concerts had a little concession been made ... The concerts as a whole did not reveal in Mr Boult a master of programme designing ... The strongest impression ... is of a very great gain in note accuracy, a much improved ensemble, and a high standard of playing from the string group. The advance made within a single season is so considerable as almost to be remarkable. It could only have been achieved by a conductor fully equipped in the technique of his art.

Sheldon then examined the quality of the different sections of the orchestra and continued:

Were Mr Boult to take his stand upon quality there can be no manner of doubt as to the support he would receive from the musical public ... It is not too much to assert that many compositions cannot be adequately given because a proportion of the personnel of the orchestra is unequal to their demands ... He would be a bold man who asserted that the orchestra as at present constituted was good enough for its conductor. Of Mr Boult as an interpreter it is difficult to generalize as yet ... Difficulty brings the best out of him. To some of us his sympathy with the hyper-romantic in music may seem incomplete, yet none can gainsay the general success won in music of many schools widely separated in their aesthetic aims.

Boult's own 'first-term report' survives in his diary. The season was

quite as successful as I hoped. The two great difficulties are inadequate hall and the orchestral contract. I took the job on because I thought it was a chance of founding a permanent orchestra ... I had an idea that we might get people to take over the orchestra during the summer so that we could gradually make up a 10 or 11 months' contract. So I went off to Walford Davies whom I've seen a good deal of lately and ... he made the obvious point – that I never thought of – that no musician is worth anything as a performer who doesn't *teach*. It is equally true to say no artist (of any kind). That being so, why not aim at the ideal (he is going for this in Wales) of the man who is paid a whole-time screw to do whatever is needed as player, coach or teacher? It is absolutely right and I'm going for it, though it is probably a long way.

There then follows this significant passage:

He also talked about my conducting, particularly two Brahms performances (No. 4 at Aberystwyth and No. 1 at RCM) and said that he felt sometimes that heart was getting the better of head and that the thought was obscured. This is a fine swing of the pendulum for dull unemotional me. No doubt Sheldon has something to do with it, for he obviously wants the virtuoso conductor who lashes everything to his own will and cannot leave the music alone, and I have gradually come to feel that I must put more stuffing into things in order not to lose the B'ham audience. I am glad to know that I *can* overdo it on that side, though Heaven keep me from too much of it! W.D. made the pleasant rehearsal tip of 'letting the procession go past' as one plays. That brings the inside straight out of the music instead of via the conductor. W.D is a marvellously fertile person in ideas.

In May 1925 Boult went back to Prague to conduct the Czech Philharmonic in Vaughan Williams's *A Pastoral Symphony* at the second concert of the festival of the International Society for Contemporary Music, of which Dent was president. It was placed last in a programme that also included Kósa's *Six Pieces for Orchestra*, Paul Pisk's *Partita* and Martinů's *Half Time*, all conducted by Talich. The symphony was enthusiastically received and Vaughan Williams was repeatedly called to the platform. He had written to Boult before they left England: 'I feel rather alarmed at meeting the freaks,' freaks being his playful word for the *avant-garde* of successive generations. Of the orchestral works performed at the festival, only the symphony and Bartók's *Dance Suite* have survived in the repertoire. While in Czechoslovakia, Boult met Leoš Janáček; in the following year he was one of a committee who organized the composer's visit to England. A month later, on 21 June, Boult went to Amsterdam to conduct the Concertgebouw Orchestra in Vaughan Williams's *Wasps* overture, Holst's ballet music from *The Perfect Fool*, Parry's *Symphonic Variations* and Elgar's Violin Concerto with Alexander Schmuller as soloist. The Parry, he wrote in his diary, was 'the great success of the concert.' A week later he conducted Vaughan Williams's *A Pastoral Symphony* at the Aberystwyth Festival.

While in Prague he had experienced another example of composers' uncertainties about tempo. 'When I originally read the *Pastoral* before the first performance (1922) I imagined every movement very much slower than he wished it, so I got used to them quicker, and now he confesses that he knows the work better now and has conducted it himself a good deal and likes everything except the scherzo (I *was* quite wrong over this) much slower.' What Vaughan Williams said to him was 'I find it's not such a boring work as I thought.' Boult attended the Three Choirs Festival at Gloucester in September. We are given a glimpse of him there with Schuster in the Sassoon diaries,[6] driving Frankie and Sassoon to the concerts in his car which he called 'the hearse,' and declaring Parry's *Job* to be 'a very great work.' They heard Elgar conduct the First Symphony ('scrappily performed,' Sassoon thought) and afterwards Boult told Sassoon he was 'losing faith in all Elgar's works except

The Kingdom, the Second Symphony, the *Enigma Variations* and the
"fiddle concerto." "I thought *The Apostles* sounded awful last night!,"
he added.' The works in which he kept faith were the only ones he had
so far conducted with any regularity, except *The Kingdom*.

The advance publicity of the programmes for the 1925–6 Tuesday
series in Birmingham proclaimed that at the October concert Sibelius
would conduct his 'new symphony' – the Seventh, which had been
completed in 1924 and was destined not to be performed in England
until 1927 because illness forced the composer to cancel his visit in 1925.
In his place Boult engaged Holst, who conducted Haydn's Symphony
No. 99 and his own *Beni Mora* and *Fugal Overture*. The *Fancy scherzo*
from his new *Choral Symphony*, of which he had made an arrangement
omitting the chorus, was conducted by Boult, because Holst found it
too difficult. 'Adrian is an Angel with Brains,' Holst wrote to Vally
Lasker. During the season Boult conducted Vaughan Williams's *A
London Symphony*, Brahms's D minor Piano Concerto, with Harold
Samuel, Rachmaninov's C minor Concerto with Pouishnoff, Elgar's *In
the South* (twice), Strauss's *Tod und Verklärung*, Bantock's *Pagan
Chants* (first performance) with Frank Mullings as tenor soloist, and
the Delius Double Concerto with May and Beatrice Harrison. Talich
was to have been a guest conductor on 2 March but had not allowed
himself time to travel from an engagement in Stockholm on 28 February – he had forgotten that February had only 28 days, the audience
was informed! In his place Boult conducted and introduced Bartók's
Dance Suite, repeating it three weeks later.

Boult's letters show that he was growing sensitive to Sheldon's notices.
It seems to be an inevitable part of British provincial musical life that
the principal conductor and a local critic find themselves at odds. It
could scarcely be otherwise. No conductor can be all things to all men;
no critic can assert that one conductor is supreme above others or is
equally effective in all composers. Boult would not have expected to be
spared criticism, but undoubtedly he felt that Sheldon 'had it in for
him.' At the opening Sunday concert Sheldon disparaged the Parry
Variations and said that the first movement of Beethoven's Fifth was
'so tamely handled and poorly played as to take away all zest for the
remainder.' In *Elijah* he 'just yearned for five minutes of Sir Henry Wood
to stir things up.' His notice of Vaughán Williams's *Pastoral Symphony*
did not even mention that Boult had conducted it. He said Boult's
Beethoven Eighth was the best since Richter and found 'stern intel-
lectuality' in his *Eroica*; in *Messiah* 'one had always the sense of a love
for the music'; in *In the South* 'Mr Boult got into its treatment a truly

Elgarian type of nervous intensity.' He ended by describing the season as 'tainted by dullness.' Boult, he said, was 'nearer to greatness in the technical art of conducting than a conductor who can inspire his men to feats of interpretative playing.' He urged an increase from eight to ten Tuesday concerts and called for more guest conductors and a larger orchestra. He was surely right to do so.

But the notice that riled Boult was of a performance of Elgar's *Enigma Variations* on 7 February 1926:

> After the fine performance secured by Sir Landon Ronald some time ago from the same players, last night was a disappointment. It had the damning effect of dullness; in the slow movements it was even somnolent . . . Even the theme was made to suggest a hymn-tune; the Nimrod variation was dragged until it bored us; and the Dorabella variation was so poorly connected that its joints were bared.

Three weeks later, writing home, Boult commented:

> I must tell you a great joke about A.J.S. You remember the Elgar *Variations* notice? Well someone (he wouldn't say who) wrote to the Editor to say that he had heard Wood and Ronald do the Elgar recently and mine was easily the best. He supposed that S. was annoyed at losing his job on the pro-grammes and was taking it out of me this way!! The cream of the joke is that S. *himself* told Michael Mullinar[7] and pointed the moral that everyone in B'ham was ill-natured and advised M.M. to leave B'ham as soon as possible. If only he'd take his own advice!

In the same letter, though, he remarks that the burden of administration he was undertaking would, if it continued, affect the quality of his work. 'I felt it last week when I was tired and Mrs Lee Matthews was horrified when I told her that I didn't open the score of most things until the rehearsal. It's all wrong and can't go on. But there is a heap of work in B'ham (3 or 4 hours' a day at least) that a competent sec. could do for me – I mean the kind of sec. a big politician or businessman has, and I'm trying to get one . . .' He had found time in this season to found a magazine, the *Midland Musician*, with Sydney Grew and to conduct the city police band.

Perhaps the greatest pleasure to him in 1925 was the chance to conduct Wagner's *The Valkyrie* in the British National Opera Company's season at the Prince of Wales Theatre in Birmingham. In the cast were Walter Hyde as Siegmund, Robert Parker as Wotan, Robert Radford as Hunding, Florence Austral as Brünnhilde and Rachel Morton as Sieg-linde. The company had been under Frederic Austin's direction since 1924 and he was busy recruiting new singers and conductors. Sargent conducted operas by Vaughan Williams and Holst in 1924–5 and in the autumn of 1926 John Barbirolli made his first appearance with the company on its visit to Newcastle upon Tyne. Reviewing Boult's début on 1 December 1925, Sheldon pointed out that there had been no chance for a complete rehearsal but

> a sense of security ran through the performance. If he preferred to guide rather than assert a commanding control ... there can be no doubt that in the circumstances he chose well. He gave us the melodic and harmonic loveliness of Wagner ... His tempi were often slower than those adopted in recent years, but they were the tempi of tradition.

When the company returned to Birmingham in March 1926, Boult conducted Verdi's *Otello*, with Frank Mullings as Otello and Miriam Licette as Desdemona. 'Among the finest things he has done here,' was Sheldon's verdict.

Not many conductors of a rival provincial orchestra would have written, as Boult did, to the *Manchester Guardian* on 1 February 1926 to express admiration for the Hallé Orchestra and its conductor Sir Hamilton Harty, after he had heard two of their Berlioz performances, of the *Symphonie Fantastique* and the *Requiem*. The Hallé, he asserted, could take its place with the best of European and American orchestras and he urged Manchester to send its orchestra to Paris to play Berlioz to the French. But he was still haunted by a conductor from the past – Nikisch. On 28 December 1925 he wrote in his notebook:

> A most extraordinary dream. We had had a very nice Wagner programme last night, including the big 1st Act slice of *Parsifal* which makes me think of Nikisch always and the night we sang it in Leipzig (after which my heart went wrong!) ... I dreamed a good deal, but finally just before I woke I was doing a concert in some strange place and as I was coming away I met old Nikisch in the doorway – I had no idea he was there. He said: 'It was very good, but let me tell you something: you must be careful to keep your hand well in to the body, for when it gets too far forward it takes the power away from the stick.' Now I have felt for some time that this was happening (the hand was taking power from the stick), but this simple solution hadn't occurred to me for a moment. Where did it come from?

CHAPTER 15

Opera

IN July 1926 Boult conducted Wagner's *Parsifal* at the RCM. Two complete performances, sung in English, were given, each spread over two evenings, Hyam Grünebaum conducting the first. Boult's performance led to one of his last letters from Frank Schuster, who was to die in 1927. 'You were the cause of a great joy to me,' Schuster wrote from Bray on 20 July,

> because you were not only able to revive old memories & particularly *old thrills* of Bayreuth early days (the most intense musical emotion of my life), but to add new ones. Also you gave me the gratification of fructifying to the full my belief in you from the very first (and assuredly I *was* the very first as I shall most certainly *not* be the last). I knew you would make a *good* conductor – but it was your interpretation of the last act yesterday that revealed you to me as a *great* one. Illuminated & illuminating, it brought home to our hearts the inner significance of the subject & the music. And for this you have the blessing of Your old friend Frank S.

For Birmingham's Sunday concerts in the 1926–7 season, the CBO moved from the Futurist Cinema to the larger West End Cinema. Its main series was given in the Central Hall, the Town Hall having been closed for repairs to its roof since October 1925. (Boult used to tell an amusing story of how in this season a new venue was found for the children's concerts. He and Gerald Forty went to see the Chief Constable, Charles Rafter, who summoned an inspector. 'Jones,' he said, 'who was that little man we prosecuted for indecency three weeks ago?' 'Mr X., sir.' 'Ring him and tell him to come round.' Mr X. was the manager of a hall. He came quivering along and of course he was delighted to house the children's concerts.) Early in the season Boult repeated the *Enigma Variations*, this performance evoking practically no comment from Sheldon. Albert Sammons was soloist in Elgar's Violin Concerto, Boult conducted four of *The Planets* and Schubert's

Great C major Symphony. (Later in the season Bruno Walter also conducted the Schubert.) All the Beethoven symphonies were played during the season, 1927 being the centenary of the composer's death. ('Yes, I'm afraid I *do* think the *Pastoral* the weakest of the Beethovens,' he told his father.)

The RCM *Parsifal* led to an invitation to Boult to conduct British National Opera Company performances of this opera on its autumn tour. He opened in Newcastle upon Tyne in September and later conducted it in Glasgow, Manchester, Liverpool and Birmingham. The cast included Walter Hyde as Parsifal, Gladys Ancrum as Kundry, Percy Heming as Amfortas and Norman Allin as Gurnemanz. Critics in these provincial cities were generally appreciative of Boult's conducting; thus A. K. Holland in *The Liverpool Daily Post*: 'A very sensitive and restrained treatment of the orchestral score ... the playing was singularly homogeneous and impressive,' and Sheldon in Birmingham, though highly critical of the orchestra's performance, wrote:

> Mr Adrian Boult conducted with an obviously intimate acquaintance with the score and with a feeling for what may be termed the *religioso* cast of the work, though it goes far beyond that ... He was specially to be admired in the scene of Amfortas's long soliloquy, where the chromatic pain-infested climaxes were allowed to stream down from each climax in a most affecting way. One liked him least in the valse music for the flower maidens ...

The performance in Manchester on 16 November marked Boult's first appearance as a conductor in the city and he came under the scrutiny of the *Guardian*'s famous Samuel Langford:

> Mr Adrian Boult proved himself ... finely adapted for the work, and while his style is perhaps a little demonstrative in the energetic passages, he has an admirable quietness in all the more restful passages of the work which is indeed more essential to it. Poignancy does not appear a strong point with Mr Boult and there is a too clear sense of satisfaction in all he does. One follows his work without any very definite aesthetic interest, but with a consistent admiration for its musical quality ... He made himself many friends by this his first appearance here ...

On the following afternoon, in *Madam Butterfly*, another conductor made his Manchester début – John Barbirolli.

In the midst of his *Parsifal* performances, Boult also involved himself in a three-week season of opera at the Theatre Royal, Bristol, where the CBO played in the pit. It opened with Mozart's *Così fan tutte*, performed in English as *The School for Lovers*, with Steuart Wilson and W. Johnstone Douglas as Ferrando and Guglielmo, Louise Trenton and

Dorothy D'Orsy as Fiordiligi and Dorabella and Judy Skinner and Arthur Cranmer as Despina and Don Alfonso. The other operas performed were Vaughan Williams's *The Shepherds of the Delectable Mountains*, Stanford's *The Travelling Companion*, Falla's *Master Peter's Puppet Show*, Philip Napier Miles's *Markheim*, Purcell's *Dido and Aeneas* and Smyth's *Entente Cordiale*. Boult conducted all the operas, and the festival owed its existence to the munificence of Napier Miles, at whose beautiful house, King's Weston at Shirehampton, Boult, Wilson, Vaughan Williams and others stayed. What might have been an idyllic and prolonged country-house weekend to the socially-minded was no such thing to Boult, who was at this time consulting the psychologist William Brown about a cure for his hampering shyness. Though used to the parties and gatherings of the upper-middle-class mode of life in which he had grown up, Boult was retiring by nature and avoided such occasions if he could. He also found that often he was not invited – especially in Birmingham – because it was assumed he would be either tired or too busy. He was also, as he confessed to Christopher Bishop many years later, intensely nervous before he conducted any concert and this continued for most of his life. At Birmingham he lived a bachelor existence in an Edgbaston guesthouse, Wyddrington, which he shared with his cousin Lowis Barman, going to bed at 10 pm and having breakfast at 8 am with unchanging regularity. There were no women in his life; and in today's climate his association with Schuster's circle would have been enough for him to be labelled homosexual. He was no such thing, but his shyness with women was well known and he would run away if he thought he was an object of interest to a woman.

One of the few women with whom he was at ease was Steuart Wilson's wife Ann, to whose son Richard he had stood godfather with Vaughan Williams in 1925. He felt 'safe' with a married woman and during the Bristol season asked her to accompany him in his car on the drive from Shirehampton to Bristol 'because so-and-so is angling and I don't want to get involved.' Each night at King's Weston he would return from the performance, creep into the house hoping not to be noticed – although his fellow guests were usually sitting after dinner in the big hall into which the front door opened – and go to his room. Even on the last night he did this, whereupon Mrs Napier Miles was heard to exclaim: 'Well I think he ought to have stayed up and joined us for a short time tonight.'

Boult ended the year 1926 by conducting Vaughan Williams's *A Sea Symphony* in Liverpool and *A London Symphony* in Birmingham. He began 1927 excitingly in Birmingham by including the *scherzo* from Bruckner's Sixth Symphony in a concert on 30 January and by conducting Mahler's Fourth Symphony on 3 February. The latter occasion drew the London critics to Birmingham, for this was only the third public performance of a Mahler symphony in Britain since Wood had conducted the Seventh in 1913. (Wood had also conducted the Fourth Symphony at a Liverpool Philharmonic concert in the 1923–4 season, when the soprano soloist was Maria van Dresser.) Boult's performance was well if cautiously received. No likelihood of a Mahler cult seizing London, *The Observer* declared, because of 'difficulty of over-statement and of confused thought' (on Mahler's part, one presumes!). The *Times* critic thought the symphony was 'an astonishing artistic accomplishment,' the *adagio* justifying claims made for it as 'one of the most lovely slow movements ever written.' Sheldon made little mention of conducting or playing but decided we ought to hear more Mahler in Britain, adding prophetically: 'His may prove the revivifying influence needed to restore the orchestral concert to the exciting experience it used to be when Strauss, Elgar, Debussy, Delius and others seemed to be pouring out new works in rivalry with one another.' The soloist in the *finale* (sung in Steuart Wilson's English translation) was Dorothy Silk.

Later in the season Boult conducted Somervell's *Thalassa* Symphony, which Sheldon found lacking in 'sheer musical imagination.' Sheldon was enthusiastic about Strauss's *Don Quixote*, in spite of there being too few strings. Boult, he wrote, 'had not merely a fine grip of the work, but also a vision of the humanity, the humour and the wisdom that live in it ... *Don Quixote* is a work of supreme genius in its kind.' On 20 February Boult conducted the Festival Choral Society at Birmingham University in Byrd's *Great Service*, which Dr E. H. Fellowes had recently unearthed from the archives of Durham Cathedral. Boult had written to Fellowes and received this advice: 'As to tempi, do whatever seems good to you ... If at any point it seems to flag in interest one may go faster or slower ... You express it admirably when you speak of "giving the amazing expressiveness of the work full play." Do that and you can't go wrong.'[1] Schumann's Second Symphony, Strauss's *Burleske*, Bantock's *Dante and Beatrice*, Delius's *Paris* and Vaughan Williams's *The Lark Ascending* (violinist Jelly d'Arányi) were also played during the season. Boult conducted a gala evening for the re-opening of the Town Hall on 12 April.

During March he conducted some BNOC performances of *The Valkyrie* at Golders Green – the critics complained of slow tempi and thin strings. Later in the month the Bristol *Così fan tutte* was performed, with almost the same cast and Boult conducting, at the Kingsway Theatre (its first London performance for about 16 years). The theatre was made available for three or four weeks by Sir Barry Jackson, but the opera was such a success that it was transferred to the Court (now The Royal Court) – a total run of 56 consecutive performances, played to crowded houses. Also in March, Boult and the CBO gave two concerts in Cheltenham to honour Holst, who was born in the town. Holst conducted several of his own works. Organizing these concerts was not plain sailing. The CBO players were not on exclusive contract and several had accepted engagements with Sir Ivor Atkins, organist of Worcester Cathedral. Boult made a personal appeal to him and he reluctantly released four players.

The orchestra's finances were still of acute concern, but had improved since the first season. Boult's father became a patron and in January 1926 the senior trustee, Sir David Brooks, wrote to Boult about this 'most generous gesture,' adding 'I am still much concerned about the bank overdraft ... I hope that some day I shall find some good friend or friends who will come to our rescue.' Lady Brooks was one of Boult's greatest admirers in Birmingham. 'I just love the atmosphere you have created, it is so different from what it was!' she wrote on one occasion. And on another: 'Sheldon is truly exasperating but be comforted in the knowledge that your performance last night was truly great.' One source of income since 1925 had been the (modest) fees paid by the BBC for broadcast relays, but the relays ceased in 1926. In 1927–8 the BBC complicated matters by changing the terms under which it engaged certain CBO players for its Birmingham-based Birmingham Studio Orchestra. The musicians had to choose between CBO and BBC and the latter won.

Boult's busy routine continued throughout 1927, although he found time for his favourite relaxation of motoring, and wrote detailed letters home about it and about the office he was trying to find in the centre of Birmingham where he could work. He also regaled his family with accounts of the rigours of conducting at the Kendal Festival:

Rehearsed from 2–5.30 on Saturday afternoon, so I earned my money, I think! ... Today we went to church and after lunch we went up in the car to the top of the first high hill you see on the left, opposite you as you start up Shap from Kendal ... They are very nice in the way of making one happy and planning expeditions, etc. ... (this afternoon's was done simply for me) but they have *no idea* of feeding the brute or of warming him. *Every* window open and *no* fire lit till lunchtime (Miss Luard-Selby complaining bitterly of the cold and doing nothing!) and they all eat very fast and give you 2- or 3-course meals at most and *nothing* between, not even early tea! Thank goodness for cartouches and beef lozenges which I always take there!

Four days later:

The car is making an awful noise under my feet. I thought 'speedometer' at once, but the garage says gearbox bearings want renewing. Would you ask Webb [family chauffeur] if he thinks that sensible and if so if I am to let them do it? Newtown want me on 15th probably, but I don't want to go there with a dicky car and if I bring it home on 13th Webb can't possibly get it right, and I can't get back in time to shoot unless I come by car. The noise is a loose heavy rattling sound just under my feet and it does *not* vary with the speed of the engine (surely this points to speedometer?) ... I wish I thought it *was* gearbox.

But a week or so later he was back to musical matters:

Various more or less tiresome things are on hand, but too long to bother to write about. This kind of thing:

(1) A row with the 1st clarinet, who has been angelic since I ate him 3 years ago. I suppose I must prepare for another meal ...

(2) Sheldon has let loose two *awful* notices. To be discussed by committee on Monday.

(3) R.V.W. is resigning the London Bach Choir and they all want me to take it on?????

(4) Usual propaganda ramp for the BNOC who are coming in Nov. They want me to conduct *Götterdämmerung*. I'm hedging.

(5) Wireless (London) are arranging 9 o'clock orchestral broadcasts almost every Sunday night. Our concerts finish at 9.5 sometimes which gives the orchestra insufficient time to (1) get their coats on (2) light their pipes or cigarettes (3) walk 500 yards to a certain pub (4) have the essential drink (5) cross the road, climb two flights of stairs (6) get their coats off and begin playing.

I may have to go to see Reith to get the thing put back to 9.15!

Feeling stale and in need of a change, Boult went for a holiday in North America in April 1927. He had always wanted to see the Grand Canyon and made fulfilment of this ambition his principal aim. After a few days in Washington, where Vincent Massey was Canadian Minister, he went to Chicago to board the train 'The Chief'. He spent three days walking and climbing in the Canyon, watching the setting sun change its colours gradually to 'an all-pervading blue and finally black.' Then he 'rubbernecked' in Los Angeles and went through the forest of Oregon to Tacoma and the wild flowers in Mount Rainier national park. His next stop was Vancouver, where he found some distant relatives. From Capilano Canyon early in June he travelled on a humble railway line called Kettle Valley through a countryside of lakes and hills to Nelson, B.C. There he took a lake steamer for 20 hours up the Arrow Lake to Arrowhead, near Revelstoke, where he joined the intercontinental train. While travelling through the Rockies to Calgary he heard that his mother had died. She had been ill before he left and he had wanted to cancel his trip and stay at Northlands with her. But, as Cedric Boult wrote to Adrian's friend Lawrence Tanner, 'she was rather better and pressed him so much that he yielded. No one dreamt that the end was so near.' On his return to England Boult himself wrote on 1 July to Tanner:

It *is* hard to bear, and it is only, as you say, by letting the memories and thoughts (which at the time seemed so volatile) become the realities that one can gradually make the earthly things fall behind them into the background and thus seem to matter less. This side of it helped me perhaps more than ever because the news found me on the west side of the Canadian Rockies, at least a fortnight's journey from home and with only one understanding friend on that side of the Atlantic. Poor Father and Olive had all the work, of course, that I would have helped in, and have been wonderful ... You heard, I expect, that the dear creature died in her sleep, most peacefully, just when she seemed to be getting over one of her asthma attacks, and at a time when we all thought she was steadily gaining strength. Father and Olive had taken her over to Bournemouth for some electric treatment, as she usually had this to help her finish off the attacks. She went to sleep quickly in the evening at the nursing home and breathed her last about midnight.

The 1927–8 CBO season began with Boult conducting Sibelius's Fifth and Brahms's Fourth Symphonies. At one of the October Sunday concerts he was taken ill and he handed over to the leader Paul Beard. A persistent cough had been troubling him for some time. A week afterwards he wrote to his father: 'There is a scheme for *all* B'ham concertgivers to go in a body to the *B'ham Post* about A.J.S. I wonder if it will come off? If we *all* exclude him he won't have much work to do!' Boult's doctor, Bardswell, whom he consulted in place of John Weir, urged a holiday abroad, followed by a routine which allowed as much outdoor exercise as possible – 'there is absolutely nothing wrong now, but I need a good rest.' Boult left London on 23 November 1927 bound for Egypt, sailing in the SS *Arabia*. Writing home during the voyage he said:

Today I wrote 51 postcards and did some more Schubert and read a good deal of Carter's *Tutankhamen* ... It is quite interesting. A fellow-passenger also lent me Weigall's *Ecknaten* (in a German translation of course). It is rather an interesting account of the father-in-law of Tutankhamen who nearly wrecked Egypt by adopting what was *almost* Christianity (in 1500 BC!!) and being entirely unpractical about it [the subject 60 years later of Philip Glass's opera *Akhnaten*] ... I suppose I am being a very 'superior person,' and it seems most unpleasant, but really the combined brains of everyone on this ship seem as if they would barely equip the proverbial peacock. Really the Germans are the best of the bunch ... We have two 'handles': Lady Willoughby de Broke (dowager, I think), who looks a dear but sits about sewing and doesn't talk to people much, and the Hon. Mrs Buller, who has the most awful drawl and is almost an imbecile ...

He rarely referred to his health except to say that he felt well, but there was once a wry comment on medical advice: 'O. [Olive, his sister] is quite right about Weir. When I told him of my more violent days, weeks or months, which I often did, he used to smile and say "there isn't much wrong with you then." Why couldn't he tell me to stop? If he had said I *must* not work 7 days in the week, etc. etc., as Bardswell did, I should have done something about it.' In a notebook Boult kept a list of the books he took with him to Egypt. They give a good idea of the catholicity of his taste, ranging from Conrad's *Lord Jim* and Walpole's *Portrait of a Man With Red Hair* to Sinclair Lewis's *Elmer Gantry*, Galsworthy's *Strife* and *The Silver Spoon* to Loti's *Le Désert* and Boccaccio's *Decameron*.

Writing home on 6 January 1928 he said he had been able to 'think things over' about Birmingham:

There is no doubt that by this time, after 4 years, we ought to be having bigger audiences in Birmingham and there can be only 2 reasons, (1) my conducting and/or my programmes don't appeal to the audience or rather don't make the kind of appeal that will catch a wider audience – for I *know* that the people who do come are happy, *or* (2) A.J.S. is really keeping a lot of people away. I certainly find among my non-concert-going acquaintances that they always know what S. has said of me on Monday morning! Now, whatever the reasons are, it seems to me that the solution is *not* to concentrate more on Birmingham, as I have been rather thinking I should like to do, but to accept the London Bach Choir (if it is offered me), keep in the College, and fix up some kind of deputy arrangement in B'ham. This will very soon prove whether reason (1) or (2) is the trouble, and if it is (2) and something got A.J.S. out of his job, I could always chuck outside things and go back to doing most or all of the B'ham work if I felt like it ... Just heard today in Luxor that Toscanini will have left Milan before I get there, so I am rather thinking I'll go to Nice for one night, get a performance at Monte Carlo Opera and then I shall probably be *quite* certain I never want to go to the Riviera. It is rather silly to say that *before* you've seen a place. But I'm quite sure it *is* so and 2 days will settle it!

In Egypt he was alarmed by the 'pandemonium' that accompanied any request for service, with a dozen porters 'screaming and fighting for each passenger,' as he wrote in his autobiography.[2] He spent Christmas Day in the Valley of the Kings – he went there several times, walking the seven miles from and to Luxor. The deepest impression was made on him by Karnak, to which he walked by moonlight.

Boult returned to Birmingham in January 1928. He was now provided with an office in No. 11, the Bull Ring, hidden behind the shops. It was a spacious room, 36 feet by 24 feet, formerly the upper floor of an imposing house. This building was 'rescued' from use as a warehouse for timber and building material by the Midland Red Bus Company and Boult, who became leaseholders and tenant respectively. It had a high, vaulted ceiling, with two arches formed by bent trees split to form the two sides of the arches. Like the arches, the roof beams were of oak. It was late 15th or early 16th century, with later additions. Boult put antique furniture into it. It has, of course, long since disappeared. On his return, there seems little doubt that his phobia of Sheldon was the principal factor in his mind. His associates knew it too, and perhaps knew it would rob them of him in due course, for there was a disposition to counter-attack in some way. Councillor G. F. McDonald, chairman of the executive committee of the CBO, wrote Boult a warmly welcoming letter and also translated his words into deeds, as Boult told his family:

McDonald came to rehearsal as well as concert to make welcoming speeches, and the row at the concert was really surprising. It went on and on and McD. and I stood looking idiotic and wondering what to do next. Forty said he had rarely *felt* such warmth in a B'ham audience. Sam Dushkin had a great success too. I had a long talk with Forty on Monday before the conference [on the orchestra's future]. Re. finance he said that my holiday was entirely due to the fact that I had given B'ham far more energy than was of the contract, or ever expected, and why therefore should I pay? Re. Sheldon, he is also feeling stronger than ever about it. The Chief Constable last Sunday at one of his concerts in aid of CBO said 'Don't you worry about what silly people say in the papers. You go and hear the City Orchestra and see how you enjoy yourselves.'

Ten days later his letter home reported: 'A.J.S. has written so enthusiastically (says I'm improving!) that McD. thinks Ford [Lt.-Col. B. J. T. Ford, a member of the committee] must have spoken to him.' Support in the columns of *The Birmingham Post* came from an unexpected quarter, the pen of Dame Ethel Smyth, in characteristically generous mood after one of her works had been played. In a letter to the editor she wrote:

> I should like to express my amazement at the change in the orchestra. Not only is there a striking difference in the quality, particularly in the strings, but an energy, a keenness and above all a warmth ... Having last Sunday conducted a new and exceedingly difficult MS work[3] with what all concerned know was the usual and absolutely unavoidable shortage of rehearsal, I was astonished – and so were my two soloists who know the work backwards – at what was nevertheless achieved by the orchestra ...

As Boult wrote to his father, 'Dame Ethel is pleasant, isn't she? I'm asking people to follow it up. Alfred Hayes has promised.' And sure enough Hayes, of the Midland Institute, wrote to the *Post* that Dame Ethel's letter 'should silence, once for all, the uninformed disparagement of our City Orchestra ... If means were forthcoming to enable all the members of the orchestra to be "full-time" players, instead of being obliged to supplement their salaries by other arduous work, if means could be found to allow them the daily rehearsals to which the perfection of certain continental orchestras is mainly due, both they and their conductor would have a much happier time ...' This, to be fair to Sheldon, was the main burden of his criticisms – he wanted the best for Birmingham and was determined not to become self-satisfied with what, as he frequently admitted, had been remarkably achieved. It is nonetheless irritating and depressing for those who are doing the achieving to be constantly reminded of how far short of the ideal they are falling. Gerald Forty wrote to Boult in February 1928, giving an account of a talk McDonald and he had had with G. W. Hubbard, editor of *The Birmingham Post*.[4]

> Provided that Sheldon is amenable to his editor, we may look for an improvement in the tone of his criticism. Hubbard certainly had gone into the matter very exhaustively. He had a huge collection of criticisms – everything that S. had written for some time past – and evidently he had read them carefully. He had talked to S. and I gather that S. is considerably perturbed. H. read to us a long letter that S. had sent him on the subject after a sleepless night ... I am anxious that you should know – and feel – that things are moving in a better direction, and that I am convinced that we have lost nothing by keeping back the letter ... I wish devoutly that you would try to dismiss [this matter] from your mind, with the knowledge that those who have asked you to leave this matter in their hands are determined to secure fair play for you and for the Orchestra.

Looking back over 30 years later,[5] Boult described Forty as 'a particularly good person for pouring oil on troubled waters. I am afraid I cannot claim an unruffled temper now and I certainly could not in those days and he was very good with it. It is a pity that benevolent kind of musical tradesman is disappearing.' Boult's temper was already notorious. Some felt that he emulated Hugh Allen who was well known for 'exploding' at rehearsals. A friend who attended Boult's rehearsals once told him she would not come again if he was going to subject the orchestra to anger and bad temper and reminded him of Holst's remark, 'When a person loses his temper, he just looks silly.'

What of music after Boult's return? Beatrice Harrison played Delius's Cello Concerto and a fortnight later Boult's conducting of Delius's *Paris* earned him a letter from Grez-sur-Loing where the composer had heard the broadcast: 'I felt you were in entire sympathy with the work and your tempi were all just as I want them.' Another Holst festival concert was given in Cheltenham, where the composer conducted the first European performance of his Hardy tone poem *Egdon Heath*. Boult conducted Schubert's C major Symphony and noted an eccentric remark made to him by Holst: 'The essential thing about Schubert is his tunes. If the tunes are inaudible what's the good of the music, therefore why not touch up the scoring?' Ernest Ansermet was guest conductor on 23 February in the Franck Symphony and Stravinsky's *Firebird* suite. In *My Own Trumpet*, Boult describes the Prelude to Act I of *Lohengrin*, which opened the concert, as 'a revelation,' but writing on the night of the event he said: 'People seemed to have enjoyed it enormously so I say nothing, but I wasn't moved an inch by the whole night!' He envied Ansermet his schedule with the Orchestre de la Suisse Romande in Geneva where, he told Boult, the orchestra gave 80 concerts in the six winter months but only about 20 programmes, for each of which he rehearsed five or six times.

If Boult sometimes felt unappreciated in Birmingham, he was acknowledged elsewhere during 1928. He was invited to join the BBC Music Advisory Committee and was elected president of the Incorporated Society of Musicians for 1928–9. Allen and Bantock had tackled him about the latter, he told his father: '... it is a great honour; the society has been overhauled and there has been a glorious row, I believe ... and they say they want a name which will give confidence to everyone. Mine was the first name suggested apparently ... Bother them! But it doesn't mean much work.' The BBC connection arose through the withdrawal of Sir Donald Tovey. Boult's friends Allen and Walford Davies were on the committee and would obviously have suggested his name. 'Why must I have these responsibilities?' he wrote to his family. 'I wish people would leave me alone in my vinegar bottle: I fear that I shall be able to do much less work in B'ham in future, but I suppose I must take on these national things: the BBC doesn't meet more than every 3 or 4 months, but it is a responsibility.' Boult kept the reply his father wrote to him:

My dear Boy. Putting you on the BBC is a great compliment! Yes, there is no doubt that the older you get the more responsibility will be thrust upon you, mainly because you have shown yourself an honest, straightforward man, one who has no 'axe to grind' and, as a matter of fact, would not grind it if he had one! By your education you are far better fitted to fill such posts than the majority of people. But there is no reason whatever why you should let them seriously interfere with your real work – conducting. Rather should this help you, it seems to me, to get the best of that that is going. I congratulate you heartily on both positions. They show clearly that even tho' you are so young, your steadfast, honest work is being appreciated, so don't mind Sheldons *et hoc genus omne*! Now about the car ...

The letters home at this time were again full of car problems – should he sell his Standard and buy a new Wolseley, Talbot or Vauxhall? Another problem was the recurrent one of Dame Ethel, this time at a Cheltenham concert.

I got to the hall to find no parts of the *Wreckers* overture. You can imagine Dame E. under such circumstances: 'I might as well go back to London' was her most practical suggestion. I was violently rude to her twice. Mr Shephard [A. H. Shephard, general secretary of the CBO] took a train back to B'ham to try and find them while I telephoned to London. Meanwhile Dame E. rehearsed the *Boatswain's Mate* Ov. and Intermezzo for nearly 1½ hours (they can't last more than 15 minutes) so she was happy. They [the missing parts] didn't come so she played the *Boatswain* twice.

Boult wrote to her afterwards and received a memorable reply written on 29 March:

Your letter made me so happy – as long as people are fond of each other nothing else matters & what made me so *miserable* was feeling that you seemed to have got me all wrong & to hate me ... Dear Mr Boult ... once you say that to yourself – once you realize how the thought of your (apparently) hating me gave me real sharp pain, I *know* I shan't get on your nerves (if I do I shall say 'Basingstoke'!). It was only because you were frantic, (of course) at the *Wreckers* incident ... & so was I (equally of course) – and *not* because you & I can't be trusted to wield the stick on the same evening without beating each other – that bourasques occurred! ... I do admire you & your work so – and I know what you are *in your heart*. And I believe you know (*really* down below) what I am in mine. And that, my dear friend, is all that really matters ...

Boult was much concerned with his methods of rehearsing, arising from dissatisfaction with a Birmingham Festival Choral Society performance of Bach's Mass in B minor. He wrote in his diary:

The idea [of rehearsing] is not to get perfection but to raise the standard as far as possible in the time allotted. People like Mahler do not rest until they achieve their ideal in performance. This means enormous friction for all concerned – and do they really achieve their ideal, any more than a man like Walter who year after year works to raise the standard by hard work himself, by making everyone round him revel in working as hard and as well as he can?

In the summer of 1928 Johnstone Douglas again staged a seven-week opera season at the Court Theatre. Boult conducted *Così fan tutte* and Cimarosa's *The Secret Marriage* (the latter was not a success with the public). For the rehearsal period he stayed with Steuart and Ann Wilson and their children at their home 23, Chepstow Villas, W.11. 'We had a marvellous morning at Kew,' he wrote to his father, 'went off at 10 in the car and found a seat far from the madding crowd and settled down. I was at once ordered to take off my coat and we then played bears, Indians, every kind of ball game, with a sunbathe thrown in. We have now fallen into a sleep-after-lunch habit. The two girls come in to tea about 4, and after that it is rather hard not to spend the time till the 6 o'clock meal playing with them, they are so entertaining.' This kind of almost frivolous behaviour has not previously been encountered in Boult's letters. During the run of the operas occur: 'Now I'm off to fetch Ann, who is doing dresses at the theatre, and take her home. Then on to Miss Schuster for lunch,' and 'After lunch I took the children on the Serpentine, and tea with an aunt of theirs close by here.'

While in London Boult conducted the College orchestra in Mahler's Fourth Symphony with Mabel (later Margaret) Ritchie as the soprano soloist – 'a surprising success,' he reported, 'I was *very* doubtful about ... Allen's opinion of it. Well, he was delighted and said he had enjoyed every minute (55!) of it, and when he heard new music like that it made him feel five years younger.' One of Boult's most assiduous students at the RCM from 1925 to 1929 was Michael Tippett, who had spent some time in Sargent's junior conducting class but found that he was not learning as much as he had hoped. He graduated to Boult's Friday afternoon senior class. Boult thought Tippett was concerned principally with conducting but the embryonic composer was really concerned with listening to orchestras. For four years he stood beside Boult at the Friday rehearsals. After a while Boult invited him to stand inside the rostrum rail and from that privileged position what Tippett learned was, in his own phrase, 'nobody's business.' He acted as répétiteur for the *Parsifal* performances and was enthralled by the *Pelléas et Mélisande* rehearsals. He discovered years later that he had been known by his fellow students as 'Boult's darling.'[6]

CHAPTER 16

The Bach Choir

BOULT spent August at the Munich and Salzburg Festivals, which he reported for *The Times* in an article printed in its issue of 15 September 1928. From Munich he wrote home: 'Back in this lovely place and wondering how on earth I could have let six years go by without a pilgrimage here!' But Bruno Walter, who Boult said in *My Own Trumpet* 'has brought the beauty of music to me perhaps more than anyone else, particularly in later life,' was no longer director of the opera and there was a difference in *Figaro*: '*Nothing* like Walter's performances 6 years ago. Some quite poor singing and the orchestra is very slack owing to sheer bad conducting, I think.' The conductor concerned was Hans Knappertsbusch. In *The Times* Boult described him as 'a great conductor in certain ways,' but 'there is a curious lack of decision about his beat which must make it almost impossible for the orchestra to put any crispness into their Mozart playing.' In Act I of *Tristan*, though, 'even those who remember the two monumental performances under Nikisch at Covent Garden in 1907 could hardly claim that a more terrific climax was then achieved than by Knappertsbusch . . .' In Salzburg, Boult heard Walter conduct *Così fan tutte*: 'It is difficult to imagine more perfect orchestral playing.' He also heard him conduct Schubert's Eighth and Ninth Symphonies:

> It must be granted that the tempo often changes through the movements and this has a tendency to interfere with the stream of the vhole, but every change so obviously comes as a result of deep thought and everything in itself is so extraordinarily beautiful that surely one can regard this simply as a sign that the art of interpretation is moving forward from the steady tempi that English music-lovers will always associate with the great memory of Hans Richter . . .

In Salzburg Boult spent some time with the young English baritone Keith Falkner, whose professional career began in 1925. Falkner had been drawn to Boult's attention by Allen, for he had been a New College choir boy from 1909 to 1913. In March 1927 he had sung under Boult in Parry's *Job* at Winchester: 'It was marvellous the buoyant feeling he gave,' he had written to Mrs Boult, 'and made me feel that everything I wanted to do, he also wanted – and so heaps of things "came off" which never had before.' Falkner was in Austria in 1928 having lessons from Boult's former teacher, Theo Lierhammer. Boult and Falkner saw Hofmannsthal's *Everyman*, 'then dinner up at a sort of terrace restaurant overlooking the town, and down to another palace courtyard where, at 10.30, a little orchestra played 50 minutes' Mozart serenade under ideal conditions: quite dark except the orchestra candles, and moon above, and a gorgeous warm night: finishing with a walk along the river bank with the castle on the hill high above us.' Because he wanted to return to give a lecture in Oxford, Boult decided to fly home, his first experience of an aeroplane.

As so often after a holiday, a bout of self-examination was in order. This time a former College pupil occasioned it:

Listened in to Ernest Parsons who has just been appointed mus. dir. at Lozells Picture House. Everything just too slow and dead. I wrote to him that Malcolm's success (no name mentioned) [Malcolm Sargent] was largely due to his doing almost everything a shade faster than most other people. Reminded him he must not be too much influenced by my slowness as he has a smaller orchestra, a less patient audience, less experience than I. But it's true that practically all of the greatest performances that I can remember have been slower than average. In Egypt, when I had a long slow time over the Schubert C major, I realized that I was really learning a score for the first time. I also began to find out that only in times of real physical rest does one really begin to think (eg. William Brown, who sticks one on to a sofa before one begins to talk). Barry Jackson said the same thing the other day: it is only when he gets away to rest and think that he gets real work done. The shows of Schubert C major at Oxford and Cheltenham afterwards were amongst the best things I've ever done. To memorize a score is the only way to get a real perspective of the whole. How trite that sounds and yet at 39 I'm only just beginning to understand the truth of it. I'm working on the 'Unfinished' now and realize I knew nothing about it though I've conducted it 13 times...

Before the Birmingham season began in earnest, Boult went to the Leeds Festival where Allen and Beecham were the principal conductors. He heard Allen conduct Beethoven's Mass in D and Parry's *Job* (in the one day). Keith Falkner was one of the soloists in *Job*. He wrote to Boult afterwards: 'I shouldn't be upset by T.B.'s genius – I used that word about him to a friend the other day and they at once replied "So's the devil!" '

In Birmingham, the orchestra faced yet another crisis. The BBC had increased the complement of its studio orchestra in the city and had offered contracts which attracted several CBO players and also ensured that they could not accept CBO engagements. The BBC's sop to the CBO was to offer to broadcast 13 of its concerts at a fee of £100 per broadcast. Boult favoured a complete merger of interest with the BBC on the grounds that Birmingham was not big enough to support two orchestras. This point was taken up by Sheldon in two extremely fine and sympathetic articles, each a column in length, in which he examined the CBO's problems. 'Mr Boult,' he wrote,

> after hard and not too well rewarded work with the ensemble of the City Orchestra must begin again. The many fine players who remain in the ranks, too, may well feel discouraged ... The ideal, however, may be stated. It is a first-rate, fully balanced orchestra operating during the winter months and based upon an amalgamation for concert purposes of the two bodies which this season will be heard separately ... Such a body, when playing in the concert room, must be locally controlled. Its musical policy must be Birmingham's and not London's. In the writer's view, the musical policy of the Birmingham studio should also be Birmingham's and not London's, but that is not the concern of the present argument ... It ought not to be impossible to devise a working arrangement which would encourage and not hamper the development of the orchestra under Mr Boult's direction and yet give the BBC what it wants for its own purposes.

It was a problem which six years later was also to face the Hallé in Manchester when the BBC Northern Orchestra was formed. On 18 October Boult went to Manchester to hear the opening concert of the Hallé season and to discuss BBC affairs as they affected Manchester at that date. Harty conducted the concert, which included Schubert's C major Symphony and Kodály's *Hary János* suite. 'One rehearsal,' Boult noted,

> and the first concert of the season: a really fabulous performance. They naturally spent a good deal of the rehearsal time on the Kodály and hadn't much left for the other things – but the C major was full of subtleties with which I didn't agree musically, but which could only amaze one as sheer orchestral virtuosity. They have an ensemble, and a capacity for under-standing Harty, which must be unmatched in Europe. I think the lesson for me is to play for safety a little less: my rule of covering practically every bar of every work in rehearsal (because B'ham players have such gaps in their equipment) is all very well for security, but to rehearse parts thoroughly

and take risks with the rest will probably get better performances and ginger the orchestra into a more alert and independent crowd. After all, seeing the risks Beecham took with his memory etc. at Leeds makes me feel that safety is not everything in orchestral performance!

The programmes in the 1928–9 season included Joachim's orchestration of Schubert's *Grand Duo*, Busoni's *Indian Fantasy*, Dohnányi as conductor and pianist in his own *Variations on a Nursery Tune* and as conductor of his *Ruralia Hungarica* and Beethoven's *Eroica*, Egon Petri as solo pianist in the Franck *Symphonic Variations* and Prokofiev's Third Concerto and a repetition of Mahler's Fourth Symphony. The one-armed Austrian pianist Paul Wittgenstein was among the Sunday soloists (he played Franz Schmidt's *Variations on a Theme of Beethoven*) and the season's climax was two performances of Bach's *St Matthew Passion* on 26 and 29 March 1929 with what the critic of *The Times*, who went to Birmingham for the occasion, called 'the best solo singers possible' – Dorothy Silk, Margaret Balfour, Steuart Wilson (Evangelist), and Arthur Cranmer (Christ). Boult had engaged Wanda Landowska to play the harpsichord continuo but she was ill. 'The great merit of this performance was its consistency, a quality obtainable only where orchestra and choir are permanently under the same conductor.' Boult attended Wood's concert early in the season and wrote home:

> I found Enery's concert rather stodgy ... He had (and paid for) an extra rehearsal: 8 hours in all – 5 of them on the day of the concert. I wonder the orch. weren't dead with a lunch-hour concert as well. He turned up smiling of course. I enclose Sheldon. As sniffy and qualified as if *I* had been conducting!

Another guest conductor was Beecham, in the West End Cinema. He thus could not repeat the famous remark he made when first rehearsing in Birmingham Town Hall: 'Mr Beard, what is that monstrosity facing me?' 'The organ, Sir Thomas.' 'Mr Beard, do you think it would be possible to have it *removed* before this evening's concert?'

Boult had accepted the conductorship of the Bach Choir in London. His predecessor, Vaughan Williams, who had gone to live in Dorking because of his wife's health, sent him some practical advice: 'Don't wait to start practice till everybody is ready – or you will never start at all. I always used to kick off at 5.30 sharp whoever was or wasn't there & however much row was going off at the bargain counter behind the curtain. Always insist on 2 band rehearsals. The extra rehearsal only costs about £25 which is a drop in the ocean compared with our total loss on each concert.' Boult began rehearsals in October for his first concert in December. 'I tackled the Kodály (new work) right away,' he wrote home

> and we looked through it first, playing bits, but mainly dissecting it musically and looking at its construction. (I was told afterwards that they were all saying that no one had done that with them ever before, and it was so interesting.) Then we sang right through it – solos and all, so that we could get an idea of how it was built up ... Then dinner with Dr Daymond [the Parry scholar, Emily Daymond] and as she had to go on somewhere, I went to see Steuart (Ann had gone to bed).

The concert, on 19 December, won the critics' admiration. Frank Howes wrote the notice in *The Times* (as he confessed in a letter to Boult, for notices in that paper were then unsigned) and praised the way Boult brought the LSO back to life. Besides Kodály's *Psalmus Hungaricus*, the programme included Wolf's *The Fire-Rider*, two songs with orchestra by Ernest Walker, Bach's cantata *Ich habe genug*, with Keith Falkner, his aria *Hört doch*, sung by Dorothy Silk, and his *Magnificat*. Boult's appointment was welcomed by Ernest Newman, who wrote of him as 'never having received in London the recognition that is his due.' Among the audience had been Holst who wrote to Boult a few days later from his holiday hotel in France to describe the concert as

> a real triumph and one that will have a lasting effect. You were quite right in thinking that some (not all and particularly not the end) of the *Magnificat* needed more rehearsal and I hope you'll do the work again. But the concert as a whole was something out of the ordinary and something to remember ... His [Keith Falkner's] was some of the best Bach singing I have ever heard and the 'Slumber' moved me most deeply. It was another proof that the mastering of technical problems is the highest source of emotion!

The outstanding concert in 1928 was on 19 October when Ravel visited the College and heard the orchestra under Boult play his *Daphnis et Chloé*.

Boult paid two visits to the United States in 1929. In June he attended a conference of the National Federation of Music Clubs in Boston, Mass., and saw Vincent Massey receive an honorary degree at Yale University. His second trip, in December, was with Keith Falkner. At some of Falkner's recitals Boult acted as accompanist. He spent some days of his summer holiday in 1929 on the Riviera – evidently he had not disliked it as much as he feared. He had begun 1929 by presiding at the ISM's annual conference, held that year in Buxton, and he presided at the opening dinner of the Society's summer school in New College,

Oxford, in August. He sounded a warning that has often been echoed in the succeeding half-century: 'Many people turn on the wireless as soon as they enter the house and then proceed to dress or cook, or do any little thing like that, only turning their attention to the music occasionally. This is the very worst way of teaching people, particularly children, how to concentrate. Nobody can concentrate on two or three things at once.'

Another August event was the ambitious first Canterbury Festival of music and drama. This was the brainchild of Dr George Bell, who had just become Bishop of Chichester after some years as Dean of Canterbury. In 1928 he had commissioned John Masefield's *The Coming of Christ*, with music by Holst, for Whitsuntide performances in the cathedral, which had been a huge success. He admitted that the enlarged August event was an attempt to found an 'English Salzburg' – *Everyman* was performed in the open air outside the West Door and Marlowe's *Dr Faustus* in the Chapter House. Boult was musical director and the orchestra was provided by the BBC – Bell referred to it in a letter to *The Times* as the BBC Symphony Orchestra, though this was premature. The opening concert comprised three Boult favourites, Bach's Third Brandenburg Concerto, Brahms's Third Symphony and Elgar's *Enigma Variations*. The cathedral proved too resonant for Elgar's quicker variations and the critic of *The Times* complained of only two double basses in 'GRS'. At the second evening concert Boult conducted the Grail scene from Act I of *Parsifal*, followed by Beethoven's Fifth Symphony. Then at 9 pm a serenade concert was given in the cloisters. Eric Blom's account in the *Manchester Guardian* of 22 August conveys the essence of what must have been a magical occasion:

> The graveyard in the centre lay in darkness and the listeners were seen but vaguely hovering here and there, while in one corner the small orchestra sat in a pool of light. Here and there the decorated window frames were outlined by a faint glow, and one of the west towers rose above the cloisters with a beam of light, tapering upwards into the starry sky, thrown on it by some unseen street lamp. The music came across the square so clearly and yet so discreetly that one listened ravished to the charming programme chosen and conducted by Dr Boult. The playing was delicious. Nothing could have been better than the dreamy tenderness in the two small pieces by Delius, the elegance of Hugo Wolf's *Italian Serenade* and the discreet fervour in Wagner's *Siegfried Idyll*. The other numbers were a Purcell suite arranged by Arthur Bliss, Dame Ethel Smyth's *Two Interlinked French Melodies* and Holst's *Fugal Concerto*. Curiously enough, the sounds from outside were not at all disturbing. The cathedral bells, the barking of a dog, and even the whistles

of railway engines gave the music that delightful casualness that is the charm of a serenade. They helped everyone to fancy that such night music is a matter of course in an old English town, something upon which one may stumble by a charming accident any fine evening.

Among the works Boult conducted during the festival were Vaughan Williams's *Pastoral Symphony*, Delius's *Brigg Fair* and Schumann's Fourth Symphony. His summing-up of the festival in his notebook was:

24 hours' rehearsal in previous week. The last two days' concerts were mostly familiar music, but I made a mistake over Schumann IV, which they had played 2 or 3 weeks earlier (with Frank Bridge). They rehearsed it well, early in the week, but had forgotten a good deal 10 days later and the show was bad. It is a problem making programmes for the *end* of a week's festival, so far away from rehearsal.

For his sixth Birmingham season, 1929–30, Boult introduced six free concerts in the Town Hall for schoolchildren during school hours, in addition to the children's concerts on Saturday afternoons. The main Tuesday series in the Town Hall included Schumann's Third Symphony, Dvořák's Violin Concerto (Isolde Menges), Bax's *November Woods*, Vaughan Williams's *A Pastoral Symphony*, Schumann's Piano Concerto (with Fanny Davies), a Wagner evening of extracts from *Tristan*, *Tannhäuser*, and *Götterdämmerung* with Rosina Buckman and Frank Mullings as soprano and tenor soloists, Berlioz's *The Damnation of Faust* and Bantock's *Omar Khayyám*.

But the highlight was the performance on 13 February 1930 of Mahler's *The Song of the Earth*, with Astra Desmond and Steuart Wilson as soloists. This was only its second performance in England, the first having been given under Wood in London in 1914. It led Boult for the first time to answer Sheldon in print. 'He says the tempi were frequently too slow,' Boult wrote to *The Birmingham Post* (18 February 1930).

How does he know? Has he formed a standard by comparing the renderings of various conductors? If so, his experience cannot include Mengelberg's, whose association with Mahler over his own works was probably as close as Bruno Walter's. His performance has on two occasions, to my certain knowledge, taken several minutes longer than we did on Thursday. May I also ask whether there is anything to be gained by continuous abuse of the Town Hall? We all know it to be inadequate, but I cannot feel that the reiteration of this depressing fact can have any effect other than that of keeping away potential concert-goers. This damages concert-givers without influencing to any degree those in whose hands the decision to build a new hall may rest.

Boult may have felt that he could pay off these two scores because it had been known since May 1929 that the 1929–30 season would be his last: he had been appointed the BBC's Director of Music in succession to Percy Pitt as from 1930. Just when he was approached is not known, but in a letter to his father written in the Athenaeum on 10 June 1928, he says: 'BBC – letter from Reith and Eckersley: "Some misunderstanding." Will I see Eck. alone first? Well, I suppose I must, though we've said *everything* in words of one syllable already!' What followed is material for the next chapter, but Birmingham had every right to regard it as ironical that its conductor, whose orchestra had been seriously affected by the BBC, should have been chosen to administer the policy of the 'enemy.' For there is no doubt that the BBC was regarded inimically by concert-giving societies at this time. Beecham and Harty were outspoken in their condemnation of broadcast concerts; and both Birmingham and Manchester, with established orchestras, had been in conflict with the BBC over its establishment in those cities of studio orchestras which, of necessity, included many players from the CBO and the Hallé. At the time of Boult's last season, the BBC was on the defensive, reducing its studio orchestras to small chamber groups, an octet in Birmingham and a nonet in Manchester.

At his last Town Hall orchestral concert on 27 March, the Lord Mayor and Councillor McDonald spoke in praise of Boult's six years in Birmingham. 'Entirely free from petty feelings,' a leader-writer in *The Birmingham Post* wrote, 'he has taken interest in all the musical activities in the city, and on numerous occasions has adopted the rôle of the inconspicuous listener in the auditorium instead of that of the cynosure of all eyes on the platform.' Sheldon saved his summing-up for an article on 'Music in Birmingham' in the April issue of *Monthly Musical Record*:

> He has won respect on all sides and made friends by the zest and impartiality with which he has thrown his energies into a difficult task. It would be too much to say he has caught on with the populace; on the other hand, he has made no concessions to that end. That nobody goes to the concerts to see him conduct is not against him. Nor can it be held a fault that, taking a high view of the responsibility imposed on him, he has given Birmingham what he thought it would do Birmingham good to hear. If contemporary music has been a little fitfully represented in his programmes, allowance needs to be made for financial considerations and the performing material available ... And he has worked hard as well as effectively: during six years he has conducted in Birmingham alone an average of fifty concerts every winter.

Boult said his farewell to Birmingham with two further performances of Bach's *St Matthew Passion* on 15 and 16 April. He had also conducted it in London with the Bach Choir on 5 and 6 April. The only cuts he made were the substitution of the opening *ritornello* for complete repeats *da capo*. On all these occasions Landowska played the harpsichord continuo. Her services were paid for by Boult, whose father also guaranteed £50 towards the cost of the two performances. Audiences were small, however, and the two concerts resulted in a loss and the reserve fund had to be called on. Thus did the London public respond to Bach in 1930. But the critics were more percipient. 'Devotion that had no sentimentality,' was the summing-up in *The Observer*. In *The Morning Post* Francis Toye had high praise for Falkner (the other soloists were Steuart Wilson, Arthur Cranmer, Hubert Eisdell, Dorothy Silk and Margaret Balfour) and of Boult said that to interpret the work so worthily 'argues gifts and insight of no common order.' Boult kept several letters he received after the London performances. Two are still interesting. The Hon. R.H. Lyttelton wrote as one who had heard Richter and Sullivan conduct the *Passion*:

> I remember Richter telling me that the B'ham [Festival] performance was the best he had ever heard. One point he specially mentioned was Santley's singing of the sacramental 'Take, Eat' and it was grand that Keith Falkner's was as good ... The last chorus is nearly always taken too fast but not by you last night.

From Dorking came a letter from Boult's predecessor as conductor of the Bach Choir, Vaughan Williams:

> Quite frankly I was rather dreading it because I hadn't heard it since I tried to conduct it myself – and as you know yourself, when one has lived in every note of a work one gets rather morbidly sensitive about it. But those opening bars, so beautifully slow and yet flowing, put me right for the evening and everything followed as it should. I sometimes feel rather jealous that you apparently with one wink of your eye can make those people do things that I couldn't make them do with hours of grind. The whole thing – though of course it wasn't my way – was yet a right and good way and absolutely convincing. I didn't care for the lady at the harpsichord – partly because I couldn't tell in the least what notes she was playing from my place in the hall, partly because of the unconscionable way she dragged out her cadences when everything pointed to swift action and partly because I imagine it is her fault that Steuart's interpretation is to my mind not so good as it used to be. But after all what I was there for was to hear the choir and they covered themselves with glory.

A few days later he wrote again: 'I heard the M.P. from Leipzig over the wireless on Friday. Thank God we've got the Bach Choir.'

It was after one of the two London performances that Boult had one of his most savage encounters with Ethel Smyth. 'As I remember it,' Keith Falkner wrote[1]

> the St Matthew had just ended, the six soloists and A.C.B. left the platform in dead silence. As we passed through the curtain and moved across the anteroom and on into the artists' room I heard someone following us into the room (from the stalls). I then heard Ethel's voice loudly, 'Adrian, when are you going to do *The Prison* [her recently completed choral work] with the National Chorus?'[2] or something very similar. The air became electric. Adrian turned his back but suddenly rounded on her and shouted 'Get out, how dare you speak to me like that.' E.S.: 'Adrian, I don't understand' and much disturbed went out. As she went Steuart said loudly 'Thank God that woman's got it at last ...' Adrian was full of remorse for what he had done and told me he must write a letter of apology. Later I heard from him that E.S. had sent a small piece of sponge to wipe out the whole incident.

Another witness recalls Dame Ethel's remark as 'Adrian, when are you going to do *my* Mass?' and that Boult yelled 'GET OUT!' so violently that she just turned and ran. Everyone was stunned by the episode. Boult himself left the room and sat in the orchestral seats until he had regained his composure.

After the first of the Birmingham performances Boult's friend Professor de Selincourt wrote to him: 'I do not believe that there is anyone else living in England with that rare combination of musicianship and character which enabled you to lift us out of the slough in which we were wallowing and set us on our feet ... If the orchestra has any success in the future we shall not forget that it is only you who have made it possible.' De Selincourt and his like and most musicians appreciated Boult's qualities, but Sheldon had been right in diagnosing a lack of popular appeal. Boult at this time was not what today we should call charismatic. Whatever may have constituted the general public's idea of a conductor, it was not Boult. He could not rival the characterful, avuncular popularity of Wood; he had none of Beecham's raffish charm and daredevilry; he lacked the brilliance and panache of Sargent; he had not the magnetic intensity of Barbirolli. Even his physical appearance was against him; with his baldness, his full moustache and formal dress he looked more like a country solicitor than a musician. His courteous manner seemed even then slightly old-fashioned. As a friend affectionately said of him, he was born at the age of 40.

But Sheldon was less than just to Boult's musical achievements in Birmingham. It is easy today, pontificating in a world where there are almost too many orchestras, where music surrounds us on radio, television and on compact discs, where subsidies run into millions, where pressure-groups exist for the most extreme manifestations of the *avant-garde*, to look askance at Boult's 1924–30 programmes. No Stravinsky beyond *Firebird*. No Schoenberg. The only Bartók the easy *Dance Suite*. No Hindemith. Yet in how many other European provincial cities would one have found a regular diet of these exotica? Compared with today, the 1920s in an English provincial city were a Stone Age musically. Boult's players would have been hard-pressed to play some of those scores, even if the public had been willing to listen. We too easily forget that for public – and critics – in 1924 a Brahms symphony was still an adventure. And how often would a music-loving citizen of Birmingham, Glasgow or London be likely in those days to hear Beethoven's Ninth Symphony? Boult showed courage in conducting even a Bruckner *scherzo*, and his Mahler performances fuelled the interest, slow to ignite, in this composer's music in Britain. (He conducted the CBO in the Fourth Symphony in February 1927: Harty did it in Manchester in November 1927. He conducted *The Song of the Earth* in Birmingham in February 1930: Harty followed suit in December 1930.)

Popular appeal or no, Boult was the man chosen by Sir John Reith to direct what can without exaggeration be called the nation's music, for no other post affected the musical entertainment and education of all parts of the kingdom.

PART III

At the BBC, 1929–1950

CHAPTER 17

Savoy Hill

THE British Broadcasting Company was formed in October 1922 with John Reith as general manager. Its first official broadcast was on 14 November. The broadcasting of music began almost at once in London, Birmingham, Manchester and Newcastle upon Tyne. No concert promoter would co-operate with the BBC, which was regarded as a potentially fatal competitor. But the British National Opera Company allowed its Covent Garden performances to be relayed and Reith soon invited the company's musical director, Percy Pitt, to be the BBC's part-time music adviser from May 1923. Pitt did not belong to British academic musical circles and was regarded askance in some quarters because of his interest in what was happening in European contemporary music. Seven weeks after accepting the post he conducted the first broadcast symphony concert. He expanded the eight-piece studio instrumental ensemble to an orchestra of 18, augmented to 37 on special occasions. Pitt built up the first BBC music staff. He appointed Edward Clark music director of the Newcastle station (where Clark included Mahler's Fourth Symphony in programmes), and had him as a programme planner in London from 1926. Clark had studied with Schoenberg and was entirely au fait with the continental contemporary scene. Kenneth Wright became Pitt's assistant. Also in the Music Department was Victor Hely-Hutchinson who launched an important series, 'The Foundations of Music,' which ran for a considerable period.

Reith and Pitt decided that the BBC should promote its own series of public concerts in 1924, to be broadcast from the Central Hall, Westminster. Various orchestras were engaged and the conductors, besides Pitt himself, included Elgar, Landon Ronald, Harty and Goossens. The BBC's studio orchestra in August 1924 comprised 22 players contracted for six concerts a week. It was known as the Wireless Players. Yet the deputy system spread there, too, and the personnel was fluid. In November 1925 Pitt became full-time Director of Music and augmented the Wireless Players to a Wireless Symphony Orchestra for a new series of concerts from Covent Garden which were conducted by Bruno Walter, Ansermet, and Pierre Monteux.

On 1 January 1927 the BBC became a corporation and Reith became Director-General, with a knighthood. This came in the midst of the 1926–7 season of BBC public concerts given by the Wireless Orchestra in collaboration with the Covent Garden opera orchestra. This 'National Orchestra' boasted 150 players and the series was truly international. Strauss conducted his *Alpine Symphony*, Harty the Berlioz *Requiem*, Holst his BBC commission, *The Morning of the Year*, and Siegfried Wagner a Wagner evening. Other conductors were Hermann Scherchen and Gustav Brecher. Unfortunately the playing, particularly by the strings, was poor. The BBC tried to introduce a no-deputy clause into the players' contracts but in the conditions of the time it was impossible to enforce it.

A major event in 1927 was the BBC's agreement with Sir Henry Wood to run the Promenade Concerts in Queen's Hall. A side-effect was that it gave its 1927–8 season of concerts in this hall, again co-operating with Covent Garden's orchestra. The programmes were ambitious, including the first performances in Britain of Schoenberg's *Gurrelieder* and Janáček's *Sinfonietta*. But once again the performances were deemed inadequate – 'the worst ever heard in London,' the *Musical Times* said, adding that the orchestra sounded 'as if it were composed in great part of "substitutes"' (as no doubt it was). Ernest Newman, who in 1925 had written that the LSO 'compares not unfavourably with the orchestras in some of the New York picture houses,' wrote in the *Sunday Times* of 21 August 1928 that London needed 'one first-rate orchestra.' Two concerts by the Hallé under Harty early in 1928 had given London an unwelcome example of what could be achieved by an orchestra rehearsing regularly under one conductor and not plagued by the deputy system. Even more sensational was the visit in December 1928 of the Berlin Philharmonic under Furtwängler. The marvellous sound of this orchestra convinced the BBC that it must form its own permanent orchestra. As early as February 1927 Sir Walford Davies floated the idea of making the Royal Philharmonic Society's orchestra into a permanent body in collaboration with the BBC.

Things began really to move just over a year later when Sir Landon Ronald told Roger Eckersley, BBC Director of Programmes since 1924, that Beecham was interested in forming a permanent London orchestra and was no longer an enemy of broadcasting. Beecham too talked to the Royal Philharmonic Society but did not mention the BBC. He had begun the long and tortuous game of which he was a master, of playing off one party against the other to gain his own ends. He was as devious as only he knew how to be, leaking news to the Press announcing salaries, saying the orchestra would be called the London or the Royal Philharmonic Orchestra, and scarcely ever mentioning the BBC. Eckersley was immensely pro-Beecham and put up with Sir Thomas's Macchiavellian strategy in the hope of finally hooking him. He booked the Queen's Hall for 22 Fridays for 1929–30 for an experimental season 'with a view to the establishment twelve months later of a permanent symphony orchestra ... of about 90 players selected from the best talent available.' The Press were told, but now Beecham was chasing the hare of a new concert-hall as the orchestra's home. Another complication was that the LSO, with which Beecham had been associated in recent years, recognized the threat of the proposed new orchestra and got together guarantees (with HMV) for 151 concerts a year for 75 contracted players. By 29 March Eckersley was seriously worried where the BBC would find the right players if the LSO took them first. So Albert Sammons and Lionel Tertis travelled round Britain listening to string players at auditions in the BBC's regional centres. A list of 27 players who ought to be approached without their having to attend auditions was agreed by Beecham, who took part in some final auditions. But despite Eckersley's persistence, Beecham never came up with the guarantors for his financial share in the scheme and at the beginning of 1930 all negotiations with him ceased.[1] But at least jobs had been offered to a nucleus of 27 players.

The experimental season was duly given and included part of the 1929 Delius Festival which Beecham organized as a tribute to his friend. *A Mass of Life* was performed on 1 November. Other events in the season were Bartók playing his First Piano Concerto and Wood conducting the first British performance of Mahler's Eighth Symphony and the first performance of Bax's Third.

While the 1929 negotiations with Beecham drifted inevitably towards breakdown, the BBC appointed its new Director of Music. Percy Pitt reached 60, the retiring age Reith established for BBC staff, in January 1929. It is said that he read of his forthcoming 'resignation' in the evening newspaper. Walford Davies, supported by Allen, suggested Boult as Pitt's successor and, as has been seen, this appointment was announced in the Press in May. It has to be stressed that at the time he accepted, Boult knew that Beecham was involved in the formation of the new orchestra. Reith had told him that his job was to direct the music, not to conduct it. 'If conducting now and then could be added to direction without impairing it, well and good but the direction was the principal thing ... The best musicians in the country were quite hopeless administrators,' Boult wrote in his autobiography.[2] 'My father had done pretty well in business: I knew I could do it. I realized it was my job to cope.' The idea of Boult as an office bureaucrat was not easily swallowed, however. Francis Toye, writing in the *Morning Post* on 21 January 1930, was shrewd:

> Having known Dr Boult well for the best part of twenty years, I would wager that of all men he is the least likely to be dictated to except under sheer necessity. He is a man of remarkable strength of character, in independent circumstances, with a sense of duty compared with which that of Frederic in *The Pirates of Penzance* pales into insignificance. Some people may not admire him, but everybody trusts him ... I do not think it will be far wrong, therefore, to assume that Dr Boult, in taking office, intends to direct BBC music in fact as well as in theory. At any rate the public will make such an assumption, and will be right to make it. With all my heart, I hope they are right ... The more autocratic Dr Boult is in the exercise of his executive functions, the better pleased many of us will be ...

A less reverent approach to the new appointment was taken by a pseudonymous writer in *Musical Opinion* in July 1929. 'Sinjon Wood', who had been at Oxford and the War Office with Boult, wrote:

> The BBC is in a parlous condition. All its best people are leaving it ... they're fed up, or attracted to the talkies or gramophone companies and other things. This always happens in England – the good go, the bad remain ... As is only to be expected, influence is as powerful at the BBC as elsewhere. Music is mostly run in England – serious music, I should say – by the academies, the head of whom is Sir Hugh Allen ... No one could accuse him of genius, but as an organizer and personality he is *it* ... He seems to think that no musical good can come out of England except through the academies and the universities. He likes pleasant young men with Oxford voices. So do I, if they are clever, but as a rule they are not ... The rise of Mr Boult is typical. He is a clever man and a rather good sort. No one can say he is a superman ... I welcome his appointment to the BBC in many ways ... Good luck, Adrian, and don't forget that music is not confined to the Royal College 'and similar institutions.'

Reith soon encountered the strength of character Toye had mentioned in his profile of Boult, who in the late summer of 1929 received a letter, as a member of the BBC Music Advisory Committee, informing him of a series of popular BBC concerts arranged at the People's Palace for the winter and spring. He was furious. As Director-elect of Music he should have been consulted about concerts which continued after his term of office had begun; and he was amazed to find that none of the concerts was to be conducted by Wood. He wrote to ask that his appointment should date from May 1930, when the series was over. Various BBC officials and finally Reith himself tried to make him change his mind, but he was adamant and said he would prefer to stay in Birmingham. Eventually the BBC agreed to a 15 May starting-date, paid him from 1 January and offered Wood some of the popular concerts. Commenting in his notebook on these 'rows and negotiations' with Reith, Boult wrote: 'Negotiating seems to be a game and he enjoys it for its own sake without regard to the end that is supposed to be in view.'

Boult flitted to and fro between the BBC's London headquarters at Savoy Hill and Birmingham for the first five months of 1930, during which Kenneth Wright's secretary, Mrs Gwen Beckett, worked for him too. She was to remain Boult's secretary until his death – loyal, efficient and unfailingly tactful. She recalled how, when Boult was reorganizing the Music Department, he said that 'bright ideas' often came to him in the night, so he bought a dictaphone and installed it by his bed. Next day he would take the cylinder to his office to be transcribed and Mrs Beckett would get so far, only then to hear 'So sleepy, no more now.' With the Beecham scheme on the verge of extinction, Boult had to consider a new plan for the permanent orchestra devised by Clark, Julian Herbage and Wright. This was, in fact, to have five different orchestras from the 100-odd players: the full symphony orchestra, a smaller symphony orchestra of 78 players, a theatre orchestra of 36, a light orchestra of 67 and a 'popular' orchestra of 47. In addition, he had to accept that several key players had been selected and that Percy Pitt and Cecil Graves, Assistant Controller of Programmes, had given undertakings to some members of the Wireless Orchestra that their services would be retained. He was happy enough about the principals but was adamant that some of the Wireless Orchestra players were unsatisfactory and would have to be compensated and replaced. Eckersley told Boult that he had asked Sir Hamilton Harty if he would object to the BBC's approaching members of the Hallé, 'and he told me that he would not mind our so doing.'[3]

As leader of the proposed new orchestra, the BBC had appointed Arthur Catterall in October 1929. Since resigning the Hallé leadership in 1925 he had been a freelance soloist and chamber-music player. Sub-leader was Charles Woodhouse; Bernard Shore, a friend of Boult for a decade, was principal viola, Lauri Kennedy was principal cello, Eugene Cruft was principal double bass, Aubrey Brain first horn, Ernest Hall first trumpet, Alec Whittaker principal oboe, Robert Murchie principal flute, Frederick Thurston principal clarinet, Richard Newton principal bassoon, Jesse Stamp principal trombone, Harry Barlow tuba, Charles Bender principal timpanist and Sidonie Goossens harpist.

The public was given a sample of the new orchestra during the 1930 Promenade Concerts. Only 90 of the eventual 114 players were on the Queen's Hall platform, led by Woodhouse, but the sound they made under Wood impressed the critics – 'in the nature of a glorious adventure,' the *Manchester Guardian* remarked. But two of the appointments listed above had ignited a new controversy. Whittaker and Barlow were prized members of Harty's Hallé and the BBC had also approached its principal bassoon, Archie Camden, though at Harty's urgent request it broke off the talks. (That, at any rate, is the BBC version. Camden, in his autobiography,[4] says that Harty left the decision to him and that he decided to stay with the Hallé for as long as Harty remained.) Harty, who had seemed willing to co-operate with the BBC, was now incensed. Speaking at Torquay on 30 August 1930 in his inaugural address as president of the Incorporated Society of Organists, he said it was 'morally wrong and quite indefensible for it [the BBC] to enter into direct competition with private musical interests ... With sublime self-confidence and an almost infantile disregard of the problems and difficulties involved, the BBC has now developed into a huge concert-giving concern. I contend that it has absolutely no right to do so.' He then attacked the formation of the new orchestra and the 'financial inducements' offered to members of other orchestras. 'It is no secret to anyone,' he added, 'that these amiable bandits of Savoy Hill have raided as far north as Manchester.' Other organizations, notably the LSO and Royal Philharmonic Society, attacked the BBC's concert-giving policy and alleged it was acting 'beyond the powers of its charter.' Some common sense was written in the *Manchester Guardian* of 6 September 1930 by Neville Cardus:

> We might as well get the fact into our heads once and for all that broadcast music is with us and has come to stay ... It is inconceivable that in time a craving for good music and for real performances will not be stimulated in all sorts of out-of-the-way places, and that this craving will not lead to a new lease of life for a musical profession which a few years ago had little enough to live on in this country.

It was characteristically British that one of the first matters to involve Boult as Director was a BBC wrangle on when the National Anthem should be played. He sent his views on 2 June 1930, describing it as 'a tune which can be played with overpowering effect on great occasions, but I do not feel that it is appropriate either as a nightcap or as an accompaniment to the process of fishing one's hat and coat out from under one's seat. I gather from the draft letter attached that this is not in keeping with previous decisions, and I do not want to press my point of view because I know how strongly many people feel that "God Save the King" should be played on every possible occasion.' A few days later he wrote to Elgar, seeking his opinion on the penultimate bar of the anthem. Its arrangement for BBC orchestras was:

'I see that your version gives it two semiquavers,' Boult wrote, 'and so I imagine that this is at any rate a personal preference of yours. Would you be willing, as Master of the King's Musick, to give your pronouncement that this is the right version? I am afraid I am not scholar enough to have explored the origins of the tune ... I can hardly believe that there is any justification for Adkins's[5] method of playing the first six bars pianissimo followed by a tremendous crescendo, though I understand that the King himself likes this method of performance very much. The problem seems to me insoluble ... If you prefer to leave it alone, I will, I think, do the same.' Elgar did prefer, although he consulted Sir Clive Wigram, the King's Assistant Private Secretary.

One curious story relating to Boult's early days at Savoy Hill concerns his choice of baton. He used one 21 inches in length 'because I am lazy and I like to work on a high gear: a very little work with the fingers will project the point of the stick a long distance, and I do most of my work with the fingers, and wrist and elbow do very little.'[6] He liked a well-roughened cork handle or, better still, several rubber bands wound round the handle. His final choice of baton was made from an assortment of samples brought to him at Savoy Hill by a Colonel Porteous. Boult found they were the most comfortable he had ever used. Porteous explained he had moved the natural point of balance nearer to the hand by inserting lead in the cork handles. Not until some years later, when Boult read his obituary in *The Times*, did he realize that his baton-maker was an eminent irrigation engineer who had done exceptional work in Asia Minor.[7]

CHAPTER 18

The 22nd of October 1930

NOTWITHSTANDING Reith's wish that conducting should be secondary to administration, neither he nor anyone else seems to have suggested that anyone other than Boult should conduct the new orchestra's first concert, to be given in Queen's Hall at the opening of the BBC's 1930–1 subscription series. Conductor and orchestra first met in July when the Central Hall, Westminster, was hired for a week of rehearsals. Reith welcomed the players before the first rehearsal and Boult then conducted Wagner's overture to *The Flying Dutchman*, which was played at sight. As he said nearly forty years later:[1]

> I'm sorry to say that at the end of that performance I was very forcibly reminded of a very bad dream that I had since I was a very young man, and that was that I should suddenly get a wonderful chance of conducting one of the greatest orchestras in the world. And I should stand up and play the first piece for rehearsal and it would be so perfect that there would be nothing I could say at all, and I should have to own myself a really incompetent person compared with the orchestra I was supposed to be conducting! Well, we did find a few things to rehearse afterwards, but I must say I was very much impressed by the striking power of that opening performance.

It can be assumed, too, that the orchestra was very impressed by Boult. Some of them – Bernard Shore, Ernest Hall, Marie Wilson (violin), Eugene Cruft and Frederick Thurston – knew his methods already from RCM or other occasions, but to the majority he was an unknown quantity. So he was too to the London public. He had not conducted a major concert in London, apart recently from the Bach Choir, for seven years. He had never taken the CBO to London as Harty did the Hallé. Out of sight, out of mind is never so true as when applied to the concert-going public of the metropolis. Luckily one of his players in the 1930 orchestra was not only a close observer but a talented writer, so we owe to Bernard Shore a factual impression of Boult at work. From the first

144

desk of violas Shore watched and compared many conductors and published his observations in the still unique *The Orchestra Speaks*.[2] His account of Boult is authoritative. 'Listen, for instance,' he wrote, 'to the *Flying Dutchman* overture under his direction. At those moments marked by Wagner for special fury, the winds scream with far more violence than is felt if the utmost is made of the top of every chromatic scale.' Shore quotes Boult's remarks at rehearsal with a vividness that brings him before our eyes and the sound of his voice back to our ears:

Take out all those slurs in the Bach! It is only one of those infernal editors again – there is no trace of anything of the sort in the original ... How on earth can you expect the clarinet to play his tune decently when you are lumbering along underneath like that? For goodness' sake, listen! Keep alive! ... No, no! It all sounds dead. Do swing the rhythm over from the end of each second bar to the third, and so on ... Horns, I don't want you to spoil your lip now, but give everything you've got tonight. You see that the trombones don't support you at that point. You must carry the weight of the whole orchestra yourselves ... Wind, those chords on the off-beat were all over the place. They must be on time to fit the violin octaves. Strings, at the opening of the *allegro* you simply sat on those dotted minims and then bumped your last crotchet of each phrase. Think of the time in two-bar groups, with perhaps the slightest push at the beginning of each alternate bar. Basses, be careful too of your Cs. Don't make them all alike. Then the great crescendo never really grew at all. You had used everything up before you got to the *ff*, which was a very poor affair. And I want still more power five bars later ... And at the *sempre ff*, five bars later, all you're worth!

The famous temper would flare out occasionally. Marie Wilson first encountered it at the RCM when (unjustly as it happened) Boult accused her of talking at the back desk of the First Orchestra: 'You! ... No, you! *Out.*' Some of his remarks were often quoted by players: 'What's the matter – don't you like it?' (To the player who complained to him that he did not like the piece they were rehearsing he replied, stroking his moustache, 'You might like it better if you could play it better'). 'Only taxi-drivers smoke at work.' 'What have I just said?' (to an inattentive player).[3] Boult expected his players to use their understanding in the performance of music; he expected them to give of their best. 'Every movement he makes is controlled,' Shore wrote. 'He relies almost entirely on the stick itself, which often follows the line of the phrase in a curve and rises just a fraction before the bar-line to make clear the swing. His left hand is used sparingly and never unnecessarily. In *pianissimo* his stick scarcely moves at all, and it has then to be very carefully watched by those who are some distance away. For the really great moments his right hand will go back behind his body with an extra effort, but only at the top of a climax.' Colin Bradbury pointed out that 'the beat, especially at rehearsals, is terrifyingly vague on first acquaintance; one end of the enormous stick remains stationary, whilst the other swishes through a two-foot arc, always a little ahead of the players ... the stick flows as the music flows, rhythmically.' He could give players unexpected practical advice. For instance, a cymbals player, uncertain how to manage the *pianissimo* stroke at the end of Debussy's *Fêtes*, was surprised when Boult showed him just how to do it, by having the cymbals touching and taking them apart just at the fleeting moment.

Another candid and vivid view of Boult on the rostrum is given by Audrey Napier-Smith, a violinist and violist, who played under him at the RCM and then many years later when he conducted the Hallé in the 1960s and 1970s:

Although he grew older and (in his own words) more 'tetchy' he changed very little. I always enjoyed the rehearsals far more than his concerts, as they were a real joy to me (at that time) as a back-desk player. First, he had a big, resonant voice, speaking intelligent, musical and instructive things – and one could *hear* (not very usual, this, at the back!). Then, his psychology was perfect: he treated us all as though we were excellent, responsible human beings, doing (of course!!) our musical utmost. Then, of course, you just can't let him down! He also had a delightful way of putting things (his English was most full in vocabulary). He asked once: 'Brass! Do you crouch before the final spring?' His concerts I didn't enjoy so much, not because they were not excellent always (though not always very thrilling) but because he had this theory – from Nikisch? – that orchestras should play like giant string quartets and listen to each other, and the beat should be at a minimum – almost a token beat. He didn't play, ever, in an orchestra, I believe, and didn't realize that the 'fringes' can *never* play like a quartet as they can't hear much of the solo wind, or the leading violin or cello solos, and the music as a whole never comes over in proper balance as it does to the conductor. Boult's beat used to 'flap' at us, in an amiable sort of way, but gave no feeling of confidence. I used to sit on the edge of my chair and live on a knife-edge. It took so much from the enjoyment. None of the people in the centre of the orchestra felt this, of course.

Some players in the BBC Symphony Orchestra and later in the London Philharmonic felt that Boult had a touch of the amateur about him compared with the superb professional musicianship of a conductor like Frank Bridge, who was also an excellent pianist, violinist and violist in addition to being a composer. In particular they thought he knew too little about the strings and noticed that sometimes he had to be told by the leader when they were not together. An orchestral violinist remembers a rehearsal when a celebrated soloist showed all too clearly by the expression on his face what he thought of the playing during the long *tutti* at the start of Beethoven's Violin Concerto. Boult stopped the orchestra and asked, 'Is anything the matter?' to which the reply was: 'Can't you hear it – they're not together – can't you hear?'

The first visitor to the rehearsals of the BBC Symphony Orchestra was Holst. Later he took along his students from St Paul's Girls' School, to whom Mrs Beckett issued passes. He formed what he called his BMB Club 'to deal with these urgent matters.' He told Boult 'BMB of course stands for Bother Mrs Beckett which the members of the club pledge themselves to do when in difficulty.'

Before the first concert a pleasant occasion awaited Boult. On 13 October Birmingham University conferred on him the honorary degree of Doctor of Laws, with Lady Astor, Philip Noel Baker, Sir Henry Hadow and Professor Robert Robinson, among others. Two congratulatory letters gave him pleasure. Reith wrote: 'I know it has no connection with your present post, but it is none the less a matter of great gratification to us.' From Hugh Allen came: 'I salute thee, Honourable and thee Honoured Doctor of Laws! I can think of no degree or faculty more likely to be of use in the unruly life you are at present forced to live.' Although entitled to Dr Boult ever since his Oxford degree, Boult disliked and discouraged it as a form of address, but from 1930 onwards the Press made him Dr Boult instead of Mr and he became Dr Adrian Boult on printed programmes.

As often happens, two important events coincided on 22 October 1930. The BBC Symphony Orchestra gave its official first concert and at the Norwich Festival Arthur Bliss's *Morning Heroes* had its first performance. Boult and Bliss had lunched together in mid-September. 'Funny that his great day and mine should both be Oct. 22,' Boult noted afterwards.

> He was very interesting about the staging of my show. Taking up my remark that I felt I had such a far higher standard than that of Birmingham to work for now with this marvellous orchestra, he stressed the behaviour of American conductors, who see no one on days when they conduct, who consider no one ('you walk past a music stand and knock it over without noticing') – of course they do it in a theatrical way which isn't necessary. One can be oneself at rehearsals, but a ruthless egotist at the performance.

Telegrams of good wishes poured into Queen's Hall on the day of the concert, including one from the City of Birmingham Orchestra and from his successor as its conductor, Leslie Heward. Among his other colleagues who wished him well were Sargent, Wood, Ronald, Warwick Braithwaite, Joseph Lewis and Stanford Robinson. The programme opened with Boult's arrangement of the National Anthem. There followed:

Overture, *The Flying Dutchman*.........Wagner

Cello Concerto in A minor.........Saint-Saëns

Symphony No. 4 in E minor.........Brahms

Suite No. 2, *Daphnis and Chloë*.........Ravel

Soloist.........Guilhermina Suggia

The hall was full. It was, Boult believed, the first time an English orchestra wore white ties and white waistcoats. A coloured postcard of Augustus John's portrait of Suggia was given with every programme and the evening was a major success. All the high hopes for the orchestra were realized. The critics next day and at the weekend were unanimous and almost lyrical in their praise for players and conductor. 'It was a welcome sight to see every bow in each section of the strings moving as one, and the resulting tone was more than welcome to the ear. The precision of the wind-band was no less admirable, and the tone of the brass magnificent. The virtuosity of the orchestra [in the Ravel] ... wiped out any reproach Englishmen may feel in the face of visiting orchestras from abroad. But the highest achievement of the evening was in Brahms's Symphony in E minor' (*The Times*). 'At last! In the very sonority of "God Save the King" ... we felt that London now possessed the material of a first-class orchestra. And as the evening proceeded the feeling became a certainty ... There can be no doubt at all that last night at the Queen's Hall we had, from the technical point of view, the best English orchestral playing heard since the war ... Boult's whole performance entitles him to rank definitely as one of the conductors who really matter' (*Morning Post*). 'In [Brahms] it was made evident that a fine conductor and sensitive musician has returned to London. There is nothing new to chronicle about his reading of the E minor. It was orderly, details thought out and properly placed, nothing unduly prominent, always a sense of sensuous thrill and sway to call on (or not to call on, as was sometimes felt). It was the reading of one who seemed to know so much about Brahms's music as to be aware that one could

never know enough of the surprising experience to be found therein ...'
(*The Observer*). Curiously, the only critic to suggest outright that Boult
should *not* continue as conductor was *The Birmingham Mail*'s. 'An
instrument of such capabilities ... ought certainly to be placed in the
hands of our most dynamic and accomplished conductor,' he wrote. He
meant Sir Henry Wood, he explained, and failing him Sir Landon
Ronald. On the other hand Ursula Greville writing in *The Sackbut*, the
magazine once edited by Philip Heseltine, said: 'If a great conductor is
a person who reveals hidden beauties in well-known works, who never
gets between you and the music, whose conception of a work is not of
a point-to-point race but of a carry through, knowing the perfect
moment for a climax, and having the ability to get it from his orchestra,
then I should say Adrian Boult was that much abused word – great.'

But what did Boult himself think about what may possibly be regarded
as the most important night of his life? The notebook carries the entry:

22 October 1930: BBC first concert – four rehearsals. I took the course of
letting *nothing* pass, with the result that there wasn't enough time for
rehearsal! The show was much admired; though I was bothered in that
the essential difference between rehearsal and performance which we all
understood so well in B'ham was not so evident here. The performance did
not glow so much in comparison to rehearsal and I felt the Brahms E minor
very nearly failed in its climax because they didn't spring to the beat.

Much admired it certainly was, as the congratulatory letters from
colleagues and old friends show. Reading them after over half a century
has passed, one can recapture the sense of excitement over something
new and special that elated those who were in Queen's Hall and those
who listened to the broadcast. Lawrence Tanner, oldest of friends,
wrote: 'I thought of many things last night and among others of a small
boy called A.B. who, somewhere about 1904–5, dreamed a dream at a
Sunday concert that one day, perhaps, he too might stand where Sir
'Enery stood and conduct the finest orchestra in England to an audience
crammed from floor to ceiling almost (but alas! not quite!) too thrilled
to cough.' From Robin Barrington-Ward: 'Adele and I purred in the
warmth of the observations round us last night. "A very fine band –
and a very fine conductor, too!" said the connoisseur next me. I am no
expert, as you know, but my personal opinion is that you gave us the
best orchestral playing I have heard in London.' From St Paul's Girls'
School just 'Congratulations from Gustav'; and from Ann Wilson, 'Oh,
bravo, what a tip-top evening. I would not have been in Norwich for
all the Arthur Blisses – I shall never forget that *exquisite* opening to

Daphnis and Chloë to mention only one small part. Continuez mes enfants!' Boult's father wrote:

> You have won a very wonderful position for yourself and I congratulate you very deeply about it. You have worked hard for it and deserve every bit of it. Some of your success you owe to dear Mum's training which I could never have given you and some of it you owe to your brains which God gave you, but most of it you owe to your own good sense, hard work and straight-forward honesty, which has impressed everybody you have come in contact with. You have won a position which might turn anyone's head, but I know well that it won't affect yours. Altogether I cannot tell you how pleased I am. Goodbye, dear boy, much love, your Father.

Two other letters made significant points. That from Percy Cater contained advice Boult would always find it difficult to take: 'Now you must grasp all the opportunities to come into the limelight. You know your job – now you have got to collect your following – you have one, of course, but I mean what is generally called the "box office" crowd. Beecham has it, Henry J., Ronald and Gene [Goossens]. You have got to get it. I know it's distasteful to you but it's the way of the world.' Sir Landon Ronald was characteristically outspoken and evidently felt the critics' notices had been muted: 'You are a great conductor and need have no fear of any rivals ... Your demeanour on the platform was a special delight to me, who has fought all my life to avoid any idea of *showmanship* ... The orchestra is a fine one, particularly the strings, but I found definite weaknesses in the woodwind and one or two of the brass. I am referring to solo playing and not the ensemble. But the *quality* of the woodwind cannot be compared with that of the strings. I have just read *The Times* with great pleasure, but I think the rest of the criticisms which I have seen in other papers is beneath contempt ... I prophesy that it is only a matter of time for you to become one of the great conductors of the world. I hope I may live to see this ...'

On the following evening in Queen's Hall, Beecham opened the Royal Philharmonic Society's season with a Mozart programme. *The Times* said this was performed 'to the satisfaction even of those who have been loudest in their condemnation of the engagement ad hoc of orchestral players. There was a certain piquancy in the fact that Sir Thomas Beecham was the chosen man to demonstrate the possibility of making good music without the aid of a permanent establishment ... If the BBC Orchestra goes on as it has begun, we may yet see the permanent organizations increasing and multiplying to meet whatever coincidences of London concerts and provincial festivals may occur.' The writer of

Adrian aged two and a half

Olive, Adrian's sister, aged nearly three

Adrian's mother, Katherine Florence Boult

Adrian aged 12 with the family pet

Adrian as a Westminster schoolboy

In 1904, aged 16

At Oxford, 1911

In the Army, 1915

A cartoon of Arthur Nikisch

Boult with Hilda Gammon and Ralph Vaughan Williams, godparents at the christening of Richard, son of Steuart and Ann Wilson, in Worcester, 1925

Boult with his father Cedric at a shoot

Kapp's drawing of Boult

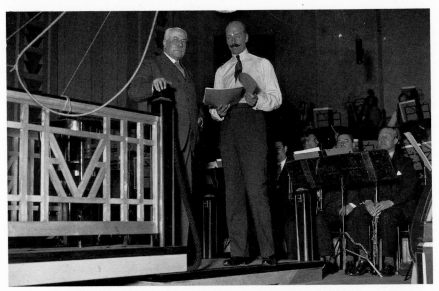

With Sir Edward Elgar at the HMV studio in May 1932 during the recording of Elgar's transcription of Chopin's Funeral March

At a fête to celebrate the award of the OM to Vaughan Williams, 1935

Boult in Coronation Year, 1937

Rehearsing the BBC Symphony Orchestra, 1934

Ann Boult at Northlands, 1938

A shot from 'The Conductor Speaks',
BBC television 1939

this article, H. C. Colles, was also concerned about the effect on the BBC orchestra, in its first season of 23 concerts, of playing under seven conductors. 'We must hope that the other six will handle it with the discretion which Mr Adrian Boult has shown at the outset.' The orchestra's second and third concerts, both conducted by Boult on 29 October and 5 November, won praise as high as its first. Arthur Rubinstein played Tchaikovsky's B flat minor Piano Concerto at the second concert and Boult conducted Strauss's *Don Juan* and Beethoven's Eighth Symphony among other works. On 5 November Adolf Busch was soloist in Beethoven's Violin Concerto and, after the interval, the first English music to be performed by the new orchestra was Vaughan Williams's *A Sea Symphony*, with Dorothy Silk, Roy Henderson and the Philharmonic Choir. Robin Legge, in the *Daily Telegraph*, wrote of 'the tremendous beauty' of the work and 'this truly magnificent presentation of it.' The composer wrote from Dorking: 'That was splendid. I thank you over and over again. *Some* orchestra and the chorus fine.' Vaughan Williams's wife Adeline wrote to a friend: 'Adrian Boult must be overworking, he is nothing but a black streak in a white waistcoat – alarming – he is making a wonderful orchestra.'⁴

A modification of the Clark–Herbage section plan for the orchestra now took effect. Joseph Lewis, who had come to Savoy Hill from the Midland Region in Birmingham, conducted light concerts, Stanford Robinson choral works, and chamber-orchestral works were directed by Percy Pitt and others. On Sunday evenings there was a studio concert given before an 'invited audience' in 'Studio 10,' a disused, rat-infested, smelly but acoustically excellent warehouse in Commercial Road in the East End. 'Here,' Nicholas Kenyon wrote,⁵ 'in these makeshift surroundings, many of the orchestra's most memorable early experiences occurred – in which it was visited and conducted by Schoenberg and Webern, Stravinsky, Richard Strauss and Bruno Walter.' At one of the first studio concerts in November 1930, Percy Pitt conducted a concert performance of Debussy's *Pelléas et Mélisande*, with Maggie Teyte, and Sir George Henschel, Casals and Albert Coates were guest conductors. Schoenberg conducted *Erwartung*, Vaughan Williams his *Job*, and Webern conducted more Schoenberg.

Of the remaining Queen's Hall concerts of the first season, Wood conducted five and Ronald one; Hermann Scherchen conducted the first British performance of Schoenberg's *Pelleas und Melisande*, and Beethoven's *Missa Solemnis*; Ansermet had three concerts, the last of which was all-Stravinsky, with the composer as soloist in his Piano Concerto (Stravinsky conducted a studio concert). In Boult's two further series of concerts in this season the works he conducted included Bax's *November Woods*, Holst's *The Planets*, Brahms's D minor Piano Concerto (soloist Dohnányi) and the B flat (soloist Gieseking), Dvořák's Cello Concerto (Suggia), Elgar's Violin Concerto (Sammons) and Second Symphony, and Mahler's *Lieder eines fahrenden Gesellen* (Maria Olcszewska). The London première of Bliss's *Morning Heroes* was conducted by the composer who asked Boult specially to let him conduct it because of its deep personal significance (it is dedicated to Bliss's brother, killed in action). Boult's return to the rostrum in February led *The Times* to remark that he 'recalled the players to certain first principles of ensemble playing which have rather been lost sight of in recent programmes given under visiting conductors from abroad.' Colles also singled out for praise Boult's awareness of style. He taught the orchestra precise characterization for the performance of 18th-, 19th- and 20th-century music and to differentiate between German, French, Italian and British styles of composition. Boult was so often praised for his 'architectural' approach to a work that it is a surprise to find Edwin Evans in *Time and Tide* of 8 November 1930, complaining that he gave 'practically all his attention to phrasing and tone. He moulds every inflection with loving care ... But in doing so he sacrifices a great deal of the virtue that resides in impulse ... one has the impression that the orchestra is being trained in the "prunes and prisms" of musical speech.' That idiosyncratic critic W. J. Turner, in the *New Statesman*, was bowled over by Boult's conducting of the *Eroica*:

> ... the best I have ever heard of a Beethoven symphony under an English conductor ... The BBC's expensive and carefully selected orchestra can play very erratically ... when I say that it plays better under Mr Boult than under any other of its conductors the credit must be given wholly to him ... Mr Boult is a strange figure; under a catholicity of taste which might have hidden a complete lack of real judgment there is apparently a very solid and definite musical character, for performances such as these cannot come by inspiration or accident during the concert.

CHAPTER 19

Double Harness

W. J. TURNER's opinion that the BBC Symphony Orchestra played its best under Boult was widely shared and, in particular, by the man who mattered most, Sir John Reith. Towards the end of the first season Reith sent for Boult and said: 'Now look here, everyone tells me the orchestra plays better for you than for anyone else. Will you become the permanent conductor? And do you want to remain Director of Music? I must warn you that if you opt for conducting only you must, of course, be on the staff of the Director and not in any way independent of him.' Boult elected to undertake both jobs. 'It now seems an outrageous proposition,' he wrote in his autobiography,[1] 'and I was immersed often in a seven-day week, and administrative decisions had to go down the telephone in the short intervals of long rehearsals ... The thing would have been impossible without the most efficient and loyal staff.'

In the summer of 1931, at Oxford, at the invitation of Clark and Wright, the International Society for Contemporary Music held its festival in England for the first time. Fifty-one of the orchestra's players gave a concert, repeated in the studio, of works by Halffter, Wellesz and others; at the Queen's Hall, music by Webern, Berg, Lambert, Gershwin, Vaughan Williams, Szymanowski, Roussel, Vogel and some composers whose names no longer mean anything was played at two concerts. Boult helped to choose the ISCM works with Berg, Koechlin, Alfredo Casella and Gregor Fitelberg. The orchestra again played at the Canterbury Festival and on 16 September and 2 and 12 October Boult returned to Covent Garden to conduct *The Valkyrie* (sung in English). Wotan was sung by Horace Stevens, Siegmund by Francis Russell, Sieglinde by Josephine Wray (by Odette de Foras at the third performance), Hunding by Norman Allin and Brünnhilde by Monica Warner. One of the performances was broadcast and was heard at Ayot St Lawrence by Bernard Shaw who wrote to Boult:

Blessings on you! I have at last heard 'Nicht weis' ich dir mehr Helden zur Wahl'[2] properly conducted, and consequently properly sung, after hearing one wretched Wotan after another whacked through it as if he were the Count di Luna trumpeting 'Per me ora fatale'. And at Covent Garden too! What is the world coming to? Also 'Der Augen leuchtendes Paar'[3] taken at the right time. And the band not a mob but a concert. Don't trouble to acknowledge this. I thought I'd send it because people who know the difference ought occasionally to say so as a sort of tuning note.

Alas, not enough others knew the difference to invite Boult to conduct more opera. In 1932 Covent Garden, having broken off its association with the BBC, persuaded Beecham to return to conduct a four-week Wagner season and from 1933 to 1939 he directed the theatre's fortunes, using his own London Philharmonic Orchestra in the pit. Boult never again conducted opera at Covent Garden. In his old age he declared: 'Beecham kept me out of the opera house,' and his attitude to Beecham was more fully expressed in a letter written in 1976:

> Somehow I used to find him absolutely repulsive both as man and musician, and his treatment of people I knew – Willie Reed and Geoffrey Toye particularly – so absolutely beastly that his complete neglect of me didn't seem to matter a bit. Fate evidently meant me to stay out of the opera house which I might have enjoyed a good deal, but if fate preferred me to sit in a BBC office for some years, so be it – there are worse things in life.[4]

Of the BBC Symphony Orchestra's second public season of 22 programmes at Queen's Hall, beginning in October 1931, Boult conducted 13. Guest conductors were Strauss, Stravinsky, Ansermet, Nicolai Malko, Wood, Weingartner and Walter. Boult's contributions included Schoenberg's *Five Orchestral Pieces* (played, Constant Lambert wrote, 'with a touch of the embarrassment and circumspection shown by a really polite Protestant who has found himself involved in a religious ceremony of some totally differing creed'), the London première of Walton's *Belshazzar's Feast* a few weeks after its first performance at Leeds, Holst's *Hammersmith*, Bax's *Winter Legends* and Bliss's revised *Colour Symphony*.

One can quite see from this list how the label British-music-Boult came to be hung round his neck, but his repertoire was wider than that. The performance that season with Albert Sammons and Lionel Tertis of Mozart's Sinfonia Concertante for violin and viola (K.364) was remembered for years. And the critic Felix Aprahamian is quoted by Kenyon[5] as saying that he was so overwhelmed by the concert performance of Act III of *Siegfried* conducted by Boult on 20 January 1932, that he could not recall how he reached his home afterwards. In preparation Boult had called an extra three-hour rehearsal for the strings. As he related it later,[6] 'I forget what the word is when you're jumping a horse over a fence, but I put them at the most difficult passages I could find in that act and they read them practically impeccably straightaway. Our rehearsal was finished in about an hour, because they were ready for their association with the wind and ready for the next stage. There was no need to work at all those passages.'

In a Friday evening studio concert on 13 November 1931, Boult conducted Schoenberg's *Verklärte Nacht* and followed it with the first British performance of the *Variations*, which had had their first performance under Furtwängler in Berlin in 1928. In a letter,[7] Schoenberg thanked Boult for a 'remarkably beautiful, clear and vital performance.' Boult's stance was that he could not 'enjoy' the *Variations*, 'but I did admire their craft, and myself found a craftsman's pleasure in seeing that his H.S. and N.S. (*Hauptstimme* and *Nebenstimme*, chief subject and subsidiary strand) were faithfully observed, serving as they did as a check on the dynamic signs in the score, which he placed so wisely that they almost always tallied perfectly.'[8]

Among English conductors of the day, perhaps only Wood besides Boult would have been willing to conduct so many works simply because they were regarded as important and therefore ought to be performed, irrespective of the conductor's personal predilections. This was one area in which the BBC had made an ideal choice in Boult. He felt it his duty to present a wide conspectus of music and though the BBC always tried to engage a specialist (Ansermet for Stravinsky, for example), if one was not available, Boult would step in. He had 'a very small black list' of composers he would not conduct, but it would be difficult to deduce which they were. Also he was as happy in the studio as at public concerts. 'I was far more comfortably dressed,' he wrote,[9] 'and the red light seemed to give me the same stimulus that one gets from an audience. Perhaps I am deceiving myself. I certainly admit that when we went to halls in foreign capitals, the general tension and excitement left me with a more vivid memory than most concerts in the studio.' Boult was unusual, too, in being willing to cede the rostrum to foreign conductors whom he thought would be of benefit to the orchestra's standards of playing and interpretation – Weingartner, Walter and Koussevitzky among them (although he had to be persuaded by Edward Clark that the last-named would be a good idea). It is equally true that the visitors benefited from the sound training in fundamental principles instilled into the orchestra by Boult. Most of the players admired his methods but a few, according to Bernard Shore,[10] found him dull. 'We never admired him in Delius,' Shore said, but a performance of *Brigg Fair* broadcast on 21 February 1932 brought a letter from the composer at Grez-sur-Loing to say he had 'never heard a better.' Beecham's first engagement with the orchestra was three months later, on 20 May, when he conducted a studio performance of the opera *A Village Romeo and Juliet*. Boult also championed his own enthusiasms among composers off the beaten track – Busoni, for example, whose *Comedy Overture*, Violin Concerto and *Turandot* Suite were performed in the studio on 22 January 1932.

A critical and intensely musical ear was being turned to the early BBC Symphony Orchestra concerts by a schoolboy who was a month short of his seventeenth birthday when the orchestra gave its first concert. The boy's name was Benjamin Britten. Like Boult when he was a Westminster schoolboy in the early 1900s, Britten kept a diary in which he recorded his opinions of the concerts he heard and attended. Where Boult was concerned, Britten was a prejudiced listener, for, out of a natural loyalty to his teacher, he had hoped that Frank Bridge would be appointed chief conductor of the BBC Symphony Orchestra – as Bridge himself had hoped, and possibly we hear Bridge's views in Britten's diary entries. Until not long before he died, Britten resented the fact that Bridge had been passed over and asked Bernard Shore what the orchestra's opinion of him had been. Shore said that from a technical standpoint Bridge had unrivalled qualifications but he would never have been appointed because of the 'big chip on his shoulder.' Britten, by then wise in the ways of the world where such appointments were concerned, said emphatically: 'Oh, I *see*!' In the musical climate of the time, Bridge, a former professional viola player in orchestras and string quartets, was *persona non grata* as far as the BBC and RCM hierarchies were concerned. Another British conductor with a similar background, Barbirolli, was not offered a BBC engagement with the main Symphony Orchestra between 1930 and 1936, the year in which New York invited him to follow Toscanini! Bridge's 'chip' was his contempt for what he regarded as the amateurish and parochial attitudes and standards pertaining in the British musical establishment as represented at the RCM by Vaughan Williams, Allen and others. He saw the same attitudes and 'musical politics' in the hierarchy of the BBC and he was therefore not surprised, but nonetheless resentful, that a 'safe' choice like Boult should be preferred to him for the conductor's post.

Britten went to the BBC Symphony Orchestra's second concert on 29 October 1930. He recorded in his diary: 'Go to BBC Symphony concert with Mrs Bridge in evening. The orchestra is most magnificent material;

but I dislike Boult; he doesn't play a stringed instrument & you can tell it by listening to the strings.' On 4 February 1931 the complaint against 'beastly' Boult was that he 'played about' with Schumann's Fourth Symphony, but the *St Matthew Passion* on 22 March was 'a very good performance on the whole, & very moving. Keith Falkner and St. Wilson were great and Dorothy Silk also.' But the 1931–2 season – the first with Boult officially the chief conductor – found Britten, now approaching eighteen, in vitriolic form. He went to the Queen's Hall with Mrs Bridge on 14 October 1931: '... Adrian Boult – muck! Brandenburg Conc. no. 3 – heavily played – tone wonderful. Ensemble of Beethoven Symph. 4 bad, other wise moderate – not sparkling enough ...' On 4 November: 'BBC concert ... Adrian Boult (*terrible, execrable* conductor) leads the show. Elgar Intro. & All° – nice spots but terrible ...' A performance of Beethoven's Seventh Symphony soon after was 'dull & unscholastic (especially in treatment of grace notes in 2nd mov.) ... Orch as before – material marvellous – but badly trained in ensemble & everything by that worst of all conductors (?) Adrian Boult.' Then a broadcast of Beethoven's Ninth Symphony on 4 May 1932 was 'uninspired ... Some instrumental parts played v. well; but on whole v. ragged considering amt. of rehearsal. Boult is beginning to fool abt. with things – he has dropped his so-called "letting the music speak for itself." ' Within five years, Britten would have heard one of his major early works given its first London performance – conducted by Boult.

Boult did not choose the BBC programmes, but he fully supported the enterprising policy of Edward Clark and Julian Herbage. He always insisted on approving their programmes before they went to *Radio Times*. Clark was usually late supplying his and whenever he included Scriabin Boult deleted it – he said it was 'evil music' and he would never conduct it. The programmes soon encountered severe criticism for their championship of new music. Yet the gloomy prophecies that the existence of the orchestra would be detrimental to established organizations were soon falsified. The LSO, after being let down by Beecham and Sargent and losing its agent and promoter Lionel Powell, who died in 1931, engaged Sir Hamilton Harty as conductor of its main series of concerts. Meanwhile Beecham still pursued his idea of a new orchestra. In the summer of 1932 he assembled players from his Covent Garden opera season, 'poached' some from the LSO, arranged a recording contract with Columbia and formed the London Philharmonic Orchestra, backed financially by Samuel Courtauld and Robert Mayer. The Royal Philharmonic Society engaged it for its winter series of concerts (its own ad hoc orchestra now ceased to exist) and so did the Courtauld–Sargent concerts organization. The LPO gave its first performance in Queen's Hall on 7 October 1932 and at once proved itself a formidable challenge to the supremacy of the BBC orchestra. The principal work in its first concert was Strauss's *Ein Heldenleben*, a Beecham speciality. Of the performance of Berlioz's *Carnaval Romain*, Ernest Newman wrote in the *Sunday Times*: 'Nothing so electrifying has been heard in a London concert room for years. The tone was magnificent, the precision perfect, the reading a miracle of fire and beauty.' Cardus, writing in the *Manchester Guardian*, called the LPO 'the best in the land, because it enjoys both a great conductor and a liberal amount of rehearsal.' The BBC Symphony Orchestra, he said, was a 'beautiful music machine ... usually wasted for want of a great conductor.'

Savoy Hill closed in May 1932 when the BBC moved to Broadcasting House in Portland Place. The music department was on the fifth floor (though it moved within four years to Marylebone High Street) but the Concert Hall in the new building was too small for a 119-piece orchestra, so Studio 10 remained in constant use. Of the 1932–3 Queen's Hall concerts, Boult conducted 12 (and another 34 in the studio). Wood conducted the season's major première, Hindemith's *Das Unaufhörliche* ('The Perpetual'), and Schoenberg conducted his *Variations*. Boult's principal new offering was the first performance on 1 February 1933 of Vaughan Williams's Piano Concerto, with Harriet Cohen. 'You have made impossible the composer's time-honoured excuse that the work would have sounded all right if it had been properly played,' Vaughan Williams wrote to Boult. 'I could not have imagined a better performance.' Nevertheless the work was not a success.

The emotional core of the 1932–3 season was the three-concert celebration, in Queen's Hall on 30 November, 7 and 14 December 1932, for Elgar's 75th birthday, which had fallen the previous June. With the healing of the breach between them in April 1931, Boult at once involved Elgar in the planning of what amounted to a festival. Already in 1931 he had conducted the Second Symphony, the *Variations* and the Violin Concerto and Stanford Robinson had conducted *The Dream of Gerontius*. Then, in February 1932, at Fred Gaisberg's suggestion, Boult invited Elgar to orchestrate Chopin's Funeral March especially for a gramophone recording by the BBC Symphony Orchestra, which was made on 30 May. At the three birthday concerts, Elgar conducted *Cockaigne*, the Violin Concerto (soloist Sammons) and the Second Symphony, Ronald conducted the First Symphony and Boult conducted the *Enigma Variations*, the *Introduction and Allegro* and *The Kingdom*.

At the final *Kingdom* rehearsal, Elgar twice said to Boult: 'Don't let them go away, Adrian. I want to come and speak to them when you have finished.' He went on to the platform and 'gave a most charming speech of thanks to them for their support and friendship all his life.'[11] To a formal letter of thanks to Boult, Elgar added an informal final paragraph: 'To you, my dear Adrian, I will say that the renewal of the atmosphere of the Second Symphony at the People's Palace under your direction [1 December 1921] was one of the happiest events of my life and I thank you ... I am your affectionate friend.' On the night of the final concert the BBC announced that it had commissioned a Third Symphony from Elgar. This was at the instigation of Bernard Shaw and Landon Ronald. The first performance was scheduled for the autumn of 1933, but Elgar put it off until May 1934. By then he was dead and the symphony consisted only of a handful of disjointed sketches, beyond hope of completion.

On 1 December 1932 Boult substituted for Donald Tovey at a Reid concert in Edinburgh University. The programme (which was broadcast) was a Haydn symphony, Walton's Viola Concerto, with Lionel Tertis, and Glazunov's *Scènes de Ballet*. The audience received the concerto frigidly, so Boult told them he would repeat it in place of the Glazunov! Tovey wrote to him two days later: 'I should like to think that I might have had the gumption to do it if I had been there ... I hope the audience took it well the second time.'

In March 1933 Boult went to Vienna as guest conductor of the Vienna Philharmonic Orchestra, his first encounter with that august and volatile body. (He had once been told by Egon Wellesz that 'any conductor who doesn't disturb the Vienna Philharmonic gets on quite well with them.') It was still led by Arnold Rosé, Mahler's brother-in-law (the celebrated Rosé Quartet was the solo string quartet in the performance of Elgar's *Introduction and Allegro* with which Boult began the first of his two concerts on 2 March). Rehearsing Mozart's G minor symphony Boult was surprised when the violas, followed by the second and first violins, slurred their first two notes in the slow movement. The orchestral parts have the slur but it is not included in the full score. Boult asked Rosé if they usually played the slur – 'we do what the conductor directs,' was the reply. Boult said he would like to do what the composer directed, and reminded them that the autograph manuscript was 'upstairs in this very building.' After this had been consulted, the slur was removed. The orchestra was so impressed by this that it later sent Boult a folio signed by all the players and with a photograph of the first page of the minuet (the wrong movement!). Although Joseph Marx wrote that Boult 'visibly enjoys himself' over the 'heartfelt Viennese tone of the Philharmonic fiddlers in Mozart's G minor symphony,' most of the critics found Boult's Mozart too staid and un-Viennese, one even comparing its sobriety to a 'machine rhythm.'

From 23 to 26 June Boult was in Wales to conduct the first Gregynog festival of music and poetry, given in aid of a fund to help the unemployed. Staying at the hall as the guest of Gwendoline and Margaret Davies, Boult was always astonished 'to find fresh visitors as well as old friends and fresh devices for their entertainment, almost every time we went there.' Beautifully bound copies of the music to be performed awaited Boult and Walford Davies in their rooms on arrival each year at Gregynog and after the festival, very often, a copy of the latest book to be printed by the Gregynog Press would be sent as a present. The programmes of the festivals, printed by the Press, are collectors' pieces. The Gregynog Choir was recruited from the estate and the nearby village of Tregynon and was trained by W. R. Allen, who sang the part of Christ in the Bach Passions. Gwen Davies once asked Boult whether he had liked the second bass soloist who had sung the arias. He had. 'I'm so glad,' she replied. 'I was a bit doubtful. You see, I heard he was leaving the village in search of work. We really haven't got enough work for a second estate carpenter, but I felt I couldn't let him go away.'

The atmosphere of Gregynog, an idyll from a vanished world, it now seems, has been well described by Ian Parrott in his book *The Spiritual Pilgrims*.[12] In June the rhododendrons were in full bloom, the grounds glowed with colour. From your bedroom you walked 'down the broad staircase, past the large vase of magnificent long-stalked sweet peas, into the dark oak-panelled dining room for a meal ... And so along to the Music Room, past the sculptured heads of Rodin and Epstein ... As you listened to the music, you will have noticed the decorative hydrangeas and gloxinias which were usually to be set against the delphiniums, spiraeas, heleniums, eryngiums and other flowers from the herbaceous borders ...' At the concert you might have heard d'Arányi as first violin in Schubert's C major quintet and Walford Davies as pianist in a Brahms sonata. 'As you left the Music Room, you took a last backward glance at the impressionist "Effet de Neige", a study of the Pont Neuf, Paris, painted from his room by Pissarro ...; and before stepping out into the sunshine you were halted by the Blue Lady – "La Parisienne" of 1874 by Renoir. As you walked past, was that Holst outside, with sunken lawn before him and the woods beyond, on his way to the lake?'

The festival programmes were a mixture of choral music, chamber works, madrigals and poetry readings (often by Lascelles Abercrombie). In 1933 Boult conducted Holst's *Ode to a Grecian Urn*, Parry's *Blest Pair of Sirens* and Vaughan Williams's *Toward the Unknown Region*. The 1934 festival commemorated the recent deaths of Elgar, Holst and Delius with extracts from Elgar's *The Apostles* and Muriel Brunskill as solo contralto in *The Music Makers*, songs by Delius and short choral pieces by Holst, including the motet *O Spiritual Pilgrim* he had written for and dedicated to Gregynog the previous year after he had been a visitor to the festival with his daughter Imogen. Vaughan Williams's new *Magnificat* and his Mass in G minor were performed. Writing to thank Boult after this festival, Gwen Davies said: 'It is lovely also that Ann is also becoming inoculated with the Gregynog "virus"!!! ... Everyone seems to have been very deeply impressed by the festival this year and one feels almost frightened at the immense possibilities and repercussions – the pebble has been thrown into the quiet pool and one can never tell where the ripples will spread.' Of Gwendoline Davies, who was appointed a Companion of Honour in 1937, it was said: 'To own such fantastic wealth and to be so utterly and completely uncorrupted by it is a marvellous proof of the quality of her character.'

At the third festival in 1935, Boult conducted Bach's *St Matthew Passion*. The soloists were Elsie Suddaby, Mary Jarred, Tom Pickering, Keith Falkner, W. R. Allen and Cecil Cochrane, and there were six string players, an organist and a pianist (Michael Mullinar). In 1936 Keith Falkner sang Stanford's *Songs of the Fleet*, Mary Jarred sang in *The Music Makers* and there was a performance of Vaughan Williams's *The Shepherds of the Delectable Mountains*. The main works in 1937 were the *Gloria* from Bach's Mass in B minor and Vaughan Williams's *Coronation Te Deum* and the *finale* of his *Sea Symphony*. In the following year the whole of *A Sea Symphony* was performed in an unusual form, with Lascelles Abercrombie reading some of Walt Whitman's text. At one of the concerts four Mahler songs and Kodály's song-cycle *Énekszó* were sung and an organ toccata by Duruflé was played by George Thalben-Ball. There was no festival in 1939 but Boult conducted the *St Matthew Passion* on 6 April.

*　　*　　*

On 1 July 1933 Boult married Ann Wilson, whose divorce from Steuart Wilson had been made absolute on 21 November 1932. The Wilsons' marriage had been drifting towards the rocks for some years and Ann had asked him in desperation why he had married her. He replied:

'Because I wanted to leave children and my name in case I should be killed in the war.' On one occasion she said: 'You really cannot go on behaving like a bachelor when you are a married family man.' Wilson retorted: 'I can and I do, you get out and leave me alone.' Eventually divorce became inevitable. Ann Wilson was granted a decree nisi on 12 May 1932. All but their closest friends were taken by surprise and Wilson's biographer, his third wife Margaret Stewart, found that after nearly 40 years many people in Petersfield and Steep districts were unwilling to talk about it, but took sides.[13] Divorce then still carried a severe social stigma and Wilson's professional career was affected: he was, for instance, barred from taking part in the Three Choirs Festivals for 25 years until Worcester engaged him as the narrator in Honegger's *King David* in 1957.

Ann had little money and before the decree nisi was granted she and her four children left the London house in Chepstow Villas to stay with an aunt of Ann's at King's Langley in Hertfordshire. Among friends in whom Ann confided at this time was Boult. But it was to her aunt that, in the six-month period between the decree nisi and its being made absolute, Boult one day forcefully declared: 'I know now, I know, I shall marry Ann and take them all on.' Aunt and niece were alike flabbergasted, but he was unshakeable. 'We will be married on New Year's Day and you will start a new life.' Ann, however, was not to be hurried and insisted on time to think it all over. Her principal concern was that she could be secure in the knowledge that, if anything should befall her, the best would be done for her children. Boult – 'Uncle Adrian' – had always delighted in the Wilsons' children and they in him, and with this certainty in mind she accepted his proposal and they were married at Ditchling, Sussex, at the Old Meeting House. The bridegroom was 44, the bride 35. Ann's parents and sister and Boult's father and sister were present, as were two old Boult retainers, with Sir Walford Davies, who played the harmonium, and Lady Davies. The critic Scott Goddard, one of Boult's first RCM pupils, lived at Ditchling and was invited at the last minute, bringing with him a sheaf of delphiniums from his garden. The wedding was followed by a picnic on the Downs. They then drove to Dover. 'Ann, who began the day with a bathe at Brighton, finished it with another at Calais,' Boult recalled.[14] On their honeymoon they visited Marie Hedmondt at Ragaz, walked in the hills north of Innsbruck and spent some days at Portofino Vetta, at the top of the promontory. Ann was somewhat aghast that he planned that they should walk down to the sea and back again, 1,200 ft down and up, 900 of them in steps, but thinking 'I didn't marry him to spoil his fun, so I must do it,' she agreed, 'humming the *British Grenadiers* the while!'[15]

At Portofino they opened the envelope Gustav Holst had sent to them marked 'To be opened in Italy and not before.' It contained the manuscript of a canon 'for A and A from GH for use in Italy, King's Langley, Gregynog and other nice places.' It was a setting of part of Marlowe's 'Come live with me and be my love.' They were cheered, too, by the good wishes of Ralph and Adeline Vaughan Williams. Both Holst and Vaughan Williams, like Keith Falkner, were also good friends of Steuart Wilson and remained so. So had been Boult, but henceforward, though they met professionally, their relationship inevitably was touched by frost. In his autobiography, published several years after Wilson's death, Boult neither mentions him nor that Ann had been married before. It can be gleaned, too, from the pages of *My Own Trumpet* just how fully he 'took on' Ann's children, for he refers to them as his own, which was how he treated them. On return from honeymoon, there was no more 'Uncle Adrian.' The family, including his sister Olive, called him 'Jonesy,' a nickname arising as such things do in families, and it stuck for ever afterwards. To his wife he was always 'Joss.'

CHAPTER 20

Beecham Again

CRITICISM of the BBC's policy of giving public concerts flared again in 1933. There was also savage hostility to the BBC's championship of Schoenberg, Berg, Webern and Hindemith, which was blamed for a falling-off of attendances at the Queen's Hall concerts. No longer could it be said that the BBC was taking the bread from others' mouths: both the LSO concerts and Beecham's very fashionable LPO were drawing bigger London audiences. When Boult conducted the first British performance of Bartók's Second Piano Concerto with the composer as soloist on 8 November 1933, Cardus described it as 'tedious and crude.' Nor did the critics show any enthusiasm for the first British performance of the original version of Bruckner's Ninth Symphony, which Boult conducted on 29 November. (But this was the dark age in Britain where understanding of Bruckner was concerned. When Klemperer conducted the Seventh Symphony in London in February 1932 at a Courtauld-Sargent concert, the critic of the *Musical Times* described it as 'not merely naive, it is uneducated, badly conceived, badly worked out, badly orchestrated. In fact, it is not worth discussing.') Beecham's appearance as guest conductor in a miscellaneous programme was ecstatically received. The BBC was worried and Eckersley asked Boult to report on the orchestra's workload. 'It is obvious,' Boult wrote,

> that the orchestra cannot keep up a continuous standard of super-efficiency ... the amount of work that is generally done is not productive of over-strain, but is only just inside that limit ... I feel it certainly desirable that some alteration be made in the working-hours of the orchestra, which I fear would reduce the hours in which the orchestra is available for broadcasting.

Julian Herbage diagnosed one cause of staleness as rehearsals under inadequate conductors, especially Edward Clark and Victor Hely-Hutchinson. This was supported years later by Archie Camden in his autobiography.[1] He had joined the BBC Symphony Orchestra as principal bassoon when Harty left the Hallé in 1933, but he found it an irksome life and resented 'clumsy, aspiring conductors ... cutting their teeth on us.' He also thought that the players' lot was made 'unnecessarily difficult and irritating by the extraordinary choice of orchestra manager – Mr R. C. Pratt. He appeared to take the view that all members of the symphony orchestra were potentially delinquent children ... and that it was his vocation to thwart their evil tendencies.' Because of his post as Director of Music, Boult was unable at this time to feel the pulse of the orchestra's morale and to be a spokesman as often as permanent conductors of other orchestras who were not in such an ambivalent position. His pride in it, however, was unshakeable. He wrote many years later: 'I do wish you could have heard the orchestra in 1931 or so. It was sad that there were so few recordings. Did I tell you that Master T.B. paid the LPO boys (1932) extra for recording – so of course ours refused to do it for less, and we didn't make any records at all for several years. I'm afraid I absolutely agreed with our players' refusal. The LPO was *not* a better orchestra then, whatever E.N. [Newman] thought of it!!'[2]

Any suggestion that Boult was aloof from his players is dispelled by two anecdotes, the first of which he told himself. One of the woodwind principals was 'a lovely player, but also a pretty hard drinker. One day he had a bad cough and I shouted for some water for him. When it came I noticed a good deal of levity round where he was sitting and as they didn't settle down quickly I shouted "What is the matter with you? – haven't you ever seen a man drink some water before?" Back came the answer in a strong unison from a dozen people: "Not *that* man!"' Perhaps it was the same player who had lunched rather too well and his interruptions at the subsequent Maida Vale rehearsal became difficult to handle, not for the first time. The orchestral manager considered he should be dismissed. Boult sent for him the following day to deliver the *coup de grace*. The player arrived looking very smart, smoking a cigar, with a flower in his buttonhole and carrying a gold-topped cane. He went into Boult's office from which, to Gwen Beckett's amazement, peals of laughter came. Later, when she asked how things had gone, Boult replied: 'Oh, I couldn't sack him, he plays so beautifully.'

The three bones of contention – public apathy towards the BBC's Queen's Hall series, the increased concert-giving by other orchestras and the workload of the BBC players – were eagerly seized upon by Eckersley to return to a stratagem he had never willingly abandoned – collaboration with Beecham. He met Beecham socially and had been most impressed by Beecham's BBC concert. Writing to Cecil Graves, Controller of Programmes, on 28 February 1934 he outlined Beecham's plan for the BBC and London Philharmonic Orchestras to alternate each week in a series of 24 winter concerts. Beecham would conduct 12 concerts, six with each orchestra, and Boult 'at least eight.' Beecham added a memorandum saying: 'I am aware that in respect of this joint series this would mean that I shall be occupying the position of conductor-in-chief of both orchestras.' Eckersley threw all his weight behind this scheme, which was to be put forward as a collaboration between the BBC and the Royal Philharmonic Society, which promoted the LPO concerts. As had happened in 1930, however, Beecham again neglected to inform the directors of the Society.

When Boult saw Beecham's plans he was furious. He wrote on 5 March to Eckersley, sending a copy to Reith. He reminded him that Beecham had formed the LPO in direct opposition to the BBC and must only be approaching the Corporation now because collaboration was vital to his own orchestra's existence.

> We cannot expect reliability from him: he is often changing programmes and cancelling engagements ... It is not to the BBC's interest and mine that I should conduct the LPO much ... To the alternative possibility, Sir Thomas Beecham's frequent conducting of our orchestra, there are even graver objections. He gets magnificent results with them, but at such a cost that I shall feel called upon to insist on a drastic curtailment of the orchestra's broadcasting hours in any week in which Sir Thomas Beecham is conducting. He usually arrives late for rehearsal and keeps the orchestra overtime ... No one admires him more as a conductor of certain schools of music, but I feel that the Corporation must be fully prepared before entering into any kind of undertaking with him. As a conductor of the occasional, carefully-chosen programme he has the greatest value for us.

The BBC's programme division still decided to approve the scheme and wrote to both Beecham and the Royal Philharmonic Society. The usual prevarications followed, with both Beecham and the Society making difficulties, but it did not matter. Reith had begun to take an interest. Basil Nicolls (Administration Controller) wrote to him to oppose the reduction in the number of public concerts and added that the Eckersley plan practically involved 'removing Dr Boult from his position as permanent conductor of the BBC Symphony Orchestra and substituting someone who, on the face of it, has an allegiance to two orchestras. I am quite confident that in the long run the result would be disastrous...' What happened next was described by Boult thus:[3] 'Roger Eckersley (my chief, who had a strong Beecham complex) ...

asked Reith to call a meeting [to discuss the proposals] ... Reith did not share R.E.'s ideas and the meeting lasted about 8 minutes! Reith scrapped the scheme in one sentence.'

Unfortunately he did not scrap the reduction in public concerts from 18 to 12, which was implemented in 1934–5. The music department had strongly opposed this on the grounds that it would be bad for morale and might lead to the departure of some 'star' players. But the reduction was supported by the Music Advisory Committee, which was continually being pressed by outside organizations to persuade the BBC to withdraw from the public arena. As a sop to Boult, his plea for the orchestra to be allowed to tour abroad and in the provinces was conceded.

This administrative unpleasantness was taking place while Boult was deeply involved in three demanding and ambitious musical projects. On 7 February 1934 he conducted the first London performance of Mahler's Ninth Symphony; on 21 February the first broadcast performance of Busoni's Piano Concerto, with Egon Petri as soloist; and on 14 March the first complete performance in Britain of Berg's opera *Wozzeck*. Apart from Hermann Biterauf, who sang the title-rôle, the cast was English and was coached for three months by Kurt Prerauer, who had recently left Berlin where he had worked with the composer on a stage production. Marie was sung by the soprano May Blyth, who had sung some of her music in a BBC studio concert on 13 May 1932 when Wood conducted the *Three Fragments*. Others in the cast were Mary Jarred, Walter Widdop, Parry Jones and Tudor Davies. With a few exceptions, the critics gave unstinted praise to the performance and Boult was delighted by a letter, written the next day, from Berg, who had heard the relay clearly at Waldhaus in Austria.

> I can measure, as no one else could, what an immense preparation must have preceded this concert. It equalled the finest stage performances with the work in the regular repertory ... It gives me only joy and happiness to think of the performance – and to think long of it. The greatest happiness of all, perhaps, is the implied *understanding* with which this (one might say) up to then strange music was revealed. That is owing first of all to *you*, dear Mr Boult ... What emerged here under your sovereign direction was a performance as if from the regular repertory of the greatest stage! And that is one accomplishment which – as I have cause to know, from 2 or 3 dozen *Wozzeck* productions – appears very seldom.

Berg was sad that 'such great *love* for one work' was expended on only one performance. Boult had already tried to involve Covent Garden – Geoffrey Toye, Beecham's assistant there, said that the Garden 'would

Lassen Sie mich, sehr werter
Herr Boult, aller innigst
dafür danken! Sagen Sie
bitte meinen Dank auch
allen, aber auch allen Ihren
wunderbaren Mitarbeitern,
u. sagen Sie ihnen dabei, daß
ich gern jedem Einzelnen von
diesen Künstlern einen Dan-
kesbrief schriebe — Daß ich
dies aber (ich weiß ja nichtein-
mal ihre Namen!) nur im
Gedanken tun kann!
Und nun grüße ich Sie, Mr. Boult,
(den persönlich zu kennen ich mich
erst recht freut) auf das allerherzlichste
als Ihr aufrichtig ergebener Alban Berg

*) Dürfte ich um ein "Programm" bitten!

The last page of Berg's letter to Boult

not have anything to do with *Wozzeck*' and Boult privately described Beecham's attitude as 'maliciously obstructive.' After the success of the concert the BBC offered *Wozzeck* to Covent Garden free of charge. The opera house showed interest and tried to borrow scenery from Europe, but the high cost of a risky project finally killed the idea and the opera was not staged there until Erich Kleiber conducted it in 1952. Boult admired and was thrilled by the music of *Wozzeck* but always maintained it became greater when it was diatonic. Another letter, written in English from Universal Edition, Vienna, was from Erwin Stein, with a 'heartiest congratulations' postscript from Alfred Kalmus. Stein called the performance 'one of the finest I ever heard. Also the singers were excellent, above all Wozzeck, and remarkably good also was the Captain, who almost gave a lyrical bel canto character to his part. Most of all I admired, however, your orchestra, how it mastered the most difficult passages with full superiority and beautiful sound. We were all of us very pleasantly surprised about the brilliant reception given to the work.'

The year 1934 had begun with six public concerts of British music which were the BBC Music Department's reply to a body that had been a thorn in Boult's side since he had become Director – the Music Advisory Committee, of which he had once been a member. This committee bitterly resented the amount of time and money spent on Schoenberg, Berg and others and seemed to believe that British music and musicians should be the primary, if not sole, concern of the BBC. Boult conducted four of the concerts, Beecham and Ronald one each. Symphonies by Elgar, Bax (No. 4) and Bliss were performed, a *Sinfonietta* by Goossens, works by Lambert, Walton (*Belshazzar's Feast*) and Moeran. The new works included R. O. Morris's symphony (a disaster, it was generally agreed), Arthur Benjamin's Violin Concerto and Bridge's *Phantasm*. The exclusion of Parry and Stanford was deplored by Sir Frederic Cowen, and others would have liked to have heard works by Finzi, Rubbra and Warlock. Later in the regular series Boult conducted Walton's Viola Concerto and Holst's *Choral Symphony*. He also conducted the first performance of Holst's *Lyric Movement* for viola two months before the composer died.

This was the 'black year' for English music, Elgar dying in February and Delius in June. The memorial concert for Elgar by the London Philharmonic Orchestra on 1 March was the occasion of Boult's first Royal Philharmonic Society appearance for 12 years, a hiatus which clearly reflected the influence of Beecham on the Society in those years. The BBC's tribute to Delius was *A Mass of Life* conducted by Beecham in September 1934. It was less prompt in commemorating Holst, whose music was regarded as box-office poison by most administrators of the time. There was no Holst concert in the 1934 Proms, but Boult conducted *The Planets* in the 1934–5 season and the first performance of the *Scherzo* from an unfinished symphony on 6 February 1935. He spent part of August 1934 at the Salzburg Festival, hearing concerts and operas conducted by Bruno Walter – *Der Rosenkavalier* and *Don Giovanni* among the latter – and attending a Toscanini performance of *Tristan und Isolde*.

From 16 October 1934 the BBC Symphony Orchestra's studio concerts were given in Delaware Road, Maida Vale, where a disused roller-skating rink had been converted into five studios built to the most modern specifications. The main studio, Maida Vale I, became (and still is) the orchestra's principal home. Two months later Boult took the orchestra on its first provincial visit – Daniel entering the lion's den, for the charge of unfair competition against the BBC was still being pressed by many organizations. The first visit was to, of all places, Manchester on 5 December. Even though Harty had gone, the BBC's alleged 'poaching' of Hallé players had not been forgiven.

This foray into enemy territory was informally agreed with E. W. Grommé, the Hallé chairman, but other members of the committee, particularly R. J. Forbes, principal of the Royal Manchester College of Music, covertly organized a boycott of the BBC concert even though the Hallé at this time owed its existence to an arrangement whereby its star players were guaranteed year-round work with the BBC Northern Orchestra. Boult wrote an article for the *Daily Dispatch* in which he hoped for an end to 'insularity in this matter of musical prowess,' but on the evening of the concert (and even though Arthur Catterall was the solo violinist in *Ein Heldenleben*), the orchestra on the platform was nearly as big as the audience in the Free Trade Hall. Glasgow and Edinburgh would not be hosts to the orchestra but it played to an audience of 3,000 in Dundee. It also visited Bristol and Birmingham. In the latter city, for a programme that included Bach arr. Schoenberg, Delius's *Dance Rhapsody No. 1* and Busoni's *Two Studies for Doktor Faust*, the Town Hall was sold out, which pleased Boult immensely.

Sometimes dissensions within the orchestra impinged on Boult's personal life. His friendship with his principal violist, Bernard Shore, went back to 1921. They spent holidays and walking tours together, and their wives were also friendly. It was from a remark by Olive Shore to Ann Boult that Boult learnt of Shore's dissatisfaction, which had begun when he was not offered the solo viola part in Strauss's *Don Quixote* alongside

the cellist Casals. Boult's letter to Shore on 29 December 1934 is characteristic of his open-handed method in such difficulties:

> Olive's very nice letter to us, though it of course washes out anything that
> might have been questionable about the *occasion*, cannot prevent my realizing
> more than before that what I had rather thought of as an ambition which is
> rightly in the mind of any artist is, with you, something more like discontent
> and irritation against the BBC – for whose irritations *I* am largely responsible.
> You have always managed any difficulties that might arise from the cir-
> cumstances of our friendship with such delicacy and skill, making it all so
> easy for me always, that I do hate to feel that you are unhappy when I am
> responsible for the conditions under which you work.
>
> What are those conditions? Except for Tertis you are recognized as the
> leading viola player in the country. Your salary is probably double T's
> professional income (I guess of course it is probably as big as that of any
> player in America and easily the biggest in Europe). The trouble therefore
> does not seem to be material – it must be artistic. Olive mentioned the *Don
> Quixote* business. I did not answer your letter to me about it – I thought it
> would be more friendly not to, though I disagreed with you on one point:
> the solo cello and solo viola are handled identically in the score; *both* are in
> and of the orchestra. As a matter of courtesy the names of both are printed
> in the programmes; but surely when the greatest living cellist is engaged for
> one part, it is up to us to put beside him the greatest living violist, particularly
> when he is an Englishman. Tertis had played it before so there was nothing
> new in his engagement – the programme people *do* keep you in mind, and
> opportunities like the Walton will come again ... There may be still dull
> patches – more studio work – I hope fewer than formerly but you mustn't
> forget that there are few people in the world (from the King downwards)
> who *don't* have dull patches in their work. Ann certainly seems to be one,
> but she has a rare gift for extracting enjoyment out of anything, even
> scrubbing floors and washing clothes ...
>
> The BBC may be an unwieldy machine but everyone I know in it is out
> for disinterested work, and everyone is very proud of the orchestra. I expect
> that no one in the orchestra gets as much solo work as he wants, but two
> things are apt to be forgotten: any solo engagement given to a member of
> the orchestra may create problems, particularly of rearrangement of duty
> and may involve the payment of an extra sub-principal; further, it will usually
> take away a solo date from someone outside who is not already in receipt
> of a comfortable BBC income ... I'm sorry to have gone on at such length,
> but if any thought I have thrown out can help to make the world a more
> cheerful place I should be very happy.

*   *   *

Koussevitzky invited Boult to conduct the Boston Symphony Orchestra in January 1935 and delayed his departure on holiday so that he could introduce his guest to the orchestra at the first rehearsal. The programmes included four British works, the largest of them Elgar's Second Symphony. These were its first Boston performances since 1911 and the critics' reaction to it was generally dismal and unperceptive. Boult also conducted Haydn's Symphony No. 88, Brahms's Fourth and Schubert's Great C major Symphonies. He was somewhat daunted on entering the 'artists' room' to find 14 paintings, sketches and busts of Koussevitzky. A Boston official whispered to Ann Boult: 'If you ask me, my dear, I think there is just *one* too many.' The Boults' host there was an old friend, Dr Archibald T. Davison, a member of the Harvard Faculty of Music, conductor of the renowned Glee Club, and friend of both Holst and Vaughan Williams. Known as 'Doc,' Davison took the Boults to see the glorious estate of 200 acres at Tanglewood, about 100 miles from Boston, which had just been given to the Boston Symphony Orchestra by two female benefactors and where Koussevitzky was already planning to establish a permanent summer school. From Boston, Boult went to Toronto to see Ernest McMillan and was invited to conduct the *Meistersinger* overture – without rehearsal – at the start of a concert, an alarming compliment. The Toronto orchestra's concerts, he wrote in a report for the BBC, were the city's social backbone: 'I felt I was really back on British soil in discovering that one of the evening papers had half a column on the dresses worn at the concert and not one word about the music!' He sailed for home from New York.

As a result of his Boston experiences, Boult made some suggestions to the Director-General in a lengthy memorandum. He had been impressed by the policy of repeating programmes several times and urged that the BBC should repeat on the following Sunday any 'work of real importance which is not often heard' from the preceding Queen's Hall Wednesday concert. He cited Busoni's Piano Concerto as an example. He had also been deeply impressed by the care and courtesy shown over arrangements for his personal comfort. 'I should like to feel,' he wrote,

that the reception of artists from abroad, if necessary at the station of arrival, particularly if they do not speak English, might be systematically watched and the money allocated for it. I also feel that it might be made somebody's business to consider an occasional lunch or dinner party on behalf of some of our guests. People like Richard Strauss and Siegfried Wagner have, I think, come and gone without any recognition other than the inevitable cheque. I cannot help feeling that some of our Governors would be happy to join us sometimes on these occasions ...

On return Boult had to take over a Handel 250th anniversary concert from which Beecham had withdrawn (it included a complete *Acis and Galatea*) and to continue his service to Berg by conducting the first British performance (20 March) of the *Symphonic Excerpts from Lulu*. Earlier in the month he conducted the premières of Tertis's transcription (for violin and viola) of Delius's Double Concerto and of Malipiero's Sinfonia No. 1. On 10 April he conducted the first performance of Vaughan Williams's F minor Symphony (No. 4), a work that shocked and baffled its first listeners by its violence and aggression. The composer said after the performance that 'Adrian had *created* the slow movement. I didn't know how it should go, but he did.' Boult wrote to Vaughan Williams on 22 April:

> If there was an inspiration about the performance it was the *work* that put it there. And if I got the bit between my teeth it was simply because the music made me feel like that. You know I feel that it is all very well for conductors to have their readings when works have taken their place in the repertory. While they are new it is *really* his business to absorb the composer's mind as much as possible – his own will emerge later; in fact, all too soon usually ... So don't worry if I ask too many questions – the thing will shake down after a performance or two – & then you may cease to recognize it!

A month before the Vaughan Williams première the BBC Symphony Orchestra had given its first concert on European soil. On 12 March Boult conducted it in the Grand Salle du Palais des Beaux-Arts in Brussels. The programme was Weber's *Oberon* overture, Vaughan Williams's *Fantasia on a Theme of Thomas Tallis*, Delius's *In a Summer Garden*, Paul Gilson's *La Mer*, Beethoven's Seventh Symphony and Ravel's *Daphnis and Chloë* Suite No. 2. The Belgian critics were ecstatic. But the climax of the orchestra's first five years awaited it in London in June when one of its guest conductors at the London Musical Festival was to be Arturo Toscanini.

CHAPTER 21

Toscanini

ARTURO Toscanini's eminence in the musical world of the 1930s was unchallenged. In New York, Milan, Bayreuth and Salzburg he reigned supreme. He and only he, his admirers said, gave audiences the music and nothing but the music. He was legendary in another respect too: his violence and terrorizing tactics at rehearsals. Scores were hurled at players, batons broken, watches ground to pieces under foot. The BBC Symphony Orchestra thought it knew what to expect when it heard that the great maestro was to conduct them in four concerts. The festival began in May 1935 with Boult conducting Bach's Mass in B minor. Then Koussevitzky returned for three concerts at which he conducted Beethoven's Third, Tchaikovsky's Sixth and Sibelius's Second Symphonies, Stravinsky's *Rite of Spring*, Vaughan Williams's *Tallis Fantasia* and Holst's *Fugal Concerto*. Toscanini's first concert was on 3 June.

He had never before conducted a British orchestra and had only once appeared in London, when he brought the New York Philharmonic in June 1930. On arrival in 1935 he stayed at Claridge's where a nervous Boult met him to take him to the first rehearsal. Boult introduced him to the orchestra as 'the greatest living musician.' At this he was interrupted by 'a hearty thump on the shoulder: "No, no, no; not that at all! Just an honest musician." '[1] Boult went to a seat in the circle to await the first explosion, which never happened, even though Koussevitzky at his rehearsals had assured the players that it would! Toscanini had demanded 20 or more rehearsals, but after his first rehearsal he shortened the remainder and cancelled some of them. He began with Brahms's Fourth Symphony, a Boult speciality. It was played through with hardly an interruption, Boult recalled. ' "Bene, bene, bene," he said, "just three things." '[2] Boult was deeply impressed by his colleague's memory, his power of concentration and his uncanny ear.

I have heard him correct a player who began a long diminuendo one note before it was marked ... His whole rehearsal scheme is a model of economy and reasonableness, granted his insistent demand for nothing less than his ideal ... He will never repeat one bar at rehearsal after he has been once satisfied. His greatest colleague at Salzburg [Bruno Walter] said to me 'I never miss his rehearsals; he is like a great high priest of music, caring only for beauty and the mind of the composer.'[3]

In performances of Brahms, Beethoven, Wagner, Elgar (the *Enigma Variations*), Cherubini, Rossini, Debussy (*La Mer*), Mozart and Mendelssohn, Toscanini and the orchestra earned critical superlatives without exception. 'The most important events that have occurred for years in the orchestral life of this country,' Cardus wrote, momentarily deserting Beecham. Toscanini said that the orchestra was one of the best he had ever conducted and promised to return.

It did not escape notice that Toscanini's placid behaviour was largely the result of his encountering a disciplined orchestra, well trained by Boult. This success came at an opportune moment, for in 1935 the BBC was being investigated by the Ullswater Committee preparatory to expiry of its charter at the end of 1936. Here was another chance for those organizations which still felt they had been harmed by the BBC to give evidence against it. They did not forgo the chance. They appointed the Incorporated Society of Musicians as their spokesman and found an ally in Reith's and Boult's *bête-noire* the Music Advisory Committee, which still considered that the BBC ignored British musicians. Boult gave evidence to the Ullswater Committee, saying his aim was 'to guide musical opinion ... we look on our public concerts as the apex of our work, concerts where we give the public the great classics together with such novelties as we consider to be of prime importance.' Boult's evidence boldly stated that some witnesses had lied to the Committee and were 'phenomenally ill-informed' about the BBC. 'The latest figures show an average of 5,500 engagements to British solo artists and 330 to foreign artists per annum.' The BBC, he said, kept the Hallé and Birmingham orchestras in being by employing a nucleus of their players. No substantial increase in employment could be given by the BBC in the immediate future without lowering the standard of its programmes.

Boult then summed up the orchestra's first five years and its contribution to raising standards. He cited Toscanini's visit and the Brussels critics' views that the orchestra was the best in Europe except the Berlin Philharmonic. And he remarked that he placed 'a high value on the disinterested advice of the senior members of the music profession, but I seldom get that advice from the Music Advisory Committee, of which

Sir Hugh Allen, Sir John McEwen and Sir Landon Ronald are all members.' If Allen, Davies and Ronald had felt that by suggesting Boult for the BBC Directorship of Music they were ensuring an 'Establishment' voice in the Corporation's counsels, they must by now have been seriously disappointed in their protégé. At any rate the BBC emerged relatively unscathed in the Ullswater report.

Boult's conducting in the BBC Symphony Orchestra's 1935–6 season included a repeat of the Vaughan Williams Fourth Symphony, Three Pieces from Berg's *Lulu Suite*, Copland's *Music for the Theatre*, Conrad Beck's *Innominata*, Roussel's Fourth Symphony, Bantock's *Pagan Symphony*, Elizabeth Maconchy's Piano Concerto and Bartók's *Cantata profana*. 'Self-conscious and forced' was *The Times* description of the Bartók (it had earlier described Stravinsky's *Oedipus Rex* as 'monumental nonsense'). During the season Boult conducted an unexpected first performance at a studio concert on 22 January 1936. Hindemith was to have been viola soloist in his own *Der Schwanendreher* but this was felt to be unsuitable because of the death of King George V. So Hindemith sat for six hours in a studio on 21 January and composed his *Trauermusik* for viola and orchestra. This was rehearsed the next day and performed in the evening. 'It was very moving,' Hindemith wrote to a friend. 'Boult was, by English and his own personal standards, quite beside himself and kept thanking me.' Later in this same concert Boult conducted Elgar's First Symphony for the first time, although he had rehearsed it in 1932 for Elgar to conduct.

On his visit to conduct the Vienna Philharmonic in Salzburg in August 1935, Boult wanted to include a major Vaughan Williams work and asked the composer whether it should be the new symphony or the masque for dancing, *Job*. Boult had first conducted *Job* in a studio concert on 19 February 1933. A year later, on 13 February 1934, he rehearsed it for a Queen's Hall performance and was amazed, on opening the manuscript full score, to find that it was now dedicated to him.[4] 'On the whole I prefer *Job*,' Vaughan Williams advised on 14 April. 'For one thing I want to make a few slight revisions in the Symph ... Also I feel that *Job* is less like what they are accustomed to, which I feel is what we ought to give them.' So *Job* it was, with the first performance of Bliss's *Music for Strings* and short works by Bax and Holst. Boult was disappointed at his first rehearsal to find that Rosé was not leading,

> but I knew that these concerts were led by several people in rotation. However, I ran into Rosé on the same evening after the opera and he asked when I was to begin rehearsing. On hearing that I had begun, he said he

wanted to play at my concert ... and he would get the duties changed over. Next morning I happened to walk through the Mirabell Garden when I heard a violin playing something familiar. I listened, and it was the first violin part of the first scene of Vaughan Williams's *Job* ... I had heard that some of the orchestra were staying in the Mirabell Palace and when I went back a little later, sure enough, the solo violin (Elihu) scene was being carefully played and practised. Dare I suggest that some of our bright young people might note that the most famous leader in Europe, having missed one rehearsal of an unfamiliar programme, felt he must put himself through the experience of playing every note of that programme (including the obviously slow and easy parts) before going to the second rehearsal?[5]

In April 1936 Boult took the BBC Symphony Orchestra on its first continental tour, with concerts in Paris, Zürich, Vienna and Budapest. Arrangements were made by Edward Clark, who planned that each concert should contain a work by a composer of the host country, an English work, a classic and a showpiece. His proposed programmes were altered without his being consulted and this precipitated his resignation from the BBC before the tour began, although there had been increasing strains for some time in his relationship with his employers.

The first of the four concerts was in Paris at the Salle Pleyel on 20 April. The French audience enjoyed Lambert's *The Rio Grande*, Roussel was there to hear his *Pour une fête de printemps* and the showpiece was *The Rite of Spring*, which Boult ceded to other conductors in London but here obtained such a precise and secure performance that the orchestra remembered it for years as one of their highspots. On the train to Zürich, Boult's large suitcase fell from the rack on to his head while he was studying scores. After half an hour he fainted and remained unwell. He missed the short rehearsal, ate a good dinner and conducted Busoni, Walton (Viola Concerto), Honegger and Brahms superbly. On the journey to Vienna, Boult was snowballed by members of the orchestra when the train stopped at the summit of the Arlberg Pass. In the city they were greeted by Bruno Walter and given a tea party by the Vienna Philharmonic. The programme in the Konzerthaus on 23 April was Brahms's *Tragic Overture*, Schoenberg's *Variations*, Vaughan Williams's Fourth Symphony and Ravel's *Daphnis and Chloë*. The critics remarked on the presence of women in the orchestra and found the symphony 'important.' The Schoenberg was receiving its first public performance in Vienna. It was not much liked and the shell-shocked President of Austria asked Boult: 'Who is this Schoenberg, anyway?' A more appreciative member of the audience was Franz Lehár, who wrote to Boult and said he had gone round to the artists' room afterwards but, on seeing a crowd, decided not to trouble Boult. While in Vienna Boult took the opportunity to hear Bruno Walter rehearse and conduct a performance of Mahler's Second Symphony.

On 24 April the Vienna Philharmonic were on the station platform to play Strauss waltzes and marches as a farewell to their colleagues. Vienna had less than two years left for that kind of spontaneity. The Budapest concert was given in the municipal theatre ('a most uncomfortable place,' Boult reported, 'with built-out stage quite inadequate for our orchestra'). Eighty per cent of the tickets were sold, much the highest of the tour. Elgar's *Introduction and Allegro*, Bax's *Tintagel*, Bartók's *Four Pieces* and Beethoven's Fifth Symphony were played. Boult thought the tour was too demanding and was furious that only half of each concert was broadcast in Britain.

The London Music Festival for May 1936 was cancelled. Koussevitzky was peeved because he had been overshadowed by Toscanini the previous year, and Toscanini took umbrage over a piece of BBC bureaucracy about his fee. After the Proms season, Catterall resigned as leader of the orchestra – he had only led at the Queen's Hall concerts, never in the studio or at the Proms – and was replaced by Boult's former Birmingham leader Paul Beard, who since 1932 had been leader of Beecham's LPO. Boult could face Catterall's departure with equanimity. Even the gentlest suggestion had often been resented and there was a considerable air of self-importance. During this year, too, Boult was provided with a deputy as Director of Music (Dr Reginald Thatcher, director of music at Harrow School) who from 1 October relieved him of some of his administrative work. Chief events of the 1936–7 Queen's Hall season were the visit as guest conductor of Willem Mengelberg and the first public performance in Britain of Berg's Violin Concerto, which Wood conducted (the work had received its first British performance on 1 May 1936 in a studio memorial concert for Berg conducted by Webern). Ansermet, Beecham and Leslie Heward were the other guests. One of Boult's first concerts was a repeat of Vaughan Williams's *A Sea Symphony* on Trafalgar Day. Next day the composer wrote a fulsome tribute to Boult:

There seem to me to be two essentials of great conducting: (1) Faithfulness to the composer. (2) The power of the conductor to express *himself* to the full *at the moment*. I always know I shall get (1) from you but sometimes without (2). Thank heaven I have never heard from you (2) without (1) – & I know I never shall. Yesterday we had (1) and (2) – result a great performance & great conducting for which I thank you from the bottom of my heart –

and your singers & players too ... You made me like the old work again & the awkward places seemed to have disappeared by magic ...

On 27 October 1936 Boult conducted a studio performance of Bruckner's Sixth Symphony and in the Queen's Hall on 18 November Casals was soloist in Elgar's Cello Concerto, an interpretation regarded by most of the critics as fatally 'un-English'! On 27 January 1937 Boult conducted the first London performance of Vaughan Williams's Norwich Festival choral work *Five Tudor Portraits*. He gave London a chance to hear his interpretation of *The Rite of Spring* on 17 February, but the event of the season was the concert performance of Busoni's *Doktor Faust* on 17 March. Several scenes were omitted 'to bring it into a reasonable concert shape' (Boult wrote in 1974) and the composer's widow Gerda attended. Ernest Newman called it 'an ambitious failure,' but a young critic, Desmond Shawe-Taylor, wrote in the *London Mercury* of 'a work of such originality and imaginative power that the memory of it must overshadow for some time the ordinary round of London music-making ...' (Just how far in advance of public taste Boult was may be measured by the fact that no stage performance of *Doktor Faust* was given in Britain until April 1986.)

In the studio that winter Boult conducted the first performances of Kodály's *Te Deum*, York Bowen's Fourth Piano Concerto, Edmund Rubbra's First Symphony and Schoenberg's arrangement of Handel in the form of a concerto for string quartet and orchestra. On 30 April he introduced to London another work from the 1936 Norwich Festival, Britten's audacious symphonic song-cycle *Our Hunting Fathers*. The young composer wrote in his diary: 'I have a rehearsal with Boult of H.F. at BBC at 11.30 – it goes quite well tho' he doesn't really grasp the work – tho' he is marvellously painstaking.' The performance in the evening, Britten conceded, went 'very creditably.'

On 1 February 1937, in the first Honours List of the reign of King George VI, Boult was knighted.[6] Telegrams and letters poured into the BBC and to his home. From the Royal Naval College at Dartmouth came a letter from his former music master, H. E. Piggott:

I do feel very proud today to see in the paper that high honours in recognition of the most distinguished work have been given to two I taught at Westminster in those far-off days – you and Tizard.[7] It was very little I could do for either of you, but I knew you were both destined for great things and the peculiar satisfaction is that you both became knights together ...

From Birmingham Gerald Forty wrote: 'That your great services to British orchestral music have been thus officially recognized affords the

Dear Adrian

There seem to me to be two essentials
of a great conducting

(1) Faithfulness to the composer

(2) The power of the conductor to express
himself to the full on the moment
— to feel himself in the music
& the music in himself

I always know I shall get (1)
from you but sometimes not (2)

(2)
Thank heaven I have never heard
from you (1) without (1) — & I have

First page of Vaughan Williams's letter to Boult

keenest pleasure to all your friends.' A few weeks later, from Florence, came the letter that probably meant most to Boult, from Bruno Walter:

> I just heard that you have been knighted (is this the right English word?) and I want to congratulate and tell you that I feel a real satisfaction by this distinction, that this time rewarded the real merit ... I think in a distinction like that you have received is recognized who you really are – the honest and enthusiastic work you have done – and this is in every sense a most satisfying event for you and your friends. So you may follow up your way further as you did before and feel in some way encouraged by a well-deserved public honour.

Boult was asked by Sir Walford Davies, who in 1934 had succeeded Elgar as Master of the King's Musick, to help with the music for the Coronation of King George VI on 12 May 1937. Ernest Bullock, Abbey organist, was in charge of the service proper and the choral music; Boult conducted the orchestral music before and after the service. This included the March *Crown Imperial*, specially written by Walton for the entry of Queen Mary.[8] In the studio on the following evening Boult conducted the first performance of John Ireland's choral work *These Things Shall Be*, which nobody seemed to notice quoted the *Internationale*! Coinciding with the Coronation was the BBC's London Musical Festival, for which Toscanini returned to conduct Boult's orchestra. He returned later in the year to conduct the second and third concerts of the Queen's Hall 1937–8 season.

Boult was determined to learn from Toscanini's methods, particularly in regard to memorizing scores. But after his summer holiday he wrote in his notebook:

> Working very hard this holiday at Sibelius 2 and Elgar's *Falstaff*, and trying to get back the knack of intensive detail work (Toscanini's), I found that the results were most unsatisfactory and a whole month's free time (ie. going up to London only twice a week) wasted. Happened to see Miss McKinnon [the pianist Lilias McKinnon] on 16/9/37. She said I had obviously been spending far too long at a time on one thing – told me how she had got hold of Strauss's *Burleske* in a fortnight working 10 minutes a day (after a good deal of comparatively fruitless preliminary slogging). Is the right way to go on in short spurts, concentrating on movement (keys etc.), dynamics, bar groups, only going on to details after all this is finished?
>
> Miss McK. says she often has half a dozen works on the bench together. I had thought this induced 'retro-active inhibition,' but this must be induced by too much work on *one* thing. Perhaps my enforced haste in studying scores all these years has been a blessing in disguise. Possibly, too, Toscanini's method has misled me, and is a law unto itself, not applicable to smaller fry.

It is for us to get the framework complete and fixed, only putting details in at the very end.

In August 1937 Boult began his 'conferences for conductors' at his beautiful country home, Quaker's Orchard, at Peaslake, near Guildford. The 'pupils' stayed in the village for a fortnight, at Boult's expense, and went to his house for talk and tuition in the mornings and evenings. Boult would talk on musical matters and they fired questions at him, all in a happy and informal manner. In the afternoons there was swimming, clock golf and tea on the lawn round a table-tennis table. Sometimes Vaughan Williams would come over from Dorking to swim and join in the talk. Among those who attended were Trevor Harvey, Herbert Murrill, Gordon Thorne, Leslie Woodgate, Julian Herbage, Mansell Thomas and Reginald Redman. This work continued after 1945, when Boult taught at many conductors' courses, especially those run by Stephen Moore, and he enjoyed one for nuns! In the late 1950s he found a kind of Gregynog at Bromley, Kent, in 'Ripley,' the home of the sisters Marjorie and Dorothy Whyte. There, for a fortnight each summer, the young conductors could rehearse a string orchestra of about 18 players led by Marjorie Whyte. Over 100 conductors received help and instruction at 'Ripley.' But that is looking ahead.

Boult's chief contributions to the orchestra's 1937–8 season were Elgar's *Falstaff* (a rarity then), Tovey's Cello Concerto with Casals ('the first movement seemed to last as long as my first term at school,' Lambert wrote), Walton's Symphony, Hindemith's *Symphonic Dances* and Malipiero's Second Symphony. On 20 October he also conducted Debussy's *La Mer*, of which Toscanini's performance had been electrifying. In the audience was a young musician, Robert Simpson, who recalled after Boult's death:

> Adrian was never a competitive man, but something must have got into him that night. The top of his bald head went a fierce red, his whiskers bristled, his eyes flashed, and his nose seemed about to impale the nearest member of the orchestra. The performance was hair-raising and Toscanini must have heard the climax of it in New York. Years later I reminded Boult of this and he said 'Yes, it did go rather well.'

The most publicity in this season was given to the disinterment of Schumann's Violin Concerto, suppressed as 'unworthy' in the composer's lifetime and the subject of a ban, to last until 1956, imposed by Brahms, Clara Schumann and Joseph Joachim. The violinist Jelly d'Arányi claimed that the spirit of Schumann had asked her at a séance to perform the work, the score of which was in the Prussian State Library, Berlin. She was so insistent that Joachim's son agreed to release the manuscript from its custodians. D'Arányi gave the first British performance, with Boult conducting, on 16 February 1938. In the studio he conducted a Szymanowski memorial concert, including the Second Violin Concerto, the first performance of Krenek's Piano Concerto, the British première of Berg's *Three Pieces*, op. 6, and on 4 March Alan Bush's Piano Concerto with the composer as soloist. The concerto's *finale* was a setting for baritone and male chorus of verses by the composer's fellow-Communist Randall Swingler (Britten set his words at this date also). It has since been related by Sir Michael Tippett and John Amis that Boult was so perturbed by the revolutionary text that he cut short the applause for the composer by launching into the national anthem. It is a good story and no doubt true, but it was a studio, not a public, concert – given before an invited audience – and Boult's action may have been dictated by some strict adherence to the programme schedule (many years later he was dissuaded by Sir William Glock from observing the extra repeat in the *scherzo* of Beethoven's Fifth Symphony because it would cause an over-run into the 10 pm news bulletin). Since Boult on the previous Sunday, 27 February, had given a broadcast talk about the concerto in the 'Music of the Week' series, in which he described fully the sentiments of the choral *finale*, it is unlikely that he was particularly shocked by them. Yet, in the political climate of 1938 it is equally possible that he suddenly took fright and decided on this course of action (it was, after all, the custom to play the anthem *before* a concert, not at the end). One has forcibly to remind oneself that this was the time when Broadcasting House was swamped with complaints from listeners when an excited commentator on the Derby shouted: 'It's a *hell* of a race!'

Eight days after the Bush performance Germany invaded Austria. Bruno Walter, conductor of the Vienna Philharmonic Orchestra, fled to Monte Carlo where Boult wrote to him. In his reply on 21 March, Walter wrote: 'I know that you feel with me and that you understand – better than anybody else – what besides my personal sufferances the death of Austria means to all of us. It is indeed tragic beyond belief and it is a difficult task to adapt oneself to this new Europe.' Boult went to Reith and offered to step down as chief conductor of the BBC orchestra so that Walter could take the post for however long or short a time he wished. This noble gesture appealed to Reith, but he felt he needed to refer it to Sir Hugh Allen as chairman of the Music Advisory Committee. Allen rejected the idea out of hand. It would never do, he said, for a

BBC orchestra to have a foreign conductor. Boult wrote to Walter inviting him as a guest conductor and received this reply:

> I thank you thousands times for your dear letter – it was entirely and genuinely Adrian Boult ... My season is 'sold out' except March which I reserved for America ... I am glad in the thought to come again to England and make some music there and let me hope to see you there – it would do me so good to have a 'heart to heart talk' with you, to be again with you for some time: our personal life is not less important for us than our artistic life – perhaps even more. And we, slaves of our work, let it pass and remain the losers in the play.

In April 1938 Boult conducted a section of the BBC orchestra at a charity concert with Josef Hofmann as solo pianist in Schumann's Concerto and Beethoven's G major. He wrote his opinions of this famous virtuoso in his notebook: 'He never practises and it shows, of course, curiously not in *pp* where the runs are as clear and lovely as they could be, but in the climaxes, which are rather muddled.' In this same month, still perturbed by his contact with Toscanini's methods, he went to Professor Francis Aveling 'with a number of queries arising out of the memory chapter in his *Conserving Mental Energy*, and out of the mess I made of my devotion last September to the scores of Sibelius II and Elgar's *Falstaff*.' Boult noted:

> As you read you probably become conscious that a detail is not becoming clear. Then is the time to stop and ferret it out ... It is not wise to work on more than two or three things at the same time. Prof. A. never does serious reading for more than 2 hours a day. If he works longer he finds he forgets ... No harm in missing days. It all depends how soon the work must be ready. The longer one takes, the deeper the impression ... In working, always take the line of least resistance, and never press yourself too far ... It looks as if the *necessity* of my busy days (just working in short bursts when the occasion offered) has been a blessing in disguise and prevented my overdoing things. Prof. A. never gives a lecture (even when this is simply reading old notes) without spending an hour or two on the notes first. Toscanini is evidently an exception on this. It shows that one ought to prepare every first rehearsal as if it were the show.

Toscanini conducted six concerts in May and June 1938, including two performances of Verdi's *Requiem*. Boult meanwhile had sailed for New York on 30 April, having been invited to conduct Toscanini's NBC Orchestra in two concerts. He conducted Busoni's *Comedy Overture*, the first New York performance of Copland's *El Salón México*, Walton's Viola Concerto (William Primrose), Vaughan Williams's Fourth Symphony, Holst's *Fugal Concerto* and Elgar's *Enigma Variations*. 'I unwisely chose also to include Beethoven's Seventh Symphony,' he wrote in his autobiography.[9] 'This was one of the misjudgments of youth (though I was old enough to know better) to try and do that kind of work on Toscanini's home ground. Everyone was polite, but I realized (after the event) that no one could possibly stand up to Toscanini in such a work.' In fact his younger colleague, John Barbirolli, in his second year as conductor of the New York Philharmonic, was submitting himself almost weekly to similar comparisons. While in America Boult visited the Davisons at Harvard and went to Ottawa and Toronto. He returned to London in time for Toscanini's last concert on 10 June. At the end of this month, Boult lost a staunch ally when Reith resigned as Director-General to become Chairman of Imperial Airways.

Boult conducted nine of the 16 concerts in the 1938–9 Queen's Hall series. Wood, Basil Cameron, Goossens and Beecham were the guest conductors, as was Bruno Walter, who in January 1939 conducted Mozart's *Requiem* and Beethoven's Ninth Symphony. Boult's principal undertakings were Honegger's *King David*, Holst's *Hymn of Jesus*, Busoni's Violin Concerto, Walton's Symphony, Berg's *Three Fragments from Wozzeck*, and Mahler's *Song of the Earth*, sung in English by Mary Jarred and Walter Widdop. In the studio Boult conducted three first performances – Howells's *Concerto for Strings* and the Second Symphonies of Rubbra and C. B. Rootham. He was abroad in Oslo and Stockholm when Walter was in London, but received a letter from his friend praising the orchestra and adding: 'You help to make musical history in England. Culture in Central Europe has gone down; musical culture here is rising, by your merits and those of your excellent collaborators.'

The year 1939 was Boult's busiest for overseas visits. In January he conducted Vaughan Williams's Fourth Symphony in Oslo and Bliss's *Music for Strings* and Vaughan Williams's *A Sea Symphony* in Stockholm. In February in Monte Carlo he conducted Bax's *Tintagel*, Vaughan Williams's Fourth Symphony and Bliss's *Things to Come* Suite. In June he sailed to New York to conduct two concerts by the New York Philharmonic in Carnegie Hall as part of the World Fair. First performances were given of Bax's Seventh Symphony, Bliss's Piano Concerto and Vaughan Williams's *Five Variants on Dives and Lazarus*. (Walton's Violin Concerto, which was to have been played, was not yet ready.) He then spent a brief holiday in Massachusetts with the Davisons and went with them to a Mozart concert conducted by Koussevitzky at Tanglewood, now established as a summer school. Between 29 June and 9 July he conducted the Chicago Symphony Orchestra in eight concerts at its Ravinia Park summer home. English music was strongly represented in his programmes – Vaughan Williams's *Job* and *Tallis Fantasia*, Elgar's *Enigma Variations*, Holst's *Beni Mora* and works by Ireland, Bliss and Smyth. (A first-desk player described Boult as 'the best rehearser we ever had.') Finally he went to Toronto. His last pre-war trip was in August to Lucerne.

Before his trip to New York, Boult had taken part in the London Musical Festival when he conducted two concerts of Beethoven concertos. These were addenda, as it were, to the six Toscanini concerts comprising the nine symphonies and the Mass in D. Boult noted what Toscanini said to him about the *Praeludium* in the Mass: 'It is so wonderful. I close my eyes when I conduct it – I close my eyes and then the organ comes in at the end and it is a light from heaven.' Toscanini told Boult of his 'terrific anxiety about the danger of covering the solo violin in the *Benedictus*. He actually consulted me as to whether he might cut out the *sforzandos* in brass and timps.'

All this musical activity took place under the shadow of impending war. Hitler's annexation of Austria and Czechoslovakia left few in doubt that a major European conflict was imminent. The BBC's advance plans involved the dispersal throughout the country of several of its major departments. Bristol was chosen for the symphony orchestra. On 1 September, the day after Hitler invaded Poland, the orchestra was in the midst of its Promenade Concert season under Wood. Reith's successor, Frederick Ogilvie, told the players after the concert that evening that the Proms were suspended and they must be ready to go to Bristol. The signal for them to do so would be the replacement in the 9 pm news of 'This is the BBC' by 'This is London.' At 9 pm the following evening the signal was given. On Sunday 3 September, war was declared.

CHAPTER 22

War

WHERE music was concerned, the first weeks of the Second World War were not the BBC's finest hours; many of its employees felt that had Reith still been in charge, matters would have been ordered differently. Theatres and concert-halls were closed throughout the country, and the BBC merged all its programmes into one network. This it filled with news, records, variety shows and seemingly endless cinema-organ recitals. As Boult wrote:[1] 'My friend Sandy Macpherson, the organist, who did a grand job, had a sixteen-hour day. The variety department ran out of jokes, while the symphony orchestra went for long walks exploring the lovely country round Bristol.' He did not take it so phlegmatically at the time. On 17 September he wrote to Ogilvie: 'Musical culture cannot be allowed to lapse any longer now that the emergency period is over and that theatres etc. are reopening. The BBC should be early in the field with a weekly public symphony series.' Over a month later he wrote again: 'If I had had my own way I should have been conducting the Beethoven C minor Symphony on September 6th, and I think I should have been right. Actually Berlin broadcast the 7th of Beethoven and the *Haffner* of Mozart from a Furtwängler concert on September 17th before I had conducted a classical symphony.'

On the outbreak of war over 40 of the orchestra's 119 personnel were released for military service, so the orchestra that went to Bristol was only 70 strong. Shortly, however, agreement was reached whereby certain key players were 'deferred' from call-up and almost 20 players returned on 26 November. But the BBC also signed contracts with a number of outstanding non-BBC players, such as Reginald Kell the clarinettist, to form a salon orchestra to play 'high quality light music.' In the meantime the BBC Symphony Orchestra arranged a series of public concerts in the Colston Hall. Only the second half of each was broadcast. At the first, on 1 November, Vaughan Williams's *Five Variants on Dives and Lazarus* had its British première. Harty, Wood

187

and Clarence Raybould were guest conductors; when Boult conducted some Wagner extracts, with Eva Turner as soprano soloist, a parson objected that they were the 'musical embodiment of German brutality and unprincipled domination.' During November Boult wrote a paper on music policy, maintaining strongly that, in general, war conditions should in no way change its basis. He called for 'rigorous ruling-out of the mediocre both as regards music and performance' and stressed that

the importance of keeping abreast – if not in advance – of the musical world becomes even more necessary if music is to hold its place as a cultural force. ... We must consider ways and means of bringing such conductors as Toscanini and Bruno Walter into our programmes again, as well as the leading international soloists ... It becomes even more necessary that our programmes and policy should show no obvious signs of insularity ... In the first week of war the musical world was temporarily paralysed, partly on account of our momentary failure to fulfil the needs of the music-loving public. It is necessary during the next few months that every effort should be made for the BBC to regain its former rôle of leadership in musical England.

In a broadcast talk on New Year's Eve 1939, Boult outlined his musical policy and held out hope of a monthly series of modern works. Only he and the orchestra, with Julian Herbage as programme planner, were in Bristol; the rest of the music department, under Reginald Thatcher, went to Evesham. Boult therefore invited his former Westminster schoolmaster, H. E. Piggott, to help Herbage. Piggott had retired from the naval college at Dartmouth. After July 1940 the BBC became agitated about broadcasting 'copyright music by composers of enemy nationality.' Someone decided that transcriptions were all right if the composers were of 'staple reputation' e.g. Bach-Busoni, Rossini-Respighi. But special permission had to be obtained from Boult for 'any work of exceptional character as long as it is not infected by the "German spirit."' Viennese operetta was banned.

Among contemporary works conducted by Boult in the first half of 1940 were Bliss's Piano Concerto, Bax's Seventh Symphony, Lambert's *The Rio Grande* and the first broadcast performance (12 April 1940) of the complete *Les Illuminations* of Britten (with Sophie Wyss as soprano soloist). Other conductors conducted other British works, yet a group of composers including Bantock, Ireland, Smyth and Vaughan Williams attacked the BBC for its failure to give 'genuine' music by British composers a larger share of broadcasting time!

With the fall of France in June 1940, the bombing of Britain began in earnest and Bristol became a prime target. It had over 200 raids in the year after the first in June. Units of Local Defence Volunteers (later renamed the Home Guard) were formed throughout the country, Boult serving as a lieutenant until the move to Bedford in 1941 when he resigned his commission and served in the ranks. There is a story, perhaps exaggerated but in character, that on one occasion he marched his unit to a crossroads near Bristol and upon a turn to the right said: 'This way, gentlemen, please.' Concerts were recorded in the afternoons and the orchestral players wore tin hats when walking to and from the studio.

Boult lived first in a rented house at Avon Grove overlooking the gorge and later moved to Leigh Woods, which involved him in crossing Clifton suspension bridge at least twice a day on his way to his offices in Pembroke Road, Clifton. He noticed that the men who collected the toll fees had no tin hats, so he gave them his own until all were equipped, much to the puzzlement of the Home Guard quartermaster, who could not understand what Sir Adrian did with them. (He was in any case careless about his civilian hats, made by Woodrows and very expensive. He carried them more often than he wore them and often forgot where he had left them, so Mrs Beckett would have to retrieve them from clubs, shops and restaurants all over London.)

On the June night when bombs were first dropped on Bristol, the BBC Club Choir, which Gwen Beckett had founded and in which Boult sang as a bass, was giving a concert in the garden of a large house. It was a balmy evening, the listeners were sitting casually in the garden, and the singers stood on a long row of steps leading from the house. The sirens sounded at the beginning of Purcell's 'Draw on, sweet night'. Thereafter the wail of sirens was a continual counterpoint to the daily work. Boult and Mrs Beckett abandoned going to the shelter in Pembroke Road or they would not have got through their work. The church opposite their offices was destroyed one night and they arrived in the morning to find all their windows blown out and their garden full of charred and smouldering debris. During the bombing, one of the orchestra's double bass players, Albert Cockerill, was killed with his wife in their flat. On another occasion the orchestra's instruments were saved from destruction in their garage when the orchestral driver had a premonition and drove the van out of the city on to the downs. Paul Beard played the *Air* from Bach's Third Suite in the 'Epilogue' (a nightly religious broadcast) during one raid kneeling beside a microphone under a table.

Early in September 1940, while Boult was rehearsing in the Colston Hall, he had a phone message saying his London flat in Avenue Close had been severely damaged by a bomb. His first question was: 'What about my music?' and he was told that his library of beautifully bound scores had been destroyed. 'Then I shall have to conduct from memory in the future.' He returned to the rostrum but ended the rehearsal early, pale and visibly shaken. The raids themselves seemed to leave him impervious. One of the orchestra remembers arriving in the rehearsal room one bitterly cold morning after a night of bombing to find it inches deep in water. They all hoped and prayed Boult would call it a day and let them thaw out over a hot drink, but he just seemed not to know the conditions existed.

During these tense months Boult had made his second appearance as conductor of the London Philharmonic Orchestra, which was struggling to survive after its founder, Beecham, had left the country. He conducted a Bach programme in Queen's Hall on 15 May 1940. It was after conducting the LPO in Westminster on 30 August that, during an air raid, he walked past Queen's Hall where the Proms were being held. Until the 'All clear' sounded and the audience could safely leave, the promoters of the concerts had devised 'siren sessions' to amuse those who chose to stay after the programme proper was over. Boult entered the hall at 11 pm and found Basil Cameron conducting sea shanties with piano accompaniment, and two-thirds of the audience sitting happily on the floor and singing lustily. Boult told an anecdote he had just heard from J. B. Priestley and then played the triangle in 'a sort of inverted Farewell Symphony,' someone impersonated Beecham, members of the LSO gave solos, and Boult and Cameron went round with the hat to collect donations to the musicians' pension fund. Dickens sketches and musical contributions by members of the audience passed the time until 3.55 am: 'It had been a noisy raid, we were told, but we had heard none of it,' Boult recalled.[2]

Bristol had the first of its really heavy air raids on the night of 24 November 1940. The Clifton arts centre, where the harpist Sidonie Goossens was living, was destroyed and all Alan Rawsthorne's manuscripts with it. Constant Lambert and others joined the firefighting. When dawn came, it revealed a ruined city. 'Bristol has been wiped out,' the Germans claimed, and indeed the devastation was appalling. Further massive onslaughts, involving terrible loss of life and destruction of property, occurred on 2 and 6 December and on 3, 4 and 16 January 1941. The blitz was renewed on 16 and 29 March, with further very heavy raids on 3, 4 and 11 April. These were not all, only the worst. With Harry Vowles, a BBC administrator, having persuaded London that the orchestra should be moved from Bristol, the search had begun for an alternative refuge. This was not easy, as what was required, to quote Boult, was '250 beds, 40 offices under one roof, 10 studios of varying sizes, including two really big ones for orchestras.' The search lasted several months until Bedford was settled upon. Meanwhile the orchestra continued to give lunchtime concerts in Bristol, including the first performance on 20 December of Vaughan Williams's *Six Choral Songs in Time of War*, conducted by Leslie Woodgate. During the last six months in Bristol, Boult conducted Rubbra's Third Symphony, Khatchaturian's Piano Concerto and Bach's *St Matthew Passion*.

Walford Davies and his wife had also moved to Bristol with the BBC at the beginning of the war. In February 1941 they went to live in the Somerset village of Wrington. A month later Sir Walford died, after only three days' illness. Boult conducted a memorial service for him at Gregynog Hall on 19 April.

The raids on Bristol lessened after Good Friday (11 April) 1941 and there was only one after the BBC orchestra had left. With Hitler's invasion of Russia in June 1941, the German attempt to subjugate Britain by bombing was no longer a strategic priority. Boult urged a reversal of the decision to leave Bristol but was overruled. He later persuaded himself the decision was wise, as is clear from a letter to Bernard Shore dated 19 June (Shore was serving in the RAF in North Wales):

> We move about August 1 and are terribly sorry for many reasons: the Colston Hall audience is terrific now and almost anything is packed, including lunchtime shows. But I'm satisfied we're right to go, for we simply couldn't do another winter of those foul records — we simply had to go where we could have a reasonable hope of playing live in the evenings ... The orchestra is in *grand* form still.

When the orchestra travelled in a special train to Bedford on 30 July 1941, Boult did not accompany them but made the journey on his bicycle, spending a night en route at Christ Church. At Bedford the orchestra played in the Corn Exchange ('a reasonably good studio, but a rather overpowering concert hall,' Boult described it) and when this was used by others there was the Great Hall of Bedford School, where the wooden galleries contributed to excellent acoustics. The music department was housed in two adjacent small hotels and Thatcher's staff from Evesham moved in with their orchestral management colleagues. Boult lived in Clapham, two miles north of Bedford. 'Bedford,' Boult wrote in his autobiography, 'welcomed us in a very friendly way,'[3] but he was, as so often in his book, being excessively polite. His secretary, Gwen Beckett, tells a different tale. Her landlady there told her that if she had any visitors they must go to the back door. As she wrote[4]:

> Bedford hated us. They didn't know there was a war on, and all they saw of it was a stray Heinkel one sunny morning which dropped a bomb on a dirty little theatre which their watch committee had been trying for years to shut! After the Americans arrived near by, Bedford shops had a wonderful time, but the drunkenness was awful. My billet hostess locked me out on my return from early Mass on Christmas Day and I spent some of it in the BBC canteen with the young King Peter of Yugoslavia, whom all the royal friends had forgotten to invite. He had no settled home then, and as Adrian had given him lunch now and then, he was looking for him. Adrian was very tired after all the Christmas work and had gone to bed.

There were, however, compensations. Boult usually spent the rehearsal-break in Woolworth's where one of the staff had a beaker of Ovaltine ready for him. On one occasion he found that Laurence Olivier shared his preference and learned that the actor had been one of his audience at Birmingham while he was a member of the Repertory Theatre company. A friendship began with Yehudi Menuhin, who flew from America to play the Brahms Violin Concerto. And there was also the pleasure of keeping up a correspondence with Bruno Walter and Toscanini in New York. 'Your greetings and love which I reciprocate moved me to tears,' Toscanini wrote. 'Sursum corda and we will win.'

Broadcast concerts from Bedford started on 17 September 1941. In the preceding weeks Boult undertook more engagements with the LPO, with whom he shared the wartime hardships of travel and accommodation. As he wrote to Bernard Shore:

> I have been doing a good deal with the LPO while their tours are on and enjoying it. It is a plucky fight they're putting up without T.B. If only the halls would take twice the money they would be doing quite well, but they have to do two shows almost everywhere in order to make ends meet.

One of these 'shows', at Derby on 31 August, proved memorable for non-musical reasons. Boult travelled there by train in company with the soloist, Eileen Joyce, who was to play Rachmaninov's Second Piano Concerto. The journey was slow and they reached the Grand Theatre an hour before the concert was due to start. There was time only for a hurried seating rehearsal. Miss Joyce discovered that the rake of the stage meant that the keyboard was not level and, worse, the piano stool was much too high and could not be lowered. As it was Sunday, no representative of the hirer of piano and stool could be found, nor was an alternative stool available. Miss Joyce said she could not play unless a suitable stool was provided, so Boult called for a saw and 'adjusted' the legs. He claimed to be the only conductor who had saved a concert with a saw and enjoyed the subsequent heated correspondence with the owners of the stool.[5]

The first Bedford concert included Bliss's *Music for Strings*. During the orchestra's 1941–2 season Boult also conducted Khatchaturian's Piano Concerto, the first performance of George Dyson's Violin Concerto, the first British performance of Prokofiev's cantata devised from his music for the film *Alexander Nevsky*, Elgar's *Falstaff* and Vaughan Williams's *A London Symphony*. The last-named was in the same programme (16 November 1941) as a new work by Vaughan Williams, his choral song for baritone, double chorus and orchestra, 'England, my England,' a setting of Henley's poem. This had been commissioned by the BBC in September 1940. The composer, listening to the broadcast in Dorking, was disappointed by the performance – 'rather dismayed' were his words in a letter to Boult.

> The whole thing was sung without conviction as if they did not know it (which according to your account they do not) ... I was particularly sorry because the tune is rather a ewe lamb of mine ... I felt on Sunday night that it had been strangled at birth ... I did not listen to L[ondon] S[ymphony] – it evoked the past too painfully 'nessum maggiore dolore etc ...'

Boult conducted the Hallé in Manchester (in the Opera House) in November 1941 and returned to the Liverpool Philharmonic on 28 February and 7 March (*Gerontius*) 1942. 'Travelling isn't much fun nowadays,' he wrote to Shore, 'but I've got plenty of it ahead of me, so there's no use in grousing.' He also told Shore: 'It's interesting you should have pounced on the weakness of the horns in the Corn Exchange. Several other people did, and we have now got a board which we put behind them with improved results, I think.' The orchestra was beginning to travel more. It visited Cheltenham, Luton, Kettering, Nottingham, Rugby School, Oxford and Cambridge. A series of special concerts was given in Cambridge between October 1941 and March 1942, and in June Boult conducted eight concerts in five South Wales towns. The orchestra also gave concerts exclusively for members of the Armed Services. After playing to Americans on one occasion, Boult was amused when the officer in charge remarked 'My wife says she's the daughter of a guy called Nikisch, who was in your line, I believe. Was he any good?'

Boult's only trip outside England was a visit to conduct an orchestra in Dublin in April 1942. Louis Kentner went with him as solo pianist. Boult's diary of the tour barely mentions music but concentrates on the contrasts between Britain and a neutral country: 'Food, of course, is marvellous. No restriction in anything except bread ... It is queer to see no blackout, and to find shops so full of everything ... Dashed out early to shop. Odds and ends like soap and hairpins.' He was taken to see Eamonn De Valera, the Irish Prime Minister. 'He seems tired ... and I think he is very anxious about his present policy. We talked mostly about music – he knows quite a lot.'

On 28 May and 4 June 1942 the BBC Symphony Orchestra played in London for the first time since the outbreak of war. Each programme was planned to contain a major first British performance in homage to Britain's two chief allies, but the score and parts of Shostakovich's Seventh (*Leningrad*) Symphony did not arrive in time. At the first concert Boult conducted Roy Harris's Third Symphony. *The Times* described the orchestra as 'on the top of their form' with performances 'as memorable as those of the historic concerts with which Sir Adrian Boult launched the orchestra on its career ... Here indeed was a reassertion of standards free from the defects of wireless transmission and routine difficulties.' News of the performance reached the Chicago Symphony Orchestra's librarian and percussionist Lionel Sayers, with whom Boult (as with many American friends) kept in touch throughout the war. 'I wondered if it was the symphony written for our 50th anniversary two years ago,' he wrote. (It was.) 'All I remember of it are the percussion parts which were written on a nasty bilious green paper and these parts were never twice alike. I don't remember any living composer that had different ideas after each performance the way he did ... I still scan the record news in the hope that you have found it possible to record *Job*.'

Boult still, whenever possible, attended guest conductors' rehearsals and was in Bedford on 13 and 14 June when the orchestra was conducted (in a programme that included Debussy's *La Mer* and Brahms's Fourth Symphony) for the first time by John Barbirolli, who was making his first visit to Britain from New York since 1939. 'Smoking,' Boult noted disapprovingly, but added: 'Lovely transparent results everywhere [in *La Mer*], but climaxes came off just because they were heavier, and not inevitably.'

CHAPTER 23

No Longer Director

AN important change in Boult's status occurred in April 1942 when he was unharnessed from the double position of Director of Music and chief conductor. On returning to Britain from the United States in 1941, Arthur Bliss was put in charge of the BBC's overseas music department. He soon felt himself to be underemployed and suggested to Boult that he should take over as Director of Music. 'I want more power as I have a lot to give which my comparatively minor post does not allow me to use fully,' he wrote to his wife on 31 August 1941.[1] Boult was agreeable, but Sir Hugh Allen was discouraging and suggested a triumvirate. Ogilvie's retirement as Director-General in January 1942 brought joint directors, R. W. Foot and Sir Cecil Graves, in his place. Graves supported Bliss, who was confirmed in the post from April.

Boult's friends were delighted that he was now freed from administrative work, and so was he. He replied to one letter: 'Yes, I think I am much to be congratulated at getting out of the office during the war. I never expected it, but Arthur Bliss is so very much the right person that it seemed the psychological moment.' His conducting took on a new authority and zest. After playing Schumann's Piano Concerto with him in September 1942, Myra Hess wrote: 'It was entirely due to you that the miracle happened ... your complete sympathy enabled me to concentrate entirely on the music itself – a rare experience in concerto playing! ... It was one of the happiest days in my long career ...' H. E. Piggott, now at Canford School, Wimborne, had been writing reports on music broadcasts for Reginald Thatcher at Evesham but gave them up because he was often up all night because of air raids and found himself falling asleep while listening to music! However on 24 June 1942 he wrote of

> ... the very marked change in Adrian's touch with the orchestra since he has been relieved of administrative duties. Many of his readings of familiar works

195

have acquired a new depth and a new fire. Many times he has seemed to me like Toscanini at his greatest in the glow that he has imparted to the music. The 'New World' [Dvořák] can never have sounded so magnificent as under him recently ... It took on a classical quality without losing its Czech romanticism ... The same was true of the Fourth [now known as No. 8 in G] ... He and Pouishnoff made of the Liszt concerto [No. 1 in E flat] a magnificently inspiring piece of music with all its tawdriness ripped off. I cannot think how it was done.

Boult was still trying to persuade Bruno Walter to resume his contact with the BBC orchestra. 'My dear Adrian, you cannot imagine how your suggestion to follow Barbirolli's example and come to England lives in my mind,' the conductor wrote from New York. 'Nothing could be more thrilling for me, but there is a "but", it is the voyage ... I think my wife would not survive the time until my cable would tell her about my safe arrival ... Anyhow my first concert outside this country will be in London and it will be one of the happiest moments in my life.'

Out of administrative office, Boult soon felt the cutting-edge of BBC bureaucracy. Bliss and he had been forbidden by Sir Cecil Graves, joint Director-General, to send a message, suggested by the Soviet Tass news agency, protesting about the German invaders' violation of the Tolstoy and Tchaikovsky museums. The reason given was that the message was not 'representative of English music.' Then came another request from Tass's London correspondent, Andrew Rothstein, for a New Year message to the Soviet peoples. Boult's memorandum of 31 December 1942 to Graves is a classic example of his skill in turning the tables on pinprickers:

The same surely applies to this. 'Who am I to send a message to the Soviet peoples?' It seems to me quite clear that part of Mr Rothstein's job is just simply to collect messages from all and sundry to send, presumably in a fairly ill-sorted mass, to Russia on any occasion. This being so, do you feel that it is a right policy for me to go on inventing excuses whereby I cannot do it? The Russians evidently are not particular in these matters, and it would seem that if the message is reasonably carefully worded in fairly general terms there might really be very little objection, but of course I have no idea about the national policy angle on this. I do feel, however, that I ought to write to Mr Rothstein and tell him to stop sending these telegrams, giving him some reason, if it is decided that I am never to do anything of this kind. Perhaps you would very kindly give me some kind of ruling?

He also now felt free to send to the Music Department his programme suggestions – 'as I have so much less administration on my mind now, I seem to find ideas cropping up.' He urged less of what he called 'second-rate Delius,' adding 'The *North Country Sketches* on the 2nd [January 1943] seemed to me quite without meaning. Perhaps a more correct way of putting it is that I as an interpreter am quite unable to give them their proper meaning, in which case they ought to be removed from my repertoire.' He urged performances of Bantock's *Hebridean Symphony* and of Schumann's Second Symphony ('It seems to me years since I have conducted the Second or Third Symphonies of Schumann and Second, Fourth and Sixth of Beethoven') and wanted to do single movements from Bruckner and Mahler symphonies. He wanted to give Elgar's *Cockaigne* a rest in favour of *In the South*, and pressed the claims of Holst's *Egdon Heath* and *Hammersmith*. An unusual choice was Wagner's *Love Feast of the Apostles*.

During the 1942–3 Bedford season, he conducted Holst's Double Violin Concerto, Rawsthorne's Piano Concerto No. 1, Bax's First Symphony, Vaughan Williams's *Pastoral Symphony* and music by Stravinsky, Bartók and Szymanowski. He also conducted a studio performance of Beethoven's *Fidelio* on 17 March 1943, with Laelia Finneberg as Leonore, Frank Titterton as Florestan and radio actors providing the spoken dialogue, and, at Leicester, the *Missa Solemnis*. These evoked a helpful letter from H. E. Piggott, who had found the broadcast balance in the Mass poor.

> I liked all the tempi and the general feeling. The orchestra were not at their best – one or two ragged places ... But, whatever criticisms and reservations, it was a glorious and thrilling experience to hear this majestic work again. I did not tell you what a thrill I got out of *Fidelio* ... I thought it the best operatic broadcast ever. You do seem to be doing a lot of conducting nowadays.

*　　*　　*

In 1940 and 1941, the BBC had withdrawn from association with Sir Henry Wood's Promenade Concerts but was reunited with him in 1942 when the season was shared between the LPO and BBCSO, with Wood, Basil Cameron and Boult as conductors. The concerts were given in the Royal Albert Hall, the Queen's Hall having been destroyed on 10 May 1941. Boult wrote to Wood at the end of the season:

> It has been a great experience for me and I have learnt much from it, but I keep harking back to 41 years ago when you first began to teach me. I think I should have gone mad if anyone had told me then that I should one day act as your assistant at the Proms! And it has really happened.

Nevertheless Boult never really enjoyed the Proms. He thought four weeks at a stretch was too much to ask of the BBC orchestra and, he told Bliss, 'I like at least several days to prepare an important performance, and I cannot help feeling that nightly work of this kind is in danger of becoming very superficial. This applies also to the orchestra which, as a rule, gets only one single rehearsal for everything it does.' (Today Boult's views prevail at the Proms and the workload is much more widely spread.) In the 1943 Prom season Boult conducted first or first British performances of works by Shebalin, Chavez (*Sinfonia India*), Copland (*A Lincoln Portrait*), William Schuman (Third Symphony), Khatchaturian (*Lezginka*), Rubbra (*Sinfonia Concertante*), William Busch (Cello Concerto), Kabalevsky (*Colas Breugnon* suite), and Moeran (*Rhapsody* for piano and orchestra).

He had new scores to learn also for the 1943–4 Bedford season, including Stravinsky's Symphony in C, Bax's Violin Concerto, Lennox Berkeley's *Divertimento for Strings*, Tippett's *Fantasia on a Theme of Handel*, and Vaughan Williams's new Fifth Symphony which the composer had introduced during the 1943 Proms; Boult took it up eagerly. The orchestra was now giving many more public concerts to help to meet the extraordinary wartime appetite for music. This appetite had led to the establishment of a full-time independent Liverpool Philharmonic Orchestra in 1942 (previously it had drawn largely on Hallé players) and to the Hallé's invitation to Barbirolli to direct its fortunes now that it, too, offered an 11-month season to its audiences and had vastly expanded its activities. Competition for good players was therefore keen, and Boult became increasingly aware that the BBC after the war could not expect to have things all its own way. The 'star' players of the BBC Salon Orchestra, disbanded in July 1942, became the nucleus of the re-formed Liverpool Philharmonic.

In the spring of 1944, Bliss resigned as Director of Music (such a course had been suggested to him, and violently rejected, a year before by Lady Cunard who wanted the post for Beecham), but now he wanted to concentrate on composition. He was succeeded by Victor Hely-Hutchinson. News of the impending change was current in the BBC at New Year 1944 and it led on 11 January to a letter from Ernest Hall, chairman of the orchestra committee, conveying to Boult the unanimous wish of the orchestra that he could see his way 'to reshoulder the position of Director of Music. The orchestra has only the happiest memories of your previous occupation of this position.' Boult was touched but pointed out that the decision had been made. 'In Professor Hely-Hutchinson we have a staunch supporter and, I think I may say, an admirer.' As it happened, Hely-Hutchinson did not take up his duties till 1 September (he was Professor of Music at Birmingham University) and Boult ran the administrative side of the department until then.

The 1944 Proms marked a double Henry Wood event: he was 75 on 3 March and 10 August was the 50th anniversary of his first Queen's Hall Prom. Boult was one of four conductors of a special birthday concert on 25 March. The Prom season itself opened on 10 June but the launching of Hitler's V1 ('flying-bomb') campaign against London in the same month led to curtailment of the concerts after 29 June. Those works which were to have been broadcast from the Royal Albert Hall were now broadcast from Bedford. Wood, after conducting an inspired performance of Beethoven's Seventh Symphony on 28 July, was taken ill and was too ill even to listen to the relay of the jubilee concert that Boult conducted on 10 August. He died nine days later. The V1 attack was followed in September by the even more deadly V2 rockets. This flare-up of blitz conditions ended plans to move the orchestra back to London. The players were becoming restless in Bedford, where studio conditions were far from satisfactory, and there were continual complaints that the place was unhealthy because of its proximity to the River Ouse. Although they had to stay there, they gave more concerts in London, some of them of the 'Tchaikovsky-piano-concerto' variety from which the BBC had hitherto held itself aloof. But a major event in the Bedford studio on 20 September was the first British performance of Bartók's Violin Concerto (now known as No. 2), with Menuhin as soloist and Boult conducting.

Another event that has lingered on as a legend was when Boult conducted the strings of the American Band of the American Expeditionary Force, stationed in Bedford and normally conducted by Major Glenn Miller.[2] A verbal invitation was given to him by the radio director of the band, Sgt. Voutsaf – the BBC had asked that Miller should not make a direct approach to BBC personnel such as Boult. This simple matter became the subject of memos flying to and fro between Hely-Hutchinson and Bedford before approval was given for Boult to accept something he had said he wanted to do. To think the BBC once imagined that Beecham could be its chief conductor! Reminiscing in a radio programme on 8 June 1953, Boult said he 'often dropped in' on Miller's rehearsals in the Corn Exchange. 'He was a thorough craftsman: he knew just what he wanted to get from his band and how to get it, and he didn't mind how hard he worked himself or them. Of course it was the string section which interested me most – 20 players, all from famous orchestras (there were actually some who had played under me in America). I always enjoyed their programme "Strings with Wings" although I wished they could have been playing better stuff.' When Boult conducted these strings at Maida Vale on 6 November 1944 they played Elgar's *Serenade* and an arrangement by George Ockner, leader of the string section, of Debussy's 'Nuages' from the *Nocturnes*. Ockner gave Boult a copy of the arrangement (in which the cor anglais solo of the original was given to a viola playing with a mute on the strings near the bridge, an effect which Boult said was 'terrific!').

In the Royal Albert Hall on 9 December Boult was presented with the Gold Medal of the Royal Philharmonic Society by Theodore Holland, Chairman of the Society.[3] This is one of the most coveted honours in British music and Boult characteristically insisted that it was really an award to the orchestra.

> I am continually being reminded that a great many people still feel that the BBC Symphony Orchestra has been leading a sheltered existence in some comfortable funkhole ... May I just tell you that one of our members was killed with his wife in his home by a direct hit an hour or two after taking part in a broadcast; that our leader was unceremoniously lifted off his bicycle by a rather too affectionate bomb and planted in a neighbouring field; another of our principals had the grim experience of seeing a large staircase window collapse on the top of his young daughter; several others, including our principal harp and the BBC chorusmaster, had their homes bombed over their heads and only escaped with the clothes they stood up in; and my secretary came to the office one morning with a sizable dent in her tin hat. Of course she is Irish, but I know she was fire-watching and it was a pretty tough night so I don't think she had been fighting any of her friends. There are plenty more stories like this, but I will only mention the night when we – the whole lot of us – played Borodin's Second Symphony by the light of six hurricane lamps. Again, we quite recently had to spend three hours playing in a studio at a temperature of 49 degrees. You may remember we were 119 strong in peacetime. Well, our 30 youngest members left us at one pre-arranged stroke on the first day of the war. The remaining 90 went off to their first funkhole. We are still 90 strong, but only 51 people on this platform are peacetime members of the orchestra.

Few people on that evening knew that less than a month earlier Boult had learned of the death in action of his wife's son, Jonathan Wilson. It affected him more than he allowed to be known. His close identification with his orchestra in this speech should have set off warning-bells in the BBC hierarchy. It pleased him that together they had recently recorded one of his great interpretations, Elgar's Second Symphony, and this was issued in January 1945. As its transfer to LP has shown, this was a performance that blazed with excitement and passion and is documentary evidence of the excellence of the orchestra in 1944. They had made no recordings since 1940 and their representation in the pre-war catalogue was relatively sparse. Thanks to Walter Legge's presence at HMV, classic recordings followed over the next 18 months – of Vaughan Williams's *Job*, Holst's *The Planets* and Elgar's Cello Concerto, the last with Casals as soloist. It was on this occasion that the engineers complained that the microphone was picking up Casals's grunts as he played. 'Well, then you can charge double for the records,' was the disconcerting reply – and the grunts are still there, for all to hear. Before the war the London critics had attacked Casals's interpretation of the Elgar concerto because it was 'not English enough.' Now they had only superlatives for it. Asked what difference there was between the earlier and later interpretations, Boult replied: 'None.' In November 1944 he pre-recorded Vaughan Williams's *Thanksgiving for Victory*, commissioned to anticipate the event. It was broadcast during a special thanksgiving service on the morning of 13 May 1945, five days after VE-Day.

In February 1945 Boult and Moura Lympany were invited to liberated Paris by Charles Munch. Boult was given a room in a flat overlooking the Champ de Mars. He conducted the Orchestre du Conservatoire on the 25th, with Lympany playing Rawsthorne's concerto. 'In the interval,' he wrote to his wife, 'I was summoned to the bandroom and Munch gave me a lovely copy of the original score of the Berlioz *Requiem* which had belonged to Saint-Saëns and had his initials on it.' Next day Munch took him to lunch 'with a Vicomte de Canson who is interested in a sort of British Council ... We were transported into the 19th century. A marvellous lunch, of course, served by two men on an immaculate table with coronets even on the table-napkins and gold spoons and forks with a double crest of arms on them! Everything in perfect order with an open fire with great logs in it.' He returned home from Le Bourget: 'My squadron leader friend said that it became an absolute routine in France that if the RAF were bombing they never bothered because they knew that only the factory or station or whatever it was would be hit; but if they were Americans everyone ran for shelters and stayed there till they had gone.'

The end of the war was to herald a difficult new period for Boult and the BBC.

CHAPTER 24

Post-War Problems

As far back as April 1941, when victory in Europe or anywhere else seemed remote, Boult was noting in a memorandum: 'The Berlin Philharmonic is broadcasting at pre-war strength. We have got to stand up to this.' On VE-Day and the day after, not a note played by the BBC Symphony Orchestra was broadcast. Boult felt it was symbolic of a new attitude to the orchestra. He wrote to Hely-Hutchinson: 'A number of things have cropped up in V-Week which make it very clear to me that at any rate some people in the upper reaches of the BBC simply do not understand what the orchestra is and what it stands for.' He attacked the 'pathetic vacillation' over programmes and claimed that the orchestra had outgrown some of the requirements of general broadcasting for which it was founded 'and may claim some of the privileges of a thoroughbred.'

The first clash occurred over the departure from Bedford. Hely-Hutchinson went there just after VE-Day and gave two possible dates: before or after the Proms. The delay was necessary because the Maida Vale studio would not be ready in time. The orchestra voted to return before the Proms, but this was rejected and the players were told to renew their Bedford tenancies on a monthly basis after 24 September. Boult explained the situation to his players at an angry meeting in the Corn Exchange on 22 May at which it was unanimously agreed that 'we definitely refuse to come back to Bedford after the Proms.' The clarinettist Frederick Thurston asked why other BBC orchestras, like the Variety, always got what they wanted while the Symphony Orchestra had to put up with everything. Another player stressed the 'constant bad health' in Bedford. The town lies in a 'saucer', often covered by cloud, and with the very wide river almost to the doorsteps of some buildings it was a damp place. In Boult's office in the Cavendish Hotel, for example, the bannisters were nearly always wet.

Boult told Hely-Hutchinson that he associated himself completely with the orchestra's decision and asked that any disciplinary action against it should also fall on him. Hely-Hutchinson knew that many of the players only stayed out of loyalty to Boult and, if they left, could swiftly find employment elsewhere. The BBC backed down, but the new Director-General, W. J. (later Sir William) Haley, was angry. Boult wrote to him on 31 May, saying that the orchestra had felt that the time for formal protests was long past.

> Half of them now know that they could earn far more money in the open market at present, but only two players have left us ... They are living, many of them, with strange families, in a most unhealthy climate, and I really feel that we can hardly expect high-spirited and not always logical artists to remember that a number of almost unknown senior officials 50 miles away are thinking and working continuously for their welfare ...

A result of the wartime boom in music was a transformation of the London orchestral scene. Walter Legge founded the Philharmonia in October 1945, Beecham the Royal Philharmonic. Although overworked, Barbirolli's Hallé in Manchester had won a new prestige for Manchester music, and other provincial orchestras were spurred by rivalry with it. There was dissension in the BBC hierarchy over a proposal to restore the Symphony Orchestra to its pre-war 119. Haley would agree only if extra use was made of the orchestra. Boult still wanted duplicated programmes; in that way, he maintained, standards could be kept up and 'productivity' increased to Haley's satisfaction. Haley delayed his agreement until March 1946, but by then Boult knew that the 20 new players would not be easy to find. In addition, there had been a 27 per cent change in personnel in a year. This was a crisis, for the majority were principals and sub-principals, including all the principal woodwind and the principal horn (Aubrey Brain). Between 1939 and 1946, Boult had lost 40 out of 90 players, including Marie Wilson, Laurance Turner (leader of the Hallé) and Bernard Shore.

Boult had some respite from these anxieties on his trips abroad. In November 1945 he became the first foreigner since the war to conduct the Concertgebouw Orchestra of Amsterdam. He included Elgar's *Variations* and short pieces by Bliss and Ireland in his three concerts and when he went to Brussels two days later he included Britten's *Scottish Ballad* in the first of two programmes. Returning to the People's Palace on 17 November, he accompanied Ginette Neveu in her unforgettable playing of Sibelius's Violin Concerto. On 29 December 1945 he sailed for New York in the *Queen Mary*, which was taking 12,000 American troops home, for his first post-war visit to North America to conduct seven Boston Symphony Orchestra concerts in Boston and a further five on a tour of New England. He had been invited to Boston in 1944 but preferred to wait until the war was over. 'I had the feeling (perhaps quite wrongly),' he wrote at that time, 'that the management were beginning to think of finding a successor to Koussevitzky and it was indeed an honour that I should be thought of in this connection, if it was the case.' He commented on this towards the end of his life[1] in an interview in a Canadian magazine:

> I always kick myself that I might have been offered the Boston job if I hadn't insisted on having my way with the seating. I am absolutely adamant about classical seating for the orchestra [first violins on his left, seconds on his right], though I do not mind if I am guesting. In Boston we played the Brahms First Symphony on the small tour they do three times a year to about seven places ... As the tour went on, the Brahms became more and more Koussevitzkyish and I couldn't stop it. I did not have the guts to say we must have a rehearsal to get it the way I want. But I was uncomfortable, and they wanted to have a second look at me after that. In a way I am glad because I don't think America is really my cup of tea.

On his 1946 visit he included eight British works, among them *The Planets*, *Job*, and the *Enigma Variations*, and his favourite Brahms symphonies. He kept a diary, which he sent home, and it makes entertaining reading:

> *3 January 1946.* Got away from the dock finally about 11.30 and found Mrs [Hamlin] Hunt waiting at the hotel [Westbury, Madison Avenue], also the BBC representative Charles Brewer (son of Sir Herbert Brewer, organist of Gloucester)[2] who began his BBC life in Birmingham when I was there ... The shops here are simply staggering – just like peacetime – everything there; one is tempted to buy up the whole place – well, I've got no money yet, so I can't!

> *8 January* ... Lunch with Bruno Walter and his daughter. It was grand to see him again and he seems no older. He is working very hard and loves it. It is rather a calamity he is already booked for the London Philharmonic in November. The BBC too late again ...

> *10 January* ... To a show called *Oklahoma!* It is a musical comedy (with a staggering ballet in which cowboys whirl young women round their shoulders) with pretty good music and not a bad sort of Wild West story. I think it will certainly find its way to London some day ...[3]

> *13 January.* In good time to the station to catch the 10 o'clock to Boston. A most comfortable journey except that I went to lunch just too late and had to queue for about 20 minutes. I had taken a book with me, so I was

quite happy ... The hotel is Ritz-Carlton, and seems as nasty as most Ritzes.

8 February [back in New York]. 11.30 appointment at Schirmers, the big music publishers, with several people, including Samuel Barber ... Feed at the hotel and then to the Lowenbachs, whom I knew originally in Prague ... He is now doing work at the consulate here. Olin Downes, the redoubtable *New York Times* critic, Georg Szell the conductor, who sent us several parcels during the war, and Martinů, a Czech composer who is living here. We talked so hard no one noticed the time till it was 12.45.

9 February ... Supper with Elisabeth Schumann, who has a lovely flat miles away beyond 90th Street with a roof garden looking out over the East River ... She still has her Viennese cook, so we had a wonderful meal, of course.

10 February ... Toscanini broadcast at Radio City. It is 50 years since he conducted the first performance of *La Bohème* and so he did Acts 1 and 2 last Sunday and we heard 3 and 4. He had a fine cast of Metropolitan singers, and it went very finely, bar one little accident near the end which upset him terribly ...[4]

11 February ... Lunch with Szell at 12.30. He is a nice creature and terribly devoted to England and his friends there.

13 February. Decided to buy another pair of shoes, so I went off to get them and some golf balls for Weir and various orchestral people ... Boston Orchestra concert, Prokofiev's new symphony [No. 5], rather exciting I think ...[5]

14 February ... Philharmonic-Symphony concert conducted by Rodzinski. I'm afraid I didn't care for Brahms No. 1 very much. The leader, Corigliano, played the Szymanowski concerto well.[6] Rodzinski was very cordial and asked me to tea tomorrow.

15 February ... *Fidelio* with Walter conducting; a lovely show, with Arthur Carron, the English tenor, doing very well as Florestan. Got on board at 11 to find almost the same cabin waiting for me.

He returned on 21 February to England and to the worries over the BBC Symphony Orchestra's depleting personnel. He urged the promise of a foreign tour as a likely bait for recruits, and continued (in a report to Hely-Hutchinson):

Put bluntly, does the Corporation wish me to try and bring the orchestra up to its 1939 standard or would it prefer to have a useful and efficient working body that will accede to all the demands of the various services ...? It might be simpler to yield to all planning demands, work our schedule on a minimum of rehearsal and a minimum of public appearances, and give up inviting our

Toscaninis and Menuhins, or at any rate acquiesce in their refusal to visit us when they discover what is happening ... There is no compromise.

Hely-Hutchinson was no ball of fire in these matters and took two months to ponder Boult's words. He eventually evolved some recommendations in November which were placed before Basil Nicolls, Controller of Programmes. 'He swallowed most of H-H's proposals whole,' Boult wrote to his sister and father on the 30th, 'so I suppose he will persuade the Board to agree to them. The main things were that the orchestra should work more closely with me (fewer guests); should be more stable in its divisions, and that choice of programme should rest more with the Music Department so that we can repeat programmes more on the different services and not be eternally rehearsing fresh things.' In mid-December the Board agreed to abolish the division of the orchestra into the old Section A, Section B, etc. but set its establishment at 96, a decrease of 23, and agreed to a reduction to four performances a week, perhaps with repeats. Nicholls told Haley: 'Boult naturally prefers conducting an orchestra which is about 20 players bigger than the standard orchestras of America and Europe ... Ensemble is more important within reasonable limits than the individual eminence of the players.' The Reithian note is conspicuous by its absence. Yet Boult, in a report on his Boston visit, had stressed that 'individually there are only two principals in the Boston orchestra who could in any way be considered superior to their opposite numbers in London.'

A new factor had by now entered into the BBC's calculations: the foundation of the Third Programme on 29 September 1946. This was to be a cultural channel, concerned not with listening-figures but with appealing to an intelligent minority by offering the best of drama, music, poetry and talks. For the post-war generation, many of whom had missed the chance to go to university, the Third *was* a university and its virtual dismantling some years later was a victory for philistinism. Its first Controller, George Barnes, was not satisfied with the standard of the BBC orchestra in 1946 and, like Boult, wanted it to be restored to its 1939 position. Boult conducted the new wavelength's first concert, a programme of English music which opened with a commissioned *Occasional Overture* from Britten, whose *Peter Grimes* at Sadler's Wells in June 1945 had placed him in the forefront of British musical life. It was not a happy commission. There was trouble over inaccuracies in the parts, and the composer, as has already been seen, was never particularly happy with Boult, who had disapproved of Britten's departure to America in 1939. In 1943, after Britten's return, Boult was asked

206

to conduct Britten's incidental music to *The Rescue*, a play by Edward Sackville-West, and (according to Bliss's report of 25 October) 'declared that he was antagonistic to the composer and his work and would rather not conduct. Clarence Raybould expressed the same opinion . . .' Britten was persuaded to write the 1946 overture by Etienne Amyot, one of the Third Programme planners, who met him and Erwin Stein, of Boosey and Hawkes, on 1 July of that year. Amyot's report to Barnes stated:

> It was a very sticky dinner until drink made both of them a little more amiable. The first half . . . was a tremendous attack against the BBC by Britten which threatened at moments to become quite hysterical. He said he had no faith in the new programme, and that though we might for a week or two spend a lot of money and time in trying to get the things we wanted, the service, like the Home and the Light, would disintegrate by Christmas and be indistinguishable from either A or B. I found the real difficulty with Britten was that he spoke not so much his own thoughts as the thoughts of Mr Stein, who is obviously his Svengali . . . By . . . concentrating entirely on Britten . . . I was able to change his point of view . . . he said he would very much like to write a Festival Overture for our opening concert. My own impression of Britten is that he is charming and that I can always get on with him. I think Stein is a stumbling block and at the moment seems to control with an iron hand all Britten's movements.

After the concert Britten withdrew the overture and it was not heard again until 1983, seven years after his death.[7]

Whatever Boult may have felt about Britten's music during the war, he conducted the first London performance of the *Four Sea Interludes* from *Peter Grimes* at a Prom on 29 August 1945. He conducted the *Scottish Ballad* in Brussels in 1946, as has been already stated, and he conducted the *Grimes* Interludes together with Vaughan Williams's *Pastoral Symphony*, Ireland's Piano Concerto, Eugene Goossens's Oboe Concerto and some Elgar when he went with Moura Lympany and Leon Goossens to conduct the Czech Philharmonic in Prague on 23 and 24 May 1946. He renewed his friendship with Václav Talich and Rafael Kubelik and his love for 'this wonderfully green city, trees everywhere.' President Beneš attended the second concert, after which there was 'an enormous party: rooms and rooms of people and incredible food, including wonderful Prague ham, strawberries, cherries, etc. etc. etc. Kubelik says that Czechs are like Russians, when they entertain they go right out of what is reasonable . . . Soon after I had had enough to eat (about 11.45) I started off home and found that Sam Barber, that very nice American composer also in our hotel, was of like mind, so we walked home . . .' A few weeks later, from 1 to 6 July, he went to The

Hague to conduct the Residentie Orchestra in Vaughan Williams's Fifth Symphony – 'I was surprised at their reading and command of style – though of course they are only in the second rank really.'

In London the BBC orchestra played during 1946 either in the Royal Albert Hall or in a hall Boult knew well from 25 years earlier, the People's Palace in Mile End Road. In the 1945–6 season Boult conducted Bach's *Christmas Oratorio*, Dvořák's Cello Concerto with Casals, and Bartók's Second Violin Concerto with Menuhin (its first London performance). On 6 March 1946 he conducted the British première of Bartók's *Concerto for Orchestra* and continued his championship of this composer on 27 November when, with Louis Kentner, he gave the first British performance of the Third Piano Concerto, repeating it in the Third Programme studio a few days later. On 16 March, in the Royal Albert Hall, Boult repeated a pre-war success, the concert performance of *Wozzeck*, with Heinrich Nillius in the title-rôle, Suzanne Danco as Marie and Otakar Kraus as the Doctor. Other novelties he conducted in 1946 included Moeran's Cello Concerto, Berkeley's *Nocturne* and the first British performance of Strauss's Oboe Concerto. In July, as he told his sister, he had 'a letter from a Boston friend who is saying that if Koussevitzky goes, I *must* succeed him as it would be the finest thing for international relations that could possibly happen etc. etc. Well, all I say is, I hope Koussevitzky won't go yet!' (Koussevitzky did not retire until 1949.)

The year 1947 began happily for Boult with the return of Bruno Walter to the Maida Vale studio. 'Everything there as always,' he noted, 'some of it intensified. He deprecated Paul Beard's saying he would save his tone at rehearsal, as he believes in full power at rehearsals (not necessarily full emotional pressure?). Strauss's *Don Juan* and the "Jupiter" were very fine.' Gradually some distinguished guest conductors returned, among them Enesco, Ansermet and Munch, but the hope that Toscanini might return in April and May 1947, mentioned by Boult in a letter to his sister written on 3 August 1946, was not fulfilled. In February and March Boult had 10 concerts with the LPO. It played, he wrote,

> ... the usual way until the fifth concert, in a freezing Albert Hall, when Beethoven 7 was in the programme. It became a new orchestra: at the start of the rehearsal there was at once a far greater intensity, a far greater perfection of ensemble, eg. the 9th bar of the Introduction. Also some lovely diminuendos and pianos (eg. last movement, just before second subject, against the *sfz* crotchets). Even the attack in *f* was quite different from what I had been getting (but exactly what I had been trying to get) in the Mozart

E flat. It transpired that about six months ago they had done it after intensive rehearsal work with de Sabata. So perhaps there is something in John Barbirolli's rehearsals which I always said rehearsed the orchestra rather than the programme: in other words that he was doing the work of a permanent conductor and going far beyond the work in hand. This method annoys quick musicians like Fred Riddle [violist], who resents the elementaries of a rehearsal. I think that explains my impatience of those things, though I can always do them when I have wind or strings alone.

Boult went to Vienna (still divided into Russian, American and British zones) in the latter part of March to conduct the Symphony Orchestra. He travelled by the *Golden Arrow*. He wrote home from Munich:

> I got the impression that the Germans have gone back 100 years in civilization since 1912. We occasionally pass local trains hanging about, and the people in them all look as if they had settled down for the day (or longer) with all their worldly goods and that time doesn't matter any more. It's like descriptions of Russia.

In Vienna he was the guest of the British Council.

> We went to the hotel for breakfast. Sacher's was the old-fashioned feudal hotel – it used to have the best food in Vienna. Now it's the principal English officers' hostel. My bedroom is incredibly 19th century and sumptuous: great leather chaises-longues and curtains weighing a ton ... Dinner with Mr [Richard] Hiscocks, who is the director of this branch of the British Council. He has a lovely flat in an old palace, and it was a pleasant party of 12, including the Deputy C.-in-C. here, General Winterton, also Lady [Susi] Jeans[8] (the astronomer's widow) who before her marriage was an organist here: she is giving a recital tomorrow. The general was very entertaining about the Russians. He gets on very well with them because he always tells them what he thinks of them, and the tougher he is the more they like it ...

His diary goes on:

> 23 *March* ... At 4 I went to a concert conducted by a Hungarian named Somogyi[9] – not very good. Klemperer came in just as I left – he is conducting next week ... [He went to Verdi's *Otello* that evening] ... the only really first-class singer was Iago, Paul Schöffler.

> 24 *March*. Rather a formidable rehearsal ... We got a good deal done, though I should have liked another half-an-hour on the Britten [*Sea Interludes*]. They read very well, but it is a very difficult programme.

> 26 *March* ... The concert was full, and the orchestra played with a good deal more spirit than yesterday. The audience were respectful to the new things – I hardly expected so much – and there was the usual Viennese

scene after the Beethoven symphony – given Beethoven, I don't think they mind in the least whether it is well or badly done!

27 March ... We went across to the Opera House.[10] It is quite incredible: you go in by the old grand staircase, which is in perfect order with all its statues: then they take you into the Imperial drawing-room, and this is also perfect. You step out from that into what was the centre box, and there is nothing at all except the bare framework of the circle boxes, the proscenium arch, and on the far side just the outside walls of the stage – open to the sky. Every stick of scenery and dresses was burnt. They have put a concrete floor in where the stalls were, and then they take you downstairs. Underneath this new roof the whole thing is untouched. An enormous power plant – steam and electricity – carpenter's shop where they are now making scenery for the new productions in the temporary opera house (Theater an der Wien), and a great painting room. It is the most extraordinary mixture of destruction and activity you could possibly imagine ... Saw Dr Hilbert, who is the Lord High Austrian Theatres. He wants me for Salzburg this summer, but I'm afraid it can't be done. He is an amazing little man who spent 4 years in Dachau ... Then to a tea party with the orchestra ... After about half-an-hour we had to go off to fetch an opera singer, Elisabeth Schwarzkopf, who was giving a recital for the British Council ... She is a charming singer, and sang a lot of old English things as well as Schubert, Mozart and Wolf.

In May of this year Boult received the honorary degree of Doctor of Laws from Liverpool University. On 8 June he conducted his first concert with the Philharmonia Orchestra, in the Royal Albert Hall. One of his wishes was fulfilled later in the month when he took the BBC orchestra to play in Paris, Brussels, Amsterdam and Scheveningen. Each programme contained a British work – Rawsthorne's Piano Concerto (Kentner); Bax's *Overture to a Picaresque Comedy*; Bliss's *Music for Strings*; Walton's Violin Concerto (Arthur Grumiaux); Vaughan Williams's Double Piano Concerto (Sellick and Smith); and Britten's Violin Concerto (Theo Olof). Boult stayed at the British Embassy in Paris where Duff Cooper was Ambassador. 'As we went down to lunch,' he wrote home on 18 June, 'we found Mr Bevin [Foreign Secretary] sitting on the verandah outside the window. He hastily retreated to a man's party which the Ambassador was giving for him elsewhere. Lady Diana did the honours for us.' The soprano soloist, a last-minute substitute, in Ravel's *Shéhérazade* on the 19th was Janine Micheau. 'After the concert we had a party in the hall, given by the Radio. It consisted only of champagne and no food, so we nearly died, and rushed off to get some food afterwards.'

Boult in 1947 still had not succeeded in disentangling himself from

the Proms. After the 1946 series he told Hely-Hutchinson that a 'fundamental overhaul' in attitude to these concerts was needed. 'We are giving
programmes of identical calibre with our symphony concerts, at greater
length and at half the price ... This is not only an absurd situation, it
is dishonest, for the slipshod nature of our performances cannot be
understood by most of that young audience, and even our professional
critics seem to assume that we have three rehearsals for every concert.'
Winter Proms were revived in January 1947, at one of which Boult
conducted the first performance of Patrick Hadley's *The Hills*. In the
summer series he conducted Walter Piston's Second Symphony, a concerto for bassoon, strings and percussion by Gordon Jacob, and a suite
by Elisabeth Lutyens. In the BBC Symphony Orchestra's 1947–8 winter
concerts he conducted Mahler's Eighth Symphony (10 February 1948)
and the first performance of Finzi's *Ode on St Cecilia's Day*.

In a studio concert on 3 September 1947 he conducted Mahler's
Fourth Symphony (with Elisabeth Schumann), on 29 November the
Third Symphony, its first performance in Britain (the contralto soloist
was Kathleen Ferrier) and on 20 December the Fifth Symphony in a
Third Programme concert that included Busoni's Violin Concerto. These
Mahler performances came a decade before the British revival of interest
in the composer. Many another conductor would have cried from the
publicity office 'Look what I'm doing for Mahler here!' Boult just
conducted it. It is worth mentioning that he conducted *Das Lied von
der Erde* in 1942 and 1945, the Seventh Symphony on 31 January 1948
and the *Adagio* of the Tenth on 28 October 1949.

On 21 April 1948 he conducted Vaughan Williams's Sixth Symphony,
the first of 100 performances this work was to receive in its first two
years' existence. Britten's *Scottish Ballad* was in the same programme
as the new symphony, which was repeated in the studio on the Third
Programme four days later. Another Vaughan Williams first performance (of a revised work) had been conducted by Boult in the studio
on 20 March. This was the *Partita for Strings*. When Vaughan Williams
conducted the BBC orchestra in this work's first public performance, in
a Prom a few months later, he consulted Boult about the use of vibrato
and decided to indicate nothing in the score. Boult's rejoinder, on 11
June, was to

> put in a plea for the stupid performer. You have no idea, I expect, what it
> feels like to hanker for the composer's instructions when you are working
> out a score ... it is the greatest comfort to have metronome marks and
> indications like *vibrato* or *non vibrato* or a note about the general treatment
> at the beginning of the score or the beginning of the movement, so please do

not expect too much from the interpreter. He may misunderstand your intentions, but that is one stage better from having none.

A further Vaughan Williams occasion which pleased Boult was when he conducted *Job* at Covent Garden on 20 May 1948, its first staging with the full orchestration. Robert Helpmann danced Satan in the three performances during the month.

In the summer of 1948 Boult took the orchestra to the second Edinburgh Festival. 'Relieved from Promenades,' he wrote in his notebook in August. 'Thank goodness. I hope permanently.' He made two overseas visits in 1948. He conducted two performances of Vaughan Williams's *Job* with the Concertgebouw Orchestra of Amsterdam on 29 and 30 January and two of Elgar's *The Dream of Gerontius* on 1 and 2 February. The Elgar was a thanksgiving to Britain for its help to Holland in the war and was organized by the Toonkunst Chor, who invited Boult. His soloists were Parry Jones, Mary Jarred and Harold Williams. At the interval Eduard van Beinum, the Concertgebouw's conductor, echoing Richard Strauss over forty years earlier, said to him: 'But this is a masterpiece!' On 20 June he crossed the Channel to travel by train to Vienna, where Richard Hiscocks was again his host and took him to Mozart's *Die Entführung* on his first evening. He was to conduct the Vienna Symphony Orchestra in Britten's *Sinfonia da Requiem* and rehearsed them at 9 am on 22 June. 'The orchestra is overworking badly: they do about 40–44 hours a week which seems frightful. But we got through pretty well as I did all I wanted to the Britten symphony and the Prokofiev 3rd concerto; the soloist is a very clever boy of 18 named Gulda.[11] I hope he won't get spoilt, as he seems pretty sure of himself now!'

Some of Boult's comments in his diary shed a noteworthy light on the state of de-Nazified Vienna:

> *24 June* ... Concert was almost full – rather unusual they say nowadays, and the two modern things went very well. I wasn't so happy about the Brahms [Fourth Symphony], but most people seemed to think it was all right. After the concert a very grand party given by the C.-in-C. (General Galloway) at the officers' club in a wonderful and enormous town house of the Kinsky family. It is full of treasures of every kind and is a museum rather than a club. Even the books are still there, including a volume of telegrams of congratulation to Count Kinsky when he won the Grand National! They are still in existence, but seem to be living now on the rent they get from the British. The Esterházys, who employed Haydn for most of his life, are scattered and the head of the family is in prison in Budapest. They are hoping to get him out.

25 *June*. 9 o'clock and still a rehearsal, but this time only to listen; a girl
fiddler named Lubowska of quite exceptional promise is playing the Delius
at a students' concert at the Academy, conducted by a student ... On to
a party given by Josef Krips and his wife. He is first conductor at the
Opera. A *very* nice creature and a fine conductor, though he is getting a
bit snuffed out by the restoration of the local (and artistic) Nazis of the
Furtwängler and Karajan order ...

Staying at Hubertushof in the Styrian Hills Boult was able to go for
long walks, like the one he took on 27 June: 'Upwards to a hill about
4,200 (the hotel is 3,500) and back along the wrong shoulder! I don't
know where we should have gone to if we hadn't run into a forester
who unceremoniously pushed us down the deepest valley and round the
corner, where we saw the wretched place, miles high of course. We got
back just at 1. Hiscocks had to go back directly after lunch, and took
me about 10 miles as we had discovered a short cut up a valley on the
map. This worked out most successfully ...' On 2 July he conducted in
Graz. 'It is a beautiful hall – I had forgotten that Schubert wrote the
Unfinished Symphony for this society – he and Beethoven were both
honorary members of it. I was shown their names in the guest book.
Everything went well – a lot better than Vienna – the cellist Krotschak
did the Elgar very well though of course far more sentimentally than
we do; and the Brahms went far better than Vienna and impressed the
audience obviously – it is funny they play it so seldom.'

While Boult was abroad, important meetings were being held at the
BBC in London with one aim in view: to find his successor as conductor
of the BBC Symphony Orchestra.

CHAPTER 25

'The Axe Must Fall'

BOULT says in his autobiography[1] that he tried to obtain 'a special gratuity' for Walter Birch, the orchestral van driver who saved the BBC's instruments in Bristol when he took the van up on the downs during a raid that demolished the garage. 'I never heard of his being given a penny,' he wrote, and added: 'Bureaucracy is a stubborn thing.' So he should not have been surprised by the events of 1948–9 which led to the end of his 20 years' employment by the BBC. Nevertheless, although there was nothing of malice in his nature and he was philosophical about the ways of the world, he remained bitter to the end of his days about the fact and the manner of what amounted to his dismissal. Nothing else would have led him to forget himself to the extent of blurting out to Princess Elizabeth (now the Queen) when presented to her in the interval of a concert: 'They have just sacked me. I mean the BBC' (an embarrassing moment eased by the Duke of Edinburgh's immediate intervention: 'Then I hope they have given you a pension'). Although, as will be seen, it was not as clear-cut as that, it was handled in a way that can be charitably described at best as distasteful.

The BBC rule for the retirement of its staff is when they reach 60. In Boult's case this was 8 April 1949. Some time before that he received a two-line chit from a clerk in Programme Contracts saying, in effect, that on that day 'the axe must fall.' It might be thought that so distinguished a servant of the Corporation, who had created for it one of the world's great orchestras, would have been interviewed by the Director-General before such a note was sent. 'A casual remark made by one whose position was much senior to mine gave me hope of extension, and this was not uncommon at that time,' Boult wrote later.[2] He was referring to Reith, who had said to him more than once: 'We shall never sack you. When you get to 60, tell us what extra help you want and we'll draw up a new contract accordingly.' But Reith had been gone for ten years; and although Boult would have expected this verbal promise to be honoured, a new climate prevailed at the BBC in 1948. Senior officials concerned with finance, for example, were not pleased by reports that Boult sometimes did not use all his available rehearsal time – they had no sympathy for his concern for his players, some of whose homes were still requisitioned in an 'austerity' Britain where food rationing was sometimes severer than it had been in the war. There was also a personal element in the affair which pained Boult deeply, though he never referred to it.

In March 1947, Hely-Hutchinson died at the age of 46 after three well-meaning but ineffectual years as Director of Music. For a year Kenneth Wright held the fort as Acting Director. In 1948, with the post renamed Head of Music, the new incumbent was announced – Steuart Wilson. What Boult must have thought when he heard this news can be imagined. Yet Haley, the Director-General, did not discover until over 30 years later that Boult's wife had formerly been married to Wilson. Since there was no mention of this in reference books, there can be some excuse for him, but the matter was common knowledge among musicians and in the BBC generally and it is extraordinary that nobody thought to mention it to Haley. (He did not know of it until 1986.[3]) Wilson had worked for the BBC from 1942 to 1945 as Overseas Music Director, a post in which Boult's and his paths scarcely crossed. He had then become Music Director of the newly-founded Arts Council of Great Britain. Two months after taking up his BBC post in 1948 he was knighted. As soon as Wilson was established in Yalding House, where the Music Department was housed, Boult moved out and in future worked only at Maida Vale.

Wilson arrived at the BBC with a long-term strategy. On 26 May he informed Haley his 'first priority' was 'to plan for the future of the Symphony Orchestra, gradually replacing Boult while looking for his successor within or without the present music staff.' He immediately began making lists of names, narrowing it down to two British candidates, Sargent and Barbirolli. His target-date for the new man was the 1951–2 season. In the meantime 'Boult could be retained as the permanent conductor provided that it was made quite clear to him that after the autumn of 1948 he would be free to accept outside engagements.' While Boult was in Vienna, there was a meeting on 22 June between Wilson, his ally Basil Nicolls (Director of Home Broadcasting) and R.J.F. Howgill (Controller, Entertainment) at which invitations to Sargent and Barbirolli were approved for a kind of trial period, although 'it does not follow that we shall in the event offer the job to either of them.' Be that as it may, Wilson offered it a few days later to Sargent, who said he did not want the full-time post but would co-operate with Barbirolli, leaving him the responsibility for the orchestra. A few days later, at the Cheltenham Festival, Wilson made detailed proposals to Barbirolli, inviting him to conduct at the 1949 Proms and to take an increasing share in the orchestra's work, leading to his appointment as Boult's successor. Barbirolli rejected the Proms but agreed to think about the chief conductorship. The BBC brought forward the starting date to October 1950 and gave Barbirolli until 1 January 1949 to decide. In October 1948 the news of the offer appeared in the Press and was followed by alarm in Manchester at the prospect of Barbirolli's leaving the Hallé. On 28 December Barbirolli wrote to Wilson declining the BBC post. His heart was with the Hallé and was to remain there until he died in 1970.

Meanwhile, on 21 October 1948, Nicolls had written a report to the BBC Governors which, although it mentioned as one of Boult's 'indispensable' qualifications his 'absolute willingness to conduct any music, classical or modern,' gave several specious reasons why he was dispensable. First was his age, coupled with 'the fact that he has asked to be excused from conducting the orchestra in the current Promenade season, which constitutes an important fraction of the year's output.' He gave Boult 'most of the credit' for a recent improvement in the orchestra, the decline of which since 1939 'is attributable to loss of players through military service and to war conditions generally' – a palpable untruth. He also mentioned the orchestra's lack of *esprit de corps*, its resentment 'of the amount of rehearsal which conductors other than Sir Adrian require.'

Deprived of Barbirolli, Wilson's next idea was for a triumvirate – Sargent, Rafael Kubelik, who had left Czechoslovakia after the Communist takeover in 1948, and Boult, with many guest conductors. Nicolls amended this to Bruno Walter, with Kubelik as assistant and Boult as 'distinguished guest.' In all this, Wilson and Nicolls took Boult's acquiescence for granted – they did not consult him. He was told he had to go, yet he was expected to be available as of old when wanted. On 3 December 1948 Wilson was writing to Nicolls about offering Boult 'renewal of his contract on a yearly basis from 9 April 1949' because 'it is clearly desirable in every way that the BBC should not lose his services.' On 6 January 1949, the Governors decided to ask Kubelik to become Boult's assistant as soon as possible. Boult would be given an extra year until April 1950 when Kubelik would take over. Later that day Wilson wrote privately to Boult telling him about the year's extension and Kubelik's succession. He then told him 'that you should

216

consider yourself free to take any engagements at all that may come your way in 1950, having regard to the fact that the BBC would certainly wish you to continue a considerable amount of conducting in that year, but no detailed proposition can be made now... I feel we must make it clear that whatever you do for the BBC, or stop doing for the BBC, you have not retired from public conducting ... I want to see justice done all round, which includes you.'

Boult was in Holland and Italy and did not reply for over three weeks. Writing on 27 January he gave his reactions under three headings:

1. A real pleasure that Kubelik may take over – there is no one I would rather make way for.

2. Considerable disappointment that it is all to happen so soon. Quite frankly, I would much rather go on with the orchestra I know, at any rate till sixty-five, even if the Associate does more work than he has up to now. I had, too, hoped that I might still be with them during the special concerts of 1951, the twenty-first year of my work with them and the year in which I become sixty-two. If anyone else is No. 1 conductor at that time the position will be much more difficult – the retired headmaster is always a nuisance, and I cannot think that Kubelik, with the interests of his visits abroad, should mind being Associate Conductor at any rate until the end of 1951 ...

3. If I am once retired, I can't help feeling that to come back is going to be difficult and awkward. The conductor emeritus business does not appear to be working well in Boston, and I think it is a bad idea. If I am really to begin looking for other work in a year's time I feel most reluctant to accept the position. The experiences of this last month, wonderful though they have been from many points of view, have only confirmed me once more in my feeling that I am no guest conductor; I want to work with a permanent body. Please let it be a BBC one.

The preamble to Wilson's reply on 7 February contains the only hint during the negotiations of their 'special relationship' – 'it must be very clear that it has been a difficult job for me to make any suggestion to you about your retirement, but it has been equally clear to me that I should have to do it, however short my own tenure was to be, and that I couldn't "leave it to the next man."' He then rejected any delay until 1951. Boult's contract would end in April 1950, 'but it is quite clear that in planning the Festival of 1951 you and the BBC Orchestra would play a very important part... The new contract with you will then be specific for certain periods during which you will be returning as a welcome guest.' This uncomfortable letter ended with acknowledgment of 'the debt which music in this country owes to your work for it over all these years. There has been nothing like it before – and there will never be a need to do such a pioneer job again, I hope. We are the gainers, all of us, but there must come the decision to change, and in my opinion we must not put it off any longer.'

Those were almost the last civil words written during this episode. Wilson's memorandum to Boult of 11 May is in a sharper tone:

> ... There will be no doubt that we will implement the suggestion that three complete free days and two half-days every fortnight will be left free by us during the winter season of October 1949 to April 1st 1950. I hope that you will, on your own initiative, refuse any other casual or lengthy invitations which might prejudice this amount of free time, which I agree is essential. In particular, I am thinking of the letter from the British Council of 26 April inviting you to Budapest. It would hardly be justifiable for me to say that this amount of free time is essential for you if you accepted such a proposal as it put forward, ie. to go for ten continuous days in Hungary in which you would quite certainly get nothing approaching the amount of free time which you would reasonably stipulate in the BBC. It also raises the question of the American tour this summer, and I hope that you are taking steps not to be too consistently overworked in that spell, for when you return for the Proms it will be impossible, so far as I can see, to implement this decision in the fortnight's work as planned ...

The gloves were off. Next day Boult wrote to Wilson: 'It is now becoming urgent that I should know what is to happen to me after April 1950.' He sought a 'closer definition' of when his services were required in 1950 and 1951.

> If it means eight or even six months in each of those years with a reasonable prospect of further work after 1951, the matter becomes less urgent. Anything less than this will make it necessary for me to think very quickly, as I do not contemplate a life of guest-conducting with any satisfaction, and I must take steps to find a permanent post, if I can, as soon as possible, but I am most unwilling to do this until I am definitely and finally removed from association with the BBC Orchestra. Another job will be undoubtedly difficult to find ...

Wilson replied after 12 days offering January–March 1951, 'considerable participation in the projected Festival of 1951 in April, May and June,' and not more than eight or nine weeks of continuous contract in 1951–2.

By the end of 1949, Wilson knew that Kubelik would not be going to the BBC. Because of his wife's illness and her wish to stay in America, Kubelik accepted the post of conductor of the Chicago Symphony Orchestra. Thus the BBC post fell into the lap of Sir Malcolm Sargent. He fixed himself a contract to run initially from July 1950 to July 1951 and thereafter without limit, subject to a year's notice. There was no mention of retirement age. On 6 January 1950 Haley at last wrote to Boult confirming that his 'retirement' took effect on 8 April 1950 and paying him the appropriate compliments. 'I have had a very nice letter indeed from D.G.,' Boult wrote to Nicolls on 25 January. 'He did however mention 8 April 1950 as the end of my contract though Music Department tell me that they will want me continuously until June 17th. ... Though there is no hurry I should be interested to know on what basis the Corporation proposes to pay me for my services.' Haley, incidentally, had received a deputation from the Symphony Orchestra, led by Ernest Hall, which asked him to retain Boult, but he merely told them 'I will consult the Director of Music.'

Meanwhile Boult in 1949 had conducted the first performances of Rubbra's Fifth Symphony and Arnold Cooke's First Symphony and the first British performances of Copland's Third Symphony, Caplet's *Epiphanie* for cello, Roussel's first *Bacchus et Ariane* suite, Barraud's Piano Concerto and Nystroem's *Sinfonia Espressiva*. When the Third Programme relayed all Bruckner's symphonies, Boult conducted two studio performances of the Fifth. According to Robert Simpson,[4] he 'slammed through it' in 50 minutes (a reasonable time would be 75 minutes) so that the orchestra 'could hardly articulate the notes and was unable to be other than grossly insensitive.' He opened the orchestra's 1949–50 season in the Royal Albert Hall on 12 October, Vaughan Williams's 77th birthday, by conducting *Job* and Elgar's *Introduction and Allegro*. In the first five months of 1950, his last period as chief conductor, he conducted the first British performance of Hindemith's Piano Concerto and Matyás Seiber's *Ulysses* and the first performance of Elizabeth Maconchy's Symphony. He also conducted Parry's *De Profundis*, which was heard over the air by his old friend Bruce Richmond (former editor of the *Times Literary Supplement*) who 'sat by firelight and listened – and flew back to Hereford (1891) and C.H.H.P. hustling it along and adding to the general confusion. But I thought then and I think still that it's about the old man's top notch.' His public farewell concert was in the Royal Albert Hall on 19 April. The programme was Brahms's *Variations on a Theme of Haydn*, Elgar's *Falstaff*, the Prelude to Act III of Wagner's *Die Meistersinger* and Schubert's Great C major Symphony.

On his 60th birthday itself, 8 April, Ann and he were entertained to dinner at the Savoy by the orchestra. No BBC staff were there except Gwen Beckett. Ernest Hall, principal trumpet, was in the chair and proposed Boult's health. The guests' health was proposed by Sidonie

Goossens, and Vaughan Williams replied. There was a 'magical enter-
tainer' and, as a surprise, the comedian Gillie Potter 'contributed some
of his inimitable fun,' as Boult put it. Haley and some BBC colleagues
gave Boult a lunch party in Broadcasting House on 21 April at which
Haley, again to quote Boult,[5] 'spoke in such kind terms that I began to
wonder whether I had really been asked to go or had insisted on going,
to their great regret.' Three days later, at a more formal farewell dinner
in the Connaught Rooms, Boult was given what Haley called 'a Mozart
of inkstands' in silver – 'which your wife will have to clean,' one of the
women Governors remarked. Haley wrote in his own hand to Boult on
28 April:

> Your letter touched me. I do hope that you will always look back on your
> twenty years in the BBC with happiness, even though – as I hope – you may
> have still greater happiness to come. Nothing will ever efface the memory of
> the part you have played here. The way of the pioneers is hard, but they do
> have the consolation that their achievements remain sharply etched. And
> what an achievement yours has been. We have not met often, but I have
> always found it a great pleasure and I trust it will not be unwelcome if in
> the future I still occasionally pay you an interval visit in the abysses of the
> Albert Hall.

Yet perhaps the most touching and imaginative farewell gesture was
a party on 15 July held by the gardening section of the BBC Club in
their newly-made garden at St Hilda's, Maida Vale. All who attended
signed a book which began with a letter expressing pride that 'the
greater part of your broadcasting with the BBC Symphony Orchestra
and other orchestras has been from the studios at Maida Vale ... We
shall remember always your charm and courtesy towards us and your
friendliness and modesty.' Boult planted a tree (*falix pendula aurea*)
during the afternoon. Letters pasted into the presentation book included
tributes from Ralph Vaughan Williams, Arnold Bax, Thomas Beecham,
John Barbirolli, Ernest McMillan, Eugene Goossens, Enrique Jorda,
Eduard van Beinum, Victor de Sabata, Bruno Walter, Charles Munch
and Rafael Kubelik.

Boult's chagrin can be understood, but friends had been warning him
for some time that his position was at risk. They sensed, particularly
after the Bedford episode, that there was a certain 'anti-Adrian' faction
in the post-war BBC and tried to persuade him that, after 20 years, a
change might be to everyone's advantage. They reminded him of Bruno
Walter's belief that a change every ten years was to the good. Vaughan
Williams took this view; it was pointed out to him that what hurt Boult

more than his 'retirement' was the way it was being arranged. 'Oh, we all know the hash the BBC makes of these things,' Vaughan Williams replied. Boult wanted to stay so that he could bring the orchestra back to its pre-war pitch and hand it over in prime condition to a successor. But he was not to be given time for that. In a sense, his removers did him a good turn, as his subsequent career showed. For too long he had been protected from the jungle of guest-conducting. He had never had to concern himself much about programme-building. Nor had he much say in the choice of soloists (though obviously he had some favourites). As he wrote some years later:[6] 'I very seldom have had to act on my own judgment where singers are concerned and I have got into the lazy way of taking what I find and doing the best with it (eg. – recordings. I almost always accept what EMI suggest and, if necessary, have a private rehearsal). Also, I *cannot* separate the artist from the person, and I'm afraid I get easily turned off if I hear unpleasant things (or meet them) about people.'

The particular circumstances of working with the BBC Symphony Orchestra and his acquiescence in conducting too many works for which he had no real enthusiasm undoubtedly took its toll of Boult's artistry on occasions, and damaged his reputation. Where Beecham or Barbirolli would give an incandescent account of a work for which they had a genuine, even if only transitory, passion, Boult – often with inadequate rehearsal – would turn in a middle-of-the-road performance, sound but uninspired (and, equally, very rarely bad). In Elgar and Vaughan Williams, Schubert and Ravel (*Daphnis and Chloë*), Brahms and Beethoven, he had few equals. A contemporary composer would know that his work would be faithfully presented by Boult, whereas some of Boult's colleagues might convince even the composer that he had written better than he knew. E.J. Moeran, for example, was disappointed by the first performance of his *Rhapsody* for piano at a 1943 Prom, partly because he disliked Harriet Cohen's interpretation, but a year later when the BBC Symphony Orchestra under Barbirolli gave the first performance of the *Sinfonietta*, Moeran wrote 'Thank God we have escaped Boult for it!'[7] Moeran referred to Boult as 'the Dame' – Beecham having dubbed Boult as 'Dame Adrian' as a jibe against his abstemious tastes – and commented to his wife, the cellist Peers Coetmore, that Boult 'said he would play my works more often were he allowed to do so. I'm afraid he's a bit of a yes man, especially as he's reputed to have said at a luncheon party recently about me that I am not appreciated today, except by a minority of connoisseurs, but that in 25 years' time I shall be a household word.'[8] Moeran, who admired the performances and lengthy rehearsals his music was accorded at this time by Barbirolli's Hallé, is a good example of some musicians' attitude to Boult. When Boult conducted Moeran's Symphony at a BBC concert in February 1949 he wrote: 'Boult rose to the occasion and gave it a fine performance, really good. I heard he spent hours on it. So he did on Wednesday when I was there. He knew the score backwards and has his own ideas and suggestions and played it like he does Elgar.'⁹

It is unlikely, had he stayed, that Boult would have enjoyed developments at the BBC. He was succeeded, but he has never been replaced. Let the last words in this matter be from Sir William Haley: 'His departure from the BBC was an unhappy business. It continued to worry me as the years went by.'¹⁰ In 1976 Haley was invited to give a Radio 3 talk on the 30th anniversary of the inauguration of the Third Programme. 'There at once flashed into my mind the thought that it would give me the opportunity to pay tribute to you,' he wrote to Boult from his retirement home in Jersey. 'You may like to listen to my talk. ... You will hear what I have long wanted an opportunity to say and will, I hope, take it as an *amende honorable*.' In the talk Haley said that

Third Programme music could not in its early days have been the cornucopia it was without Sir Adrian Boult ... The Third Programme rostrum was international. Those occupants of it were transient ... Adrian Boult was always there; ready to take on the most outlandish work and to give it a careful performance, whether it appealed to him or not. Sir Adrian says in his memoirs that my speech at the farewell luncheon for him in Broadcasting House on his retirement under the age limit was so kind that he wondered if it was he who was insisting on going. I spoke as I did because I had already begun to realize that I had listened to ill-judged advice in retiring him. Happily, it released him for other achievements.

The olive branch was accepted.

It remains to record the happier parts of 1949, visits to Amsterdam, Milan and Rome and to Toronto, New York and Ravinia Park. Boult conducted the Concertgebouw Orchestra on 5 and 6 January when the soprano Jo Vincent sang Bach's cantata *Mein Herz schwimmt im Blut*. 'I think it all went well,' Boult wrote after the first evening. 'Jo Vincent at the top of her form, and the extraordinary sensation after the Brahms symphony [No. 3] of turning round and finding the whole audience on their feet. I think they often do it here, but it is always a shock for the stranger.'

On the train to Milan he went through the 'staggering' St Gothard tunnel:

I looked right down and saw a train crossing the valley and diving right into the hill below us; when in the tunnel we met the train, and on coming out we looked up and saw it coming out where we had first looked down on it. I should awfully like to do this trip by road, and come back up the Brenner. It would be fun to see what Hannibal really did with those poor elephants.

In Milan he conducted Holst's *Fugal Concerto*, Bliss's *Music for Strings* and Berkeley's *Divertimento*; and in Rome he conducted Vaughan Williams's Sixth Symphony. While in Milan he dined with the city's Federalists. After the war he had wanted to find an extra-musical activity to which to devote some time and energy, and Lady Snowden, then a BBC Governor, interested him in Federal Union. He was elected to the executive committee, but later became a vice-president of this body, the aims of which were an anticipation of the European Economic Community.

In Rome he was greeted by Keith Falkner, who was British Council Music Officer in Italy. He was pleased that the audience liked the Vaughan Williams but his first visit to St Peter's stole its thunder in his diary.

For some time I could only walk up and down and gape, because the size somehow eludes you. They have the length of other cathedrals marked in the floor, but the size of the dome can only be appreciated gradually as one walks about under it. The place gains enormously from its emptiness (no pews anywhere) and of course suffers from some pretty awful tombs. I visited the Sistine Chapel next (it is next door on the map) but found I must walk right round the Vatican City and then back through the galleries. This again is a staggering experience. So many things one has always known sitting there: Laocoon, Hermes of Praxitiles etc. The Sistine itself was disappointing as it was a dark day. One sees far more in reproduction, or perhaps on a sunny day.

While in Italy he renewed his friendship with the critic Francis Toye, who lived in Florence.

Boult sailed for New York in the *Caronia* on 18 June. On 30 June he conducted in Toronto. On 3 July he went to Tanglewood on the day the summer school began. 'It is a most lovely place ... Saw Koussevitzky – he has a house high on a hill above the estate and was in great form.' He went on to New York, where Isaac Stern was his soloist at a concert in the Stadium. At his second concert Claudio Arrau played the *Emperor* Concerto. Back in Boston with Archie Davison he went to a party given by Unitarians for Albert Schweitzer. 'He was in great form – seems younger than ever, and has decided to come to Europe for six months every year. The Africa hospital [Lambaréné] can look after itself in between, he thinks, as he has so many workers there.' On 24

July he went to a Mozart concert at Tanglewood. 'Koussevitzky was delighted I was there – he is a comically child-like person; but there are nasty stories about his jealousies. The Mozart programme was beautiful sometimes, but a lot of it seemed not Mozart to me.'

On 26 July he conducted the Chicago Symphony Orchestra at its summer festival venue, Ravinia Park.

> I found a great many former players there, and wonderfully responsive. I cannot make out why the East always cries down this orchestra. It is absolutely in the New York–Philadelphia–Boston class in my humble opinion. They played the fourth Beethoven most beautifully, I thought, in the evening ... Just as we were finishing the interval I became conscious of some disturbance outside, and there was the whole audience RACING for the shelter, as torrents of rain had burst upon us. They have rebuilt the whole thing wonderfully well after the fire only three months ago. The platform is splendid, and still better for sound than before, and over the audience an enormous marquee thing is stretched, covering three thousand people. There are still more seats outside, and the unfortunate occupants of those crowded into the middle, of course. We started the *Siegfried Idyll*, but the noise was terrific and finally thunder very close made us stop. We waited about ten minutes and then tackled the Elgar *Variations* – playing rather loud, and apparently loud enough for most people to enjoy quite a lot of it. They were very enthusiastic at the end, and the rain mercifully stopped just as we did. Then home for some welcome sandwiches and milk.

At other Ravinia concerts he conducted Vaughan Williams and Brahms – 'they played *Job* very well and also the Brahms symphony though one paper thought it was dull.' The critic's words were 'a sluggish, lifeless performance.' But Eugene Stimson in the *Chicago Daily News*, writing of Boult's Brahms and Schubert, described him as 'not a cold conductor, as many professed to find him ... He has the ease of a scholar, the zest of a gentleman, the clarity of a plate-glass window pane and the simplicity of a great intellect. But most of all I found him delightful because he is unselfishly, completely and naturally musical.' Boult returned to New York for a holiday of socializing and swimming, and went to several concerts including one at which Dmitri Mitropoulos 'played and conducted the Third Prokofiev. He is a remarkable pianist, and though his conducting is a bit spasmodic, there is no doubt he is one of the leading people here.' While in New York Boult had an experience he never forgot and which he mentioned in a broadcast talk.[11]

> I myself have become so much the slave of the clock that I always know what the time is (within a few minutes), and if my mealtimes are upset I am

annoyed and probably get very bad-tempered. Curiously, I quite recently had a glimpse of that freedom from the fetters of time which the East understands so well...It was very hot in New York so I took a train out along Long Island, stopped at random at a seaside village, found a room almost by accident and then spent two days on an island off the coast, amongst sandhills, alone but for a few other bathers. There was a small restaurant there, but even the need for meals seemed less urgent...But removed as I was from responsibility by three separate stages – first by the launch trip to the island, then by the railway from New York, and then by the ocean from my working base – I seemed to get release from time in a way I had never known before.

He sailed for home – and the difficulties that awaited him – on 11 August.

PART IV

Freelance, 1950–1983

CHAPTER 26

With the LPO

BOULT's last overseas visit while he was with the BBC was to Paris in the first week of January 1950. He found the orchestra of the Concerts Colonne 'a poor crowd' in Elgar's *Variations* 'with about 30 per cent interested and promising.' He was taken to a concert in the Palais de Chaillot where 'a coloured American named Dean Dixon[1] was operating not very well on sundry classics (he seems to be a sort of Yankee Vic Oliver, and about as musical) but there was a fine audience. It holds 3,000.' Boult's second rehearsal was with the radio orchestra, the Orchestre Nationale – 'splendid, and they read the Vaughan Williams [Sixth Symphony] finely. They are altogether different from the Colonne people who are quite material about the job and that's all.' At the concert on 9 January

> ... the orchestra played really finely ... The place was very well filled ... and they certainly listened to the Vaughan Williams without a cough. Several people said that *Don Juan* (Strauss) was exceptionally fine. I think the orchestra knew it well, though they had some funny French tricks, of course. [Yvonne] Lefébure played the Ravel very well too. Nadia Boulanger gave a 'small' party afterwards; ten of us sat down to an enormous meal, and got home after 1.0 am. It was very nice, and though I gather there are factions and intrigues, Paris musicians seem to get together in a very friendly way over a glass of wine!

On the day before he left, a strike which had lasted several weeks at the Opéra was settled and he went to a rehearsal of Act I of *Götterdämmerung* with Flagstad, Max Lorenz and Paul Schöffler. 'Sebastian, the conductor, is a Russian apparently and a great Walterite, and apparently he listens to us a great deal. He has a fine orchestra there in many ways, but they don't balance their chords well.'[2]

In the month before Boult finally left the BBC his father died. He had been ailing for some time. Coming when it did, this was a further emotional wrench, for Boult had consulted his father on every major decision he ever took – and a good many minor ones, too – and had come to rely on this prop. Some of this family dependence was now transferred to his sister Olive. Hardly a day went by but he telephoned her to discuss matters of moment and of triviality.

Soon after the news of his impending departure from the BBC became known, Boult was lunching in Great Portland Street and saw Thomas Russell, administrator of the London Philharmonic Orchestra. Its principal conductor at that date was Eduard van Beinum but he was not well and in any case was also conductor of the Concertgebouw Orchestra. Russell therefore invited Boult to take over after van Beinum, and Boult had the satisfaction, on 4 April 1950, four days before the axe was due to fall on him, of writing to Steuart Wilson asking that the BBC should make up its mind when it wanted his services early in 1951 because 'the LPO are very anxious to make all their plans.'

Boult shared an LPO visit to Brussels with van Beinum in May, conducting Brahms's Second Symphony, Ravel's *Le Tombeau de Couperin* and Elgar's *Variations* there on 9 May. During the summer he toured with them, conducting in Southampton, Guildford, Brighton, Folkstone, Eastbourne and at the Swansea and Malvern Festivals where he revived Elgar's *The Music Makers* and had Kathleen Ferrier as soloist in Mahler's *Kindertotenlieder*. He found the orchestra in financial peril and dug deeply into his own pocket to help them for a considerable period. The experience of being out 'on the road,' free from the BBC's bureaucratic mesh, proved exhilarating for Boult. In an article in the orchestra's magazine headed 'Thoughts of a New Boy,'[3] Boult described himself as 'an inveterate stay-at-home' and frankly admitted that he had dreaded a freelance life because, in rehearsing, he preferred 'saying fresh things to the same people rather than saying the same old things to new people all the time.' The LPO, he continued, 'is what I like to call *an orchestra*; it works together day in and day out; and no one may absent himself for any reason other than illness or an important solo engagement.' Those on the LPO administrative staff at this date recall some of Boult's performances as being among the finest he ever obtained. They also were alarmed by manifestations of his violent temper, when he flew into rages, sometimes involving physical assault on innocent and understandably bewildered and aggrieved members of the public, which suggested to witnesses that they could only arise as an outlet for something in his nature that he usually kept sternly repressed.

In another major respect Boult's career broadened when he left the BBC. He was invited more and more frequently into the recording studio. After *Job* in January 1946 he had made no records with the BBC orchestra. In June that year his recording of Vaughan Williams's *Flos Campi* was made with the Philharmonia and William Primrose. Nothing more happened until July 1948 when he recorded Parry's *Blest Pair of Sirens* with the Oxford Bach Choir and LSO. It was with the LSO, too, although the BBC orchestra had given the first performance, that in February 1949 he recorded Vaughan Williams's Sixth Symphony. In September of that year he made his first records with the LPO, of Elgar's First Symphony, and these were followed in July 1950 by Elgar's *Falstaff*, Mahler's *Lieder eines fahrenden Gesellen* with Blanche Thebom, and Beethoven's First Symphony.

When he accepted the LPO post, Boult knew that its chairman and managing director, Thomas Russell, was a member of the Communist Party of Great Britain and made no secret of it. He also knew that even Russell's adversaries admitted that he kept his politics out of his work, and so he was prepared to collaborate with a man for whose professional skill as an orchestral administrator he had the highest admiration – many good judges believe that Russell has never been excelled in this field. However, an incident in 1950 might have shaken Boult's confidence and possibly had some bearing on his conduct two years later when Russell was dismissed. On 25 October he found himself named as a member of a committee which would welcome delegates to a Communist-inspired 'World Peace Congress' to be held in Sheffield in November. He immediately denied that he was a Communist, though he supported the British Peace Committee. 'I do not remember agreeing to serve on any committee,' he told journalists, 'because I am not able to give time to this kind of work at all.' But Gwen Beckett told the *Evening Standard* that Boult had recently signed two documents sent him by the Peace Committee and 'without realizing it, he may have committed himself to serve.'

In the *Daily Express* of 26 October, Boult was quoted as saying: 'I am out for peace. Among the committee's supporters were the names of many people I respect. I signed a tear-off portion which, as far as I remember, only said I was in agreement with the committee's aims. I ignored a suggestion to serve on the welcoming committee. I did not know then it had a Communist tinge. But if the committee is out just purely for peace, I don't mind if it is organized by some Communists.'

The year 1951 was to be busy for British musicians, for it was the year of the Festival of Britain, an event lasting several months which symbolized the throwing-off of the lingering wartime mood in a celebration of industry, commerce and the arts. London and other cities were designated as festival centres, and the Festival's biggest permanent bequest to Britain was the building on the South Bank of the Thames of a spacious new concert-hall, the Royal Festival Hall. The BBC, as has been said, had engaged Boult for the early months of the year. Having conducted his old orchestra on 15 November 1950 in the first performance of Rawsthorne's First Symphony, in February and March 1951 he conducted Roger Sessions's Second Symphony, Schoenberg's *Pelleas und Melisande*, Elsa Barraine's Second Symphony and Bartók's Viola Concerto (William Primrose). But on 15 June 1950 Herbert Murrill, the Assistant Head of Music at the BBC, wrote to R. J. F. Howgill, the Controller of Entertainment, to say that Boult had written to Haley 'in some distress that he has been offered only one concert with the BBC Symphony Orchestra during the period of the 1951 Festival of Britain. He wishes to withdraw and not to appear at all with the orchestra.' At this date the orchestra was to give six London concerts in the Festival, the first two under Toscanini (who later cancelled the engagement because of illness). Of the remaining four, Murrill proposed one for Stokowski, two for Sargent and one for Boult. Howgill insisted in reply that Boult must have two concerts 'at the risk of incurring Sir Malcolm's displeasure.' Nicolls, the Director of Home Broadcasting, challenged Boult's plan to conduct a complete *Planets* 'on the grounds,' Howgill said, 'that it is a work not particularly attractive to the public in its entirety. Perhaps you would consider ... the possibility of giving him an Elgar choral work to conduct.' Wilson joined in, allotting Boult two dates only if Stokowski dropped out. Haley then intervened, to Nicolls's obvious chagrin, ruling that Boult must have two concerts and, in addition, 'Sir Adrian should be given some showing in studio concerts during the period of the Festival proper ... May to July. I should have thought that we might be having some planned programme scheme such as doing the Vaughan Williams Symphonies or an Elgar sequence and that Sir Adrian might undertake it.' In the event, Boult conducted the BBC Symphony Orchestra once during the Festival summer – in the Royal Albert Hall on 20 May – in Vaughan Williams's *Job* and Holst's *The Planets* (complete!).

In January 1951 Boult took the LPO on a gruelling tour of Germany, 11 concerts on 11 successive days from the 16th to the 26th in Essen, Hanover, Berlin, Hamburg, Münster, Dortmund, Düsseldorf, Nuremberg, Munich, Stuttgart and Heidelberg. In the repertoire were Elgar's *Introduction and Allegro*, Holst's *The Perfect Fool*, Strauss's *Don Juan*, Stravinsky's *Firebird* and Beethoven's Seventh, Haydn's 104th, Brahms's First, Schumann's Fourth and Schubert's Ninth Symphonies. There were eight performances of the Beethoven and before the tour Boult wrote to his friend Dr Hedwig Kraus, director of archives of the Vienna Gesellschaft der Musikfreunde, asking if the composer's manuscript had *crescendo* and *decrescendo* signs on the second subject of the *Allegretto*. (The society did not possess the manuscript, but Dr Kraus consulted early editions and a piano score corrected by Beethoven.) After BBC tours, the Germany visit was indeed being 'in the galleys' for Boult; and another article he wrote for the LPO house magazine in January 1952 shows that he was discovering new aspects of the domestic front:

> The Royal Festival Hall has come, and we are still learning to make the best use of it. Like all thoroughbreds it needs delicate treatment and will amply repay the trouble anyone takes to learn its likes and dislikes ... Outside Central London there are about 20 halls which the LPO visits at intervals of four to ten weeks, and nearly all of them were new to me ... Some give a pleasant mellow quality to the strings; some tend to let the woodwind get swamped (this danger is obvious whenever the orchestra is placed all on one level); some emphasise the brassiness of the brass ... Some artists' rooms are clean and spacious and warm; some are not; some are hardly there at all; there are two where David Wise [the leader] and I have to get on briskly with our changing in order that Miss [Winifred] Cockerill may also use the room, or perhaps she gets in first, and then goes on to the platform to tune her harp while we change ... In one hall we know that about twelve members of the orchestra cannot see the beat at all if they play in a normal way – well, they must manage somehow because it so happens that the quality of sound is lovely in that hall, and the audience is one of the largest and most stable that we know. The worst and unfortunately the most general trouble that we meet is inadequate space for actual playing. There are really only about half-a-dozen halls where the orchestra can be arranged in a satisfactory way so that every member is playing in comfort with ample room and clear visibility ...

As 1952 was the year of Vaughan Williams's 80th birthday, Boult was able to conduct a good deal of the music of his old friend. Since 1950 he had conducted three Vaughan Williams first performances in the Royal Albert Hall, the cantata *Folk Songs of the Four Seasons* on 15 June 1950, the *Concerto Grosso* for strings (written for a massed orchestra of the Rural Music Schools Association) on 18 November 1950 and the cantata *The Sons of Light* on 6 May 1951. The last-named was written for a massed choir of the Schools' Music Association and was commissioned by (and dedicated to) Boult's old friend and principal violist, Bernard Shore, who was then a staff inspector in music for the Ministry of Education. Shore wrote to Boult next day: 'I don't think I have ever admired you more than yesterday ... These dear people, who have had so little really nice experience, have now had a pretty big one, and they are *really* grateful. They at any rate do know what *you* mean to them. Do take care of yourself, and not be too much at people's beck and call – yet I know what you feel.' Boult also made several Vaughan Williams recordings at this time, the *Serenade to Music* and *A Song of Thanksgiving* in December 1951 and, during 1952, *A London Symphony*, the Violin Concerto (with Menuhin),[4] *The Lark Ascending* (with Jean Pougnet) and *A Pastoral Symphony*. The symphonies were the beginning of Boult's complete recording of the whole series, all but the Ninth being made with the composer present. The LPO's five-year contract with Decca was one of the best which had then been negotiated, giving it a 10 per cent commission on sales except on recordings where it only accompanied. Boult invariably handed over his share of the recording fees to the orchestra fund. An historic recording was made on 7 and 8 October 1952 when Boult and the LPO accompanied Kathleen Ferrier in some sacred arias by Handel and Bach. Exactly a year later she died from cancer.[5]

Boult continued his championship of new British works during 1952. For the BBC he conducted the first broadcast of William Wordsworth's Second Symphony (he had conducted its first performance at the Edinburgh Festival of 1951) and with the LPO Howard Ferguson's Piano Concerto, Alan Bush's *Nottingham Symphony* and Franz Reizenstein's cantata *Voices of Night*. The Reizenstein, when repeated in a BBC concert on 5 October 1954, was the occasion of a famous Boult outburst. The composer was persistently offering advice and eventually his 'could I just make one point, Sir Adrian?' was answered with a bellowed 'No!' Cambridge, too, had occasion to remember a chilling manifestation of Boult's anger when, in 1948, the university musical society's chorus joined the BBC Symphony Orchestra for Hadley's *The Hills*. The final rehearsal was in the old Exam Schools and it soon became obvious that the chorus had not learnt the work. Boult told Boris Ord he would not waste his orchestra's time and asked him to fetch a piano so that the chorus could be taught the notes. He then leaned against a wall, silent and with arms folded, for nearly an hour while Ord and six undergraduates trundled a piano from the music school quarter of a mile away.

CHAPTER 27

The Russell Case

THE last months of 1952 were clouded by an episode in which the motive for Boult's uncharacteristically devious rôle remains speculative. It showed him that he had not left musical intrigue and politics at Broadcasting House. The attitude to Communism and the Left was far less tolerant in the early 1950s than, willy-nilly, it is today. The euphoria of the Anglo–Soviet wartime alliance had evaporated after the war as Stalin's Russia became increasingly intransigent and hostile. The Berlin crisis of 1948 and the Communist takeover of Czechoslovakia in the same year had alerted the West to the aims of Soviet imperialism. The inevitable result of this tension was a general suspicion of anyone who professed sympathy with Communism and this led in the United States to the unpleasant over-reaction of Senator McCarthy's inquisition against sympathizers. It is within the context, therefore, of the Cold War that events now to be narrated must be judged.

During the summer of 1952 Thomas Russell went in his private capacity, but with the agreement of the LPO Board, to China for six weeks on a leave he was entitled to take. On the day he left a news item about him appeared in Britain on the front page of the official Communist newspaper, the *Daily Worker* (now *Morning Star*) in which he was described as 'managing director of the LPO.' This annoyed several members of the LPO Board, particularly Eric Bravington, the trumpet-player, who thought that the *Daily Worker* report compromised the orchestra politically. Like other London orchestras, the LPO was self-governing. Its Board of Directors, apart from Russell, once a playing member, were members of the orchestra. There was also an Advisory Council, at this date comprising Eric Hall (chairman), Victor Carne, Robert Cruickshank, the Hon. James Smith and Hamish Hamilton. (For some years, J. B. Priestley had been chairman of the council from its inception.) The LPO Board sent Russell a cable informing him that he had been dismissed. This was at the beginning of September. On the

15th a special Advisory Council meeting was called. Although he was not a member of the council, Boult made a diary entry for this day: 'LPO Council re China.' Two days later the matter was raised at an Arts Council meeting. On his return Russell let it be known that he would fight to be reinstated. There was an orchestra meeting during a visit to Cardiff on 3 October and the Advisory Council met on 13 and 21 October, Boult being present on the 21st by invitation. At this meeting four directors of the orchestra, led by Eric Bravington (who had been appointed to Russell's post), submitted a memorandum detailing the charges against Russell. His visit to China was never given as a reason for his dismissal. Instead it was said that his 'outside interests and frequent absences' had militated against his work for the LPO.

Up to this point Boult was supporting Russell. But between 21 and 30 October events moved swiftly and on the 30th, just before a concert in Peterborough Cathedral, he was in the vestry with Russell and Adolph Borsdorf, the LPO concert director, when he turned to Russell and said: 'Tom, I've gone over to the other side.' In this way he prepared them for the letter* he had sent that very day to the orchestra's shareholders. He had been persuaded to do this by the Arts Council, whose chairman, W. E. (later Sir William) Williams, had recently been worsted and made to look rather foolish by Russell in a controversy over policy in the columns of the *New Statesman* and had never forgiven Russell for it. The Russell affair was to be debated at an Extraordinary Meeting in St Pancras Town Hall on Friday 14 November, and Boult's letter could only be interpreted as a major blow against Russell's case. The Extraordinary Meeting lasted from 9.30 am to 4.30 pm on a bitterly cold day. Boult sat there throughout, huddled in his overcoat, its collar turned up, and never spoke. The pro-Russell case was that the dismissal was a 'witch-hunt' on political grounds. Russell made a brilliant speech in his own defence, answering effectively every criticism made in the morning session, even though he was on the point of exhaustion. (He suffered from a chronic skin complaint and was due to go into hospital on the following Monday for an operation for another condition.) It so happened that his latest book, *Philharmonic Project*, was published on the day of the meeting. It had a foreword by Boult. Russell began his speech by contrasting its sentiments with the letter Boult had circulated. He looked across to the conductor and said: 'Et tu, Brute.'

* The letter, along with the reply sent to Boult by a group of orchestra members, appears in full in Appendix 4.

Until Russell spoke in the afternoon, the tenor of the meeting was unfavourable to him, but thunderous applause greeted his speech. No one was left in doubt who had, until then, won the day. Then Thomas O'Dea, the company secretary, chose his moment to play a trump card. He revealed that Russell had relied on information from a telephone operator. Puzzled by the frequency of calls from the Arts Council to Boult urging him to write his letter, the woman operator had illegally listened in to them and had told Angela Newton, Russell's secretary, what she heard. The company secretary presented this as a smear, making it seem as if it had been organized, whereas the woman had acted on her own initiative out of distress over what she overheard from the Arts Council. But Russell had not referred to this information in his speech. There was a gasp, even from some pro-Russellites, and when the vote was taken, the motion to reinstate him was lost by five (27–22). Adolph Borsdorf and others immediately resigned.[1]

Why did Boult act as he did in this unsavoury business? He carried weight with most of the orchestra, who knew of the financial contribution he made to their upkeep and who may have feared Arts Council reprisals if Russell's case prevailed. There was also a theory among the LPO management that Boult had been reminded by 'someone' that his eligibility to conduct the music at the forthcoming Coronation of Queen Elizabeth II on 2 June 1953 might be questioned if he were to be seen in alliance with Russell. If this seems an unworthy motivation, then he must have been powerfully persuaded that the future of the orchestra would be severely jeopardized financially if Russell were to be reinstated. In *My Own Trumpet*, written nearly 20 years after these events, Boult's references to Russell are in glowing terms!

As Boult had said in his letter, the matter was not really his concern, but it is difficult to see how he could have avoided involvement, though that would certainly have been his inclination. There was considerable sympathy for Russell in the Press, even in the columns of the Conservative *Daily Telegraph*; and in the *New Statesman* of 6 December Desmond Shawe-Taylor exposed the unfairness of the case against Russell who, he said, had shown himself 'a good democrat' where the LPO was concerned. In the same issue of this magazine, Frederick Riddle and 14 other LPO players wrote a letter to the Editor pointing out that statements to the Press had failed to mention that Russell was sacked because of his visit to China. A new official of the orchestra had been quoted as saying that 'everyone is happy' in spite of the change. The signatories expressed 'extreme unhappiness' increased by awareness that the decision was arrived at 'after considerable influence from outside.'

Gradually the situation simmered down, although throughout subsequent years it has been recalled in the Press. But it left wounds which
in some cases never healed.

CHAPTER 28

Russian Visit

FOR the second time in his career, Boult was involved in directing the music for a Coronation. He shared the privilege with Sir William McKie, organist of Westminster Abbey, and conducted an orchestra which, as in 1937, comprised representatives of the nation's orchestras. Boult conducted in the Abbey the first performances of Bliss's *Processional* and Walton's march *Orb and Sceptre*. Next day Boult went to Cambridge where on 4 June in company with Nehru, Thomas Mann and G. M. Young, he was the recipient of an honorary doctorate, in his case of music. That evening he conducted the LPO in Elgar's Second Symphony in Gloucester Cathedral. It was a good year for English music in the recording studios and Boult added the remaining five of the then seven symphonies of Vaughan Williams, some shorter Vaughan Williams pieces, Holst's *The Planets*, Walton's *Belshazzar's Feast* and some Elgar.

Boult returned to the Proms in September 1953 after a three-year gap. He conducted the LPO in three concerts which were made the occasion, at the planning stage, for a further short outburst of spite by the BBC. On 12 March the Head of Programme Contracts, W. L. Streeton, wrote to the 'Music Booking Manager,' Norman Carrell, asking if it would be possible 'to get Boult to agree to a fee of £80 for each concert instead of his usual fee of £100.' This was suggested to Boult's agent verbally, but his secretary Gwen Beckett, who had left the BBC's employment at the same time as Boult in order to remain with him, demanded that it be put into writing. When Boult left the BBC, a fee of £100 per concert for future engagements had been agreed and Streeton was told that 'it has apparently always upset both Sir Adrian and Mrs Beckett that the former was not asked if he would accept this fee and Mrs Beckett periodically complains that the fee should be in guineas, since we pay other artists in guineas.' The upshot was that Boult's fee for the Proms and other concerts was revised to 100 guineas (£105). There was a further skirmish during August when Boult telephoned the Director of Home Broadcasting, Lindsay Wellington, on learning that the BBC had withdrawn an offer to him to conduct the Royal Concert on St Cecilia's Day, and pointed out heatedly that he had been told by the BBC that Queen Elizabeth the Queen Mother had said how glad she was he would be the conductor. Wellington informed the Controller of Music, Richard Howgill, that 'I spoke to Boult a second time and put the blame on us, the Corporation, apologized and said you would take charge of it all on Monday. His amiability came to our rescue in that he cooled down and said that he was ready to withdraw, provided that an explanation could be given to the Queen Mother if indeed she had expressed pleasure that he was to conduct. I think we shall not have trouble with Boult, but I'm not quite sure that we should rest content to be rescued by his amiability.'

At the 1953 Edinburgh Festival Boult conducted the Philharmonia Orchestra, having Isaac Stern and William Primrose as soloists in Mozart's Sinfonia Concertante for violin and viola, and giving the first performance of Fricker's Viola Concerto with Primrose. He also conducted the National Youth Orchestra of Great Britain at this festival. Boult was president of this orchestra and had encouraged its work from when Ruth Railton founded it in 1947. 'I thought it a fine idea,' he wrote, 'but I gathered that some of my colleagues did not.'[1] He conducted some of its early courses and concerts in Manchester and Bournemouth.

The year 1954 began with a major Decca recording session in the Kingsway Hall, a complete *Messiah* and Vaughan Williams's *Job*. Before the year was over Boult had recorded the four Brahms symphonies and others of his works, Schubert's Great C major Symphony, Mendelssohn's Third and Fourth Symphonies, Elgar's Violin Concerto with Campoli and shorter pieces by Elgar, Bax, Butterworth and Arnold. On 1 February, in a BBC studio broadcast with the LPO, he became the first conductor to perform a symphony by Havergal Brian, who was then 78 and had completed 11 symphonies (another 21 were to be composed between 1955 and 1968). His Eighth, completed in 1949, was the work Boult chose. Later in the year he conducted the first performance in England of the First Symphony by Brian's champion at the BBC, Robert Simpson (and he later recorded it). Other landmarks of this kind were Fricker's Piano Concerto (21 March) and Humphrey Searle's Symphony (1 June). Some years later he also recorded the Searle.

His visits abroad in 1953 had been to Paris in February to conduct the Lamoureux Orchestra in Mozart, Beethoven, Rawsthorne and Debussy (*Nocturnes*), followed by a supper with Nadia Boulanger, and to Frankfurt on 21 September where Vaughan Williams's Fifth Symphony was his main offering. In 1954 he went to Basle on 15 and 16 March to conduct the same symphony and Bliss's *Music for Strings*, and in April to Hilversum for two concerts in which Elgar's *In the South* and Holst's *The Planets* were played. He sailed for New York in the *Queen Elizabeth* on 10 June. Three days out from Southampton Ann and he came up from church service to sit on deck. He stooped to tuck a rug round her when he fell down in a faint through pain from a slipped disc in his back. For some years he had experienced back trouble and often wore a belt, though he found it uncomfortable. He had forgotten to pack it for the voyage but a cable home meant it was in New York when they arrived. A Finnish masseur on board attended him, and he was fortunate that one of his fellow-passengers was a homeopath, since he was a lifelong believer in homeopathic medicine. (Stooping in certain positions caused him this acute pain – he had once fainted in the Maida Vale studio at rehearsal when lunging at the trombones).

He conducted the New York Philharmonic at three concerts in the Lewisohn Stadium – in Beethoven's Seventh Symphony and Fourth Piano Concerto (Rudolf Firkušný as soloist), Vaughan Williams's *A London Symphony* and Brahms's Second Symphony. The Boults again fitted in a trip to Tanglewood, sad in some ways now that Koussevitzky was dead. But in New York, Chicago and Los Angeles Boult saw other old friends – Bruno Walter, Jascha Heifetz, Lionel Sayers, Gregor Piatigorsky, William Primrose and Alfred Wallenstein. He visited Chicago Art Gallery, stayed at the Huntington-Hartford Foundation and revisited the Grand Canyon. On 15 July he conducted at the Hollywood Bowl for the first time, an operatic concert with Eleanor Steber and Jan Peerce as the soprano and tenor. At two orchestral concerts in the Bowl he conducted four of *The Planets*, the Elgar *Variations* and Rubbra's Viola Concerto (with Primrose). Then on 27 July he conducted Handel's *Messiah*, with the Roger Wagner Chorale and Steber and Peerce again among the soloists – 'all revelling in the music,' he wrote,[2] 'with a fresh approach which we find hard to achieve at home where everyone knows the oratorio by heart.'

One pleasure in the mid-1950s was his return to Covent Garden. No one asked him to conduct opera – ironically, Steuart Wilson, after leaving the BBC, went to Covent Garden until 1955 as deputy general administrator – but he was invited to conduct two ballets, Ravel's *Daphnis and Chloë* and Vaughan Williams's *Job*, of which he was a superb interpreter. In 1955, too, he recorded Delibes's ballet scores for Nixa, the company with which the LPO had a recording contract from

November 1954. For them, too, Boult recorded Suppé overtures in addition to Bartók's *Divertimento* and *Music for Strings, Percussion and Celesta*. More Elgar was recorded for HMV, also Sibelius's Violin Concerto with Menuhin, and for Decca he recorded Rachmaninov and Franck with Clifford Curzon. Yet his most surprising recording sessions of the year were in Paris in June when, as he put it, Decca 'chose to send an elderly British conductor to record Russian music with a French orchestra.' The results, with the Paris Conservatoire Orchestra, were Prokofiev's *Lieutenant Kije* suite and Tchaikovsky's *Italian Caprice*, *Francesca da Rimini* and the *Suite No. 3* in G. Boult rated the *Suite* as 'beside the greatest of his symphonies.'

Apart from an April trip to Hilversum, where he revived Bliss's *Colour Symphony* and Delius's Piano Concerto, his principal tour in 1956 was his visit to Russia with the LPO. Originally he had not wanted to go. It involved flying and that upset his ears, while long journeys hurt his back. So he helped to choose other conductors and planned a rest while the orchestra was away. During August, however, a Soviet official went to the LPO's offices and asked to see the programmes. He noted Boult's name was not there and said: 'If Boult does not go, the trip is off.' This led to Boult's being summoned to the Foreign Office where a powerful appeal was made to him. He realized that cancellation of the tour might mean bankruptcy for the orchestra, so he agreed to go. Ann and he left on 13 September to travel to Warsaw by train from Paris. The journey was a nightmare, with endless delays at Iron Curtain frontiers. Food was appalling – the breakfast sausages in Poland 'foamed when cut'! Waiting in Warsaw for three days for the Moscow train, they took the opportunity to visit Chopin's birthplace. At Brest-Litovsk on the 18th they joined the orchestra, who had flown from London to Berlin. The dining car on the train was barred to the ordinary passengers because of the LPO's presence – 'the Russian public is certainly long-suffering,' Boult commented.

The LPO gave nine concerts in Moscow and four in Leningrad. Anatole Fistoulari and George Hurst shared the conducting with Boult. Boult's four Moscow programmes included Vaughan Williams's Fourth and Fifth Symphonies, Holst's *The Planets*, Walton's Violin Concerto (Campoli), Bliss's *Meditation on a Theme of John Blow* and Schubert's C major Symphony. On 23 September the Boults saw Glinka's *Ivan Susanin* at the Bolshoi and next day attended Shostakovich's 50th birthday party. Their hosts were friends they had made in Vienna eight years earlier, the British Minister, Cecil Parrott, and his Norwegian wife, who took them round the Kremlin museums and on other expeditions. In

Leningrad Boult conducted the Walton and Schubert and visited the Hermitage, but what impressed him most was that as he stepped off the train 'two girls on the platform were laughing, really laughing, a sound we had not heard for a fortnight ... The atmosphere of Leningrad is much more friendly and cheerful. The audiences were kind everywhere, but in Leningrad they *looked* happier too.'[3] Boult and his wife returned to England through Germany, where he conducted a Beethoven concert in Bonn and visited the composer's birthplace. They reached London on 14 October, much relieved to be home and to find Olive Boult and Gwen Beckett waiting at Victoria.

CHAPTER 29

'Second Eleven'

AFTER the Russian experience Boult told the LPO that he would no longer be its musical director although he was ready to work with the orchestra whenever it wanted him. This at first made little difference – William Steinberg did not become music director until 1959 – and 1956 was a vintage year for the partnership in the recording studio, including Tchaikovsky's 'Polish' Symphony, Rachmaninov's Second and Third Symphonies, all the Sibelius tone poems (including the rare *The Bard*), Elgar's Second and Walton's First Symphonies, the Schumann symphonies, the Berlioz overtures, Elgar's *Falstaff*, Vaughan Williams's new Eighth Symphony and the *Partita*, and sacred and secular arias by Bach and Handel with Kirsten Flagstad. A concert that gave Boult special pleasure was at the Festival Hall on 10 December when he conducted five Holst works, including the *Ode to Death* and the *Choral Fantasia*. This was the first event to be sponsored by the Vaughan Williams Trust, set up by the composer in that year to devote his performing rights income to help other composers and musicians. Boult had been proud to share with Vaughan Williams in 1956 the award of the Harvard Glee Club Medal, an honour which had been bestowed on Holst many years earlier.

He felt free now to accept recording engagements with other orchestras and opened 1957 with the Philharmonia (some violin concertos, including Bruch's *Scottish Fantasy*, with Michael Rabin, a 20-year-old American who was to die, tragically early, in 1972). In April he recorded Dvořák's Cello Concerto with the Royal Philharmonic and Mstislav Rostropovich and another disc of sacred arias with Flagstad. The following month he went to Vienna to record Mahler's *Lieder eines fahrenden Gesellen* and *Kindertotenlieder* with Flagstad and the Vienna Philharmonic, performances of a quality to cause regret that Boult's interest in Mahler was not more fully exploited by the record companies. Four Beethoven symphonies and four Beethoven overtures with the LPO followed, but in the year of Elgar's centenary Boult was not asked to record any of his music!

The strangest recording sessions of the year were those for US Columbia in July when the American organist E. Power Biggs, after a tour of Europe, decided that the organ best suited to a recording of the Handel organ concertos was in the church at Great Packington, Warwickshire. Some of the LPO players took tents on this occasion and camped in Lord Aylesford's park. A cable was laid across the park so that the organ could be electrically blown. The organ was a semitone under pitch. When transpositions were found to be still a few vibrations under the semitone, Mrs Power Biggs, who was recording manager, summoned the organ builder Noel Mander from London to dismantle the instrument, take it to London and return it within two days. His factory worked all night to complete the task. On the first day of recording, Mrs Power Biggs swallowed some tinfoil and was taken to hospital. Then it was found that fluctuations in the electricity supply necessitated the postponement of recording until 5 pm, ending at midnight. After lunch in Packington Old Hall on one of the days, Lord Aylesford remarked 'You must get your organ grinder back on time.' 'Him?' said Mrs Power Biggs, looking at her husband, 'Him? He's only the monkey.'

Boult was severely ill with bronchitis for most of October 1957, which caused him to miss two concerts to which he had looked forward – conducting the LPO's silver jubilee and Vaughan Williams's 85th birthday. A notorious event in his career occurred in the Royal Festival Hall on 5 February 1958 when he conducted the BBC Symphony Orchestra in the first performance of Tippett's Second Symphony. This work was a BBC commission and it had originally been planned that Hans Schmidt-Isserstedt would conduct it. When he was unavailable, either Paul Sacher or Rudolf Kempe was considered, but in July 1957 Boult was engaged. At the February première, shortly before the music reached the second-subject group of themes, the performance broke down after 2 minutes 17 seconds at fig. [18] in the score. The horns had entered a bar early, with the string basses at fig. [16] instead of a bar after them. Boult turned to the audience and said: 'Entirely my mistake, ladies and gentlemen.' He then began the symphony again. It was his mistake inasmuch as he had allowed Paul Beard to alter Tippett's rhythmic groupings in the string parts; this, in addition to distorting the music, made it no easier to play.[1] Boult told Tippett at rehearsal that if Beard's amendments were disallowed, the symphony would not be performed. Tippett was surprised to find that Boult seemed unwilling to confront Beard, who was allowed to play his solo in the *scherzo* slower than the score required. There was a controversy in the Press, several critics blaming the orchestra for technical deficiencies. Eventually Howgill, Controller of Music, defended the orchestra in a letter to *The Times* of 21 February using the phrase: 'In spite of Sir Adrian Boult's public admission that he misdirected them, the blame has been ascribed to the players.' Three days after the performance, Boult and the orchestra repeated the symphony without mishap in a studio broadcast. Howgill's letter implied that the fault lay principally with the composer, probably as a riposte because Tippett's silence about the affair was taken by the orchestral players to mean that he blamed them. After a fortnight, Tippett wrote to Rudolf Schwarz (the orchestra's chief conductor) and Beard, praising and exonerating the orchestra. But after reading the letter to *The Times* (in the train from Oxted to London), Tippett told Howgill that if that was what was thought, then he would not conduct the symphony at the Proms as had been intended. Boult was engaged in his place. A few days before the performance, Howgill telephoned Tippett to say: 'We would like you at the rehearsal to show that there are no ill feelings, but you must come no nearer than 40 yards from the orchestra.' Tippett was flabbergasted and amused by this ludicrous edict and phoned Boult to tell him he would either have to shout such questions as 'Has Mr Beard bowed this correctly?' or come down into the hall to speak to him. Boult followed the latter course. Tippett, who was remarkably unperturbed by the breakdown at the first performance, felt that Boult, whom he much admired, was unable to cope with the madrigalian textures of the symphony. Boult himself attributed his difficulties to lack of understanding of some modern music. 'Nonsense, Adrian,' Tippett told him, 'there's nothing here you won't find in Brahms.'[2] The incident was a blow to the BBC Symphony Orchestra's prestige and, apart from a symphony by the American composer John Vincent in 1962, Boult never conducted another BBC first performance.

His recording sessions in August 1958 were for the Everest label, which enabled him to venture into unfamiliar territory. His only recording of a Mahler symphony (the First) was made then, together with Shostakovich's Sixth Symphony and Hindemith's in E flat. The session on 26 August proved to have a melancholy significance. It was the first of two days set aside for the Ninth Symphony by Vaughan Williams, which had had an unsatisfactory first performance under Sargent the previous April but had been excellently played by the LPO under Boult at a Prom on 5 August with the 85-year-old composer receiving a tremendous ovation. Two days later Boult went to the composer's home in Hanover

Boult addressing a conductors' course in London, 1948

'Here's to the next time . . .' Boult greets Henry Hall at a lunch on 16 February
1956 in honour of the former conductor of the BBC Dance Orchestra

Adrian and Ann Boult, September 1954

With Paul Beard in the Royal Albert Hall before Boult's last concert as conductor
of the BBC Symphony Orchestra, 19 April 1950

With Pablo Casals

With Paul Tortelier in Worcester
Cathedral, 24 September 1977

On the phone ...

With Janet Baker, rehearsing Brahms's *Alto Rhapsody*, December 1970

With Yehudi Menhuin, rehearsing Elgar's Violin Concerto, 1965

Boult and Shura Cherkassky studying Schumann and Grieg, November 1967

(*Above*) With Sir
Arthur Bliss and
Christopher
Bishop

(*Left*) With
Gwen Beckett
after she had
received her
MBE, February
1973

In the study . . .

With Herbert Howells

The last photograph: Boult, a week before his 93rd birthday, receives the honorary degree of Doctor of Music of the Royal College of Music from Queen Elizabeth the Queen Mother outside Clarence House, April 1982

Terrace to discuss plans for the recording, notably tempi. Just before he was leaving for Walthamstow Town Hall on the morning of the 26th, he was telephoned by Ursula Vaughan Williams with the news that her husband had died during the night. The recording went on and included a brief tribute by Boult to the man who had been his friend for nearly 50 years. Later in the year Boult re-recorded *Job*. He also conducted the music for Vaughan Williams's funeral service in Westminster Abbey on 19 September.

The year ended with what he described as 'four grilling Nixa sessions at Walthamstow with Mindru Katz[3] (two on the Saturday) finished at 4.45 [20 December] – after reasonable applause (he had played right through with tremendous bravura and staggering accuracy) I suddenly noticed in the usual racket of an orchestra packing up that he was quietly playing the E flat minor Prelude from the 2nd book [of Bach's '48']. I signalled to the orchestra for silence and we all felt he could not have finished the turmoil of Prokofiev 1 and Khatchaturian more perfectly. I had no idea he had that kind of thing in him.'

Concerts with the LPO and Hallé and recording with Menuhin occupied the first two months of 1959. On 15 March Boult left for Vienna where he spent most of a fortnight recording Mozart, Vaughan Williams, both Chopin and both Liszt concertos, and Holst (*The Planets*) for the Westminster label with the Vienna State Opera Orchestra. On his return to England in the week preceding his 70th birthday on 8 April, he conducted three of his favourite works, Elgar's *The Dream of Gerontius* and Cello Concerto, the latter with Joan Dickson, daughter of his schoolfriend Douglas Dickson, as soloist, and Vaughan Williams's Sixth Symphony. Among the hundreds of birthday greetings was a letter from Robert Mayer, the first of whose concerts for children Boult had conducted over a quarter of a century earlier:

> When the sages of my race envisaged 70 years as the *comble* in a man's life they could not envisage the negation of this theory by men like yourself who are easily jumping over this milestone & continuing their activities with undiminished vigour & enthusiasm. But then you were fortunate enough to have chosen a profession which is also your great love & inspiration.

He began to take life a little easier in the late 1950s, enjoying short holidays where he could go for good walks, visit art galleries and stately homes. He often went to hear opera at Sadler's Wells and he heard *Ariadne auf Naxos*, *Die Zauberflöte* and *Idomeneo* at Glyndebourne – and *My Fair Lady* at Drury Lane. In June he recorded Handel's *Acis and Galatea*, with Joan Sutherland, Peter Pears, David Galliver and

Owen Brannigan. At the Edinburgh Festival he conducted a Vaughan Williams memorial concert (the Double Piano Concerto with Vronsky and Babin and *A Sea Symphony*), had lunch with Alexander Gibson who had just become principal conductor of the Scottish National Orchestra, went to see *The Thrie Estaites* and heard a recital by Fischer-Dieskau and Irmgard Seefried. For the winter of 1959–60 he combined nostalgia and a generous rescue-act by returning for a season as principal conductor of the City of Birmingham Symphony Orchestra. Its previous conductor, Andrzej Panufnik, had unexpectedly resigned in the summer and no successor was available at such short notice. Boult conducted four Vaughan Williams symphonies (*London, Pastoral*, the Sixth and *Antartica*), *Job*, the original version of the Piano Concerto and the orchestral version (by Gordon Jacob) of the *Variations* for brass band; Elgar's Second Symphony and *Gerontius*; Brahms's Third and Fourth Symphonies; Schubert's Great C major Symphony; Mahler's Fourth Symphony (with Joan Sutherland the soprano in the *finale*); Walton's Cello Concerto (Amaryllis Fleming); Holst's *The Planets* and *Egdon Heath*; Strauss's *Tod und Verklärung*; Ravel's *Daphnis and Chloë*; and the first performance (25 February 1960) of Robert Simpson's Violin Concerto. All this and no A.J.S. in the critic's seat for *The Birmingham Post*. It was a festival of Boult.

Two major events in London during this season were his revival of Busoni's *Doktor Faust* in a concert performance at the Royal Festival Hall on 13 November with Fischer-Dieskau in the title-rôle,[4] and a BBC studio performance of Vaughan Williams's opera *The Pilgrim's Progress* (with a young singer named Janet Baker in minor rôles) in December.[5] The failure of this work at Covent Garden in 1951 had hurt the composer deeply. Although there had been memorable performances at Cambridge in 1954, Boult's taking it up was an important factor in its rehabilitation.

A warmer wind was now blowing towards Boult from the BBC, where William Glock was Controller of Music. He took part in a Christmas music quiz on the Third Programme produced by Hans Keller and later gave some talks on conducting at Keller's instigation. These were later expanded into a book and published in 1963 as *Thoughts on Conducting*. Efforts were made to engage him to conduct the BBC Symphony Orchestra at the 1960 Proms. These were thwarted because Sargent would not let anyone else conduct the orchestra, but G.J. Willoughby, BBC Concerts and Orchestral Manager, wrote to say that

... we all of us fully appreciate and applaud the attitude you take with regard to the idea of your conducting any other orchestra than the LPO, apart from

248

the BBC Symphony Orchestra, in the Proms. William has told me to tell you, and it gives me the greatest possible pleasure to do so, that we hope to be in a position to invite the LPO to perform at least three groups of two in next season's Proms and ... it goes without question that you will be asked to appear with them.

On 28 March a special kind of BBC accolade was conferred on him: he was a castaway on Roy Plomley's 'Desert Island Discs'. The eight records he chose were: Mozart's 36th Symphony ('Linz'), conducted by Bruno Walter; Weber's overture to *Der Freischütz* conducted by Nikisch; Brahms's *Der Schmied* sung by Elena Gerhardt accompanied by Nikisch; an extract from King George V's broadcast on his silver jubilee in 1935; the motet *O Taste and See* composed by Vaughan Williams for the 1953 Coronation; Rossini's overture to *La scala di seta*, conducted by Toscanini (BBC Symphony Orchestra); *Galliard of the Sons of the Morning* from Vaughan Williams's *Job* (his own – then the only – recording); and Mozart's Third Horn Concerto in E flat, played by Aubrey Brain with the BBC Symphony Orchestra. The book he chose was Bunyan's *The Pilgrim's Progress* and his 'luxury' was a warm blanket. The broadcast brought a letter from Gerhardt: 'The orchestra conducted by Nikisch brought old and wonderful times most vividly back to me. I was touched by your devotion to him ... He orchestrated some songs for me ... and in gratitude I hope you will accept the enclosed manuscript of his orchestration of Beethoven–Goethe's *Die Ehre Gottes* ... Elena.'

Boult was now conducting again at the Royal College of Music – *A Sea Symphony* in December 1960 – and during the year he conducted Parry's *De Profundis* and two Mahler symphonies. There were engagements with the Hallé and Scottish National Orchestras and with the 'Modern Symphony Orchestra'. An LSO concert at the Festival Hall on 4 December inspired a letter to the soloist, Menuhin:

Sunday was, as always with you, a wonderful experience. Have you ever played the Beethoven more splendidly? Perhaps in the first movement when I somehow felt I was not really with you, & that *must* have affected you, though I hope not – I certainly didn't hear anything: I just felt that I hadn't taken your spirit as an accompanist should. But after that it was wonderful, I felt, & hope it *all* was for you. And now I want to ask you to think over one small point about the *cadenzas*. Are they getting too fast? Your fabulous technique is of course fully equal to it all, but I did feel particularly where the two themes come together it could have sounded still more noble if it had been a little broader – I wonder?

It had been planned that Menuhin should play Elgar's concerto at the

Royal Festival Hall concert on 17 January 1961 which was the LPO's tribute to Boult on his tenth anniversary with the orchestra, but he was ill and Campoli took his place. Menuhin wrote to Boult on 9 January:

I feel so unhappy... It is an occasion which, as you must know, and must feel, is very close to my heart, as for so many years we have shared with the London public the violin concertos of Beethoven, Brahms, Bartók. We have lived many wonderful moments together, and ever since, as a child, or rather as a young man, I first came under your benign baton, I have always treasured this association.

Boult wrote in his notebook: 'A unique thing, I think – a concert planned by an orchestra as a tribute to its conductor after 10 years' service, or rather its quondam conductor. Priaulx Rainier's Dance-Concerto [*Phalaphala*], specially composed and dedicated to me, next Elgar Vn. Concerto played by Campoli (*vice* Menuhin), and the Bliss *Colour Symphony*. And beforehand a charming presentation by Y.M. of the Bliss score signed by everyone.' His old friends Nadia Boulanger and Hindemith sent messages. The latter recalled the composition of his *Trauermusik* 'in one of the BBC's dungeons' when George V died. 'I remember very clearly our playing of the piece the same night and how doleful we all were, many of the musicians weeping.' He sent Boult the original sketch 'of "our" music of mourning,' inscribing it 'To my temporary angel guardian [*sic*] and permanent friend ... with fond memories.' Another appreciative letter was from Bernard Shore, to whom Boult replied:

I'm so glad you enjoyed the Bliss so much. I still think it is a very fine work and hope it will get back to the repertoire again. No, I'm afraid I have no opinion of Miss Rainier's effort – I can't make head or tail of it. It was rather good as we had been rehearsing some time, and went on and on with the stuff, when someone said 'When is the soloist coming?' A beautifully orchestral remark.

The London Philharmonic's tribute to its conductor in the printed programme included the words:

With him duty and inclination are one. He is an artist with a public conscience. No task is too difficult, none too menial for him ... Another very characteristic Sir Adrian sympathy has been manifested in his interest in the annual summer tours of churches and cathedrals which the London Philharmonic Orchestra has undertaken in the past six years. Normally all of these concerts he has generously conducted himself ...

Boult enjoyed the churches tour and told a young conductor that he thought the acoustics of the church at Rothwell, Northants., were the finest in the country. He conducted Schubert's Great C major Symphony there and never forgot it.

Boult was, as always, generous with advice and help for younger colleagues and his engagement books at this time record meetings with Vernon Handley and talks to James Loughran and Colin Davis. The last-named consulted him about *The Planets*, which he was to conduct at a BBC symphony concert. Boult went to the performance. He never lost his interest in hearing other conductors and whenever he could he went to important new works, Britten's *A Midsummer Night's Dream* in 1961, for instance. Davis was principal conductor of Sadler's Wells Opera and in 1974 was to write, in a letter to John Warrack, of his 'apprenticeship' with Boult.

> I imbibed all my classics from Boult's interpretations [during wartime broadcasts]. He *never* put himself before the music. One heard the standard masterpieces plain – the best way to hear them. Dr. A.C. Boult was at that time my idol and my instructor ... He was instrumental in sending me to Dr Wilfrid Barlow who gave me a long course in Alexander technique.[6] Why? Boult is alleged to have said 'that young man will be a cripple if he goes on like that' ... He made me *observe* what I was *actually* doing, which was very different from what I thought I was doing. Perhaps 'objectivity' is what he was trying to get across ... 'Leave it to the orchestra': one of his favourite bits of advice which, understood correctly, saves unnecessary and useless waste of energy. Use the stick to 'throw the juice over them.' Splendid Freudian imagery from an unusual quarter!

Boult was particularly helpful, too, to a young composer from Australia, Malcolm Williamson, whose music he had first conducted in 1958. At the 1961 Proms, Boult conducted the first performance of Williamson's Organ Concerto, with the composer as soloist with the BBC Symphony Orchestra. It was dedicated to Boult and each movement was based on the notes A—C—B. 'It was a curious and humbling feeling to play under your direction,' Williamson wrote on 13 September, five days after the performance.

> There is a hypnotism which you spread over the orchestra which elevates every player and which moved and inspired me greatly. I am sure there is nobody to compare with you technically and spiritually except Bruno Walter; I couldn't believe my slow movement was capable of such marvellous life! ...

The four years 1961–5 were on the whole a fallow period in Boult's career. He was not in constant demand and could be found conducting rather second-rate organizations, perhaps only because he could conduct something he rather liked. He was less in demand by the record companies: Holst and Elgar and a new *Messiah* in 1961, Holst's *The Hymn of Jesus* in 1962, Elgar's Second Symphony with the Scottish National Orchestra in 1963 and nothing in 1964. He made two visits to Holland in 1960, but there were no overseas engagements over the next four years. He enjoyed his days at the RCM and there were engagements with the LPO and Philharmonia. Boult was conducting the Philharmonia in the Royal Festival Hall on 23 March, a fortnight after the orchestra's founder and artistic director, Walter Legge, had announced that he would disband it because 'it is no longer possible, in present circumstances, to maintain the standards which have been the hallmark of the Philharmonia ...' Boult turned to the audience and said, with great passion, 'Do you want to see this great orchestra snuffed out like a candle? It must not be allowed to die.' Legge, who was in a box, walked out. Boult and Barbirolli had been the first conductors to contact the orchestra, expressing dismay and pledging help.[7] Boult conducted the Philharmonia at the Proms in 1962 in the first performance of Schoenberg's orchestration of Brahms's Piano Quartet in G minor, and six weeks after Legge's bombshell he had conducted a Busoni programme at the Festival Hall – which other British conductor would have undertaken it? – comprising the *Comedy Overture*, the *Geharnischte Suite*, the *Tanzwalzer*, extracts from *Doktor Faust*, and Four Songs with piano accompaniment (Gerald Moore). The singers included Fischer-Dieskau and Otakar Kraus. Another memorable occasion in 1962 was on 26 June in Chester Cathedral when Boult conducted the BBC Northern Orchestra (now BBC Philharmonic) in Elgar's Cello Concerto, with the 17-year-old Jacqueline du Pré as soloist. This was one of her first, if not her first, professional performances of this work. She had made her London début only just over a year earlier, in March 1961.

There were two slight contretemps between Boult and the BBC in 1962. He had mildly objected to being relegated to what he called the 'second eleven,' but he was more biting over a programme offered to him for a BBC symphony concert in the Festival Hall – Vaughan Williams's *Tallis Fantasia*, Beethoven's Fourth Symphony, Bach's Double Violin Concerto and Elgar's *Falstaff*. He wrote on 21 June 1962 to Eric Warr, Assistant Head of Music Programmes:

> It is more than four years since I have done a Royal Festival Hall concert for the BBC and I am sure, if you look again, you will think that that programme is not a programme at all but a list of all the pieces which you find it hard to persuade other conductors to do, and anyhow has anyone ever thought of a programme that goes in this order – Vaughan Williams, Beethoven,

Bach, Elgar? . . . I am sorry to be so rude to an old friend, but you have asked for it, haven't you?

The programme he eventually conducted on 28 November was the Twelfth Symphony of Shostakovich (its first London performance), Beethoven's Eighth Symphony, and Bach's Third Brandenburg Concerto.

There had been a personal sadness at the beginning of 1962 – the death of Bruno Walter. Boult's last letter from him had been a sad condemnation of the ugliness in the world and in the art of music. Boult told a Festival Hall audience before the start of a concert of the Anglo-Austrian Music Society, of which Walter had been honorary president, that 'we mourn the loss of a great man, whose own great sorrows in life matured and glorified his own splendid performances.' As he mourned his old friend's death and thought back to Munich in 1924 and the direction his own career had taken, Boult could have been forgiven if he had felt that life had bested him to some degree. He had moulded and guided a new orchestra and it had been snatched from his grasp. From being keeper of the national gallery of music, he was back into the marketplace, spending most of his time with an orchestra that was not regarded as among the best in the country. The BBC's failure to hold on to the best orchestral players after the war had left an open field for the predominance of the Philharmonia under such conductors as Cantelli, Karajan and eventually Klemperer and for Beecham's Royal Philharmonic. These two orchestras won all the critical plaudits between 1949 and the 1960s, and Barbirolli's Hallé was also highly acclaimed, playing to large audiences throughout the country and invited to several festivals. Boult saw his BBC orchestra for seven years in the hands of a conductor, Sargent, who made it quite clear that it was not his consuming interest and refused to conduct the catholic repertoire that Boult had made his speciality. The public, however, found Beecham, Barbirolli and Sargent more exciting than Boult, and a less generous-spirited man might have interpreted Vaughan Williams's award of the premières of two of his symphonies to Barbirolli and his last to Sargent as a reflection of this judgment during the 1950s.

CHAPTER 30

On Record

IN January 1965 Boult went for the last time to Vienna, where he conducted the Vienna Symphony Orchestra in Bliss's *Music for Strings*, Vaughan Williams's *Job* and Williamson's Organ Concerto. To Boult's and the composer's surprise, the audience was highly excited by the concerto. Boult went to *Don Giovanni* at the State Opera and to the Volksoper to *The Merry Widow*, in which Hanna was sung by the British soprano Adèle Leigh: '. . . a wonderful show,' he wrote, 'and she was jolly good.' He also conducted two concerts at Graz, in one of which Sibelius's Second Symphony was included – 'curiously inserted, I feel sure,' he wrote, 'because the management had suddenly discovered that it was the composer's centenary year and they had done nothing about it. English conductors were rash enough for anything, and they decided to saddle me with it. The result surprised them and it was a great success.'[1] He was pleased (since he noted it in his diary) to be told by his friend Richard Rickett, who had been his host on all his postwar trips to Austria, that Josef Krips had said he never went to a Boult concert without learning something.

Returning to an England mourning Churchill, Boult was more active than for some time. On 2 February he conducted the concert with which the Royal Festival Hall reopened after considerable alterations and at which Menuhin played the Elgar concerto. He conducted the Hallé and Royal Liverpool Philharmonic, the Orchestra da Camera at Leicester, LPO industrial concerts and, having conducted the RCM Orchestra in Mahler's Seventh Symphony in February 1964, he conducted the orchestras and choirs of the four London colleges in the Eighth at the Royal Albert Hall on 4 March 1965. He was disappointed by the standard of the chorus and at the final rehearsal sent the orchestra away over an hour before the end so that he could 'try to get the music into the chorus's heads.' In April he conducted the Northern Sinfonia, the chamber orchestra based at Newcastle upon Tyne which had been founded in 1958 and of which Rudolf Schwarz was then principal conductor.

From October 1964 Boult and his wife had a cottage at Mark Cross in Sussex – one of what they called their 'Boult-holes' – and spent as much time as they could manage there. Boult enjoyed the walks among the spring flowers and a visit to Kipling's former home, Bateman's. They spent most of August 1965 there. In the following month Boult conducted for the first time at the Three Choirs Festival, held that year at Gloucester. The works he chose were Vaughan Williams's *Norfolk Rhapsody* and Elgar's First Symphony.

In November he returned to the recording studio with the LPO to record Grieg's and Schumann's Piano Concertos with Cherkassky for World Record Club. More significant were the December sessions in the Kingsway Hall when Boult and the LPO began their association with Richard Itter's enterprising recordings of British music on his Lyrita label. In three days they recorded nine of John Ireland's works. Then, from 28 to 30 December, Boult recorded Elgar's concerto with Menuhin and the New Philharmonia, his first recording with EMI for six years. Boult conducted for Menuhin at his 50th birthday concert in the Festival Hall on 26 April 1966. A week later conductor wrote to soloist:

When you read this you will say 'Adrian is even more cracked than usual' but I'm going on & please just *don't answer* if you aren't interested. I'm cracked enough to wonder – just to wonder – if I couldn't tell you one or two things about your *approach* to performance, both conducting and playing, that might help, although surely you have thought about all this again & again. Better men than I have illuminated my vision now & again, & I just wondered whether any of it might perhaps be of use. The serene perfection of your performance of the [Beethoven] Romances at the rehearsals was something that one *must* perpetuate if it can be done & I'm sure it can. If you think it at all worthwhile having a talk, do you ever pass by the BBC (we are across the road here)? ... *Hundreds* of people have spoken to me about Tuesday. It *was* a wonderful privilege to take part with you in it.

Menuhin accepted this offer. 'I approached Sir Adrian several times,' he wrote afterwards,[2] 'in particular for advice on the *Symphonie Fantastique* of Berlioz which I conducted in Washington. He invited me to his office and with great patience took me through the score, indicating various points which proved to be of real benefit. He was a wonderful companion on the platform, really a benevolent spirit, with the perfection of an accompanist who never failed in empathy or precision. I loved him dearly ...'

This episode reflects the position Boult now held in English musical life. At 77, his experience and continued zest for his work made him the successor to Vaughan Williams as a centre of integrity, where advice would be diffidently offered and help readily given. Gradually, too, he was becoming that much-loved British institution, a 'character.' Never one to court the limelight, repelled by any suggestion of 'showmanship,' his very modesty and reticence were now being seen as virtues which caught the public eye. He was becoming the butt of bus conductors' wit, always an accolade. Stepping on to a bus at rush hour, he was climbing the step to stand inside when the conductor said: 'You stay on the platform, sir, you're too tall to stand inside, and I know you're a member of the conductors' union.' But another bus conductor peered searchingly at him on one occasion and said: 'I know you, you're the policeman at Lord's.' Boult's reply, typical of his courtesy, was: 'I'm afraid I don't get much time to watch cricket these days' (he would not have watched cricket if he had been paid). He was also active in the mid-1960s as an adjudicator in conductors' competitions sponsored by the Gulbenkian Foundation. The first was in Glasgow in December 1965. After the competition at Bournemouth in 1967 he wrote in his notebook: 'Abortive a year ago. This time appointed Nicholas Braithwaite. Silvestri[3] said that at the Liverpool international conductors' competition the orchestra unanimously voted for a young Frenchman who had a very nice manner. His conducting, however, put him only in the honourable mention class (as seen by the *jury*). Silvestri afterwards discovered that he had practically no experience. Are orchestras really so easily misled?'

Nothing gave Boult greater satisfaction than the announcement in November 1965 that Colin Davis was to become chief conductor of the BBC Symphony Orchestra. He wrote a congratulatory letter and received this reply, dated 19 November:

> When I was a boy during the war and only music filled my whole life, to be the conductor of the BBC Symphony seemed the highest office that any man could hold. Now, although I am terribly aware of the tremendous responsibility involved and naturally unsure that I am really able to tackle such a task, I do not really feel any difficulty except that other sides of life have found more room in my mind. During my boyhood, under your leadership the BBCSO was the finest in Britain and my ambition can only be to attempt to restore it to its former position and if I fail, which I suppose is as likely as not, it will not be for the lack of example and inspiration I received from you and the orchestra at the most impressionable time of my life. One further thing I would like to say: during the talks we have had together on conducting you may have had the impression that your advice and experiences have

made little impression on me. This is far from the truth. A man can only understand what he is ready to understand; my age and the experiences I have had in the last three or four years have prepared me for an understanding of what you were trying to tell me then. I still cannot 'do' it always, but I know that the principal effort I must make is to get myself (or rather my 'personality') out of the way so that the music itself may be presented.

The decade which Boult described as 'the time they thought I was finished' was ending. Nothing about him had changed but it suddenly seemed that people were re-awakening to the musician who had been in their midst for so long. Separate performances of Brahms's First Symphony brought admiring letters from colleagues who had heard broadcasts. Colin Davis wrote: 'I didn't know who was performing until I got home and looked up the programme. But it struck me at the time that Brahms is supposed to be played like that: it was so full of grandeur and *music* ... Please excuse my excitement.'

The horn-player Barry Tuckwell wrote of 'the elation your performance of Brahms One has just given me. I tuned in at random and identified the orchestra [BBC Symphony] but could not think who was conducting. I was completely gripped by the majesty of the interpretation, and the names I thought of just did not fit – during the last movement I *knew* it was you.'

In June and July 1966 Boult made his last visit to the United States, sailing in the *France* on 17 June. He had been invited by the Boston Symphony Orchestra to take part in the Tanglewood Festival. He conducted the Boston Orchestra in a Mozart programme and the students' orchestra (with seven rehearsals) in Vaughan Williams's *A London Symphony*. He also took a seminar of a dozen conducting students. Michael Steinberg of the *Boston Globe* described the 'special sort of creative conducting' which had made the performance of the Vaughan Williams so striking as 'one of the most imposing and refreshing displays of sheer professionalism I have ever seen.' Next day the young players gave him a 'dedication scroll.' Boult's tempi in Mozart, Steinberg wrote, 'are often daringly flexible across a whole movement, but he moves from one to the next so organically that only in retrospect, say in singing over fragments of the symphony just heard, does one realize how different the speed was at the beginning of a movement as opposed to ten pages later ...'

Before going to Boston and on his return to embark in the *Queen Mary*, Boult visited old friends in New York, heard Ansermet conduct the New York Philharmonic and went to the Lincoln Center. Ann had not accompanied him, since she was supervising the move into their new Hampstead flat in Marlborough Mansions. Two days after his return he was in the EMI studios to record *The Planets* with the New Philharmonia.

On 30 October 1966, in the Royal Albert Hall, Boult conducted BBC forces in Havergal Brian's enormous *Gothic Symphony*, a work built on a Mahlerian scale, with four solo singers, children's choirs and mixed chorus in addition to a vast orchestra. The performance was to celebrate Brian's 90th birthday: '... it was an impressive moment when [he] appeared on the platform at the end and the orchestra rose to acclaim him,' Boult wrote.[4] This year was the 900th anniversary of Westminster Abbey, and he took part in several musical occasions there, conducting the LPO and the RCM orchestras. He was also shown round the Abbey treasures by his old schoolfriend Lawrence Tanner.

A melancholy Abbey occasion at the start of 1966, on 4 January, was the memorial service for the BBC commentator and war correspondent Richard Dimbleby. Tanner told Boult it was the largest congregation (except for the Coronations) in his memory. Boult conducted the BBC Symphony Orchestra in Elgar's 'Nimrod' variation. Ann Boult was much touched by an incident on this occasion. Two young men stood next to her near the Jerusalem Chamber, which was used as an artists' room. Pointing to the conductor, one of them said: 'Is he anything to do with you?' 'He's my husband.' Silence, but after 'Nimrod', when the congregation was dispersing, the young man said: 'We think he's rather good!'

Characteristically, in this year too, Boult journeyed often to Bristol to conduct the newly-formed (and short-lived) BBC Training Orchestra, its members at the stage between leaving the colleges and starting professional careers.

From 21 to 23 December 1966, with Janet Baker and the LPO and London Philharmonic Choir, he recorded Elgar's *The Music Makers* for HMV. The producer of the record was the 34-year-old musician, Christopher Bishop. It was the start of an 11-year collaboration that was to give Boult a glorious Indian summer and to provide him with one of the most warming friendships of his life. Bishop has since confessed[5] that he himself was 'overawed' by the prospect of working with Boult. 'But I need not have worried. Sir Adrian was kindness itself ... The one mishap which I remember was that I got my musical knights confused and called out over the intercom, "Ready, thank you, Sir Malcolm." But Sir Adrian's kindness passed even that test – he merely chewed his moustache a bit, but the LPO enjoyed themselves.' Bishop witnessed Boult's alarming rages with the orchestra and was taken aback by the reaction the first time he ventured a criticism of tempo. 'Oh, I hate you!' Boult shouted, 'I hate you – because you're right.'

Boult and Bishop soon established a successful working method. Boult rehearsed while Bishop in the control room achieved a basic balance. A fairly long section would then be recorded and Boult would go into the control room to hear the playback. He would then re-record any passages where balance was faulty or mistakes had been made. He tried to make as few 'retakes' as possible, feeling that he was 'letting the side down, for I ought to be able to do the thing in one. Surely we should be able to treat our recording friends exactly as we treat audiences in the concert room?'[6] After *The Music Makers* he wrote to Bishop: 'It has all been a great experience for me too – and don't forget, it is a *partnership*. I look forward to lots more happy times together.' Ten years afterwards he wrote:[7] 'Yes, *The Music Makers* is a great work, and those quotations most apposite, I always feel ... Janet is the voice for it – do you know she had never sung it before the recording and she actually made one mistake that morning, just one! Can you believe it!' Christopher Bishop was amused by an incident during the recording sessions at the point in the score where Elgar quotes a snatch of *La Marseillaise* on the orchestra. He complained to Boult that he couldn't hear it. 'You don't have to,' the conductor replied. 'But Sir Adrian, it's a pity not to let people enjoy Elgar's little joke.' 'Quite unnecessary.' And the quotation is practically inaudible on the recording, one suspects because Boult thought it was rather a vulgar little joke!

The year 1967 was to be Boult's busiest in the recording studios since 1956 and it began with such a general flurry of activity that he made a note of it: '5 January to 12 February 1967. 3 recording sessions, 20 rehearsals, 12 performances, 15 long journeys.' The journeys took him to Plymouth in the South West and to Edinburgh and Glasgow. In July he conducted the five Beethoven piano concertos at a series of concerts with Emil Gilels, who on his return to Moscow wrote to express 'grateful thanks for your imaginative and complete co-operation.' *The Dream of Gerontius* at the Proms on 28 July 1967 brought an admiring letter from a friend to which Boult replied:

The nicest thing that can possibly happen to a performer is to find that he has lit up a well-known work to a musician who knows it backwards already ... I have never thought of 'Go forth' any faster than it was the other night. So I suppose others have speeded it up since Elgar's time. It was a great pity that the Angel hadn't bothered to learn it – she was hopeless at Wednesday's rehearsal and I begged her to spend Thursday working on it. It was better on Friday certainly but did let us all down. I have various E.E. marks in my score, but I always remember the whole end of Part I quite processional ... Yes, it *is* a terrific work, but *The Kingdom* is greater still in my humble opinion.

Another characteristic Boult episode occurred at the Royal Festival Hall on 10 October when he reached the rostrum to conduct Elgar's First Symphony only to find that his full score had not been placed there. Well as he knew the piece, he asked the audience if anyone could lend him one, an appeal answered by the *Sunday Telegraph*'s critic John Warrack, whose article the following Sunday elicited this reply:

> I have never before seen in print my objectives in work so clearly stated and so charmingly expressed; in particular my wife and I enjoyed your 'brash rostrum athletes' and, seriously, I do wish it were possible to get kindly at some of these young people and point out to them that the *results* are better when you do less. However, I feel that many minds are absolutely closed on things that seem so obvious to others that I sometimes despair of getting at these people and of course one can only be an infernal nuisance to any one who is not interested. Talking of obvious things, we attended a party last night after Pitz's[8] fine performance of the Beethoven Mass and the chorus told us that it sang the whole thing at concert pitch at the rehearsal that very morning. I am quite certain that if any other conductor had done that, Mr Pitz would have been most resentful, but he, like many other conductors, seems to think that human beings can go on grinding out music all day long.

He had several sessions with the LPO for World Record Club, recording popular Tchaikovsky works, Bruch's *Kol Nidrei* and a disc of 12 well-known marches, including four of Sousa's finest and Coates's *The Dam Busters*. 'We had an enjoyable day with those marches,' he told Bishop when the record was issued, 'you see half the orchestra knew a lot of them from their service days and were all set to enjoy them.' He also recorded more John Ireland and some Moeran, Bax and Holst for Lyrita, as well as the Elgar symphonies. In February 1967 he embarked on a new series of the Vaughan Williams symphonies, beginning with the Sixth (produced by Ronald Kinloch Anderson), and recorded Elgar's *Wand of Youth* suites and other short pieces with Bishop. Vaughan Williams's Fourth Symphony and *A Pastoral Symphony*, and some of his shorter pieces were recorded early in 1968. In the Royal Festival Hall on 17 January 1968, Boult conducted Mahler's First Symphony at a Royal Philharmonic Society concert; and he returned to another of his early enthusiasms, Strauss's *Don Quixote*, on 11 April when the solo cellist was Jacqueline du Pré. This was three days after his 79th birthday which, as he learned with pleasure later, had been marked in a novel manner at St Paul's Church, Langleybury, Herts., when six of his admirers rang a peal in his honour for two hours 35 minutes – 5,040 changes in the method Plain Bob Minor.

In the spring Boult absorbed himself in the recording for BBC colour television of Elgar's *The Dream of Gerontius*. The first plan was to make the film in Worcester Cathedral, but this was switched to Canterbury. The recording was made on 27 and 28 March, with the LPO and London Philharmonic Choir and Janet Baker, Peter Pears and John Shirley-Quirk as the soloists. Boult used Vernon Handley as 'deputy conductor' to take some pressure off himself. The result was a profoundly imaginative use of television in the service of music, with camera-shots of parts of the cathedral – its windows, carvings, and tombs – making a visual commentary on the music in a way that has since become familiar (and overdone) but was then new and pioneering. The film was transmitted on Easter Sunday. Boult and his wife watched it. 'To tell you the truth,' he wrote afterwards,[9] 'the sound in the cathedral was so wonderful that the TV thing was inevitably second best and we were both disappointed. The details of ensemble sounded bad at times whereas everything was lovely in that wonderful place. You saw the distance that separated us – choir, soloists and me, so ensemble was hard, particularly as the soloists were told *not* to turn to me at all! ... P.P. surprised me too [he made several mistakes in the text]. He hadn't sung the part for 20 years, apparently, and did take a lot of trouble, but anyhow to miss "the pain has wearied me" etc. does seem queer ... J.B. and J.S.-Q. were both perfection and I don't think that any of the old guard could surpass them. I used to meet Muriel Foster at The Hut, to which she would come husbandless as E.E. would come wifeless. It was a glorious voice but my memory is quite unable to make comparisons.'

Between 23 September and 23 December 1968 Boult recorded Vaughan Williams's *A Sea Symphony*, Double Piano Concerto and Eighth Symphony, Rubbra's Seventh Symphony and Elgar's *The Kingdom*. The last project was very close to his heart. He shared Frank Schuster's view that it was superior to *The Dream of Gerontius* – 'one can only marvel at the unpredictability of human taste,' Desmond Shawe-Taylor commented – and once described it as 'without blemish.' The recording was issued to mark his 80th birthday, and on 26 March 1969 Ibbs and Tillett, Harold Holt and EMI arranged a public lecture-recital in the Wigmore Hall to promote sales of the album. 'Rather fun,' Boult wrote to Bernard Shore, 'at which we played about an hour of it and sold 50! Carice [Mrs Elgar Blake, Elgar's daughter] came, which was very nice of her.' Boult was delighted by the success of *The Kingdom* recording and recalled later:[10] 'Christopher Bishop (... he is the most sensitive possible EMI recording manager) thought "Yes, very nice" when we did the K. preliminary performance at Eastbourne [14 December 1968]. Then as we went on recording, he became more and more enthralled ... I don't know *The Apostles* as well as *The Kingdom*, so I feel it sprawls more – perhaps that will tighten up if we do record it.'

CHAPTER 31

Companion of Honour

THE year 1969 began with the announcement in the New Year Honours List that Boult had been appointed a Companion of Honour, as Wood and Beecham had been and as Barbirolli was to be six months later. The letters and telegrams flooded in. As his old friend Lord Maclean wrote to Ann Boult: 'No one will ever know what millions of people have received comfort and joys – discovery – and heart-searchings and friendships from Adrian's unlimited determination to give his "all" – all the time.'

Boult conducted the London Philharmonic Orchestra and a choir comprising representatives from six of the leading choirs in and around London at the Royal Albert Hall on his 80th birthday, 8 April 1969. He chose music by three English composers, Parry (the unison song *England* and *Blest Pair of Sirens*); Elgar (Violin Concerto with Menuhin as soloist); and Vaughan Williams (*A London Symphony*). 'We suddenly felt the close of the Vaughan Williams with its lovely mystic atmosphere and the Westminster chimes would be rather sombre at the end of this particular evening,' Boult wrote in his autobiography, 'and we added Eric Coates's rousing *Dam Busters March* for obvious reasons.'[1] He had been rather disappointed by Menuhin's performance. 'He played like an angel at rehearsal,' he wrote to a friend, 'and "it" *was* all there, but "it" was not there in the evening. This is such a tragedy and we keep wondering what anyone can do about it, it happens too often. We were so disappointed and waited and waited for him to touch the stars at the concert but he never did. Who can help him?'

A note in the programme said:

This concert is a gesture of thanks to the very many people who have supported a career lasting fifty-one years. Friends in audiences, colleagues on platforms, backroom boys and girls have all, under Providence, made heavy contributions to a life of almost unclouded happiness, domestic, social and professional. Thank you. It is much to be hoped that our enjoyment together tonight may help a little to improve the very sad lot of some of those who are so much less well off, and are dependent on the good work of Oxfam.

The sequel to that worthy aim was a letter Boult wrote on 5 November to the Oxfam treasurer: 'You will perhaps have thought that I have pocketed all the proceeds of the concert ... but owing to illness and other difficulties in the management firm, I have only just had the accounts which, I regret to say, show a deficit of about £300 ... In May we sent you a cheque for £325 from the LPO, many of whose members very kindly returned their fees, and in June I believe you had a cheque from Mr Menuhin ... If you would very kindly let me know what these amounts were, I shall hope to make up the sum to something which will help a little.' He sent them nearly £2,000.

With the birthday festivities behind him, Boult went into hospital on 7 May for a hernia operation, returning home 12 days later. He had recorded Vaughan Williams's Fifth Symphony for EMI early in April (and some Moeran for Lyrita in February) and wrote to Bishop on 30 April: 'Sorry we shan't meet (at work at any rate) for so long. I'm to be carved up next week probably, but I gather it only takes 10 days, so I *ought* to be ready for Oct. So glad the 5th sounds all right. I have a great affection for it.' Earlier in the letter he wrote: 'I hope you'll enjoy *Carmen* – a masterpiece if ever there was one – I feel so awfully ashamed when the composer has to suffer as he did, and then come all the thousands to whom it gives enormous pleasure – in fact to everyone except the poor man who wrote it.' He convalesced at Mark Cross in Sussex, enjoying the walks, visits to friends and even – in an unlikely diary entry on 28 June – 'TV cricket.'[2] During this period he began to write his autobiography, working in the mornings. Ann and he would then usually go to lunch at the Brew-House in Mayfield and he would go to bed in the afternoons. In the evenings he read aloud to Ann. As he gained strength they resumed their pastime of visiting stately homes – altogether they visited 137. One of his favourites was Hardwick Hall, Derbyshire. He was an authority on Bess of Hardwick and maintained that one could 'feel the past most strongly' at her great house.

Writing his book at a time when he was physically below par was not a good idea. He found it difficult to concentrate and often repeated himself. The book grew too long and eventually he asked a friend, Eric Gillett, to read and edit it. Even then, he was asked to cut it further and grumbled that he had been told to omit everything except what was relevant to music – 'Aren't I allowed to have any other interests?' When it was published in 1973, *My Own Trumpet* was generally found not to live up to the promise of its title. It was over-modest and over-reticent – 'not exactly "porn"!', as Gerald Moore wrote to John Warrack in 1974.

During his convalescence he extricated himself from a potentially damaging Elgarian situation. A BBC talks producer, Roger Fiske, had devised a programme about Elgar's fragmentary Third Symphony in which he had orchestrated the sketches, completed some of Elgar's unfinished scoring and 'composed' some other parts. Boult had agreed to conduct these examples and Elgar's daughter had given her approval. By lucky chance, Fiske's orchestral parts were sent for checking to Maurice Johnstone, who had retired in 1960 as head of BBC music programmes. He was appalled by what had been done and wrote to Robert Layton, head of music talks at BBC, passionately protesting against this proposal to ignore Elgar's dying wish that 'no one must tinker with it.' He went on: 'By "tinkering," Elgar surely meant the completion, the scoring or the joining-up of his "bits and pieces" by guesswork and assumption.' He sent a copy to Boult, with a hope that 'you will not commit yourself until you have compared Roger's score with the fragments as in W.H. Reed's *Listener* article or book *Elgar as I knew him* ...' Nothing more (thankfully) was heard of the idea until 1979, when a proposed BBC television feature on the symphony similarly came to grief.

He eased himself back into work in mid-July, conducting the RCM junior orchestra. On 29 July he conducted the BBC Symphony Orchestra in Elgar's First Symphony at the Proms. On 4 August he conducted Lennox Berkeley's *Magnificat* and Brahms's First Symphony, on 11th Schubert's Great C major Symphony and on 18th Elgar's Second Symphony. He then had another short holiday before going to Worcester for the Three Choirs Festival where he conducted the RPO in Elgar's Violin Concerto and Schumann's First Symphony on 29 August. 'You may get a revelation when Hugh Bean plays the Elgar,' he wrote.[3] 'After his Lark [a very fine recording of Vaughan Williams's *The Lark Ascending*] I can expect anything – but DON'T stay for Schumann I. The RPO won't know it, and on one rehearsal it will be GHASTLY. I put my faith in Gothic resonance.' Throughout the autumn he was fully back in harness, whether it was conducting the Brighton Philharmonic in Schubert – 'poor [Herbert] Menges had rather a trial because the orchestra was mostly deputies as the C.G. orchestra were recording and his Brighton Sunday orchestra is usually pure C.G.,' he wrote to Christopher Bishop, 'however we got through with one major blob' – the BBC Symphony Orchestra in Finzi, Parry and Vaughan Williams's

Job, the Hallé in Walton's Second Symphony, the LPO in Viennese evenings or the Royal Liverpool Philharmonic in Chester Cathedral on 13 November. This concert had a special significance for him – 'Hester Dickson, Joan's sister and my godchild, is playing the Mozart B flat with us, and as she has lost two husbands after nursing sad and difficult illnesses, I feel I would like to do all I can to help her now she is a real professional again ... I would very much like to get her in with the general BBC as well as the Glasgow people.'[4] Joan Dickson played Elgar's Cello Concerto in the same programme.

In November and December he was back in the recording studio, making Vaughan Williams's *Serenade to Music*, the *Sinfonia Antartica*, *Tallis Fantasia*, Ninth Symphony and *Fantasia on the Old 104th Psalm Tune*. This was his second recording of both symphonies and he was particularly concerned about the Ninth:

> It was the only one he didn't hear me do and I only went through it with him about ten days before he died and I boldly asked for 30 or 40 more bars at the end – to my astonishment he said he would think it over, but meanwhile I might like to take it a good deal slower at the end (than the record of Sargent's first performance). So I did.[5]

But it was Elgar as well as Vaughan Williams who principally concerned him in 1970. He had accepted an invitation to conduct Elgar's 1898 cantata *Caractacus*, then very rarely performed, at the Cheltenham Festival on 12 July, but had stipulated that he would not conduct it with H.A. Acworth's libretto, particularly its rather imperialistic final chorus. So a revision was commissioned from an author who undertook it only out of respect for Boult and did his best, but in retrospect wished he had not been so foolhardy. 'I wonder how E.E. ever thought Acworth any good,' was Boult's attitude. In the event Boult handed over the concert to John Sanders, organist of Gloucester Cathedral, because he fell near his Hampstead home on 10 July. 'Yes, I deserved to break three or four bones,' he wrote,[6] 'but Providence does look after fools, and pools of blood in West End Lane is the worst of it, though my lip and right hand caught it a bit.' While he rested he was able to hear a BBC feature about Hans Richter which brought forth some perspicacious comment: 'You know, as I get older I feel more and more that I have benefited all my life (and am doing so still more now) because Richter was conducting every orchestral concert I heard until I was 12. The monumental power and sweep of it were absolutely irresistible. But isn't there any record of the *Siegfried Idyll* which knows the difference between quavers which are $\frac{1}{2}$ a crotchet and those which are triplets? As

I heard it, *all* the quavers were the length of those which were in triplets, and I always feel that ♩ ♪♪ ♫♫: that bar played *properly* is the key to the whole mood of the work. Forgive all this – your bad-tempered schoolmaster.'[7] In a letter a few months earlier he had touched upon what he owed to Richter, adding: 'The static and architectural aspect of music seems to me to be more and more important and the broad rise and fall to and from climaxes (and whatever word could be used for the reverse of climax) becomes more and more important to me. I therefore deplore the increasing tendency of practically all my colleagues to pinpoint and highlight details in music which I consider comparatively unimportant and forget all about the broad overall flow; in fact they remind me of the skipper of a ship who spends his time running about the engine room with an oil can.'[8]

With the death of Elgar's daughter Carice on 16 July 1970, Boult became closely involved with the affairs of the Elgar Birthplace Trust, which administered the cottage at Broadheath, near Worcester, where the composer was born and which had been a museum since the 1930s. Carice had allowed Elgarian affairs to get into the hands of a financier who promised more than he ever delivered. Boult felt entirely responsible, although there was no need for him to do so. He went so far as to instruct his solicitor that, in the event of his death before the problems were resolved, the entire cost of making good the lost money was to come from his estate. One of his fellow trustees, Raymond Monk, assured him that the person really responsible was being investigated by Scotland Yard and that all the trustees were guilty of putting too much trust in one individual. But Boult was not much reassured. He felt that he and perhaps one other person were responsible and none of the new trustees. 'I hope I shall not slither out of it by dying and leaving you all in the lurch,' he wrote to Monk. 'Do not worry about my coming to Malvern for meetings. I really very much enjoy a long day in the train.' His friendship with Monk began on a train journey after a trustees' meeting in the summer of 1970. They found themselves at Worcester Shrub Hill station where Boult invited him for a cup of tea in the buffet, 'the best British Rail cup of tea in England.' On the train Boult studied the score of Vaughan Williams's *Job* in preparation for a recording and invited Monk's opinion of it. 'For the rest of the journey,' Monk recalled, 'he gave me a lesson in score-reading which no amount of money could have paid for. My eyes were opened to countless things I simply had not noticed.'

Boult conducted six performances of *Job* when the ballet was revived at Covent Garden between 23 April and 9 May 1970 and the recording was made in August, just after the *Enigma Variations* (which prompted him to write: 'I'm hopelessly biased: these solutions to the Enigma are *all* plausible and it doesn't matter two hoots (to *me*) which of them was the one E.E. was thinking about – the *music* is what matters'). In March he had also conducted five Covent Garden performances of another ballet based (by Kenneth MacMillan) on a work he admired and had long championed, Mahler's *Song of the Earth* (*Das Lied von der Erde*). The year had begun in the recording studio with more Ireland for Lyrita followed in March, for the same label, by Parry's *Symphonic Variations*, *Overture to an Unwritten Tragedy*, *Lady Radnor's Suite* and *English Suite*. To record some Parry had long been Boult's desire, but he had no illusions. He had recorded the works, he wrote,[9] 'with a rather unwilling LSO ... Nobody will buy them, but the R.V.W. [Trust] have nobly backed the recording for Lyrita. I'm sure it was worth doing.'

On 29 July he was saddened by the death of John Barbirolli. In strong contrast both as men and musicians, they liked and respected one another. The difference between them is delightfully illustrated by the occasion when Barbirolli went to a performance, in Leicester or a similar town, of Bach's Mass in B minor conducted by Boult with Kathleen Ferrier as one of the solo singers. Afterwards Barbirolli congratulated Boult on achieving such good results after, as he knew, a rather small amount of rehearsal, adding 'I don't know how you do it.' 'Oh well, John,' Boult replied, 'we can't all be like you and spend months studying these things and then have days of rehearsals before we conduct them. For some of us they're only sporting events!' Barbirolli was shocked to the core by such levity about the sacred art of music. Boult on another occasion remarked to Barbirolli: 'I wish I had your integrity.'

Boult now was the sole survivor of a great generation. Beecham had died in 1961, Goossens in 1962, Sargent in 1967. But he saw a line of successors – Charles Groves, Norman Del Mar, Alexander Gibson, Colin Davis, John Pritchard, James Loughran, his protégé Vernon Handley – and many more than he could have imagined when he had gone to Birmingham in 1924, having almost decided that England offered no chances to a conductor.

After the August recordings of Elgar and Vaughan Williams, Christopher Bishop found they had two spare sessions and suggested to Boult that they should record a Brahms symphony. The Third was chosen and the recording was so successful that the three other symphonies followed, in addition to Beethoven's and Bruch's Violin Concertos and Brahms's *Alto Rhapsody*. 'Having "served his time" in English music,' Bishop wrote, [10] 'I felt it was time that he put on record

his magnificent Brahms and his famous Schubert Great C major.' Boult
was delighted. He wrote to Bishop from the Mark Cross cottage on 15
August: 'I want to thank you *very* much for all you have done this week.
You know it already, but I want to say how *enormously* I am helped
by knowing that there is an absolutely like-minded musician in charge
whose judgment seems always identical with my own.'

Gerontius and Elgar's First Symphony at the Proms, *The Kingdom*
in Truro Cathedral – these were the prelude to his holiday in Suffolk.
He was now involved in plans for his next major recording, Vaughan
Williams's *The Pilgrim's Progress*. This was preceded by a concert
performance in the Royal Festival Hall on 3 November for which there
were 12 hours of rehearsals. The recording was spread over 11 days and
when it was over Boult again wrote to Bishop to thank him for 'that
thrilling experience which you alone made possible. What an adventure
it is, this recording, and how unpredictable in time (for me at any rate,
and I expect even you are surprised sometimes). Anyhow it is done ...'
Reviews were laudatory, and a Vaughan Williams enthusiast thanked
him 'for so nobly, convincingly and incontrovertibly vindicating Ralph's
belief in the power of this music of his. You really make it properly
dramatic – in the music itself – and colourful.' The sixth side of the
recording consists of extracts made at the rehearsals, from which Boult's
sometimes acerbic, always encouraging, style of rehearsing can be
enjoyed and studied by posterity. Choirs had always caught the rough
edge of his tongue, such as the Bach Choir soprano who held up a
rehearsal because someone else was in her usual place. 'Have you *bought*
that seat?' Boult asked her. Recording *The Apostles* he shouted: 'You
are not in the Upper Room – yet!'

He kept a brief record in his diary of what he did every day, where
and with whom he had lunch, whom he saw to give advice or help.
Names like Julian Lloyd Webber, the cellist, occur in 1971, and Paul
Vaughan, later to join the BBC. Very occasionally capital letters empha-
size the importance of the event. 'BOOK TORN UP' on 19 July 1971
signalled the rejection by Cassell's of his autobiography. A holiday at
Cowes, a Sunday morning walk in Regent's Park, a visit to the cinema
to see *The Railway Children*, all were recorded. The year ended very
happily for him when he spent two days before Christmas recording
the preludes to four Wagner operas. 'Although I forget most things
nowadays,' he wrote to Bishop on Christmas Day, 'I don't think I shall
ever forget your marvellous help over those Wagner sessions.' Then the
enthusiasm, bottled up for nearly 50 years, spilled out: 'It is exciting
that you think a box of 3 might be possible. I am naturally thinking

about this and have done a few notes which I enclose. I wonder if "they" would think one or two singers a good idea? If so I put Wotan's Farewell at the top of the list, and then I suppose the Liebestod and perhaps *Götterdämmerung* close, but this is long – more than 20 I think ... Anyhow, do try and get things moving before I'm too decrepit. Time is short, as old Cardus said to me the other day and he is one week younger than I am!'[11]

Apart from Wotan's Farewell, Boult recorded his Wagner boxed-set in December 1972 and January 1973 and after the sessions Bishop gave him the Furtwängler recording of *The Ring*. 'It will be a constant delight,' Boult wrote, 'and I shall be most interested because I heard Richter 3 times when I was a boy, and that is firmly stuck, and comparisons will be exciting.' Six weeks later: 'I keep forgetting to tell you that the Furtwängler *Ring* is *magnificent* – really wonderful quality. I just dip in and so far the *Walküre* Abschied is unbeatable.' After hearing his own recording of Siegfried's Funeral March he wrote to Bishop (18 November 1973): 'I'm sure I can do it better for you. Could you possibly let me try? (It *would* be the biggest orchestra in the repertoire!) I am quite certain that the semiquaver figure *must* be ♪ ♪ each time and not just ♫ ♫ as we seem to have done it. It isn't *serious*, of course, but if I *could* do it again & have it substituted for the old one, I *should* be grateful.'

During 1972 he also recorded more Bax, two Brahms symphonies, the Schubert Great C major, Elgar's Cello Concerto with Paul Tortelier and the six Brandenburg Concertos (Boult told Bishop he was 'tired of chopped-up Bach'). On 1 June, the day before Elgar's 115th birthday, he laid a wreath on the memorial stone to the composer in the North Aisle of Westminster Abbey, which the Prime Minister, Edward Heath, unveiled, and in what was Vaughan Williams's centenary year he conducted the Sixth Symphony at the Proms, opened the Edinburgh Festival with *Job* and *Dona Nobis Pacem*, conducted *A Sea Symphony* at the Three Choirs Festival at Worcester, and the centenary concert in the Festival Hall on 12 October (*Job*, Eighth Symphony and *On Wenlock Edge* with Richard Lewis). In November he conducted the Fifth Symphony and other works in Westminster Abbey and later that month was reunited with the BBC Symphony Orchestra at a Royal Albert Hall concert of Elgar and Vaughan Williams to mark the BBC's 50th anniversary. He was now in his 84th year and apologized to a friend for missing an event because 'I'm really doing nothing but work now – awfully stupid!'

CHAPTER 32

Tempo Changes

IN the 1973 New Year Honours List Gwen Beckett, Boult's secretary since 1929, was appointed MBE. He was as pleased as over any honour he had himself received and he was her escort to the Buckingham Palace investiture, taking her to lunch afterwards. More Wagner was recorded in January and more Vaughan Williams in April. He conducted the CBSO in February in *The Planets* and Vaughan Williams's Fifth Symphony and the Hallé in March in Parry's *Symphonic Variations* and Vaughan Williams's *A London Symphony*. He was thrilled to be asked by the Royal Ballet to conduct several performances of Frederick Ashton's ballet on Elgar's *Enigma Variations*. He had seen this when it was first produced in 1968 and went to the Royal Festival Hall on 12 February 1973 to refresh his memory by seeing the film of it. He thoroughly approved of Ashton's way of treating it, not by inventing some story but by basing the scenario on the actual events surrounding the work's composition, setting it in Elgar's garden in Malvern in 1899 and ending with the arrival of the telegram from Richter's agent accepting the work for performance. Boult conducted four performances at the London Coliseum in the last week in May. He gave his views on the ballet five years later in an interview:[1]

> There is one variation in the Elgar Enigma which I can hardly bear, but the tempo suits the dancers so I do it that way and the mood opens to this very slow pace ... I was always fascinated by the Enigma ballet. I knew two or three of the subjects ... Frederick Ashton took the greatest trouble to get the personalities of the people as near as he could when he was designing the ballet. He is a very great man ... Lady Elgar is the only one that's not quite right. She was a tiny little thing ... Elgar's daughter said all the others were exactly what she remembered of them ... Elgar in the ballet is the image of Sir Edward in life. It is extraordinary.

On 24 March he had returned to the Robert Mayer children's concerts at the request of his former BBC colleague Trevor Harvey. In the programme was Schumann's *Konzertstück* for four horns. Knowing Boult's enthusiasm for Schumann, Harvey was surprised to discover that this was completely new territory for him. But not for long. On 11 February Boult accepted Harvey's offer to do some early rehearsing for him, 'if you have time and could let the orchestra look at the only tricky passage I can find: O to P – the last movement – I should be grateful. If you haven't a score it's just a fast 2/4 with nasty semiquavers for the fiddles – the usual trick of poor old S. writing piano music for the strings!!' On 17 February another letter came: 'I haven't looked much at it yet, but what little I have done makes me happily share your enthusiasm. BUT, what *is* the 1st trombone doing on page 42? I suppose poor old R.S. thought the second horn couldn't play. Shall I cut the Pos. [trombone] out? That unison can't help sounding *filthy* I would say! It's a shame that *you* aren't doing it, though. Would you like to swap with something else in the programme? It's all the same to me – I'm happy with anything, and it is a shame that you have never done it.' After the concert there was a 'thank you' letter with a difference, not only for the event itself but for a talk on Boult that Harvey had given – 'that amazing broadcast: how you ferreted out all that stuff, which I had forgotten altogether, and the much too complimentary things you were kind enough to say seemed to me absolutely staggering. And all the *Gramophone* reviews – I am indeed lucky to have the things reviewed by a man who thinks of music exactly as I do, for I know most people seem to need more emotion nowadays than I care to turn on.'

Three more Elgar recordings followed in the summer. The score of a short ballet *The Sanguine Fan* had been unearthed after over 50 years of neglect and Boult agreed to record it. Eventually it was issued on the same LP as *Falstaff*, but this was not the original plan. 'I don't mind *Falstaff* being separated,' Boult wrote to Bishop on 15 April, 'it will be more awkward for you than me probably. But the more I look at the *Sanguine Fan* the more I feel that the S.F. is perhaps a bit weak for a whole side, and I'm inclined to think that the Bach [Elgar's transcription of Bach's *Fantasia and Fugue*] *should* go in as well, even if the S.F. must be cut. But perhaps you feel that S.F. as a novelty *must* go in uncut? It's really a policy thing – perhaps I'm too keen on the Bach. I told you his remark, "It's rather fun when the cathedral windows begin to rattle, isn't it, Adrian?" So I'm afraid I throw the ball back into your court.' Bishop also produced the recordings conducted by André Previn and he was most anxious that 'his' two conductors should meet and possibly collaborate, for Previn is a brilliant pianist. Boult was reluctant, but on

7 March Bishop brought them together for lunch at the Connaught Hotel. (Even Previn, not known for his formal dress, wore a tie!). 'It was a most delightful occasion,' Boult wrote next day, 'I *did* enjoy it. He is splendidly forthright about our contemporaries and great fun over it.' As a result, Previn was soloist in two Mozart piano concertos conducted by Boult which Bishop recorded in September. 'What a staggering Mozart player that chap is!' Boult wrote after the sessions. 'I *have* enjoyed it all.'

In these last years of his life Boult became deeply concerned over his tempi in certain works and re-examined his approach as it compared with recordings by the composers and other conductors. His changed views – which will perhaps surprise those who regard him as 'fixed' in his interpretations – may be summarized by this extract from a letter:[2] 'Now I ask whether you also feel that Barenboim's record of the E flat [Elgar's Second Symphony] is all right? I'm coming (rather suddenly) to *hate* the thought of *traditional* performance. I'm quite sure that R.V.W. while doing the No. 4 as he did[3] did not necessarily think that any other way was wrong. If the music is big enough it will shine through utterly different approaches. He would never *say* that of his own work, but I'm sure now that he felt it.' He had been alarmed in 1972 when Holst's 1926 recording of *The Planets* had been reissued and he heard how fast the composer took *Mars* and other movements. He wrote to Holst's daughter Imogen, a specialist in her father's music, who replied on 1 February 1973: 'I think there is no doubt whatsoever that the extreme discomfort of the recording conditions and the agony of having to go *on* (because they weren't allowed to stop) must have distracted him on many occasions . . . I think it would be quite wrong for anyone to think of this recording as "authentic." ' Trevor Harvey was also struck by the differences between Holst himself and his interpreters and wrote an illustrated broadcast talk on the subject. Boult was very helpful to him, as in this letter (dated 16 April 1974):

I well remember G. [Holst] saying that he wanted the *stupidity* of war to stand out [in *Mars*] and be the dominant mood. I heard those records and was appalled . . . I strongly feel that G., like V.W., had a pretty wide view of the *correct* tempo for anything. They often said 'You do it your own way.' BUT there is evidence that E.E. [Elgar] and others were rattled by the 4-minute slavery [the average duration of a 12 inch 78 rpm disc was four minutes] and let themselves be hurried. I greatly regretted hearing the Elgar 1 record a day or two before I did it at the Proms – I rushed it unnecessarily and disliked it afterwards when it was too late! . . . I say definitely that rushing *Mars* à la Malcolm is *not* putting its *stupidity* first. Don't you agree?

... G.H. *was* a good conductor, particularly with amateurs. His Morley [College] shows were often splendid. But the right arm neuritis was *awful* and when it was painful, as in the *Hymn of Jesus* première, it took time away thus

$\frac{5}{4}$ | ♩. ♪♩ ♫♩ (♪) | as the poor right arm laboured up from the elbow.

In August 1973 Boult recorded more English music for Lyrita: Moeran's Symphony and some Stanford and Parry incidental music. But his principal concern was the long-awaited recording of Elgar's oratorio *The Apostles*. Elgarians had been agitating for it ever since *The Kingdom*, but EMI had been wary about its commercial appeal. Bishop, however, convinced them that this was something Boult had to be allowed to do. The recording was spread over three months, the sessions being on 23, 29 and 30 October, 5 and 7 November, 20 and 31 December and 2 January 1974. He had previously conducted it only three or four times and was unsure how his interpretation would be accepted. 'I wonder what you will think about "Turn you to the stronghold"?' he wrote to another Elgarian on 1 November.[4] 'I am sure the metronome mark is too fast, but the main tempo should, I think, be faster than the start. At the same time, as John Alldis[5] pointed out, we do not want it to sound like a prayer and I am afraid that is what I have done.' Five days later:[6]

NOW – I must confess that for the first time in my life – I don't count peccadilloes like the start of 'Turn you to the stronghold': that speeds up quite soon and behaves itself after that – I have consciously and deliberately altered the composer's metronome mark. It is in the *Fantasy*. I have taken it a lot faster than 112 because I feel that at that pace it would be terribly stodgy and unvisionary. The dilemma of Mary Magdalene, who sings so slowly and with such dignity of her past sins and then suddenly rushes *prestissimo* into those quotations during the *Fantasy*, and slow again afterwards, has been met by Helen Watts gallantly doing her best with the speed. Now Vernon Handley, who is very nobly (and, please, anonymously) acting as deputy conductor says he did it at 126 and it wasn't stodgy! He is, I think, very shocked but too polite to say so ... I have Christopher Bishop on my side: he says that down the pipe it is utterly convincing like that.

After the last session, Boult replied to a note he received from Bishop:

You have written *very* kind things about my share of the *Apostles* recording, but I *really* feel that it is all the other way. I have been yapping at your heels and you have done the brunt of that *awful* schedule, which went without a hitch and proved to be perfect (except for the power strike) and the tension of the sessions was mainly with you and C.P. [Christopher Parker, balance engineer] buried in that beastly little room – *and* it was you who brilliantly chose the soloists and chorus which J.A. had done very finely too. Many thanks for it all. It is obviously my last big show (though I do hope to get the Holst before I pack up) and you have a tremendous array of possibilities ahead of you. Good luck to them all!

Between *Apostles* sessions he recorded several short pieces for Lyrita and in November, January and February for EMI he recorded string music by Bliss and Howells, more Wagner and a disc of short Elgar items. He had conducted the first performance of Howells's *Concerto for Strings* in December 1938 but it had slipped his mind:[7]

I can't think how I can completely have forgotten *anything* as I have done this ... So much about H.H. is unpublishable. When I joined the RCM staff in 1919 he was already there – the brilliant boy from the obscure West, befriended by Parry, greatly admired by Stanford, and taken up rather forcibly by several rather over-enthusiastic old ladies. He wrote songs, chamber music (I think two quartets were published by Carnegie-Stainer and Bell) and all was set for a great orchestral work. *Procession* (4 minutes) and *Puck's Minuet* (6), which I recorded this morning for Lyrita which is dated 1922 and published in 1924, were I think the first effort. Soon after this the Philharmonic announced a pf. concerto to be played by [Harold] Samuel. As the work finished in Queen's H., before the applause could begin, someone shouted from the gallery 'Thank God that's over.' I was only on friendly speaking terms with him, but closer friends told me that this rebuff dried him up for years ...

Boult was beginning to find recording sessions tiring. In November 1973 he had warned Bishop: 'I'm inclined to think we ought to avoid 3 days running in future – I shall be 85 by June!' After some discussions over the recording in March 1974 of Holst's *Choral Symphony* he wrote again: 'I simply can't think why you don't get another conductor for the whole lot – when people are a nuisance one should always sack them *at once*! I don't think I've ever been such a nuisance before. I'm so afraid that A.D. will catch us up any time, but surely 2 a week *should* be safe. This latest trick is maddening: the day after a show I'm perfectly happy, and then become a wet rag on the second, specially in the afternoon and evening. I hope I can avoid a bad show next week.' After the Holst sessions he wrote to Bishop: 'Each session we do together puts a *greater* strain on your patience (and C.P.'s too) and therefore increases my gratitude. I think everything this week has shown that we are right to do no more choral work and as soon as you feel the orchestral things becoming unbearable you must say so and we'll pack up on them.'

One pleasant task came his way in December. If there had been coolness between Britten and him it had been forgotten, and he wrote to 'dear Ben' on 16 December on behalf of the committee of the Athenaeum Club inviting him 'to become a member of the Club under Rule II which is very rarely offered, and only to distinguished people, and means immediate election with no entrance fee. I remember H.P. Allen getting it, but I rather think Elgar didn't and awaited his turn like the rest of us.'[8] Britten had during the year undergone a serious heart operation and Boult added: 'I do hope you are getting over the miserable troubles that you have suffered for such a long time now. I don't know whether life seems to invite you to a London club – if so, I know you would have a very warm welcome from the (not very many) musicians there. I'm afraid I don't go often, but it would be very nice to know you are there, and you would be honouring all of us if you care to accept. I do hope you will.' Britten accepted and Boult wrote again (4 January 1974): 'I am indeed delighted and I send all kinds of good wishes for your convalescence to speed up and get you back to proper health.'

His 85th birthday on 8 April brought him many letters and was heralded in the Press by several tributes. One of the best and longest, in an *Observer* colour supplement, was written by John Warrack. He and Boult had lunch together on 10 January, after which Boult allowed himself a rare moment of self-pity in his letter next day: 'Do you know, there is hardly a soul in the world who is kind enough to stand me a lunch? I enjoyed it all immensely.' Warrack had encouraged him to reminisce and Boult wrote:

I am now full of things that I wanted to say ... Somehow I'm not very good at assessing anything, whether it's individuals, soloists or orchestras. I always feel like taking what I find and doing what I can to help (it or them) in the time available – I never seem to have a vision of perfection, there are so many good paths up the hill. Nikisch seemed to take what he found and improve it at once but never destroy or negative [sic] anything – but don't let's forget that somewhere about 1912 when an American millionaire offered to tour an orchestra with him for a month, he chose the LSO although he was at the time permanent conductor of the Berlin Phil. and the Gewandhaus. There is no doubt that foreign orchestras are slower in the uptake. I remember Boston *asked* me to rehearse closely some of the passages in *Job* when I noted that they hadn't improved much since the first run-through the day before. An English crowd would surely have practised them before the second rehearsal!

During his research for his article Warrack received an interesting account of Boult from Gerald Moore:

A.B. is a wonderful accompanist and since hearing from you I have asked myself why; I think the answer is stick technique – the tip of his long baton literally quivers with life – watch it at the end of a long *cadenza* or the beginning of a new rhythmic pattern and the players know exactly where they are. This long baton makes the massive waving of arms unnecessary (I suspect he is a little lazy although this is uncharitable of me), he is never excited but is always at one with his colleagues. He never outshines the soloist, is never sarcastic with the men, is rarely annoyed, never rouses the orchestra to work like demons. The men, therefore, like him. No affectations, no fire if you like, but beneath the surface – bland and urbane – lurks a highly sensitive musician. In an emergency he is unbelievably quick – in a performance of the Bliss piano concerto the soloist had a bad lapse of memory, but with hardly a moment's pause Boult called to the men 'Letter M' and with an electric flick of the baton the orchestra was *in* with scarcely a break.

Replying to Bernard Shore's congratulatory letter, Boult wrote: 'As someone said, "I expect you are tired of birthdays," but I can still enjoy my friends' good wishes.' From Michael Tippett came memories of over 40 years earlier:

I did not realize it was yr 85th birthday till turning on the radio this evening – some recordings of yours. So, not a congratulatory telegram, but a letter. One of the pieces played was Brahms 3. You won't remember (tho I do, as it were yesterday) my standing beside you at the rostrum at the RCM during a term's (?) training of that piece. (The cellos always had trouble with the second subject of the finale!). It's a long time ago. But what I learnt, as a composer, through those four years of Fridays at yr side is nobody's business. A belated thank you – & for much beyond.

On 5 May Boult conducted the Hallé in Manchester in a magnificent performance of Elgar's Second Symphony, but he had clearly found it a strain (though this did not show in the performance). He wrote afterwards:9

Sir G.H. [Geoffrey Haworth, chairman of the Hallé Concerts Society at this date] was very pressing about the Schubert C major in November, but it's an awful problem. You saw on Sunday how very senile my knees are getting. How much worse will they be in November?? I expect you spotted that the third movement (which we had rehearsed thoroughly) was played by the orchestra with only slight interference from the conductor: his concentration now won't do 51 minutes at a stretch. Now, isn't it better to go out on Elgar II than risk another visit with a stool and all the rest of it? Ann is all for going out *without* any deterioration and I'm sure she's right, and anyhow one can go on recording as Bruno W. did.

It was at a rehearsal for this concert that Charles Cracknell, then the Hallé's principal bassoonist, went on the platform to find Boult already there. Boult at first didn't recognize him, then said 'Oh it's you, Cracknell' (they knew and liked each other well). Cracknell, a very tall man, jocularly replied: 'Sir Adrian, you should use spectacles.' 'Oh, spectacles,' was the response, 'I only use them for driving.'

He went to Henley in July and at the Proms he conducted Schubert's Great C major Symphony and Holst's chamber opera *Savitri* and *The Planets*. The Schubert was on the opening night. The columnist 'Pendennis' of *The Observer* went to the rehearsal to interview Boult but found it an uphill task, as he reported in his paper on 21 July. Gwen Beckett had told him there would be no interview, but a BBC official had obtained Boult's permission for him to have a talk. The journalist went to the canteen to await Boult:

> There we encountered Mrs Beckett herself, a small determined figure in tweed two-piece, sensible shoes and a civilian-style Girl Guide hat carrying a brief-case-sized black handbag. Her manner was less than amiable. Had she not forbidden us to come? Our conduct, she said, was disgraceful. She was joined by Lady Boult, tall, thin and implacable in a somewhat similar style of hat, who fully endorsed Mrs Beckett's sentiments. 'But Sir Adrian has agreed ...' we began. 'Sir Adrian,' retorted his wife, 'does not speak for himself.' She then upbraided the dishonourable practice of the Press in refusing to keep away. We said, humbly, that we only wanted to get news. 'Newspapers,' observed Lady Boult, 'are far too full of news ...' Eventually the ladies departed, out-manoeuvring us by taking up strategic positions hard by the podium in the rehearsal room itself. Schubert's Ninth Symphony came to its triumphant close. Sir Adrian, jacketless and looking for all the world as youthful as the denim and sweatered musicians around him, laid down his baton. As soldiers on guard, the ladies stepped forward. Looking slightly puzzled, Sir Adrian approached and said that apparently we had been asked not to come, therefore he must be silent. 'We cannot be defied,' said Mrs Beckett, smiling. 'The Promenade Concerts,' added Lady Boult, propelling her husband to the door, 'are not about journalists but about music and that is why we are here.' We made our excuses and left.

Finzi recordings for Lyrita followed in October and on 16 October he recorded part of a Mozart symphony for EMI. Next day he went into the Royal London Homeopathic Hospital for a major operation. This was performed on 22 October. What had been expected to be a simple matter lasting less than an hour proved to be more serious and the operation took four hours. For several days he was very ill, but gradually recovered and returned home on 19 November. Scarcely had he done so but Ann had a severe attack of shingles. He found that he tired very easily and that walking was extremely difficult. He began to read again and to play records, but found it hard to sustain interest in anything for long. He did not want to see visitors and said he felt he had been a long time away in a far country and had not the strength to cope with anyone who had not been there too. He was cheered by the issue of the recording of *The Apostles* and by the ecstatic reviews it received. Later in December Ann encouraged Christopher Bishop to call: 'He would now really enjoy a visit ... Don't ring up or announce, just "blow in." He rather dreads a set piece. We are wallowing in the Previn Mozart concertos. I think it has been more responsible than any other for relieving the slough of despond.' Early in January 1975 he was well enough to go to stay at the Spa Hotel, Tunbridge Wells, and he returned to active music in February and March when he conducted three performances of the *Enigma Variations* ballet at Covent Garden.

On 18 April Boult returned to the EMI recording studio to complete the Mozart he had left unfinished six months earlier. Some Vaughan Williams followed on 28 April. These were preliminaries to the major undertaking which Christopher Bishop had persuaded him would be feasible – a recording of *The Dream of Gerontius* to complete the trilogy of Elgar's major choral works. Boult was anxious to do it to make up for lost opportunities. As he wrote:[10] '... my *Gerontius* was generally thought boring beside those of J.B. and Malcolm and therefore I was left out.' Most of the sessions were fixed for July but on 18 May Robert Lloyd recorded the bass aria of the Angel of the Agony. On three days in June Boult recorded Wagner's *Wesendonck Songs* and some Strauss songs with orchestra with Janet Baker as the singer. 'They are wonderful songs,' he wrote,[11] 'and she does sing them marvellously – we couldn't help it!' He eased himself back into conducting concerts with an Eric Coates programme with the BBC Concert Orchestra on 11 June. His first public appearance was in the Royal Festival Hall on 30 June at a concert in aid of the United Nations Association, when John Lill was soloist in Brahms's B flat Piano Concerto. Henceforward he usually shared a concert with another conductor. Ann would accompany him on the slow walk from artists' room to the side of the platform when an orchestral attendant – Ted Lee of the LPO or Bill Edwards of the BBC – would take over and help him to the rostrum where a chair awaited him, from the back of which he hung his walking-stick. He conducted three works at the Proms, Vaughan Williams's Fifth Symphony, Brahms's Fourth and Elgar's Second. Of the Vaughan Williams the composer-critic Anthony Payne wrote in the *Daily Telegraph* (5 August) that 'if anyone was expecting our senior conductor to deliver a slow-moving, serene reading, Sir Adrian tersely dismissed such cliché-ridden ideas about the wisdom of old age and shaped one of the most taut and concentrated interpretations I have heard of the work. This is not to say that there was not an impressive serenity at the heart of the performance, but it was a hard-won serenity.'

Another preoccupation during the summer was helping the Elgar scholar Jerrold Northrop Moore to compile a collection of the letters he had received from musicians over seven decades. These were published in 1979 under the title *Music and Friends*. The *Gerontius* sessions in the latter half of July, however, took most of his energy and concentration. He was much exercised about the tempo of the final section of Part I – 'Go forth in the name of angels and archangels' – and found Elgar's metronome markings little help. A lively correspondence* followed:[12]

> After the first take the other day Bishop gently suggested it was too slow for recording, so we did two more rather faster. He has now put the thing together, made his selection and chosen No. 1! Have you noticed that the V.S. [Vocal Score] has $\quad = 76$ at [73] and *another largamente molto* 2 bars later? The F.S. [Full Score] still stands at 83 with the *allargando* and *molto larg.* It is 66 *Andantino* in the Prelude [where the 'Go forth' tune is first heard], where it has to stand four repetitions of the tune. Anyhow, musically I want it slow and I can't think that I didn't hear it like that somewhere ... E.E. never has been vaguer about anything ...

His correspondent consulted the original manuscript at Birmingham Oratory. Boult responded:

> As E.E. set the original 66 at [12], I feel that that is probably his first idea, a fundamental, but don't let us forget that even that is *sostenuto* at [15] and *largamente* at [16]. It is unlikely that this passage, which restates the tune three times, can be *slower* than [73] + 2 which surely is the combination. I therefore think that the vocal score 76 at [73] *must* be spurious, though perhaps put in later by E.E. All those [72] consonants rattle if one lets it go too fast and I'm sure he often slowed up at [73] − 2 – note the trombones.

In November and January 1976 he recorded Elgar's Second Symphony for the fifth time since 1944. A fortnight after the first session he wrote: 'A's shingles are (after a year!) showing slight signs of improvement and I'm all right (in the upper half!) apparently, as the EMI people still want me, but legs are rotten. I still have to drive [be driven] everywhere.'[13] As always he was concerned about tempi, but was less bothered by comparisons with Elgar's own recordings, because, as he wrote:[14] 'I used to put "E.E. 1928" and so on in my score against the things he did or didn't do as the annual 3 Choir performances went on – it was often quite different from year to year.' He always remembered that at one

* With the author.

of his earliest performances of the Second Symphony, he overheard W.H. Reed, the leader of the LSO, say to Elgar: 'Can't you get him to take the *scherzo* more slowly?' He was delighted that so many other conductors were taking up Elgar's music: 'I remember Julian Herbage the morning after Casals's first performance of the concerto saying "He has taken it right away from the parish pump and put it on the map as a European masterpiece." And that is what the Barenboims and Mehtas are doing too, I'm glad to say.'

Preparing for a Festival Hall performance of Walton's First Symphony with the BBC Symphony Orchestra on 3 December, he wrote to the composer about various points. Walton replied from Ischia (in the Bay of Naples) on 12 October: 'I've been thro' the work with your Nixa record and tho' the record "qua record" is abysmal, you've got it all right. The answers to three questions are right and the metronome markings correct – perhaps the *Maestoso* in the last movement might be a shade less so.' The sequel to the performance was a request from the BBC for a repeat at the 1976 Proms, but as Boult explained to a correspondent 'somehow I couldn't face all that malice[15] a second time and said so, and they finally gave way (I don't think he has ever forgiven me – he heard about it somehow) and I didn't do it. I remember how I felt about the *Coronation Te Deum*. It was really pagan.'[16] This remark was another pointer to the fascinating dichotomy in Boult's character, further exemplified in two authenticated anecdotes. Congratulated on his conducting of *The Rite of Spring*, he stroked his moustache and replied: 'Yes, but I do really think it celebrates all the least desirable aspects of Spring.' This was the same man who was seen by a BBC Symphony Orchestra viola-player in the Randolph Hotel, Oxford, seated behind a large plate of cream-cakes – 'ooh, 'e *did* like cream-cakes!'

CHAPTER 33

'Alpha Plus'

AFTER some recording sessions at the beginning of 1976 Boult took things easily for the rest of the winter. The *Gerontius* recording was issued in time for Easter and once again the reviews were highly favourable, with general approval of the choice of the Swedish tenor Nicolai Gedda to sing Gerontius. Boult wrote to Christopher Bishop on 19 April: 'We heard it all yesterday and of course I want to change things, though perhaps the second time won't sound so bad to me. Eg. the whole Prelude seems too fast! That's quite a new one, surely? I can't make it out. I rather wish we had had two basses: the characters are so different, they should *sound* different, too. But why think of that sort of thing *now*!! Gedda is alpha plus.' He sent another letter on 28 April thanking Bishop for his

> choice of and responsibility for the soloists, including the brilliant recruitment of an unlikely foreigner; all those dates and negotiations; the choice of orchestra, choir etc. (not to mention conductor!) and then the whole responsibility for balance, placing and all the other momentary problems. I know you are used to it, and have the whole apparatus at your fingertips, but even when everything is going reasonably smoothly, you can't sit back and listen! So I say a very big *thank you* and hope I may be spared for a bit longer in order to have a bit more of what I always find to be the enormous pleasure of working with you – particularly when you comment and criticize! So there it is, I just can't thank you enough.

To another correspondent he wrote: 'I almost feel I want to pack up now. This "recovery" is so beastly slow it seems hardly worth while. I hear the Janet Baker *Wesendoncks* are not coming out till *December*, and that's what I hope will be good.'

On 21 April he went to the musical *Salad Days* and on 17 May conducted Brahms's First Symphony at the RCM for the soprano Carrie Tubb's 100th birthday (it had been first performed in 1876, the year she was born). On 19 June he went to York Minster to conduct Elgar's

Cello Concerto for Paul Tortelier, with the BBC Northern Symphony Orchestra. 'That orchestra is very good indeed,' he wrote.[1] 'The rehearsal was ghastly, with a vast crowd shuffling about so that no one could hear anything. T. called the performance "unique," which meant well, I think!!' A side chapel was rigged up as an 'artists' room' and in the interval a young lady walked in and said to Boult: 'You won't know who I am, I'm the Duchess of Kent.' It reminded him of a previous occasion at the Minster when he had undone his tie and put his feet on a table for a rest when the Princess Royal was announced and walked in.

On 3 July he received the honorary degree of Doctor of Letters from Reading University. His Prom works with the BBC Symphony Orchestra were Elgar's First Symphony, Beethoven's *Pastoral*, Wagner's *Siegfried Idyll* and Brahms's First Symphony. The Elgar performance elicited a letter from the BBC's Controller of Music, Robert Ponsonby: 'It was a privilege and joy to hear your Elgar last night. I could not be more grateful. You bring to that symphony a poignant strength which I've never heard with any other conductor. And the orchestra makes a quite individual sound for you ... I was *delighted* to see you looking so well.' Martin Cooper's *Daily Telegraph* notice of the Wagner and Brahms remarked that 'the truly idyllic mood of quiet rapture in Wagner's serenade, with a perfect scaling-down of effects, needed only a flick of the wrist for the occasional *sforzato* and never lost its poetic quality ... The *finale* [of the symphony] was given an unmistakably heroic note but avoided the rhetorical and gained enormously by the sober tempo of the opening *adagio* and Sir Adrian's refusal to race the final *più allegro*. He has always been a musician of the long view, and this occasion was a great vindication of his essentially classical attitude.'

He spent three weeks after the Proms staying at Osborne House in the Isle of Wight, the former home of Queen Victoria and now used as a convalescent home. Some recordings, including Elgar's First Symphony, in the autumn and sorting through his papers to be presented to the BBC archives at Caversham Park, Reading, took him to the end of the year, with recording several works by his favourite 'light' composer, Eric Coates, as a relaxation!

Elgar and Walton marches and some Finzi works were recorded in January 1977. In February he was at Covent Garden to conduct four more performances of the *Enigma Variations* ballet; he conducted the LPO in Vaughan Williams's Ninth Symphony in February, and the BBC Symphony Orchestra in Schubert's Great C major and Elgar's First Symphonies in March, and in April and May he recorded Beethoven's *Pastoral* Symphony, with all the required repeats. 'Bars 19 and 20 of the

2nd movement *Pastoral* are still uncertain,' he wrote to Bishop on 18 April. 'The second leader thinks it hasn't been together properly.' Two days later his visitor at home was the 22-year-old conductor Simon Rattle, with whom he had shared the LPO concert in February. At the rehearsal he had introduced himself with an outstretched hand and 'Boult's the name.' (Another young conductor, Mark Elder, shared a Prom with Boult and, after a strenuous rehearsal, retired to the dressing room where his senior colleague looked at him over a newspaper and remarked: 'Ah, I see you are one of the sweaty type.')[2]

Later in April he began to record Elgar's Violin Concerto with Ida Haendel and in May conducted three performances at the Coliseum of Elgar's short ballet *The Sanguine Fan*. The concerto's second movement was recorded on 10 June and three days later he wrote:[3]

> ... Ida Haendel is playing the Elgar superbly. We have recorded movements I and II and we hope for III in July. I hadn't heard of her for years, but she *can* play! ... I seem to be jogging along with half programmes that people still seem to want, but it seems ridiculous really that I still can't walk more than 20 yards without wanting to sit down and have to do everything in a hired car.

He had begun this letter:

> I will give you our awful news – this flat (Marlborough) is falling down and will soon need drastic modernization (eg. outside painting – scaffolding everywhere; new pipes as all our water is now thick with rust: 14 new lifts – every staircase needs them and I believe it involves 3 or 4 weeks' daily banging!). Ann is always ahead in these things and she has been looking out and found a 2-acre field with flats all round it which seem to be quiet. Our present landlord is bankrupt so nothing has been done for several years. We are the first rats to leave the ship, and hope for the best!

Ann had been worried about Marlborough Mansions anyway because the six steep steps to the front door and another four inside were proving a strain for Boult. The new flat, 68, Compayne Gardens, was a mile and a half away. They were to move in on 6 July and to spare him the strain of the upheaval she arranged for him to spend a fortnight at Osborne House. From there he wrote to Christopher Bishop about their next recording session on 19 July. He had become very anxious to record the Brahms *Serenades*:

> I'm getting enormously intrigued with them and want to do them quite un-Brahmsily – more like Schubert – Tovey seems to hint in that direction too – and please may we begin with the last movement, because it will set the scene better? – that is if you don't think I am talking nonsense. I shudder to think

now what the thing sounded like when I performed it in my devotional youth! ... Poor A. has had an awful time moving – everything went wrong, eg. furniture delivered *before* the carpet men came etc. etc. I feel quite awful lazing here, but as I can't carry anything they had to get rid of me.

He returned to the new flat on 15 July. It was on the ground floor, with the big rooms they liked, and only a step at the gate and one more at the front door.

At the Proms he conducted Elgar's Second Symphony on 24 July (this was to be the last time he conducted it, and the critic Alan Blyth wrote that his reading 'sailed down the mainstream of Elgarian interpretation, noble, unhurried, elegiac'), Bliss's *Music for Strings*, Williamson's Organ Concerto and Brahms's Third Symphony. While rehearsing the Brahms, he said to one of the first violins: 'Have you got the repeat rubbed out nice and comfortably?' 'Yes, Sir Adrian.' 'Then PUT IT BACK AGAIN! What do these Prommers get for their money these days?!' On 17 August, on what was to be his last Prom appearance, he conducted the BBC Northern Symphony Orchestra in Vaughan Williams's *Job*. In his diary he made a rare comment – 'alpha plus.' During September he conducted three *Sanguine Fan* performances for the Festival Ballet in the Royal Festival Hall and on the 24th conducted half an Elgar concert in Worcester Cathedral – in aid of the Elgar Foundation's appeal for funds to finance the improvement of the birthplace – at which Tortelier played the Cello Concerto. Boult began with the Prelude to *The Kingdom*, using the concert ending Elgar devised when he recorded it with the BBC Symphony Orchestra in 1933: 'I had forgotten,' he wrote five days later[4], 'that E.E. had tacked on ten bars of the last scene to round it off again in E flat instead of veering into C major for the Final Scene. Apparently Novello's had lost the score and parts but luckily found them in time![5] I don't know about the appeal yet, but IBM backed it to the extent of £1,500. They charged up to £4 a ticket and IBM bought and gave 120 seats to their customers in that neighbourhood and backed it up with a champagne and boar's head supper after the show! They apparently do about 20 of these parties annually all over the country ... and call it *advertising*! Shades of Esterházy and Rasoumovsky!' The orchestra on this occasion was the City of Birmingham, thereby rounding off an association stretching over 53 years.

On 12 October, the 105th anniversary of Vaughan Williams's birth, Boult and David Atherton opened the BBC Symphony Orchestra's winter season in the Royal Festival Hall by conducting the *Sinfonia Antartica* and *A Sea Symphony* respectively. It was to be the last concert-hall appearance Boult would make. Again it is Anthony Payne's review

(*Daily Telegraph*, 13 October) that merits quotation. He described the *Antartica* as 'a quite magnificent interpretation in which the BBC Symphony Orchestra played superbly ... This performance proved once again how unprogrammatic it [the symphony] really is and despite sectional forms and picturesque textures, how organic as pure music and emotional experience.' Five days later Boult continued the Brahms *Serenades* recording and between 25 October and 18 November he conducted the *Enigma Variations* ballet at Covent Garden five times. Unusually for the Royal Opera House, a spotlight was shone on Boult when he arrived in the pit and the audience cheered wildly. After the fourth ballet performance he noted 'back strained,' and later diary notes curtly record 'lumbago,' 'disc.' He was to have conducted a sixth performance on 23 November but withdrew. He continued, however, to see young musicians, the conductors John Carewe, Anthony Ridley, Owain Arwel Hughes, and Jonathan Del Mar, the cellist Julian Lloyd Webber about the Elgar concerto, and a succession of Elgar Society officials and enthusiasts.

In January 1978 he completed the Elgar Violin Concerto recording and continued with the Brahms *Serenades*, which were finished during April. Bishop had been recording in Philadelphia and on his return Boult wrote:

> I have been cogitating about Serenade No. 1 and am appealing to you. We have done I and VI [movements] I think? Well, our usual practice of working would give us II, V, III, IV for order of batting, but I wonder whether II will be the best preliminary for you? It will be so very monotonous (I think of it as *misteriosissimo* throughout, so perhaps C.P. and you would prefer another?). I'm rather frightened of III – it seems so much more like *andante* most of the time, I hope you will agree?

In May he embarked on his fifth recording of Holst's *The Planets*. After the third session in July he wrote to Bishop:

> I'm sorry to be inflicting a letter on you but I'm afraid of forgetting about *Saturn*. I was thinking too much of detail and am afraid I didn't get it calm and quiet enough through the last 3/2 movement (from V to the end). I see it's all *pp* or *ppp* and it must be as quiet, including the organ, as you can possibly risk on a record. I think you said you could deal with it mechanically – if so, well and good, if it can really express *peace*. If you think we ought to do it again it will be a nuisance because it's a larger orch. than *Mercury* (which I think is the only movement left). But I hope not.

His last public appearance was on the evening of 24 June when, unannounced, he directed the London Festival Ballet at the Coliseum in

Elgar's *The Sanguine Fan*. This, too, he noted as 'alpha plus.' The Holst recording was completed on 31 July (*Saturn* was not re-recorded) and a start was made on a record of works by Parry on which Boult had set his heart – 'I do hope this will help put him where I feel he ought to be in our history,' he wrote.[6] To Bishop in July he wrote: 'I think Parry V [Fifth Symphony] is getting very impressive as I work on it – but I think his tempo marks are often idiotic – and it is worth noting that though there are two harps they are only in the last movement so we shan't want them for quite a time ... I think it will be a record worth doing.'

Yet he approached this task with misgivings. Before the 31 July session he wrote to Bishop:

> I keep forgetting to tell you that I fear the 3-hour session will soon be a bit long for an 89-year-old. What is the solution? Would it be wise to engage someone else who wants to make use of an hour or so at the end or beginning, or simply to pack up when we have had enough, or to start half an hour later, which would suit the players very much?! I don't suppose you have ever had this problem before, and I know your company looks after the shekels rather carefully and will therefore wish to make a plan! Very sorry about it.

Bishop was warned before the session that he would find a change in the old man, judgment less accurate, energy evaporating sooner, eyesight deteriorating. Nevertheless during that summer Boult wrote to many of his friends greatly concerned over the number of orchestral posts in Britain, particularly at the BBC, being filled by foreign conductors. To one friend he wrote:[7] 'No, chauvinism doesn't stretch as far as the chief (or 3 assistant) conductors of *five* London orchestras!!! Do you suppose that Rozhdestvensky[8] is the great-grandson of the worthy admiral who commanded the Russian Baltic Fleet? In the Japanese war they were suddenly ordered to go round to Japan. They had obviously had a cheery night before they started, and then they got into the North Sea and found our fishing fleet and thought they were Japs, peppered and sank about half of them. I suppose history books now forget it, but I haven't forgotten the national dailies at that time. It was of course *before* 1917.'

The Parry recordings, of the *Symphonic Variations*, the Fifth Symphony and the *Lament for Brahms* (which had not been performed since 1918) continued on 4, 9, and 19 November. The last session was on 20 December. He left the studio feeling totally indifferent to what had been achieved and later told Ann that he thought he could 'no longer be bothered with it.' He felt he no longer had the energy to make an orchestra 'mind' about what he wanted. He remembered Toscanini, whose retirement was clouded by his major lapses of memory in familiar Wagner extracts during rehearsals for his final concert (in which he broke down) with the NBC Symphony Orchestra in New York in April 1954.[9] Boult could not bear to contemplate a similar fate and – especially as Bishop was leaving EMI to become manager of the Philharmonia Orchestra – he had already decided, as he paid his last homage to his beloved Parry, that he would never again stand before an orchestra and lift his baton.

CHAPTER 34

Retirement

As Boult's 90th birthday approached, it was marked beforehand in several happy ways. On 23 January 1979 he heard that his own university of Oxford was to confer on him the honorary degree of Doctor of Letters at the Encaenia on 27 June. The Incorporated Society of Musicians nominated him as Musician of the Year. And John Rae, Head Master of his old school, Westminster, wrote on 25 January to ask if they could call the school's new music centre the Adrian Boult Music Centre. Yes, they could; he was delighted. Before the great day itself, 8 April, an article appeared in *Radio Times* written by Paul Jennings,[1] who had sung under Boult in the Philharmonia Chorus. It began:

> As an amateur choralist, I was once in a performance where the broad, elegiac, lyrical line he was beating for the Elgar of which he is such a supreme exponent didn't actually signal one entry, so we didn't come in. We were not in the league of those of whom Peter Beavan, late principal cello desk, Philharmonia Orchestra, tells the charming story of the Walton Violin Concerto. 'Gentlemen, it gets a little complicated here,' said Sir Adrian. 'I'll keep a steady two; you'll have to fish about for yourselves.'

Jennings quoted Tortelier's first impression of working with Boult in 1955:

> I thought, an aristocrat, perhaps a little cold. I still think he is an aristocrat, but there is such a great kindness too. It took me some time to measure him! ... At Portsmouth, I think it was, I heard him also conduct the Brahms First Symphony, then I realized he was a *universal* conductor. You cannot only be a national conductor to conduct Brahms like that. When you are not too precise with it you can, in some strange way, get more tension.

And Hugh Bean:

> He saves it for when it matters. Never underestimate understatement! He once called Winchester Cathedral a *room*. 'Well, gentlemen, we know this room, come in a bit earlier, then it'll go with the wind section,' he said once

... He can time and place a climax, he's so economical, when it does come
it's overwhelming. It *is* very often a beat that puts you on your mettle; but
somehow he always is able to gauge how much mettle is *there* ...

To one of those who wrote tributes to him at this time, Boult responded
that 'it reads as if I were another J.S.B. or something – instead of an
elderly bloke who has spent his life enjoying himself doing a very
worthwhile job.' But the 'job' was now too much for him. The BBC
had tried to tempt him into agreeing to conduct a studio concert in
May, but he had refused the offer. The long steep staircase in the studio
daunted him, Bill Edwards had left and he was afraid that no one would
know his needs or be able to look after him, except Sidonie Goossens
who would be playing. Moreover he had been asked to do Ravel's
Daphnis and Chloë but he had not conducted it for many years and he
was in dread of his memory letting him down, quite apart from his
failing eyesight. A year or so earlier he would have longed to do it; now
he was apprehensive and did not think he could summon up the mental
and physical energy. A short while before he would have flagged without
the musical impetus; now he knew a sense of relief. Robert Ponsonby,
BBC Controller of Music, wrote to say he was 'very saddened' not so
much by the refusal to conduct 'but because of what you said about the
slipping of your sense of pitch. This must be fearfully trying and
depressing for any musician – unthinkably trying and depressing for
someone like yourself.'

It was the same with the 90th birthday concert that the BBC planned
as a Promenade concert in the Royal Albert Hall on 8 April in aid of
the Musicians' Benevolent Fund. Boult made it clear that he would not
conduct, and in his place three British conductors were engaged: James
Loughran for Brahms's Fourth Symphony, Vernon Handley for
Vaughan Williams's *Tallis Fantasia* and Norman Del Mar for Elgar's
The Music Makers, with Sarah Walker as the solo contralto. To everyone's disappointment, Boult did not attend the concert but recorded a
message which was played to the audience before the music began. To
Ursula Vaughan Williams, the composer's widow, who had offered him
means of transport to and from the concert, he wrote: 'I'm afraid we
are to be far away from the RAH that night – the box office and BBC
all know and I'm very sorry that you hadn't been told – please help us!
I just can't face it. A. has rightly said "he isn't physically, mentally or
emotionally fit for it." You know I still can't walk 4 yards without
sitting down? I ought to have packed up more obviously at the 80th.'
The man who had walked hundreds of miles in the mountains and hills

of Britain, Germany and America did not want to be seen in public as an invalid, old and unsteady.

On the eve of his birthday the BBC broadcast Boult's 'Desert Island Discs', his second appearance as a castaway on Roy Plomley's programme. It was recorded at Boult's flat in Compayne Gardens on 1 March. His choice of eight records to take to the island this time was: 1. Mozart's Symphony No. 40 in G minor, conducted by Richard Strauss; 2. Rubbra's Second Symphony, New Philharmonia Orchestra, conducted by Vernon Handley; 3. Bliss's *Meditation on a Theme of John Blow*, City of Birmingham Symphony Orchestra, conducted by Hugo Rignold; 4. 'When I set out for Lyonnesse' (Hardy) from Finzi's *Earth and Air and Rain*, sung by John Carol Case (baritone); 5. Robert Simpson's Third Symphony, London Symphony Orchestra, conducted by Jascha Horenstein; 6. 'Requiem aeternam' from Howells's *Hymnus Paradisi*, conducted by Sir David Willcocks; 7. King George V's silver jubilee broadcast, 1935; 8. Parry's anthem 'I was glad', Choir of King's College, Cambridge, conducted by Philip Ledger. His selection of 'just one disc' to take was the Mozart, his 'luxury' was a panama hat filled with barley sugar, and his book, as it had been 20 years earlier, was Bunyan's *The Pilgrim's Progress*.

If music itself had lost its grip on him, he made no attempt to withdraw from musical affairs and was available to aspiring conductors and others who wanted to consult him. He showed his customary interest in the many societies of which he was president or a vice-patron (particularly the Elgar Society, of which he had been President since its foundation in 1951). He had been distressed by the dismissal of the LPO's principal oboist, Roger Winfield, in 1978 and when he discovered that this had been done without consultation with the orchestra's artistic director, Bernard Haitink, who had then resigned, he wrote to Eric Bravington, Managing Director and Secretary of the LPO, on 21 January 1979:

> I have heard in a roundabout way that Mr Haitink had nothing to do with Mr Winfield's sacking and, in fact, although he was still director of music to the LPO, was not consulted. Now, surely, if this has been done and the director of music not consulted about something of such great importance as the position of the First Oboe, the president must support the director of music and go too? In any case I'm much too old to be an active president and *must go* anyhow so will you please accept my resignation.

Bravington replied four days later asking him 'please do not make the Winfield case' a reason for resigning. 'As a favour to me could I ask you in any case that no more mention of this is made until after your birthday concerts. We have given them such wide publicity and sincerely want to pay this tribute to you that it would be a shame to spoil it.'

His alliance was sought in opposition to a statue of Elgar which was to be erected opposite the cathedral in Worcester. Some of those who had seen photographs of early efforts by the sculptor, Kenneth Potts, felt strongly that the likeness was poor. Boult urged the organizer to show the sculptor more photographs of Elgar and suggested that Potts should see Derek Rencher as Elgar in the *Enigma Variations* ballet. When the completed statue was unveiled by the Prince of Wales in June 1981, Boult seemed happier about it. 'The statue *could* be better,' he wrote,[2] 'but it is recognizable and in a very good place as it stands, and so much of it is good – one can't expect perfection after 50 years.' He had himself been singularly fortunate in the head sculpted in 1973–4 by William Redgrave which is now in the Royal Festival Hall, London.

The inevitable sadnesses of old age came too – the death of old friends. Lawrence Tanner, his friend from his first day at Westminster School, died at the end of 1979. Boult was sad not to be able to attend the Abbey memorial service on 21 January 1980 but was gratified when Edward Carpenter, the Dean of Westminster, wrote to him to say that 'Lawrie valued his life-long friendship with you as one of his most treasured possessions.' It was less painful when just a retirement was involved. One such occasion concerned the BBC announcer John Snagge, who replied to Boult's greetings: 'I have never forgotten and never will your everlasting patience to me when as a young and very junior announcer you treated me with patient understanding and showed me constant guidance in my task.' It was pleasant, too, to be remembered by Christopher Bishop's young son Edward and to be moved to reply: 'I want to thank you very much for your picture of Dan running into the Wye to fetch his stick and bring it back to his master. It is a jolly piece of music and now you have done a picture of it all, it makes it still more fun ... I am going to put your picture into a score of the Elgar.'[3]

He would scarcely have been human if he had not taken pleasure, too, in the way that Lionel Salter, a former Assistant Controller of Music at the BBC, introduced his review[4] of Boult's recording of *The Planets*:

Of all the crass actions taken by bureaucrats, the BBC's enforced retirement at the age of 60 of Sir Adrian Boult – who had formed its Symphony Orchestra and for twenty years made it one of the finest bodies in Europe, which every great name was eager to conduct – must, in the realm of the arts, rank among the most myopic. In a world teeming with flashy youthful talents, Boult went on for a further thirty years, increasingly recognized as a musician of total integrity and the highest professionalism, never resorting to fuss or 'star temperament' ...

That made up for a lot.

In a quiet, methodical manner, Boult prepared for his death. He had always been meticulous in keeping his diary, his programmes, even the lists of where he went on his holidays. Now he was making sure that his possessions went where he intended. This was not only a question of bequeathing papers and scores, he made precious personal gifts. He looked through the letters he had received from Elgar and sent one to Sir Robert Armstrong, son of his old friend Sir Thomas Armstrong and Secretary to the Cabinet, and one to Daniel Barenboim. Then, too, there was the success of his last record, the Parry works. 'I'm so pleased,' he wrote,[5] 'my swan song, a record of Parry, 5th symphony and other things, has been dubbed best seller by the *Sunday Times* or some other paper – Parry as a best seller!!'

On 25 July 1980 his sister Olive died, aged 98, a final severance with his childhood and the close-knit family circle. Fortunately he was concerned during this June and July with the Musicians' Union strike of over 550 BBC musicians which caused cancellation of the first 20 Promenade concerts. The strike was over the proposed disbandment, as an economy measure, of five of the BBC's 11 house orchestras, including the BBC Scottish Symphony Orchestra. The economies – to save £500,000 a year, an 8 per cent cut in expenditure on music – had been first mooted in February, though the strike vote was not taken until 16 May. Boult had from the first been involved in efforts to save the BBC Scottish Orchestra. 'There are three separate committees to get up funds for them,' he wrote,[6] 'and I quite expect the poor orchestra will be stuck in the middle of it all and get nothing done! I do hope they *will* get saved somehow. I daresay you have heard that the Scottish Opera company decided to start a new orchestra of its own two or three weeks before the BBC made its announcement – I call that pretty good!' Boult's suggestion was that the Prom concerts should be given but not be broadcast until after the dispute was settled. This was rejected by the union as 'quite impracticable.'

On the scheduled First Night, 18 July, the BBC broadcast (ironically) Boult's recording of Elgar's *The Apostles*, the work which, conducted by the BBC Symphony Orchestra's chief conductor, Gennadi Rozhdestvensky, was to have been performed in the Royal Albert Hall. The orchestra itself staged a popular Prom of Tchaikovsky and Berlioz, conducted by Sir Colin Davis at Wembley Conference Centre. Boult sent them a message of support. He was also concerned when the composer Robert Simpson, a senior BBC music producer, resigned during the dispute not only in protest over the disbandment proposals but because of his 'dwindling respect' for the Corporation's management and 'the degeneration of the traditional BBC values in the scramble for ratings.' Boult wrote to George Howard, Chairman of the BBC Governors, expressing his dismay and received an anodyne reply denying that the BBC had surrendered to philistinism. The strike was settled on 24 July when all dismissal notices were withdrawn and the BBC Scottish Symphony Orchestra was reprieved.

On 22 October 1980, the BBC Symphony Orchestra celebrated its golden jubilee. Rozhdestvensky conducted Vaughan Williams's Fifth Symphony, Stravinsky's *Rite of Spring* and Prokofiev's First Violin Concerto, with Itzhak Perlman as soloist. George Howard sent Boult a telegram: 'Greetings and good wishes on 50th anniversary of your creation from all at Royal Festival Hall and millions of viewers and listeners.' Boult contributed a brief foreword to Nicholas Kenyon's history of the orchestra, in which he expressed his indebtedness to Lord Reith 'for giving me the opportunity of working with such a fine body of players' and his admiration for Sidonie Goossens, 'who was with us at the first concert in 1930 and who graces the platform at nearly every concert still ... I would like to send her my special congratulations.' Miss Goossens was appointed OBE in the following January and retired in the summer. Boult signed the photograph of the orchestra her colleagues gave to her. 'It has made it much more precious to me,' she wrote to him. 'I cannot realize that I am no longer a member of your great orchestra ... I have wonderful memories, especially of you, dear Sir Adrian. My fond love to you.'

To mark the orchestra's jubilee the BBC Symphony Club was founded and Boult became its honorary president. He would do anything for 'his' orchestra. But he could not resist contributing a foreword to Robert Simpson's book *The Proms and Natural Justice*, published in July 1981 in which the Controller of Music's absolute rule over the Prom programmes was attacked, a means of making savings in the cost of mounting the Proms was given and a list was published of 20th-century composers who had had a raw deal during Sir William Glock's régime as Controller. Simpson showed the typescript of the book to Boult, who read it carefully and critically and said: 'That lot ought to be taught a lesson.'

On 15 December 1981 he formally announced his retirement from conducting. 'Long years of standing up have put a strain on his back,' Gwen Beckett told the Press, 'and he can now walk only with the aid of sticks.' Although it was over three years since he had last conducted in public, this news, Christopher Ford wrote in *The Times*, 'still prompts a sense of slight shock and considerable sadness.' In a leader, the *Daily Telegraph* wrote: 'Not only has he fought single-handedly for English music, making a home market for the creators, he has played an uncomputable part in raising the standards of orchestral playing. He is one of those few who created the many, the modern British audience, more sophisticated, more responsive and more musical than might have been dreamed of.' Again, as on the 90th birthday, the letters flowed in and there was still Mrs Beckett to help answer them. Since 1977 she had lived in a charming cottage Boult had bought in Farnham and which he and his wife sometimes used as their latest 'Boult-hole.'

So it was nearly over. He still saw friends for a talk – Robert Simpson, Christopher Bishop, Rodney Friend, Michael Pope – he wrote letters but the writing was noticeably shaky now. On 23 November 1980, he went through the score of Parry's cantata *The Soul's Ransom*, a work he had never seen before, with June Gordon (Lady Aberdeen), who was to conduct it at Haddo House, Aberdeen. He made no entries in his diary after January 1981 and he seemed intermittently to lose interest in listening to music. Telephone calls sometimes confused him. He told Christopher Bishop he was bored and just waiting to die. But one more honour remained. In the autumn of 1981 the Council of the Royal College of Music conferred the honorary degree of Doctor of Music of the College on Boult and Herbert Howells. Hitherto it had been conferred only on royalty. These awards, Sir David Willcocks wrote to Boult, were 'an expression of the admiration and affection which past and present members have for you, and a recognition of your loyalty and devotion to the College.' The degree was conferred by the College's president, Queen Elizabeth the Queen Mother, on 1 April 1982. The two recipients, Boult within a week of 93 and Howells 89, went to Clarence House. Howells was able to go inside but Boult could not leave the hired car and the Queen Mother walked down to the car, chatted to him, handed him the diploma and read the citation.

During 1982 he went into a nursing home in Christchurch Avenue, NW6. It had become difficult for Ann to look after him. He had tripped once on the step down from the bathroom and she had not been able to lift him. She telephoned to Bill Edwards, the BBC orchestra's retired attendant, who drove from Hammersmith to help. In the nursing home Ann sat with him during the day. His desire to hear music returned and they would listen to *The Kingdom* and other recordings together. There was the chance to have a large first-floor bedroom in a new nursing home near Tonbridge with a basement flatlet for Ann to rent, but he refused to move. Gwen Beckett had arranged for many of his personal papers from his BBC days and all his carefully kept programme books to go to the corporation's Written Archives Centre at Caversham Park, Reading. George Howard wrote to him on 16 December: 'This is typical of the great generosity of your spirit and the nobility of your approach towards the Corporation which, it is still felt in some quarters, treated you somewhat shabbily more than thirty years ago.' The final olive branch.

On 20 February 1983 he asked Ann to play his recording of Vaughan Williams's *A Sea Symphony*, the work he had heard at its first performance nearly 73 years earlier. He went to sleep before the end. It was the last music he heard, with its noble exhortation 'O my brave soul, O farther sail ...' Next day he was tired. As Ann left at 8 pm she turned at the door and called 'Au revoir.' He called back 'Goodbye.' On the 22nd, the night sister rang Ann to ask her to come early. His bed had been moved nearer the window and he was asleep. He stirred and turned over, lying with one hand under his cheek as he often did. Ann lifted his head to smooth his pillowcase; he opened his eyes but did not speak. At 10.15 am he died, his face kindly and at peace.

There was no funeral: he had bequeathed his body 'to medical science.' He also requested that there should be no memorial service, but a concert to celebrate his life was given on 9 December 1983 in the Royal Festival Hall when Sir John Pritchard conducted the BBC Symphony Orchestra and Chorus in Parry's *Blest Pair of Sirens* and Elgar's *Enigma Variations* and, more appropriately than was perhaps realized, Mahler's *Das Lied von der Erde*, with Janet Baker and Hermann Winkler as soloists. On what would have been his 95th birthday, 8 April 1984 (Passion Sunday) a memorial stone was unveiled in the North Aisle of Westminster Abbey,[7] near to the graves of Purcell, Handel, Blow, Stanford and Vaughan Williams and the memorials to Elgar, Britten, Howells and Walton. He was the first conductor to be honoured in this way. The ceremony was preceded by J. S. Bach's Passacaglia and Fugue in C minor played by Simon Preston. The first hymn was Bunyan's 'He who would valiant be,' sung to Vaughan Williams's tune. Keith Falkner read a passage from André Maurois and from Psalm 150, and Preston played Brahms's chorale prelude *Es ist ein Ros entsprungen*. Jill Balcon gave some readings, followed by the precentor's prayer of thanksgiving for the composers commemorated in the Abbey; 'Adrian Boult over many years gave us their music and that of many other composers, bringing them alive and anew before us, and we rejoice that his art can remain to inspire future generations through his recordings.' After Vaughan Williams's hymn-tune prelude for organ, *Rhosymedre*, Boult's god-daughter Hester Dickson unveiled the memorial and the Rev. Simon Barrington-Ward, son of his schoolfriend Robin, invited the Dean to dedicate it. Flowers were placed on it by Bernard Shore. The last hymn was 'Praise my soul, the King of Heaven' and Preston played the first movement of Elgar's Organ Sonata.

In his will Boult left estate valued at £173,731 (£178,781 gross). He left his music, music books, records and tape recordings, not otherwise bequeathed, to the Royal College of Music, with £1,000 given to his trustees for them to pay for rebinding and preserving his bequest. He also left £2,000 to Manchester College, Oxford, where students trained for the Unitarian ministry. Boult had been granted honorary fellowship in 1968 and had given generously to the college's organ appeal in 1973.

*   *   *

Among the tributes paid to Boult after his death was Robert Simpson's:[8]

> He had a goodness, a kindness, rare among the dangerous breed of conductors; he had so gentle and unassuming a nature that it was hard to believe that he could ever have had the urge to be a conductor. Yet he *could* bark if he liked – though it never lasted long and there was no malice in him ... Adrian never really got over the cold routine of his compulsory retirement by the BBC at the age of 60 and always insisted on referring to it as 'the sack.' The BBC lost, and could not replace, the ideal radio conductor; this was mercilessly made plain to them not only by his successors but by the magnificent Indian summer of his association with the LPO ... All the new music Boult brought out was placed against the background of the masterpieces of history; this gave it a truer perspective than one could perceive in any esoteric ghetto.

Yet, as this book has set out to show, his urge to become a conductor was the burning incentive of his life. It was only one of many paradoxes about him that he gave the impression of being almost indifferent. But none of the musicians with whom he worked was ever under the illusion that he lacked commitment and passion. A member of the LPO once told me: 'From the back, when he was conducting *Mars*, he seemed hardly to be moving. But we could see he was almost foaming at the mouth!' The baritone John Carol Case, in a letter at the time of Boult's retirement in 1981, wrote to him:

The Times remarked upon your ability to get outstanding results by the slightest of baton movement. Had the writer been on the 'receiving end' like me, he would have noticed that you share, with Vaughan Williams, the ability to get what you want by 'looking' at your soloist. V.W. (hopeless conductor that he was!) was able to draw a performance out of people by giving a piercing glance over the top of his spectacles, and without realizing what you were doing, you did what he wanted. This is something that you are able to do, and so far no one has referred to it.

A young conductor who attended one of Boult's classes was to conduct Brahms's *Requiem*. He told Boult, who took him through the score. 'He opened it and his eyes lit up as he excitedly pointed things out to me. "Look what he does here" and "Here's a wonderful thing." He had an animation quite different from his austere bearing on the rostrum.' He was a man of wide and cultured tastes, but in the last analysis music was all that mattered to him. Like Richard Strauss, he conducted as if it was just a way of passing the time. But it was deadly earnest.

Of his kindness to his colleagues and to orchestral players, the stories are legion. His hand would reach for his cheque book for anyone down on their luck. Dozens of charities benefited from his donations. Gwen Beckett remembers a young musician arriving for an interview on a very wet day, soaked to the skin and with his shoes badly in need of repair. After a long talk with him, Boult took his own mackintosh off the hook and gave it to the youth, together with money for new shoes. Such an occurrence could be multiplied many times. Yet where his own style of living was concerned he was frugal and parsimonious. He explained this to his father in a letter in 1928: 'Yes, I've plenty of money, but have been brought up not to waste it, and the worst way (to me) of wasting it is on something that disappears, and personal comfort disappears so *very* rapidly unless hard work ensues immediately on the journey. So that's why I *hate* spending money on 1st class and taxis!' In this respect he never changed. Before he needed a hired car because of his lameness, he travelled round London on his pensioner's bus card.

Composers who sent him scores he was unable to perform would receive a constructive letter when he returned the manuscript to them. No one ever heard him tell a *risqué* story – he was no prude, just not interested – and in over 50 years his wife remembers his saying 'Damn' on one solitary occasion. Even in one of his rages he never swore, and his manifestation of bad temper was to go into a deep, long silence. Friends knew that if their telephone rang and that clear familiar voice said 'I say,' then all was well, but if he said 'I say, look here,' then he was on the warpath. John Lade, who presented BBC Radio 3's *Record*

Review for many years, was told of a phone call to the BBC after one of the programmes:

'Is John Lade there?' 'No, he's no longer on the BBC staff.' 'Well, look here, he's just made a mistake and said a Tchaikovsky symphony was conducted by Vladimir Ashkenazy, but he's a pianist.' 'Yes, but he's also a conductor.' 'Is he? Well, he's a jolly good one then.'

Although for many listeners, Boult's interpretations of Elgar and Vaughan Williams are supreme, he himself knew that there were other ways of conducting their music and his was only one way. His Schubert, Beethoven and Brahms performances are those on which his admirers may base their claims for him to be ranked among the finest of interpreters of the great classics. His recordings are there in support. Yet it is when we hear the performances of Wagner that he conducted in his old age that we may begin to wonder what we have lost and why. Boult's early inclinations were for the German Romantics and post-Romantics, for Wagner, Strauss and Mahler. His aim was to be a conductor of opera, but the circumstances of English musical life in the early 1920s moulded him into a champion of British works and kept him away from the purple path of opera. His whole upbringing was devoted to instilling into him the idea of service to others and his willingness to conduct what he was asked to conduct whether, sometimes, he wanted to or not, was at once his cardinal virtue and his principal failing. Writing to a close friend once to admit he did not know a particular work by Elgar, he said: 'There is the difference between scholar and performer: we simply study what we are told. How I would like to go right through the Haydn symphonies and quartets! Some day perhaps, if I break a leg or something!' There were some puritanical colleagues who believed that because of his enjoyment of the popularity and reverence his acquiescence engendered, he failed to do as much for English music as he might have done if he had been a 'fighter' who chose his own programmes. The point is arguable, in view of the economic risks that beset the champion of the unpopular. There can be little doubt, however, that the career eulogized in the obituaries was not the career Boult himself envisaged when he set out upon it. The wind blew where it listed, and he was content, or very nearly content, to go with the wind instead of setting his face against it. Ultimately he lacked driving ambition.

But a man's life must be judged by what he achieved, not by what might have been. Adrian Boult was the right man in the right place at the right time in 1930. His temperament fitted him ideally for the unique task, given to no other conductor before him, of educating and moulding the musical taste of the nation through the medium of radio. Alien to professional jealousy, bearing no grudge over missed personal opportunities, he had the overwhelming satisfaction of opening the doors of music to tens of thousands of individuals, who blessed and will bless him to the end of their lives.

Notes

CHAPTER 1

1 *My Own Trumpet* by Sir Adrian Boult (London 1973).
2 Emmanuel Christian (Charles) Hedmondt (1857–1940) was principal tenor of the Carl Rosa Opera for many years and lived in Liverpool. He was American, born in Maine, and took the name Hedmondt instead of Hedmont when he joined Leipzig Opera in 1882. There he married a Czech soprano. He sang David in *Die Meistersinger* at Bayreuth in 1886 and Lohengrin at Covent Garden in 1891. He presented his own season of operas at Covent Garden in 1895, singing three rôles.
3 *My Own Trumpet, op. cit.*, p. 4.
4 Anton Van Rooy (1870–1932), Dutch bass-baritone, noted for his Wagner rôles.
5 Moriz Rosenthal (1862–1946), Ukrainian pianist who first played in London in 1895 and had an international reputation.
6 Presumably Dr Richter was dedicating the performance to the memory of Queen Victoria who had died on 22 January.

CHAPTER 2

1 *Op. cit.*, p. 9.
2 *My Own Trumpet, op. cit.*, p. 9. Tovey wrote the programme notes for the visit of the Meiningen Orchestra to London in 1902.
3 Richter became conductor of the Hallé Orchestra in 1899 and remained in Manchester until 1911.
4 Rodewald was a Liverpool businessman who conducted an amateur orchestra there. He was a friend of Cedric Boult. His greatest friendship was with Elgar. He died at the early age of 43 in November 1903.
5 Dent (1876–1957) was Professor of Music at Cambridge University 1926–41. He was active in many operatic ventures, especially as a translator of libretti. He was the friend and biographer of Busoni.
6 *Op. cit.*, p. 18.

CHAPTER 3

1 Dr Adolph Brodsky (1851–1929) was a Russian violinist who in 1895 settled in Manchester and succeeded Hallé as Principal of the newly-formed Royal Manchester College of Music. In Vienna in 1881 he gave the first performance of Tchaikovsky's Violin Concerto. His quartet concerts were a feature of British musical life for over 20 years.

2 *Op. cit.*, p. 63.

3 *Siegfried Sassoon Diaries 1920–1922*, ed. Rupert Hart-Davis (London 1981), pp. 293–4.

4 Letter to the author, 9 August 1967.

5 Schuster's letters are usually signed 'Leo F. Schuster,' but he was always called Frank or Frankie.

6 'I knew Edward Elgar' by Sir Adrian Boult, in *London Calling*, 12 July 1951.

CHAPTER 4

1 Winston Churchill in *The World Crisis* (London 1931), wrote: 'The Conservatives, after nearly 20 years of power, crept back to the House of Commons barely 150 strong. The Liberals had gained a majority of more than 100 over all other parties combined.'

2 Franz Schalk (1863–1931), Austrian conductor (pupil of Bruckner) who was at the Vienna Opera from 1900 to 1929.

3 Wassili Safonoff (1852–1918). As a pianist he was a pupil of Leschetizky in St Petersburg. For 20 years he taught at Moscow Conservatory, being Director from 1889 to 1905. He began his conducting career in 1889 and was conductor of the New York Philharmonic 1906–9 (when he was succeeded by Mahler). His London conducting début was with the LSO in 1906.

CHAPTER 5

1 Sir Henry Coward (1849–1944) was one of the greatest English choral conductors. Founded Sheffield Festival 1895.

2 Hedmondt, whom Boult had heard and met in Liverpool (see Chapter 1), was stage manager for the English *Ring* in 1908.

3 Sir Landon Ronald (1873–1938), conductor, composer and pianist. First conducted at Covent Garden in 1896. Principal, Guildhall School of Music 1910–38. Friend and interpreter of Elgar, who dedicated *Falstaff* to him.

4 Letter to the author from Sir Thomas Armstrong, 24 February 1983.

5 Letter to the author, 1 June 1962.

CHAPTER 6

1 *My Own Trumpet*, *op. cit.*, p. 24.

2 *My Own Trumpet*, *op. cit.*, pp. 27–8.

3 *My Own Trumpet, op. cit.*, p. 20.

4 *My Own Trumpet, op. cit.*, p. 27.

5 The programme was Overture, *Die Meistersinger*; *Till Eulenspiegel*; Brandenburg Concerto No. 3; *Enigma Variations*; Beethoven's Fifth Symphony.

6 *Music and Friends, Letters to Adrian Boult*, ed. J. Northrop Moore (London 1979), pp. 1–4.

CHAPTER 7

1 Wrongly. It was performed at a Hallé concert in Manchester on 10 February 1887.

2 *RCM Magazine*, Vol. LV, No. 1, February 1959.

3 *My Own Trumpet, op. cit.*, p. 31.

CHAPTER 8

1 *My Own Trumpet, op. cit.*, p. 39.

2 'Nikisch and Method in Rehearsal', *The Music Review*, Vol. XI, No. 2, May 1950.

3 'Nikisch and Method in Rehearsal', *op. cit.*

4 *My Own Trumpet, op. cit.*, p. 32.

5 Letter to the author, 20 February 1974.

CHAPTER 9

1 Letter from Holst to Boult, 5 February 1918, quoted in *Music and Friends, op. cit.*, p. 26.

2 The four programmes are printed in full in Appendix 3.

3 'England for music', *The Star*, 4 April 1935.

4 Quoted in *Music and Friends, op. cit.*, pp. 27–8.

5 *Musical Times*, October 1958.

CHAPTER 10

1 Letter to the author, 19 September 1969.

2 Letter of 30 September 1918, quoted in *Music and Friends, op. cit.*, p. 33.

3 Letter of 18 November 1918, quoted in *Music and Friends, op. cit.*, p. 37.

4 Letter of 14 November 1918, quoted in *Music and Friends, op. cit.*, pp. 34–6.

5 Stanford conducted his *A Song of Agincourt* for orchestra at the RCM on 25 March 1919.

CHAPTER 11

1 *The Music Student*, pp. 220–1. A long extract is included in *Music and Friends, op. cit.*, pp. 47–51.

2 Letter to the author, 1 September 1977.

3 Visit to London in June 1920. Elgar's First Symphony was among the works played.
4 *The Times*, Monday, 22 November 1920.

CHAPTER 12

1 *My Own Trumpet*, *op. cit.*, p. 85.
2 Earlier in 1923 Holst conducted at a festival at the University of Michigan at Ann Arbor.
3 Through conducting the Robert Mayer concerts, Boult became a lifelong friend of Queen Elizabeth the Queen Mother. As Duchess of York, in the 1930s, she took her daughters to the concerts and Boult on one occasion lent his miniature score of Wagner's *Siegfried Idyll* to Princess Elizabeth (now Queen Elizabeth II), who wrote him a charming letter of thanks on returning it.

CHAPTER 13

1 I am indebted to Mr Beresford King-Smith and his booklet *1920–1970, The First Fifty Years, A History of the City of Birmingham Symphony Orchestra*, published by the CBSO (Birmingham 1970).
2 *The Orchestra in England* by Reginald Nettel (London 1946), p. 227.
3 *Siegfried Sassoon Diaries 1923–1925*, ed. Rupert Hart-Davis (London 1985), pp. 230–1.
4 The prelude to Act II of Smyth's *The Wreckers* is called 'On the Cliffs of Cornwall'.
5 A member of the committee, later chairman of the executive sub-committee, and director of the music business Dale, Forty & Co. Ltd.
6 Letter to the author, 22 June 1976.

CHAPTER 14

1 Two of the Tuesday concerts were given twice in the one evening – at 6 pm and 8.30 pm.
2 Talk to CBSO Society members, 2 June 1960.
3 Sheldon was born in Liverpool. He went to Manchester for a commercial career but received some musical training and became music critic on the *Manchester Courier*. Langford was his model. He contributed to *Musical Opinion* under the pseudonym 'Schaunard' and wrote on music in Birmingham for *Musical Times*. He died after a long illness on 5 July 1931.
4 In which he said 'it would be Birmingham's fault if it had to wait long for an opera house of its own' – *The Birmingham Post*, 28 September 1924.
5 A. J. Sheldon described the Town Hall thus: 'Our principal concert building is not an abode of comfort ... Nobility marks the building, inside and out; but the authorities in charge conspire to make it a forbidding building to enter and a dour place in which to spend an evening. Nobody seems able

to get anything done to temper its disadvantages ...' (*The Birmingham Post*, 27 April 1925). When it was refurbished he dubbed the interior 'early Metro-Goldwyn-Mayer.'

6 *Op. cit.*, pp. 282–3.

7 Michael Mullinar, pianist, who at this time was accompanist for the CBO when singers included songs with piano in the concerts.

CHAPTER 15

1 Fellowes to Boult, 15 December 1926, quoted in *Music and Friends, op. cit.*, p. 78.

2 *Op. cit.*, pp. 60–2.

3 The Concerto for Violin, Horn and Orchestra (1927).

4 George William Hubbard was editor of *The Birmingham Post* from 1906 to 1933.

5 Talk given by Boult to CBSO Society, 2 June 1960.

6 Information from Sir Michael Tippett.

CHAPTER 16

1 Letter from Sir Keith Falkner to author, 28 November 1985. The account of this incident given by Boult in Christopher St John's biography of Ethel Smyth (London 1959) is notably milder!

2 The National Chorus was the BBC's chorus (since 1977 known as the BBC Symphony Chorus). It was formed in 1928, giving its first performance in the Queen's Hall on 23 November when Sir Granville Bantock conducted his new oratorio *The Pilgrim's Progress*. Dame Ethel, knowing that Boult was taking over at the BBC, was seeking a similar première for her own new choral work. Eventually Sir Henry Wood conducted it with the Bach Choir in 1931.

CHAPTER 17

1 Those who wish to follow every move in Beecham's machinations may do so in the first chapter of Nicholas Kenyon's *The BBC Symphony Orchestra 1930–80* (London 1981).

2 *Op. cit.*, p. 94.

3 Letter from Eckersley to Boult, 30 January 1930.

4 *Blow by Blow* by Archie Camden (London 1982), p. 113.

5 Captain H.E. Adkins, Director of the Royal Military School of Music, Kneller Hall.

6 *My Own Trumpet, op. cit.*, p. 179.

7 In a letter to Menuhin on 22 June 1963, Boult said: 'That Porteous stick that I describe in the book [*Thoughts on Conducting*] has stopped – the only man who could make them has died. I am very angry with Chesters for letting it drop, & have written to say so ... I can't believe that no one else can make them.'

CHAPTER 18

1 From 'The Time of My Life: Derek Parker talks to Sir Adrian Boult', broadcast on 18 June 1967.
2 *The Orchestra Speaks* by Bernard Shore (London 1938).
3 'At Work With the Orchestra' by Marie Wilson and Colin Bradbury, in *Sir Adrian Boult, Companion of Honour*, ed. Nigel Simeone and Simon Mundy (Tunbridge Wells 1980), pp. 50, 53 and 55.
4 *RVW: a Biography of Ralph Vaughan Williams* by Ursula Vaughan Williams (London 1964), pp. 184–5.
5 *The BBC Symphony Orchestra 1930–80*, *op. cit.*, p. 58.

CHAPTER 19

1 *Op. cit.*, pp. 99–100.
2 'Never more shall I point out heroes to you on the battlefield ...' – Wotan's wrath inflicted on Brünnhilde in Act III.
3 'Your bright eyes that I have smilingly kissed ...' – from Wotan's Farewell at the end of Act III.
4 Letter to the author, 22 June 1976.
5 *The BBC Symphony Orchestra 1930–80*, *op. cit.*, p. 74.
6 'The Time of My Life', *op. cit.*
7 *Arnold Schoenberg Letters*, ed. Erwin Stein (London 1964), p. 185. Letter dated 14 April 1934.
8 *My Own Trumpet*, *op. cit.*, p. 146.
9 *My Own Trumpet*, *op. cit.*, p. 98.
10 In 'Sir Adrian Boult', radio feature broadcast on 19 May 1985.
11 'I knew Edward Elgar' by Sir Adrian Boult, in *London Calling*, 12 July 1951, p. 13.
12 Salesbury Press, Llandybie, Dyfed, 1968.
13 *English Singer: the Life of Steuart Wilson* by Margaret Stewart (London 1970), p. 134.
14 *My Own Trumpet*, *op. cit.*, p. 112.
15 Letter to the author, 21 November 1985.

CHAPTER 20

1 *Blow by Blow*, *op. cit.*, pp. 125, 138 and 144.
2 Letter to the author, 2 June 1976.
3 Letter to the author, 2 June 1976.

CHAPTER 21

1 'The Secret of Toscanini' by Sir Adrian Boult, in *The Listener*, Vol. XVII, No. 440, 16 June 1937, pp. 1177–8.
2 *My Own Trumpet*, *op. cit.*, p. 101.
3 'The Secret of Toscanini', *op. cit.*

4 The date of this incident is confirmed by the entry in Boult's diary for 13 February 1934: '*Job* rehearsal and dedication.' Boult explained in an interview with Robert Layton broadcast in December 1968 that the reason for the dedication being added to the manuscript nearly four years after its completion was that the cost of the engraving of the full score for publication was subscribed by the Bach Choir as a parting present to him when he had to give up the conductorship. When Vaughan Williams heard about this, he dedicated *Job* to Boult. The score was published in 1934.

5 'Rosé and the Vienna Philharmonic' by Sir Adrian Boult, in *Music & Letters*, July 1951, Vol XXXII, No. 3, pp. 256–7.

6 The New Year's Honours List of 1937 was delayed for a month from the usual date of 1 January because of the Abdication of King Edward VIII on 10 December 1936.

7 Sir Henry Tizard (1885–1959) was principal scientific officer to the British Government from 1946 to 1952. He was rector of the Imperial College of Science and Technology from 1929 to 1942. In the years before the Second World War, his research on defence against aerial attack qualified him as one of the first 'backroom boys' and he played an important part in the development of the Spitfire and Hurricane fighter aircraft. During the war he clashed with Churchill's scientific adviser, Professor Lindemann (later Lord Cherwell), over bombing policy.

8 This was its first public performance. It had been broadcast by the BBC Symphony Orchestra (Section B), conducted by Clarence Raybould, three days earlier.

9 *My Own Trumpet*, op. cit., p. 134.

CHAPTER 22

1 *My Own Trumpet*, op. cit., p. 115.
2 *My Own Trumpet*, op. cit., p. 119.
3 *My Own Trumpet*, op. cit., p. 120.
4 Letter to the author, 19 March 1984.
5 Information from Raymond Monk. Letter to author, 23 January 1986.

CHAPTER 23

1 Letter quoted in Kenyon's *The BBC Symphony Orchestra 1930–80*, op. cit., p. 172.

2 Glenn Miller (1904–44) was a trombonist and dance-band leader whose orchestra had a distinctive and still popular style. He was lost on a flight to Paris in December 1944.

3 The programme included Vaughan Williams's *Tallis Fantasia*, Beethoven's Violin Concerto (Henry Holst), Ravel's *Shéhérazade* (Maggie Teyte) and Strauss's *Till Eulenspiegel*.

CHAPTER 24

1 'Adrian Boult at 90' in *Fugue*, June/July 1978, p. 23.
2 Herbert Brewer (1865–1928) was organist at Gloucester 1896–1928. Among his pupils were the composers Ivor Gurney and Herbert Howells.
3 When Boult saw *Oklahoma!*, by Rodgers and Hammerstein, it had already been running for three years on Broadway. It opened in London in 1947.
4 Mimi was sung by Licia Albanese and Rodolfo by Jan Peerce. 'There was an extraordinarily flabby brass attack near the end,' Boult stated in his BBC report.
5 Boult's BBC report elaborated on this: 'It is obviously a work of major importance, but I was rather alarmed to find how easy and agreeable it seemed to me at first hearing.'
6 Boult's 'official' verdict on the Szymanowski in his report was that it 'sounded pathetically dated.'
7 The first concert performance was by the Chicago Symphony Orchestra conducted by Raymond Leppard on 28 April 1983. It was played by the City of Birmingham Symphony Orchestra conducted by John Carewe on 6 October 1983 and has since been recorded by the CBSO conducted by Simon Rattle.
8 Susi Jeans (*née* Hock) was born in Vienna in 1911. She studied with Franz Schmidt and later (in Paris) with Widor. Married Sir James Jeans (1877–1946) in 1935. She has done much to revive interest in baroque organ music.
9 László Somogyi (1908–86). Founded Hungarian State Orchestra. Conductor of Rochester Philharmonic 1964–70.
10 The Vienna State Opera House was severely damaged by Allied bombs. It was rebuilt and reopened in 1955.
11 Friedrich Gulda, born in Vienna in 1930. He has also made a reputation as a jazz pianist.

CHAPTER 25

1 *My Own Trumpet*, op. cit., pp. 91–2.
2 *My Own Trumpet*, op. cit., p. 147.
3 Letter to the author, 18 April 1986. Sir William wrote: 'I am sure as I can be that I had heard nothing about Mrs Steuart Wilson = Lady Boult until your letter arrived.'
4 'Music by Radio, the Bruckner Symphonies' by Robert Simpson, in *Music Review*, Vol. II, No. 1, 1949, pp. 29–30.
5 *My Own Trumpet*, op. cit., p. 149.
6 Letter to the author, 1 September 1977. He was discussing the rôle of the Angel in Elgar's *The Dream of Gerontius* and described Muriel Foster (1877–1937) as 'ideal ... Herself a very good wife and mother as well as a religious woman she was *right* for the part herself and fitted it. The voice itself had a beautiful quality. At this distance of time I should say that it

was not unlike Janet Baker with less power. Both could really immerse themselves in what they were doing and thinking.'

7 *Lonely Waters* by Lionel Hill (London 1986), p. 37.

8 *Lonely Waters, op. cit.*, p. 145.

9 *Lonely Waters, op. cit.*, p. 141.

10 Letter to the author, 18 April 1986.

11 'Speaking for Myself', a talk in the BBC's 'English Half-Hour' in its Far East service, October 1949.

CHAPTER 26

1 Dean Dixon (1915–76). Became conductor of Gothenburg Symphony Orchestra 1953–60, Hesse Radio SO 1961–74 and Sydney SO 1964–7.

2 Georges Sebastian (originally György Sebestyén) was a Hungarian, born in Budapest in 1903. He took private lessons in conducting with Walter in Munich 1922–3. Conducted for Moscow Radio 1931–8 and spent the war in the United States, returning to Europe to live in Paris in 1946.

3 *Philharmonic Post*, September–October 1950, pp. 8–9.

4 This recording, with Bartók's Rhapsody No. 2, has never been issued.

5 In 1960 Boult and the LPO re-recorded in stereophonic sound the accompaniments for these arias and these were 'dubbed' on to a reissue. Since then they have been transferred to compact disc also.

CHAPTER 27

1 After leaving the LPO, Russell joined Collet's Holdings as general manager and later managing director. He retired in 1969 and died on 28 October 1984 at the age of 82.

CHAPTER 28

1 *My Own Trumpet, op. cit.*, p. 148.

2 *My Own Trumpet, op. cit.*, p. 145.

3 *My Own Trumpet, op. cit.*, p. 164.

CHAPTER 29

1 A recording of this broadcast is held by the National Sound Archive (a branch of the British Library), on NSA Tape T5529R.

2 Information from Sir Michael Tippett.

3 Mindru Katz (1925–78), Rumanian pianist who made his London début only in 1958. The next year he settled in Israel.

4 Others in the cast were Ian Wallace (Wagner), Richard Lewis (Mephistopheles), John Cameron (Duke of Parma), Heather Harper (Duchess of Parma). The *Symphonia*, the *Poem* and the *Intermezzo* (Chapel in Münster) were omitted.

5 The work was broadcast twice, on 4 and 6 December, from the Camden Theatre. Pilgrim was sung (as at Cambridge) by John Noble, Bunyan by Raimund Herincx, the Evangelist by Norman Walker, the Interpreter by Alexander York and Watchful by John Carol Case. The Cup Bearer and Madam By-Ends were sung by Janet Baker.
6 S. Matthias Alexander (1869–1955) was a Tasmanian who devised a method of relearning the relationship between mind and body in order to control the body so that it functions more efficiently and thus eliminates harmful tensions. The Alexander principle is now taught in many drama schools and music colleges.
7 *Philharmonia Orchestra, a Record of Achievement 1945–1985* by Stephen J. Pettitt (London 1985), pp. 120 *et seq.*

CHAPTER 30

1 *My Own Trumpet, op. cit.,* p. 170.
2 Letter to the author, 22 September 1986.
3 Constantin Silvestri (1913–69), Rumanian-born conductor who from 1961 to 1969 was conductor of the Bournemouth Symphony Orchestra.
4 *My Own Trumpet, op. cit.,* p. 171.
5 'Recording with Sir Adrian Boult' by Christopher Bishop, in *Gramophone,* April 1974, p. 1843.
6 'Making the Records' by Sir Adrian Boult, in *The* Gramophone *Jubilee Book* (Harrow 1973), p. 16.
7 Letter to the author, 29 September 1977.
8 Wilhelm Pitz (1897–1973), first chorus master of the Philharmonia Chorus, 1957–71: chorus master Bayreuth Festival, 1951–71.
9 Letters to the author, 16 and 17 April 1968.
10 Letter to the author, 27 June 1969.

CHAPTER 31

1 *My Own Trumpet, op. cit.,* p. 184.
2 Third day of England v. West Indies at Lord's.
3 Letter to the author, 27 June 1969.
4 Letter to the author, 4 November 1969.
5 Letter to the author, 25 July 1970.
6 Letter to the author, 20 July 1970.
7 Letter to the author, 15 July 1970.
8 Letter to the author, 14 March 1969.
9 Letter to the author, 19 March 1970.
10 'Recording with Sir Adrian Boult', *op. cit.*
11 Neville Cardus gave his birthdate in *Who's Who* as 2 April 1889, but since his death his birth certificate has shown that he was born on 3 April 1888.

CHAPTER 32

1 'Adrian Boult at 90' in *Fugue*, June/July 1978, pp. 22–4.
2 Letter to the author, 7 May 1974.
3 Vaughan Williams's recording of his Fourth Symphony, made in 1937 with the BBC Symphony Orchestra, is markedly faster than any other conductor's.
4 Letter to the author, 1 November 1973.
5 Chorus master of the London Philharmonic Choir since 1969.
6 Letter to the author, 6 November 1973.
7 Letter to the author, 13 November 1973.
8 In fact Elgar *was* elected under Rule II in 1903, sponsored by Parry and Stanford.
9 Letter to the author, 7 May 1974.
10 Letter to the author, 17 November 1975.
11 Letter to the author, 12 October 1976.
12 Letters to the author, 4 October and 27 November 1975.
13 Letter to the author, 17 November 1975.
14 Letter to the author, 18 July 1974.
15 The *scherzo* of Walton's First Symphony is marked *Presto, con malizia*.
16 Letter to the author, undated but after July 1977.

CHAPTER 33

1 Letter to the author, 22 June 1976.
2 'Meet the Conductor – Mark Elder' by Elwyn Jones, in *BBC Philharmonic Club Magazine*, No. 14, June 1986, pp. 13–14.
3 Letter to the author, 13 June 1977.
4 Letter to the author, 29 September 1977.
5 What Boult modestly did not say in this letter was that he very well knew this version existed but Novello's told the manager of the CBSO they had never heard of it. When this was reported to Boult he said: 'Nonsense, I saw it at Novello's myself.' 'When, Sir Adrian?' 'Why, in 1933, of course.' Novello's looked again and found it.
6 Letter to the author, 22 September 1978.
7 Letter to the author, 22 September 1978.
8 Gennadi Rozhdestvensky, the Russian conductor, was chief conductor of the BBC Symphony Orchestra from 1978 to 1981.
9 The incidents are movingly recounted in Harvey Sachs's *Toscanini* (London 1978), pp. 307–9.

CHAPTER 34

1 'The Music Maker' by Paul Jennings, in *Radio Times*, 7 April 1979, pp. 11–13.
2 Letter to the author, 27 July 1981.

3 The 11th of Elgar's *Enigma Variations*, 'G.R.S', was said by Elgar to represent the Hereford organist G. R. Sinclair's bulldog Dan falling into the Wye, scrambling out and barking.

4 *Music and Musicians*, 1 July 1979, p. 28.

5 Letter to the author, 9 May 1980.

6 Letter to the author, 9 May 1980.

7 The printed order of service gives the date of Boult's death as 23 February, but this is wrong. He died on the 22nd. Herbert Howells died on 23 February.

8 In *Tonic*, journal of Robert Simpson Society.

APPENDIX 1

Platform Planning

Sir Adrian Boult's views on the positioning of the orchestra are of such interest that a fuller exposition of them than has been given in the body of this book deserves to be included in his biography. He wrote it in the 1950s.

Concert halls throughout the world vary a great deal in their platforms, and orchestral tradition varies considerably also, so that a touring orchestra has many and unusual problems to solve every time it moves to a new hall. There are many principles involved, and it is really true to say that there is no perfect solution to all the problems at once. Indeed I have heard it said that the right plan would be to let everyone sit where he wishes, regardless of the instrument he is playing – a better ensemble might be achieved that way, and there would be no blocks of homogeneous sound. But I'm afraid that the disadvantages would also be formidable, and I personally am not exactly inclined to try this bold plan, exciting though the results might be!

But I think we might explore some of the principles and discuss the various solutions though we certainly shan't be able to agree on the perfect answers. First, are we going to place our players on a level stage or on the tiers and steps which are built into most British halls? I believe that many American stages are level, and when orchestras play in theatres, as often in France, they must bring in special boxes or platforms if they are not to be placed on a dead level. I must say I prefer the levels to be different: the Strings outnumber the Wood-wind by 6 or more to one, and it seems only sensible that the eight, twelve or even sixteen Wood-wind players should be raised: they have much solo work to do; but on the other hand their instruments do have a greater penetrating power than the Strings, and String players are often encouraged to listen to a Wind soloist as they make their contribution to the accompanying background.

I should say that the only two rules that are in almost universal observance in the orchestral world are, first, that the Leader of the orchestra sits on the Conductor's immediate left-hand, and, second, that the group of Wood-wind soloists sit in the middle of the platform with the first players in the middle, Flute next to Oboe sitting on the first rise, and Clarinet and Bassoon together behind in the middle of the second rise. But in some halls this is impossible, because the first rise is so far forward that there is hardly any room for the Strings: in this case the Wood-wind must sit higher and further back. In other halls the level space is so wide that it throws the Wood-wind group too far back. This is a nuisance because their tone can easily be submerged, particularly in a theatre where the proscenium arch comes down low and throws the orchestral sound straight upwards instead of outwards to the audience. It is possible perhaps to get some boxes and build the Wood-wind forward a bit.

I have said that this is an almost universally adopted plan, but recently in a provincial hall I saw the whole Wood-wind chorus placed in front of the platform to the Conductor's right. This might give some distortion to those sitting in front seats in the hall, but to me in a distant gallery the result was often most effective.

Having placed the Wood-wind, I think we should then see how far the Strings can be packed in. If the hall is narrow and you can't get them in, there will be nothing for it but to move the Wood-wind further back, but we will hope not. In placing the Strings it is now the fashion to start at the left with the First Violins, and radiate round, Second Violins next, Violas, then Cellos, with the Double Basses on the extreme right of the platform, sometimes in front, sometimes further back, according to the space available.

There are two things here which I dislike intensely. This plan puts all the treble artists on the left of the platform and all the bass on the right, and, I submit, gives the audience a most unbalanced picture of the orchestral sound. Those sitting on the right of the hall (facing the platform) will get a preponderance of bass; in fact I have myself found that in the Royal Festival Hall, if one sits on that side one hears the bass sound first, and the tunes trickle across the hall a fraction late!

In Vienna, in one of the most perfect halls in the world, the Basses are always placed in a row across the back of the top stage. They have the Organ case immediately behind them, and a splendid foundation to the whole texture comes forward from them. This is also possible in the Royal Festival Hall, and I much prefer it that way.

This principle of tonal balance also affects the position of the Second

Violins, and here I feel most strongly about it, although I must admit that I am in a small minority. However, on my side are Bruno Walter, Monteux, Klemperer, and a few others, including Toscanini, who was adamant about it, and insisted that the String balance should be preserved by placing the Second Violins on his right, exactly balancing the Firsts on his left, so that they shared equally the front of the platform instead of being tucked away behind the Firsts, where, I maintain, their tone is largely lost. This practice, which I so dislike, only came in about 50 years ago, and I'm sure that the shades of Richter, Weingartner, Nikisch and Toscanini, as well as the still earlier masters, are frowning at this modern idea, which thinks only of the convenience of the performers and nothing of the effect to the audience as envisaged by the composer. I admit it is easier for the First Violins to have the Seconds near them, and for the Violas to be placed between the Seconds and the Cellos, but is ease of playing and convenience to be the chief criterion which governs a great orchestra? Surely the result is what matters, and I can assert that on many occasions in many halls I have heard the give-and-take answering passages, which occur in all music from Mozart to the present day, sound completely ineffective when the answer comes as a pale reflection from behind the First Violins instead of sounding up bravely from the opposite side of the platform. If it is true, as is sometimes said, that the Second Violins are so far turned away from the audience that they can't be heard, I will flatly contradict; it is not so, unless the outside players turn inwards and put their shoulders in between their instruments and the audiences. If they do this it can easily be stopped. Another argument, that the First and Seconds often play in octaves or unison, and bow together, and therefore should sit together, is to me unimportant. If the Leader of the Seconds is any use at all he will secure a perfect ensemble, though if there is a pianoforte on the platform it does make it more difficult for him, but not impossible, and there is no doubt that a long unison line, like the slow movement of Scheherazade, was thought of by Rimsky-Korsakov as coming from the front of the whole width of the stage in a most telling way.

Orchestras vary a good deal in the space each String player needs to enable him to bow comfortably. This also affects the seating problem considerably. The famous Amsterdam Orchestra has always placed itself exceedingly close, thereby helping its wonderful ensemble, and visiting orchestras of the same size get a bit of a shock when they get on to that platform, and try to spread out as they do at home.

There are not so many considerations in regard to the placing of Brass and Percussion once the Strings and Wood-wind are settled. It must not be forgotten that the sound of a Horn emerges from behind the player's elbow, and sometimes if the Horn group is placed too near the wooden fence which separates the Orchestra from the Chorus seats in the Royal Festival Hall, their tone hits the boarding behind them, and is curiously magnified. The Brass is often divided with Horns to one side of the Wood-wind, and Trumpets and Trombones to the other, and I like the Trombones in the Festival Hall to be placed a little sideways so that they play into the orchestra and not directly out to the audience. I feel their tone blends better that way. Percussion, Harps and Celesta fit in where they can, but I like the Percussion as near the middle as possible, particularly the Timpani, which, like the String Basses, seem so often to be the foundation of the whole texture.

It is sometimes seen nowadays that in choral works, particularly where the soloists are closely involved in the choral writing, they are placed in front of the Chorus, but above and behind the Orchestra. Halls vary a good deal in the appropriateness of this, but when the front of the platform is very low, it is often better for the majority of the audience to have the Solo Quartet up near the Chorus, but of course the Orchestra must keep their accompaniment discreet. Once again I can say: trust the orchestra. They can hear the soloists, and judge the balance for themselves, far more easily than if the soloists are singing away from them with their backs turned.

APPENDIX 2

Boult on Elgar's Scoring and Tempi

In 1977 Boult and I exchanged letters over some points which concerned him in Elgar scores. This arose over the following letter which Elgar wrote to him about the First Symphony which he was about to conduct at the BBC's concerts celebrating his 75th birthday.

Marl Bank, Worcester,
22 November 1932

My dear Adrian,

I do not want to worry you unduly but perhaps one of your assistants could see to the following matter *if* you approve of my suggestion. In the First Symphony there are some passages which I have never got to my liking. In the passage beginning four bars before [30] (and occurring twice more) I want an *echo* effect – the only thing to be *heard* in the first two bars being the *quaver passage* (Clar, Cello, Viola, Vl. II) which should be slurred right over & the solo violin really *pp*.

Would you allow someone to mark the copies, one (or two) desks only to play??

These are the 'spots.' Begin four bars before [30] – 'Echo' four bars; at [30] *tutti* for four bars; then Echo eight bars. (N.B. Vio. I (*tutti*) come in at the end of bar 8.)

Again, the same sort of thing at [53]; Echo, four bars; – *più lento, tutti* two bars; – then Echo six bars; *allargando, tutti*.

I am looking forward keenly to seeing you again and hearing this symphony with your gorgeous orchestra.

Ever yours
Edward Elgar

Boult wrote to me on 30 March 1977.

78, Marlborough Mansions, NW6

... When that letter came I remember writing it all in my score, but I didn't ask why, when he had already conducted it X times in 25 years, *HE* had never succeeded in getting the effect he wanted!! I have looked at it again and now feel certain it is his own fault – the scoring doesn't allow the *echo tutti* business. Am I right?

2. I'm sure I'm right about [149]: the last 4 bars before [149] are fully scored and stuffy; the 4 bars before ([149], 5–8 before) are brilliantly scored for brass, without strings for 2 bars, & therefore they sound *more* brilliant and the climax ([149] itself) is anticipated and ante-climaxed and also anti-climaxed! Am I right?

3. I have just been asked to tell Novello's that those ridiculous signs at [17] and [44] should be changed to $\downarrow$ = $\downarrow$. . But isn't that also wrong? Surely it overdoes it the other way and makes the 3/2 too slow? Am I right?

Is it possible that there are three mistakes in one work, when the man has made no mistakes anywhere else except of course poor old W.N. (Enigma VIII) who has to scamper away at $\downarrow$. = 52 because E.E. got his arithmetic wrong.

Don't tell J.N.M. [Jerrold Northrop Moore] how frivolous I am about his idol ... I am afraid I have never been successful over [30] – in fact I had forgotten about it till I read your note[1] and realized that I had ignored it for many years!

Boult again referred to the metronome marking of W.N. in the *Variations* in a letter to me after I had mentioned the holding of the B flat on the trumpet at one bar after [149] in the *finale* of Elgar's Second Symphony. I suggested that, since I knew Elgar had approved this, there ought to be a footnote to that effect in future editions of the score. Boult replied:

> I'm sure you are right about printing a note, as Harold Brooke [a former managing director of Novello's] did about W.N. when poor old [Rudolf] Schwarz[2] took it literally at $\downarrow$. = 52. The B'mouth orchestra sent a message to me via old Piggott (an old Westminster master who had taught me many things and was then living in retirement in B'mouth and going to all R.S.'s rehearsals). I went to Harold Brooke who agreed that it was E.E.'s bad arithmetic and he meant $\eighthnote$ = 104 not $\downarrow$. = 52.

Boult then quoted to me a letter he had just received from Ernest Hall, former principal trumpet of the BBC Symphony Orchestra, who had originated the holding of the note in the symphony when he was with the LSO. Hall wrote: 'When Sir Edward asked me at a recording

[1] Sleeve note to Boult's recording of Elgar's First Symphony, HMV CDC 7472042, ASD 3330 or TC-ASD 3330.

[2] Rudolf Schwarz was principal conductor of the Bournemouth Symphony Orchestra from 1946 to 1951.

why I held my top B flat over the next bar and I replied that I was so pleased to get the note I didn't like to leave it, his reply was "I intended to write it so, but thought it would be too high to hold." ' Boult added:

> When E.E. took me through the score, he marked tr ᴡᴡᴡ in pencil at that point at the foot of the score and said 'Let him prolong it if he feels like it' and as you know they always do.

Boult erred here – most other conductors keep strictly to the printed score, perhaps because they are unaware of the licence Elgar gave them at this point.

APPENDIX 3

The 1918 Concerts

Below are printed the programmes of the four concerts in which Boult conducted the London Symphony Orchestra in the Queen's Hall, London, in 1918. Each printed programme (price 6d [2½p] for the first concert, 3d thereafter) carried the inscription: 'Any profits made at these Concerts will be given to the Wounded Soldiers' Concert Fund.'

First Concert, Monday, 4 February at 7.45 pm

Brandenburg Concerto No. 3 in G for strings .... J.S. BACH

Chaconne for viola alone .... J.S. BACH

LIONEL TERTIS

Country Song for small orchestra .... G. von HOLST

Rhapsody .... R.T. WOODMAN

(First performance in London)

Romance .... ⎱ for viola and   BENJAMIN DALE
Tambourin Chinois ⎰ orchestra   KREISLER orchestrated
                                              by York Bowen

LIONEL TERTIS

Overture to *Der Freischütz* .... WEBER

Second Concert, Monday, 18 February at 7.45 pm

Overture, *In the South (Alassio)* .... ELGAR

Song *Asie* (from the cycle *Shéhérazade*) .... RAVEL

(First performance in England)

A London Symphony .... VAUGHAN WILLIAMS

Songs – (a) *Phidylé* .... Duparc
     – (b) Variante sur l'air
          Au clair de la Lune .... Pierre de Bréville
          (First performance in England)

Yves Tinayre

Overture, *Die Meistersinger* .... Wagner

Third Concert, Monday, 4 March at 5.45 pm

Overture, *Don Giovanni* .... Mozart
Concerto in C major for flute and harp (K.299) .... Mozart
        Solo flute...Louis Fleury
        Solo harp...Gwendolen Mason
Symphonic Variations in E minor .... Parry
Concerto in D minor for violoncello .... Lalo
      Solo violoncello...Beatrice Harrison

In Shakespeare's Days – Pavane and Morris Dance .... David Piggott
        (First performance in London)

Rhapsody, *A Shropshire Lad* .... George Butterworth
Prelude and Dances from the ballet *Between Dusk and Dawn* Arnold Bax
      Prelude – Summer Night at the window;
    Dance of the wind in the garden; Midnight strikes;
   The Awakening; The Russian Dancer and the Clown.
        (First concert performance)

Fourth Concert, Monday, 18 March at 6.0 pm

Reverie in E minor, op. 24 .... Scriabin
Air of Lisa (from the opera *Queen of Spades*) .... Tchaikovsky

Zoia Rosowsky

The Forgotten Rite .... John Ireland
A London Symphony .... Vaughan Williams
        (Repeated by request)

Scherzo from Symphony 'In Memoriam' .... Oliver H. Gotch
La Chanson perpetuelle .... Chausson

Zoia Rosowsky

321

Symphonic Poem, *With the Wild Geese* .... HAMILTON HARTY

For the first concert, the orchestra, led by W.H. Reed, numbered 50 players, for the second 59, for the third 52 and for the last 76.

APPENDIX 4

The Russell Case

(See Chapter 27)

(See Chapter 27)

Boult's letter to the shareholders of the LPO, with their reply:

The melancholy controversy that has now split the Orchestra for two months does not, of course, concern me directly; I am the servant of the Company, and have been privileged to hear confidences from men on both sides, all of whom are my friends. At the same time I feel that my main task, the preservation of the artistic standard of the Orchestra, is now being brought into danger by recent events, and so I venture at last to take sides and give an opinion.

I was considerably shocked when, just before Mr Russell's return, I heard that he had been removed from his Chairmanship. I felt that this should have been done by the Shareholders at their Extraordinary Meeting, and could have waited till then. The reason for this has now been explained to you, and to me, and I have also outside confirmation of the general Company practice that any discussion of the Chairman's actions is always preceded by his vacation of the Chair. Previous experience leaves no doubt that Mr Russell would have been unwilling to conform to this practice, and a chairman so astute could well have a considerable influence on a meeting of comparatively inexperienced shareholders and might well prevent some of his opponents from gaining a hearing at all.

On October 21st I was invited to attend a Meeting of the LPO Advisory Council. Three members were present and Mr Russell was invited to make his statement in reply to Mr O'Dea's letter of September 13th and the subsequent Minute of the Council. He made a statement lasting for some forty minutes, and I confess that I found some of what he had to say persuasive enough, after which he answered a number of questions, and then was asked to withdraw. However, these three experienced and respected business men, who have shown such goodwill towards the Orchestra in its difficulties in recent years, one after the other (the Chairman last) said they felt entirely unmoved by what Mr Russell had said and they unanimously confirmed their Minute of October 15th, which you have seen. This impressed me very much.

A letter has now reached the office of the Arts Council regarding its future relations with the orchestra. This letter is, naturally, phrased in general terms, but I fail to see how the 'unity of the Orchestra,' on which they insist, can possibly be maintained if Mr Russell is returned to office. I don't think the LPO can exist without the Arts Council subsidy. It is true immense economies have been made and have been loyally accepted by you and by the staff, but we can go no further, and I must say I look on a future without the support of the LPO Council and the Arts Council (both of which supported us generously in the crisis of two years ago) with the gravest alarm.

May I now say a word about the principal personalities in this sad business? It is often a help to try and explore the motives which have driven people to take up any position. Mr Russell, founder of the present LPO, has by his courage and industry performed miracles. I have continually admired his many qualities, and I think many of you have had personal help from him. But I cannot help comparing the two years of my service with you, and feeling that in this second year Mr Russell's outside activities seem to have taken precedence over his LPO work and (in addition to his most unfortunate illness) his absences this year have been considerable. It is not unfair to tell you that this change has been noted and remarked on by some of our outside contacts.

The four Directors who have signed the Memorandum of October 21st are all well known to you, and I think you can see that they have nothing at all to gain by what must have been a most distasteful course of action to artists whose only ambition is to excel as players and as members of the LPO. If only one of them may perhaps have an ambition beyond this it certainly does not lie in the direction of an office desk in Welbeck Street.

Finally, Mr O'Dea, an experienced and accomplished Chartered Accountant, came to the LPO in order to keep some interest in life, though many men in his position would have indulged in complete retirement. I am satisfied that as this sad business developed, his position as Secretary (admirably set forth in his own statement) forced him from neutrality into support of the four Directors because he saw that any other course would cause him to neglect his duty to the Company, particularly in the matter of protecting the shareholders. I greatly deplore his decision to leave the office after the Extraordinary Meeting, whatever its outcome, but he will leave (if leave he must) with the personal gratitude of many of us quite apart from the time and energy he has given to us in this crisis.

As you know, I vigorously denied the rumour that I had said I would not remain with the LPO if Mr Russell were reinstated. It was not my place to make this threat, and I had then no wish to put pressure on the shareholders. But I think I have shown a number of convincing reasons why I now suggest to you who have votes, that your future is more than precarious if Mr Russell resumes control. I need not repeat with what personal reluctance I now take this course.

On 4 November, a group of members of the orchestra, with Frederick Riddle, the violist, as principal signatory, replied to Boult thus:

As shareholders of the Company, some of us for a great number of years, we were deeply shocked to receive your letter of October 30th. Throughout your association with this orchestra we have all been aware of your very great friendship with Mr Russell and the admiration which you felt for his work. We have heard you express these feelings on numerous occasions, but have never heard any criticism of him from you. As recently as in Swansea [where the LPO played on 13 October] your attitude indicated no disapproval, and your sudden change of front cannot fail to be bewildering.

The arguments you put forward (to which we refer later) are singularly unconvincing, and can only lead us to fear that you have been subjected to extreme pressure from outside the Company for reasons which have not been explained to us, presumably because they would not carry weight with the orchestra.

May we quote this paragraph:

'Previous experience leaves no doubt that Mr Russell would have been unwilling to conform to this practice (vacating the chair), and a chairman so astute could well have a considerable influence on a meeting of comparatively inexperienced shareholders and might well prevent some of his opponents from gaining a hearing at all.'

We should like to ask you on whose 'previous experience' you based this remark. To our knowledge you have attended only one General Meeting of the Company, on which occasion Mr Russell refused to speak in his defence until he had pressingly invited any other shareholders to speak against him. As for the expression 'comparatively inexperienced shareholders', some of the undersigned have held a share in this Company since 1939 and remember no instance of any effort made by Mr Russell to gag his opponents. Perhaps you will be kind enough to substantiate this accusation.

We note that although you found Mr Russell's observations at an LPO Council Meeting 'persuasive enough,' you were very much impressed by the refusal of three other people to accept these arguments. Could we have your opinion as to the fairness of asking our Managing Director to leave the Meeting while you discussed the matter, but allowing an employee of the Company and, indeed, yourself, to remain in the Meeting for this purpose?

We have seen the letter from the Arts Council regarding its future relations with the orchestra, but find nothing in it to justify that we shall have 'to exist without the Arts Council subsidy'; on the contrary, it may well have the reverse effect. On the other hand, we accept majority decisions as binding upon us all, and Mr Russell has always succeeded in healing temporary divisions. You speak of 'immense economies' having been accepted by us. Our individual incomes from LPO sources are higher this year than at any time since 1939, and although we have had to make some uncomfortable journeys by coach instead of train, this is due as much to increased railway fares as to the financial position of the Company which, as you know, is more prosperous than it has been since 1932, due in no small measure to your work for the Orchestra. We should also point out that during the present season we are making more – and highly successful – appearances at the Royal Festival and at other London engagements. May we ask therefore for some details of the 'immense economies' practised at our expense?

Those of us who have been Directors recently cannot agree that Mr Russell's outside activities have taken precedence over his LPO work. These activities have in any case been approved by one of the Board. Furthermore, we cannot agree that his absences this year have been considerable. Apart from holidays to which he was legally entitled, he has been away from the office only for a few days each week for a period of a month. This was made known to the Board before it took place and was made necessary by a most painful and irritating complaint from which Mr Russell was suffering. In spite of this, he attended all important meetings during that period and to our knowledge was often in the greatest discomfort at such times. Your reference to this appears extremely unworthy of you, and we cannot fail to recall that you were away for a no more serious reason for a period of three weeks at the height of the Festival of Britain 1951. If our facts in this matter are incorrect perhaps you would let us have further details of Mr Russell's 'considerable absences' and the names of those 'outside contacts' who have noted and remarked on the change in Mr Russell's work.

We do not wish to pass any comment on your estimate of the four Directors, or, for that matter, of the Company's Secretary, although it is clear that your statement regarding the latter could not have been drawn up by yourself in isolation.

We should be very glad to have your replies to these questions at your earliest convenience.

Boult did not reply.

Select Bibliography

ANDERSON, MARTIN J. (ed.), *Boult on Music* (London 1983)

BOULT, ADRIAN C., *The Point of the Stick: A Handbook on the Technique of Conducting* (London 1920, repub. 1968)
   Thoughts on Conducting (London 1963)
   My Own Trumpet (London 1973)

CAMDEN, ARCHIE, *Blow by Blow, the Memories of a Musical Rogue and Vagabond* (London 1982)

COX, DAVID, *The Henry Wood Proms* (London 1980)

KENYON, NICHOLAS, *The BBC Symphony Orchestra 1930–1980* (London 1981)

MOORE, JERROLD NORTHROP (ed.), *Music and Friends, Seven Decades of Letters to Adrian Boult* (London 1979)

PARROTT, IAN, *The Spiritual Pilgrims* (Llandybie 1968)

RUSSELL, THOMAS, *Philharmonic* (London 1942)
   Philharmonic Decade (London 1945)
   Philharmonic Project (London 1952)

SANDERS, ALAN, *Sir Adrian Boult, a Discography* (General Gramophone Publications, 1980)

SIMEONE, NIGEL and MUNDY, SIMON (eds.), *Sir Adrian Boult, Companion of Honour, a Tribute* (Tunbridge Wells 1980)

*   *   *

Programme Book for The 90th Birthday of Sir Adrian Boult CH (Promenade Concert, 8 April 1979) (London 1979)

Index

328